"Once again, Kimberley Woodhouse pens a fast-paced action adventure with enough twists and turns to keep the reader turning the page. Her attention to detail and historical accuracy makes *A Song in the Dark* stand out among WWII stories. I encourage readers to put this on their must-read lists."

Tracie Peterson, ECPA, CBA, and *USA Today* bestselling author of over 140 books

"With compelling characters and high stakes, Kimberley Woodhouse tells a tale of hope triumphing in the darkest of times. Readers will find much to love in Chaisley and Rick's romance, set against the backdrop of the brewing storm of WWII. Woodhouse's love of music and passion for telling stories of faith-filled resistance shine in this novel."

Amy Lynn Green, author of *The Codebreaker's Daughter*

A SONG
in the
DARK

A SONG *in the* DARK

a novel of WORLD WAR II

Kimberley Woodhouse

BETHANYHOUSE
a division of Baker Publishing Group
Minneapolis, Minnesota

© 2025 by Kimberley R. Woodhouse

Published by Bethany House Publishers
Minneapolis, Minnesota
BethanyHouse.com

Bethany House Publishers is a division of
Baker Publishing Group, Grand Rapids, Michigan

Printed in the United States of America

Library of Congress Cataloging-in-Publication Data
Names: Woodhouse, Kimberley, 1973– author.
Title: A song in the dark : a novel of World War II / Kimberley Woodhouse.
Description: Minneapolis, Minnesota : Bethany House Publishers, a division of Baker Publishing Group, 2025.
Identifiers: LCCN 2025000963 | ISBN 9780764244674 (paperback) | ISBN 9780764245770 (casebound) | ISBN 9781493451357 (ebook)
Subjects: LCSH: Women pianists—Great Britain—Fiction. | Blind musicians—Great Britain—Fiction. | Christian women—Great Britain—Fiction. | Spies--Great Britain--Fiction. | Espionage, British—Europe—Fiction. | Hitler, Adolf, 1889–1945—Fiction. | Europe—History—1918–1945—Fiction. | LCGFT: Christian fiction. | Thrillers (Fiction) | Historical fiction.
Classification: LCC PS3623.O665 S66 2025 | DDC 813/.6—dc23/eng/20250523
LC record available at https://lccn.loc.gov/2025000963

Scripture quotations are from the King James Version of the Bible.

This is a work of historical reconstruction; the appearances of certain historical figures are therefore inevitable. All other characters, however, are products of the author's imagination, and any resemblance to actual persons, living or dead, is coincidental.

Cover photograph of woman © Mark Owen / Trevillion Images

Baker Publishing Group publications use paper produced from sustainable forestry practices and postconsumer waste whenever possible.

25 26 27 28 29 30 31   7 6 5 4 3 2 1

This book is lovingly dedicated in memory
of my beloved grandparents:

Ray—a WWII veteran—and his beautiful wife, Dot Frappier

Two people who hugely shaped my life as a musician,
writer, and most importantly—believer.

Their legacy lives on through their children, grandchildren,
great-grandchildren, and now great-great-grandchildren.

Grandma and Grandpa—you are dearly missed.

dear reader,

This story has been in my heart and mind for umpteen years. In fact, it's been brewing since before I signed my first publishing contract. Forty-plus books later, it's coming to you through much love, sweat, and tears.

A ton of research has gone into it, and yes, there are historic dates and details which are real. But the premise is completely from my imagination.

For so long I wondered why the Jews stayed in Germany, or other parts of Europe, as long as they did. I also wondered how and why the world couldn't see what was truly happening. As the saying goes, hindsight always is 20/20.

The more entrenched I became in the research and history, the more I understood. I watched hours and hours of documentaries and testimonies of survivors. I went through countless boxes of Kleenex and learned as much as I could to at least imagine what it must have been like to walk in their shoes.

One incredible man who inspired me was Otto Weidt, a nearly blind man who employed and hid blind and deaf Jews in Berlin during the horrible years of the Nazis. What he did to aid others had a powerful impact on me. How he managed to convince the SS and Gestapo that his workshop (where they made brushes and brooms) was necessary to them for their cause and war effort completely blows my mind.

Even though Hitler and his regime knew what they wanted well in advance, they set out in a gradual process at the beginning. Whether this plan was to gain more followers and convince people that what they were doing was necessary and acceptable, or because they didn't want to shock the world too much at once and cause a global uprising, the end goal was the same. They wanted the expulsion and extermination of the Jewish people, as well as anyone deemed unworthy to live. A glaring example for us all even today to be aware, seek truth, stay informed, and be ready to stand firm.

One of the documentaries that interested me was that of Inge Deutschkron being interviewed by Claude Lanzmann. They were filming "Shoah," and you can find the interview on the site of the United States Holocaust Memorial Museum: collections.ushmm. org/search/catalog/irn1004643.

There are hours of Inge's testimony sharing how this gradual process took place. Her testimony helped me understand what it was like to live during this time.

Even though Hitler held power and systematically put his plans into motion fully beginning in 1933, the world was unaware of the truth and the threat growing. Looking back, people have questioned why the world allowed the Olympics to be held in Germany. But during the 1936 Olympics, Hitler made sure that his propaganda—and all evidence of hatred and prejudice against the Jews and others—was not seen on the world stage. He ensured Germany looked good to the world—all while advancing his atrocities in the background.

If ever the tale of the frog in the pot of water being brought to a slow boil was played out in real life—it was during this time.

Years ago, Joel Rosenberg wrote a wonderful book I highly recommend, *The Auschwitz Escape*, in which a question is asked in a concentration camp: ". . . if you ask me, the question shouldn't be 'Why are you, a Christian, here in a death camp, condemned for trying to save Jews?' The real question is 'Why aren't all the Christians here?'" That question has resonated with me ever since and I wrote a blog post back in 2016 about it. (KimberleyWood-house.com/uncategorized/apology/)

I encourage you to read and reread that quote above. Let it simmer for a while. Then read it again.

In early 2024, my husband and I went to see the movie *One Life* with Anthony Hopkins. I was already contracted for *A Song in the Dark* and deep into the research and writing. I thought the movie would provide wonderful insight, and I was blown away by the story. I highly recommend it. Once again, I was inspired by the people who saw what was happening and did something about it.

All these people who inspired me were beautiful reminders of my grandparents. That's why this book is dedicated to them. My grandpa was one of the most joyous and funny people I've ever known. He loved dessert and mashed potatoes with gravy (not at the same time, but then again, it wouldn't surprise me if he made those two foods a meal). He was an amazing saxophone player and musician. He pulled some crazy pranks in his life and reminded us all to live life to the fullest, grab onto joy, and love God with everything we had.

But a piece of his life held dark memories. He fought in World War II, and what he saw and experienced haunted him. He was awarded the Bronze Star for performing heroic acts of bravery and saved the lives of fellow soldiers.

As a history major, my son dove into researching my grandpa's journeys, battles, and role in the war. What he discovered was awe-inspiring and devastating.

Grandpa only spoke to me of the atrocities he faced a couple of times—he never wanted to share the ugliness. Didn't want to dwell on it. Didn't want to travel down that memory lane.

One time, I was a teenager when my parents and I visited Grandma and Grandpa in their RV as they were traveling and volunteering with a retired group that helped around the country. My dad wanted to get some of the stories down on paper because he was working on genealogy and our family's history, and none of us knew what Grandpa had endured.

Grandpa's hesitant stories stuck with me. How could a man who was so full of joy and fun still be so after such horrible things? The memories as he shared them shook him to his core and brought tears to all of us.

I used a story of Grandpa's—that I fictionalized—in *Out of the Ashes* (Bethany House Publishers, 2018), and it's amazing how many readers have written in to tell us that it had a huge impact on them as well.

My grandma was a phenomenal pianist and inspired me in my own musical career. Her love for God, Grandpa, music, and her family were huge in shaping not only me—but our whole, great big family. Family reunions were an incredible thing to behold with all the cousins, aunts, uncles, and our beloved grandparents. But their greatest impact and legacy is the fact that they started each day on their knees praying for each and every member of our family. As the years passed and our family grew—so did their prayer time.

World War II was awful. And that is the understatement of the century. But the history is fascinating, and we must not forget what happened lest we repeat it, right? Readers who love this era have spurred on an entire genre of fiction. Some fascinating and beautiful stories have been written highlighting this horrific time in our history.

A Song in the Dark is my first novel set during this time period. Partly because I've been waiting for the right time. Partly because I wanted to do it justice. And partly because I had to bathe it in prayer for a long, long time.

I appreciate you taking the time to journey along with me, and I pray this story touches your heart. I encourage you to go back and reread that quote from Joel Rosenberg's book.

I long to be one of the few.

Kimberley
Woodhouse

The Few

Before Hitler invaded Poland on September 1, 1939 . . .

Before Kristallnacht on November 9, 1938 . . .

Before the Munich Agreement on September 30, 1938 . . .

A culture of hatred and superiority set the stage for war in Europe. In the hearts and minds of people, it quickly spread.

Many didn't want to acknowledge what was happening because the continent still reeled from the Great War. It hurt too much. Surviving was hard enough.

Many thought the world leaders would stop it before it got too bad.

Many didn't believe the stories they heard.

Many ignored what was happening right under their noses.

And then there were the few . . .

The few that stood up to hatred and bigotry and murderous hearts.

The few that heard and saw things and didn't wait to do something about it.

The few that sacrificed everything to save even one.

Stories have been told about the few who each saved hundreds—possibly thousands—of lives. But many stories are still untold.

This story is for all the unsung heroes. The ones we may never know about.

May we remember.

May we not be afraid to do what's right.

May we never be complacent again.

May we love one another above all else.

May we turn our hearts to God Almighty.

May we be . . . the few.

—Kimberley Woodhouse

prologue

The melody inside Chaisley fought with the excited butterflies in her stomach. Which would be released first?

Light shimmered on the shiny black and white keys.

Her birthday present.

The golden letters spelled out *Steinway*.

Chaisley Frappier's heart leapt. It was all hers. She slid her hand along each of the eighty-eight keys, counting them again as she went. Their surface reminded her of touching Grandmother's silver serving dishes. Polished and smooth.

"Go on, darling." Mother stood in the circle of Father's arms. "Try it out."

Chaisley nodded. Couldn't keep the grin from her face. Father had indulged her initial curiosity by giving her an old, dusty text on musical theory. The binding was falling apart—and if she didn't hold it just right, pages would fall out—but oh, how she loved that book. The music room had been commissioned not long after she'd read the entire text and shared with them at every meal each new piece of information that fascinated her.

She'd riddled her private tutor with questions about everything she didn't understand. And soaked in every bit of knowledge as

15

she waited the long months for her very own pianoforte. Until one day, her teacher informed her parents that she needed a specialized music tutor because he no longer had answers for all her questions.

Another thing to wait for . . . but to finally have the explanation for the music that seeped from her bones? It was glorious to think about. Grandmother told her such words made her sound much older than her ten years. But all of her time was spent with adults so what other words would she use?

As she sat on the padded bench, she let her legs dangle for a moment, relishing the beauty of the instrument before her. She reached out her right hand to stroke the silky keys again.

The notes resonated within her. Her left hand joined her right.

Touching, caressing, feeling each key as she pressed them to hear the individual sounds.

Each tone.

Her eyes couldn't leave the piano. She closed the cover with the pretty gold letters over the keys and walked around the instrument. While she understood the basics—the keys made the hammers hit the strings, and they resonated with the sound—it still amazed her. She had so many questions!

"That's called the fallboard." Father pointed to the cover and followed her around.

When she stopped in the big curve on the right side, he lifted the massive lid and placed a leg-looking stick into a rounded upside-down cup on the underside. The lid stayed open and her eyes widened at the glorious construction inside.

"That's the lid prop. And look. If we want it open, but a bit lower, we simply use the shorter leg." He smiled, and his eyes danced.

Like she imagined her own must look as she took in her new treasure.

Giggles escaped, and she couldn't stop them—nor did she wish to.

She ran another circle around the piano, twirled around twice when she reached the bench, and then sat down again with a flounce. She lifted the fallboard and slid her index finger over the lettering and then tested out every one of the keys over and over again. Watching the hammers hit the strings, the reflection of her hands in the ebony mirror of the lid, and the precision of movement—she was in heaven. For a whole year, she'd waited.

And it had finally come.

Music radiated within her. Soon she'd be able to transfer the music from her heart to the keys. She just knew it. Everything was mathematical—and she adored math. Measured in half steps, the keyboard was laid out in a pattern. Different combinations of keys would make chords . . . major, minor, augmented, diminished. Everything she'd read came alive before her very eyes.

"Happy birthday, sweetheart." The faint hint of his French and Dutch ancestry came out in his accent. "We've hired a master teacher to come see you. Your first lesson is"—he glanced at his pocket watch just as the chime for the front door rang—"right now."

Chaisley did her best to stay proper on the bench. "Truly?"

He nodded and tapped the end of her nose. "Let's see if you can put all that book learning to good use." He leaned down and whispered in her ear. "Be brave, my little munchkin. He's a very tall man and looks intimidating, but he's the best of the best."

She shifted her gaze back to the six-foot grand piano. Another small giggle escaped her and she placed her hands over her lips as if she held a magical secret. And she did. "Dr. G is very tall too." Father's best friend and their family physician—Dr. Grafton—had been bringing her additional books on music for several months. Tchaikovsky's *Guide to the Practical Study of Harmony* and Rameau's *Treatise on Harmony* were her current favorites. Dr. Grafton understood her longing to release the music inside her because he said he had that longing too. Even though she'd never played an instrument in her life, Chaisley *understood* music.

"Well, I see she is enchanted by her present." Mum's voice

drifted into her awareness. "We'll be in the parlor, sweetheart, if you need us."

The hour with Monsieur Beaufort fed her soul and opened up her mind to the vast universe of music. And she didn't have to work at being brave. Several times, she'd caught her teacher with his mouth open. Then he'd mumble under his breath in French that he'd never seen a child as gifted as she.

Three hours after his departure, she remained on the padded bench. Her fingers giving life to a melody etched onto her soul.

"Chaisley, my goodness." Her silver-haired grandmother— her favorite person other than her mother and father—entered the music room. "You've been in here for hours tinkering away." Grandmother's accent was thicker than her father's, and Chaisley loved to listen to the cadence of her words. Like music itself.

Chaisley tore her eyes from the piano. "It's so beautiful, Grandmother. I couldn't help myself."

Grandmother pulled a tapestry-covered wing-backed chair up next to the bench and sat. "Did you know that Steinway pianos were founded by a man from my mother's home country? They've made the best pianos in the world since the 1850s. When your father wanted to surprise you with one, I heartily agreed that it was the only piano we should buy." She ran her hand over the sleek gold lettering, just like Chaisley had done. "It is indeed beautiful, child. As is your music. I could hardly believe my ears."

"It's like it's all trapped inside me, just waiting to burst forth and get out."

"You've always been an old soul, Chaisley. Your words, your mannerisms. You've just turned ten years old today, and yet you talk like someone twice your age." Grandmother winked at her. "Maybe that's why we get along so well, my dear. My blond-haired, blue-eyed little cherub."

Grandmother's wrinkled hand reached out and touched Chaisley's cheek. *Old soul.* She'd overheard the grown-ups whispering that about her before. Was that why she didn't have any friends her own age?

Mother and Father walked into the room and that was when she noticed that the shadows of the tall windows had grown across the floor.

Mother walked over and pulled Chaisley into her arms. "Are you happy, dear?"

"Oh, yes. Thank you so very much." Happy didn't even begin to describe everything that danced within her.

Father winked, the glimmer in his eyes just like his mother's. "Maybe this will give you something to do other than burying your nose in your books."

Mother patted her hand. "There's nothing wrong with reading books, darling. Your father is teasing. Now, let's get you ready. We've planned a party for you at your favorite restaurant this evening."

Food and a party sounded like fun, but . . . Oh, how she wanted to stay at her precious piano. With a longing glance at it over her shoulder, she pasted on a smile. The piano would be there after the party.

Grandmother cleared her throat and stood. Chaisley saw tender understanding in her eyes. "Come on, little one. I'll help you get dolled up for your ten-year celebration."

CHAISLEY PRESSED HER CHEEK against the back window of the Rolls-Royce Silver Ghost limousine. *Silver Ghost.* From the day her father showed her the new automobile, Chaisley loved to repeat the name. She could imagine it came from a fairy tale. A melody line immediately formed in her mind. As the music swelled and grew into a symphony of story, she closed her eyes and allowed it to play. The sonata of the Silver Ghost finished with a flourish, and she drew in her breath. She was . . . what? Content. Yes, that was it. Not only did the music inside her have a way to come to life now, but she'd begun to understand the structure of it. It made sense. Logical and yet beautifully mysterious. She could hardly wait for tomorrow's lesson with Monsieur Beaufort. A little chill raced up her arms and she replayed her new composition in her head.

"Perhaps we should ask Gerard to drop us off a few blocks away so we could take a stroll together. It's such a lovely evening."

Mum's words caused Chaisley to open her eyes and blink away the music. "Oh, could we? By the fountain? I could make a wish on my birthday!" She bounced on her seat as she faced her parents in the back of the long car.

Her dad chuckled. "Of course. Change seats with me, Chais." They did so, and he tapped on the glass behind him and spoke to Gerard.

If only Grandmother could have come with them! But she'd had a sudden bad headache, and as much as she wanted to come, she couldn't.

Grandmother's disappointed tears had made Chaisley want to cry herself. A party just wouldn't be the same without the one grandparent she'd ever known, who'd lived with them since she was a baby.

She sighed and looked at the sparkly lights outside and the people dressed in their finery. She loved watching out the window as they drove to the city in their motor car. But tonight, her mind drifted back to the shiny Steinway Grand sitting in the new music room. The lavish wing of the home built for *her*. And her music. A laugh bubbled up inside her and escaped once again. What a joyous day.

But as the world slid by the car's window, Father's words from earlier drifted back into her mind. Did she really read too many books? Didn't every child read books? Just because she enjoyed reading and the music that played in her mind—that didn't make her odd, did it?

The car hit a bump in the road, and Chaisley's forehead banged into the window. She rubbed at the smarting spot.

"You'd better lean back, Chais." Father grinned and shook his head at her.

She rubbed one last time. Every time they drove to the city, the same thing happened. She'd hit her head on the glass while peering out the window, Father would suggest she lean back, and she would obey and gaze out the window some more. But it seemed her forehead always inched back to where she could enjoy the cool feel of the glass against her skin.

Mum moved to the seat next to her father and took his hand. The special smiles they shared together always made Chaisley feel warm and protected.

A terrible screaming punctured her happy bubble and filled the car. Air-raid sirens!

All the air in Chaisley's lungs whooshed out as she screamed. She closed her eyes tight—wait . . . what was that sound?

The roar of airplane engines.

Her eyes popped open and she saw Father's eyes were wide. "Turn the car around! Now!"

The earth rumbled beneath them and the car shook. The blast was so loud that Chaisley cupped her hands over her ears to stop the ringing.

"Turn *around*!" Father's mouth shaped the same command, though the ringing and roar all around her drowned out his voice.

Gerard cranked the steering wheel, and Dad pulled Mum under his arm. He waved Chaisley closer, but they were so far away. The small space between their seats turned into a chasm as she felt frozen in place.

A bright light from the other side of the car made her snap her gaze to the window.

What was that? It was coming fast. Getting brighter and brighter . . .

With a sharp inhale, her hands fell to her sides and she stared as time seemed to slow down.

Mum screamed. Father grabbed for Chaisley and her mum, but his hands met air as they jostled around inside the car. An awful new sound filled her ears—screeching, screaming metal. Chaisley cried out, reached for her father, and saw something in his eyes she'd never seen before.

Fear.

She turned to Mum just in time to see her head smash against the window and bounce back. Her eyes shut. Blood trickled down her face.

"Oh God, no! Please . . . save us!" Father's words jerked Chaisley's eyes off her mother.

Chaisley swung her gaze to follow his. The lights—and whatever was behind them—were pushing them toward a massive stone wall.

She screamed and tried to reach for Father again. If she could get to him, she'd be safe.

But he was too far away.

They slammed into the wall.

The impact threw Chaisley from her seat.

Glass shattered.

The car crunched.

Her father shouted her name.

THREE MONTHS LATER

"So there's no hope?" Grandmother's whispered words from somewhere across the room traveled over the length of Chaisley's body like a tiny wisp of wind.

The last remnants of sleep disappeared and she rubbed at her face.

A man sighed. "There's plenty of hope for her life now that all her other wounds have had time to mend." She recognized the voice—her father's best friend. The only doctor she'd ever known. "But the tiny glass shards did too much damage to her eyes. I'm sorry. Her skin has healed, yes. You can barely tell the places she had stitches. Her broken bones have mended. I know you want her to be exactly like she was before. Perfect in appearance and . . ." He paused. A deep breath. "You'd like her to be perfect with all her senses intact. But God has given us a different path. She's young and strong and needs to know the truth." Footsteps brushed the carpet. An all-too-familiar sound now. "Chaisley. Can you hear me?"

Her dry throat burned as she opened her mouth. "Yes, Dr. G."

"Do you understand what is going on?" The scent of peppermint whirled around her with his words.

"Yes." Her own words cracked. She swallowed. "I can't see. I won't ever be able to see again." The words were mere facts. She'd had three long months with the dark to understand them. They didn't hurt. Not anymore.

Unlike the knowledge that Mother and Father were dead.

"Well, I want to send a new tutor over for you. You need to learn braille and other life skills. There's no reason you shouldn't enjoy a very full life. Your parents would want this for you. *We* want this for you." His tone wasn't harsh, but it sounded . . . determined. Funny how everyone's voice was different now that she could no longer see their faces. But she could feel what she used to be able to see. Like dynamics inserted into a piece of music.

Grandmother gasped. "Grafton, don't you think that's a little too brash? She's just a child."

"Celestia, your son was like a brother to me. You know very well what the will stated. And I'm taking my job very seriously. Chaisley is like my own daughter, and I won't see her bedridden. She is brilliant, talented, and capable and if I have anything to do with it, she will receive every benefit she deserves and live life to the fullest." His statements were clipped and then he cleared his throat.

The rustling of Grandmother's dress told Chaisley the older woman had risen. And when Grandmother stood, she meant business. Chaisley chewed on her bottom lip, her ears tuned to every breath, every hint of sound.

"Young man, might I remind you to whom you speak. I understand *exactly* what the will stated—I aided my son in the writing of it—but remember that we are co-guardians of our dear girl, and *I* am related by blood. This is *my* estate. *My* granddaughter. And I do not appreciate being trampled over by a mere boy who used to build mud pies in my flower gardens, *Timothy*." A thud accompanied each word, followed by several thumps at the end to punctuate.

Grandmother didn't need her cane to assist her in walking, but she said it made her feel more comfortable to carry it. No doubt to help her get her points across.

And the fact that she called him *Timothy* . . . she must really be in a lather.

"There's no need for reminders of the past." The doctor's voice sounded less on the verge of cracking as he chuckled.

Hearing Dr. G talk with Grandmother was almost like hearing Dad's voice again. Warm but firm. She let out a sigh and snuggled against the pillows.

The doctor continued. "I apologize, ma'am. I truly do. But you can't keep her sequestered and bedridden. She needs fresh air. She needs to run around. She's healthy and robust, but she won't stay that way if you continue to coddle her for fear of losing *her* as well."

No one ever scolded Grandmother. Ever. How would she respond?

He cleared his throat again, and Chaisley listened as the footsteps moved away. Possibly to the window? His voice was deeper

24

and quieter as it spanned the expanse of the room. "We have seen amazing things among the blind. Why won't you allow her to live? Not just live . . . thrive."

Grandmother huffed. The rustle of one of her lace hankies—no doubt—muffled her sniffs. Amazing how all the sounds were distinguishable now. Her sure, soft footfalls came toward Chaisley. The scent of lilac preceded Grandmother's hand touching her own. "My dearest, I never wanted you to have to go through any of this. I'm sorry you've had to overhear our discussion. But know this—I love you—"

"We both do." Dr. Grafton's gentle, firm voice again.

Grandmother cleared her throat. "Would you excuse Grafton and me? I'd like to speak to him downstairs."

"But . . . I want to hear." Why did her own voice sound so weak and mouse-like? She wanted to tell them that she *did* want to live . . . to thrive.

"I'd like to speak to Dr. Grafton alone." Grandmother's tone brooked no argument.

She nodded. "Yes, Grandmother. I'll be fine." As soon as Dr. Grafton challenged her grandmother something had shifted inside her.

The pain from her injuries had overshadowed every part of her life but her grief for many weeks. And her body had been so very tired. Then her other senses often became overwhelmed as they took up the slack from her loss of sight.

But to hear him say that she was healing and could live her life encouraged her more than she dared imagine. Today was the first day she had any gumption to do anything other than what she was told.

She wanted to live. Oh, how she desired it!

But the world was a scary place in the dark. Her room was safe. Her bed her little cocoon of comfort.

Tears pricked her eyes. *"Be brave, my little munchkin . . . God*

will always be with you." How could she be brave? She couldn't
see. . . . Her parents were gone. . . .

"Be brave . . ." Father's words echoed in her head. Whenever
she faced something new, he'd say the same phrase. She could hear
his voice, clear and strong in her mind. Oh, she never wanted to
forget his voice.

A surge of warmth rushed through her body. She *would* be
brave. For Mother and Father.

But as soon as the feeling came, it left.

How could she be brave? She was scared. Helpless. A little blind
orphan girl . . .

The tears returned in earnest. For weeks, she'd battled the dark
and the nightmares that accompanied it. Days passed in a sludge
of smothering unknowns. What would she do without her parents?
What would she do without her sight?

And what would happen to the music that multiplied and grew
inside her each day?

MARY BETH BRIGMAN, the teacher Dr. G had brought in twenty-two
days ago, coached her down the steps. "You're doing splendidly,
young lady. You've just about mastered every area of the house
without any aid."

At the bottom of the grand staircase, the coolness of the marble floor seeped through Chaisley's thin ballet slippers and she
bounced on the balls of her feet at the praise. She knew every inch
of her home now, and not just by counting her steps or touching
the walls with her hands and floors with her feet. No. Each room
had its own sound. Its own pitch. Its own smell and feel. And
in her mind, notes played across the musical staff in a different
melody for each one.

Mary Beth engulfed her in a hug. "I'm so proud of you, little
miss. It's barely been three weeks since we started and you amaze

me every day. I'll go fetch your grandmother so you can show her. You head on back up the staircase."

She nodded, unable to contain a smile. Though her guardians had indeed gone to battle over her recovery, Dr. G had won, and the very next day Mary Beth arrived with a long stick. The walking stick was great for their walks outdoors and helped her to navigate unknown surroundings, but she didn't like to be hindered by it inside. She'd much rather skip and jump and glide through her own home. Each day, she felt a little stronger. A little braver. A little more alive.

As she turned for the stairs, a strange sensation tugged at her. Melodies and harmonies and symphonies burst into her mind. Notes from the lowest of basses to the highest of trebles.

Sliding her feet back round, she hesitated. Dare she? The room called to her. The music begged her. A lone tear slid down her cheek. She hadn't wanted to venture back into that room since that terrible night. . . .

She inhaled but didn't dare move just yet. She released her breath as the music inside her swelled.

It was back. Wholly and completely.

The music exploded in her head and heart. No stopping the pull—it drew her like a magnet. She touched her right heel behind her to the stair and felt the line of it. If she turned forty-five degrees, she'd be facing her beloved music room. Without counting her steps, she headed straight toward it. The room that had been closed since her birthday and—

No. The nightmare couldn't control her any longer. The loss of her parents couldn't squelch the beauty that deep down she *knew* lay ahead.

If only she allowed the music to take over. Fill her heart. Soothe her mind.

Her right foot met the bottom of the door. Both hands reached for the brass handles she could see in her mind's eye.

She pushed and wrinkled her nose. Stale air permeated the room like a musty perfume. Still she moved forward. The warmth from the sun spilled over her. Father had built walls of windows into this room. At least the staff hadn't drawn all the drapes. The warmth on her face told her the sun was shining in.

Hands held out in front of her, Chaisley searched for what she desired most. The one thing that would bring a smile as it reminded her of her parents for the rest of her life.

She walked straight into it and jolted from the force of the bump. The slick surface felt wonderful under her hands, soothing the ache inside. As she allowed her fingers to guide her, she knew she was standing in the great curve on the right-hand side.

Working her way around to the keyboard, a sensation she hadn't felt since her birthday bubbled up inside her tummy.

Excitement.

With a swift turn to put the piano at her back, she steadied herself and then counted her steps back to the double doors. But she ran into the doorjamb instead.

Which was just as well, as she'd left the doors open.

Something she quickly rectified. With the click of the doors, she turned again and held the handles behind her back.

Using all the techniques Mary Beth had taught her, she focused and counted steps again. To the edge of the piano. Then back to the doors. This time she ran into the left door. Almost center. Better try again. Back to the piano again.

Ten times she repeated the process until it was exact and she found her way each time.

With a shaky breath, she allowed a smile and lifted her chin.

At the piano, the fallboard was down over the keys, the bench pushed in. But she fixed that within seconds and let her hands find their way. Without making a sound, she skimmed them up and down the keyboard with reverence. She remembered what it all looked like. The sets of two black keys and the sets of three black keys divided up the white keys, making the notes easy to find. From left to right, C was before a set of two. F before a set of three.

In her mind, the picture unfolded . . .

And she could *see*. Her fingers moved over the keys, the music rippling like a ribbon in her mind. The tip of her nose burned as tears rose to the surface. Her sight wasn't coming back. And neither were her parents.

She knew that.

But right now, sitting at her piano, she felt like any moment she would soar right out a window and into the heavens. A sense of purpose poured out of her into the keys, a melody swirling and rushing through her like a river in a storm.

The smile that broke through her grief warmed her to her toes.

And for the first time since the accident that stole everything from her, Chaisley had hope.

CELESTIA FRAPPIER HOOKED the ornate cane over her arm and rushed to the house to see Chaisley. The walk uphill to the manor had kept her in shape all these years, but the ache in her hip after kneeling at the family cemetery reminded her she wasn't getting any younger. More painful than the ache in her hip was the ache in her heart. The loss of her only child and his wife had taken its toll. Like part of her heart had been wrenched from her chest while the remaining pieces struggled to be put back together. But she'd done everything in her power to not let her granddaughter see it.

Melanie—the sweet daughter of Chaisley's teacher —had run out to the garden to fetch her for a 'spectacular look-see at the bottom of the stairs,' as the young girl put it. Mary Beth always summoned Celestia for each milestone her granddaughter achieved.

Chaisley had made so much progress, it astounded her. She sighed. She'd have to apologize to Grafton—he'd been right after all. But she didn't mind. Not one bit. It was a good thing the man would be there for afternoon tea. They had much to discuss.

As for her own battered heart, it would heal. Especially with the joy of Chaisley around.

Just then, Mary Beth trotted around the corner in a most unladylike manner. But the young woman beamed, and Celestia understood her excitement. The whole house brimmed with the news of her granddaughter's daily progress.

Losing sight wouldn't hold the child back.

Celestia felt the crinkles around her eyes deepen as she smiled. What joy the little girl had brought into her grief-stricken life.

But upon reaching the staircase, she gasped. No sign of Chaisley anywhere.

"Um, I'm sorry, ma'am. I'll run up and see if she's taking a rest. Or possibly a jaunt to the loo."

Mary Beth was halfway to the top when a glissando reached Celestia's ears.

What?

Her heart clenched at the memory of Chaisley's birthday and her present. With an abrupt turn, she headed toward the music room, Mary Beth close on her heels.

No. It couldn't be. Could it?

Celestia had ordered everyone to stay clear of the room since that awful night. No one had dared to enter other than the one maid that was allowed to clean in there.

Arpeggios up and down the piano sounded. Then a spectacular and flowing melody.

When Celestia reached the doors, she stopped. Her heart thundered. Her mouth dropped open. With a shaking hand, she opened one door and then stared. The song grew in volume and harmonies. The music coming from the instrument was beautiful. Unlike anything she'd ever heard before.

It jolted at a dissonant chord. The music stopped. Chaisley's mumbled words couldn't be deciphered, but then the music started again.

Celestia peered across the room. Could her eyes and ears be deceiving her?

No. It was true! Her granddaughter sat on the bench, her eyes wide open, face toward the windows, a jubilant smile lifting her lips.

Mary Beth nudged Celestia and whispered, "My goodness, Mrs. Frappier, you didn't tell me the child could play. I would've brought her in here had I known. How long has she been studying?"

Celestia could only shake her head.

"Ma'am? Are you quite all right?"

The sweet girl's question brought Celestia out of her stupor. She closed her mouth and composed herself. She swallowed and cleared her throat. How could she explain this? There was no way . . . other than divine appointment.

"We must call Monsieur Beaufort immediately." The words spilled out on a soft whisper.

"Who?" Mary Beth stepped in front of her, brows knit deep. "Ma'am, I'm confused."

"Monsieur Beaufort is the piano teacher." With a deep breath, Celestia put into words the only explanation she could give—the truth. "Three hours, Mary Beth. That's it."

"Excuse me, ma'am?"

"My granddaughter . . . she's had one lesson and only played three hours prior to today."

chapter ONE

BERLIN, GERMANY—THURSDAY, FEBRUARY 10, 1938

Tension hummed in the crowd as Rick Zimmerman pointed to the third fish on his left. Hopefully the code hadn't changed. He held his breath.

Harold the fishmonger nodded, wrapped the selection, and then handed it to Rick.

The sour and salty smell of fish mixed with the musty scent of the newspaper assaulted his senses as he allowed himself to breathe again. Swallowing hard, he tucked the package under his arm. He tipped his hat to the older gentleman and turned on his heel, taking long, steady steps down the block.

The market was busy this morning, but his contact hadn't flinched. Nazi police and soldiers seemed to be everywhere. None of the shoppers looked anyone in the eye. They made their purchases, then scurried to the next store.

Or left altogether.

Rick threaded through the crowd, the fish feeling heavier with every step. With his free hand, he turned up the collar of his jacket. The chill in the air grew with every heartbeat. Five more minutes until he was home. Until he found out the location of his next assignment.

Shrill whistles pierced the air. "Halt!"

His heart kicked into a higher gear as he broke into a jog with the crowd around him. Footsteps thundered in all directions, but who had shouted the command? With a quick turn to his left, Rick slipped into an alley and tuned in to all the voices around him. Officers in the distance spoke in harsh tones to someone. Rick slid up against the wall as close to the corner of the building as he could. Only then did he dare to glance back.

Four *Geheime Staatspolizei* officers surrounded the fishmonger. Rick flinched as they punched Harold in the gut. One of the officers let out a laugh when the old man crumpled to the ground. Another picked up basket after basket, dumping the contents into the street. Harold moaned and rolled to his side. The *Gestapo* officers jerked his arms behind his back, hauled Harold to his feet, and dragged him off.

Rick broke out in a sweat. Harold was one of the few contacts he had left in Berlin. He leaned back against the wall for a moment, his head thumping against the brick. They all knew they were in danger of arrest, or worse. Every contact was trained, made aware of the dangers of the job. Harold knew the risks. But he'd become more than a contact—he was a friend. Rick clamped his lips tight. Emotions were a weakness, but the loss tugged at him.

Please help him, Lord. Protect him.

Whistles sounded again, pulling Rick out of his prayer. He'd stayed here too long. One more glance told him the officers were headed the other direction. For now. It was time to make a run for it. He thrust the fish inside his jacket and tugged the zipper all the way up to his chin. He made quick work of the distance to his flat, running all the way up the stairs, checking at each landing to ensure no one followed.

He slipped his key in the lock, entered the flat, and closed the door with a soft click. There was no time to lose. He put his other security measures in place.

A chair under the doorknob.

Drapes pulled shut.

Glass bottles upside-down on each window ledge.

With deft pulls, he closed the extra layer of thick curtains over the first, then dropped the fish on the table. He made a survey of the room.

No one had been there since he left.

He grabbed a knife from the kitchen and slit the fish, his fingers trembling. What if he didn't have the right one? Would the Gestapo find it in Harold's baskets? He paused and held his breath for a moment before releasing it in measured bursts. If he wasn't careful, he'd slice a finger.

He cut the rest of the fish open and pulled it apart. There, the tiny message was intact! His shoulders eased a bit as he unfolded the small slip of paper.

Father says Mother is in Holland to care for her great-aunt. She misses you. Here's hoping your French and your driving skills aren't rusty.

Back to Holland, and as a driver no less. Disappointment simmered in his chest, but he shoved it away. He would take any assignment they offered, any opportunity to prove he was worthy of more responsibility. Besides, his work as a driver last year had produced an abundance of reliable intelligence. It was amazing the secrets people revealed in front of someone they considered invisible and beneath them. But the snippet about French sent a thrill up his spine. Perhaps this assignment was with a diplomat or a government official.

His superiors had often used his fluency in multiple languages when there was a higher-up involved. This could be better than he first thought! He glanced at the small clock on the kitchen wall. Ten thirty-seven. The next train left in forty-five minutes.

No more time to waste. Leaving Berlin was a relief to the side of him that was always on edge—even as he slept. Which meant he didn't sleep much. But his conscience and humanitarian side warred with the decision to leave. Would he be able to do what was needed in Holland?

He grimaced. It wasn't like it was his job alone to stop Hitler and his amassed army and followers. But with British contacts diminishing in number, would there be anyone left to stop him?

He couldn't think of that now. He had a job to do. He emptied drawers and the small closet in his bedroom, then shoved everything he owned into one bag. He burned the message—and anything else that could identify him as anything other than a Nazi sympathizer—in a small metal pail.

Harold's arrest meant one thing. Someone was onto Rick's small band of informants left in Germany. He passed a hand over his face. How could he leave when there were so many who couldn't escape the hostile regime?

He shook his head. Pushed the thought away. He had a job to do and little time to think about anything but getting on that train. He wiped down everything as he made his way backward out the door, ensuring nothing was left behind. He raced out of the building and down the street toward the train station. Whistles continued to split the air. The Gestapo were everywhere. Rick saw three more men arrested just in the time it took him to get to the station.

The Gestapo must have tortured someone who pointed them to an underground band of rebels. Was it his?

Scanning the train station, he got in line and watched several Gestapo interrogate travelers. When it was his turn, he stepped forward, purchased his ticket, and strode to the waiting train.

One hurdle down. Prayerfully, none of them followed him.

Climbing aboard, he resisted the urge to look around or behind him. A man with nothing to hide would just go about his business, after all.

He pulled out a newspaper and counted down the minutes until the train departed. Although a moving train didn't mean that he was safe, he could at least breathe easier once they were on their way.

The edge of his paper crumpled with the weight of a black-gloved hand.

Rick held his composure and met the stare of a Gestapo officer. The man wasn't one of the young, fresh-faced, eager-to-please officers Rick had seen of late. No. This man was seasoned. And the hardness of his eyes gave away his devotion to the Nazis.

"*Papiere*," the officer demanded.

Rick handed over his papers. His ticket was tucked inside his pocket. Prayerfully, the man wouldn't ask for it as well—because if it was taken away? Well . . . things could get much more difficult in an instant.

"*Wohin reisen Sie?*"

Why did the officer want to know where he was traveling? And why did the question hold a sharp edge? He opened his mouth to answer, but a scuffle in the back of the train escalated to shouting, and a woman's screams pierced the air.

The officer shoved Rick's papers back to him and shouted commands to remove the passengers from the train as he marched away.

It took several minutes for Rick's heart to return to normal as he hid behind his newspaper. Not until the train reached full speed, and his ticket and papers had been examined one more time, did the tension in his shoulders ease a bit.

Rick set aside his reading material and inspected each person in the car. All seemed safe for the moment. He slumped against the seat, but relief wouldn't come.

The barren landscape blurred before his gaze. Escape had come at a high price. The violence of the Gestapo was well-known. Could he be the only one who made it out? Rick rubbed his face, his eyes heavy. It was the middle of the day, but a nap sounded like heaven.

No. He needed to stay alert. Safety was an illusion until this train crossed the border into Holland.

Contacts for the British spies were disappearing in droves. But it was worst in Germany. And Hitler had full control of the military. His power and influence were growing at an alarming rate. Add to that the anti-Semitic laws he'd enacted in the last few years since President Hindenburg died, which had changed the landscape of *Deutschland*. Many of Rick's Jewish friends and contacts had been driven from Berlin, prohibited from doing their jobs or even sending their children to school. Jewish families weren't even considered citizens of Germany anymore.

His chest burned. The injustice was horrific. How could so many citizens be content to ignore Hitler's ever-growing power? Did they really not know of the hold he had on their part of the world? Germans were a people proud of their heritage and country.

The train whined to a stop, and Rick glanced out the window as the conductor came through, announcing the last stop before Holland. Several people stood and gathered their things, leaving Rick, one family, and a single woman alone in the car. He stood for a moment, stretching his arms over his head. The movement felt wonderful, tension easing from his muscles. Only a few more hours to go.

He sat again and looked out the window. The trees were bare, stark against the slate-gray sky. Families moved across the platform, bundled in warm coats and thick scarves. He watched one family in particular gather their luggage. A small boy was nestled in his mother's arms as a girl, no older than seven, clutched the back of the mother's coat. The dad had two shabby carpetbags clenched in his hand, and with a jerk of his head, he directed his family across the wooden planks and into the station.

Were they fleeing Germany? Or were they just one family among many heading home, oblivious to the lies the Nazi Party was feeding them?

The train lurched forward, jerking Rick's gaze away from the building. He needed to get out of these morose thoughts. Dwelling on the Nazi Party wasn't great for his mental state. Sure, he was tasked with finding out everything Hitler and his cronies were doing and how to stop them. But that task peeled back evil after evil.

Rick shoved his hands in his hair. How could he do his job and shield his heart from the horrors of what he uncovered?

It was impossible.

The writing was on the wall, but the Nazis knew how to appease people by tailoring speeches to their audience. Many were blind to what was really happening as they held out hope for a better future. A future where Germany was a player on the world stage again. Though how Hitler planned to accomplish that by leaving the League of Nations was a mystery.

The thought of what it might be like in the future if Hitler had his way caused a chill to race up his spine. If Rick's informants were correct, Germans would soon be prisoners in their own land. Revulsion twisted his stomach. In addition to losing informants, they'd lost too many allies and agents the last three months. Good men and women trying to save the world from another war.

And a maniac.

Rick's thoughts drifted to Harold. Was he still alive? Maybe it was better for his friend if he didn't survive to see his beloved country wither away even further. He winced. Cynicism and dark thoughts like that weren't helpful either. Time to focus on the job.

Did they have any chance to stop the growing evil before it was too late?

LONDON, ENGLAND—TUESDAY, FEBRUARY 15, 1938

"I know you're there." Chaisley lifted her fingers off the F#m7 chord and turned her head toward the entry. Her right foot eased off the sustain pedal and her lips tipped upward.

"You didn't resolve to the major chord, so I *know* you know I'm here. If it were anyone else, you would have finished the melody while inviting them to enter. But since you know how much I dislike dissonance and unresolved melodies, you like to torture me." Melanie, her assistant and dearest friend, chuckled. Footsteps clicked on the marble floor approaching the piano on the right. "The day you *don't* know I'm here is the day I shall worry that you are ill. Here, hold out your hand."

Chaisley did and something cool plopped into it. She closed her fingers around it. Paper. An envelope. She moved her thumb. Ah . . . *two* envelopes. "Thank you."

"The top one is from your grandmother. The other seems to be from a fan. The tour manager sent it over. I already asked Louise to have some tea sent up to your room."

Melanie's unmistakable scent of lavender and lemon teased Chaisley's nose as she turned toward the sound of her friend's voice. Her shoulders relaxed. That her friend knew her so well and looked after her . . . Her eyes burned as she fought back tears. What was wrong with her?

The clock chimed eleven times. Perhaps six hours at her piano this morning perfecting her latest composition was a bit much. Especially since she hadn't moved from the bench once in all that time. One thing about being blind was that her body had its own clock and didn't worry about when the sun came up or set. She always asked to be awakened by six each morning, but most days she was up well before that.

It would be heavenly to take a break and relax over her grandmother's words. "Thank you for arranging tea. I assume the other letter isn't in braille?" She stood from the bench and clutched the letters to her chest.

"It doesn't feel as if it is, but I didn't open it." Melanie's presence grew closer, and she slipped her arm around Chaisley's shoulders. "Working on that piece has worn you down—your emotions and exhaustion are clear on your face. But let me assure you, this latest masterpiece of yours is perfect. It moved me to tears, Chais. This tour is going to be your best yet."

The tour. Her temples began to throb. Melanie was only trying to be encouraging, but each time someone declared this concert or that tour or this appearance was going to be her best . . . the headache emerged. She puffed out a breath. No. There was no sense in giving into the pressure. She had been touted for years as the world's greatest pianist. This gift was from God, and she would use it to the best of her ability. All this anxiety was silly. Nerves were normal.

"Chais?" Melanie's voice cut through her thoughts. "Are you all right?"

Chaisley nodded, pushing through the pain growing in her head. "I practiced too long today without a break. I think tea and a letter from Grandmother is just what I need to set myself to rights. Would you come get me in an hour if I'm not back down?"

"Of course." Melanie's response was hesitant. "It will be time for luncheon by then anyway, and if the other letter isn't in braille, I'll read it to you."

"Thank you." Before her friend could ask any other questions, Chaisley moved toward the door. No one could understand what a tour meant for her. Leaving the safety and comfort of her quiet and orderly home to enter the chaotic world full of people and noise was overwhelming, to say the least. The preparation she had to do for that wasn't something a person with sight could understand.

As she counted her steps to the door and then to the stairs, the soft notes of C5, E5, and G5 met her ears. The treble C Major chord sounded happy and complete. Exactly what Melanie loved. Even though the G was a touch sharp.

She cringed. Perfect pitch often drove her batty. Every conductor she'd ever worked with had been mesmerized by her ability to hear when any instrument—especially the piano—was out of tune.

Moving up the stairs she listened to Melanie play the arpeg-giated chord several times and then all the notes together. Then a C scale. Her friend loved to tinker on the piano. Over the years, Chaisley had offered to teach her, but Melanie always declined.

At the top of the stairs, Chaisley navigated her way down the long hallway to her wing—forty-five steps—then turned left and counted twenty-two steps to her rooms. The cool handle dipped down as she opened the door. Shutting it behind her, she leaned against it for a moment. The silence was a balm to her racing thoughts.

Ah . . . the scent of roses. It was Monday. A new bouquet of two dozen roses was always delivered on Monday from Dr. G. The man was so good to her. He'd picked up the tradition after Father and Mother passed . . .

Her lips trembled, the memory washing over her. Dad loved to give her mum flowers every Monday. Not for any reason, just because. When Chaisley turned six, he brought her a bouquet as well. As soon as he found out that roses were her favorite, that's all he brought her. Every week. She wiped away a tear and spoke to the empty room. "I wish you were here. Both of you." Her voice cracked. Maybe a good cry would help. Some days the loss of her parents weighed heavier than others.

The clock on her dresser chimed the quarter hour and pulled her out of the melancholy. No time for a good cry. Melanie would check on her before she knew it, and there was still much to be done. Grandmother's letter awaited. She swallowed her tears. Tak-ing eleven steps forward and one to the right, she kept her hand at a forty-five degree angle out in front of her to find the back of the chair. Once she was seated, she opened her letter and laid the pages in order from left to right on her desk and put her fingers on the top of the first paper.

Her fingers flew over the dots on the page as she read the braille letter.

My dearest Chaisley,

All is well here, my dearest, other than the bitter cold of winter sending an ache through my bones. But that will be cured as soon as I am able to wrap my arms around you.

I must say thank you once again for agreeing to do the European tour and to spend time here in Holland with me. The world is a different place since the Great War. Hurt and suffering seem to envelop everyone. But you have the chance to spread hope and inspiration to all these people. In this time of great division and chaos, music can bring unity. I am certain of it.

I have been told that many of your concerts are already sold out of tickets. What wonderful news, although I am not surprised!

Don't you worry about a thing, I have made sure that everything is set up exactly as you requested here at my home and all of my staff know not to move a piece of furniture or anything else. Not even an inch.

Chaisley lifted her chin and listened as the wind rattled the windows in the manor that had been home her entire life. Grandmother's opening chitchat was exactly the perspective she needed. This European tour had been in the works for several years. Chaisley's schedule was always booked out at least two years in advance. But this time was different. This was a special request from her grandmother to give the people of Europe something of beauty to look forward to.

When Grandmother was involved, everything became larger than life. And how could Chaisley deny any request of hers? Not when Grandmother had done so much for her—raised her, given her every opportunity to develop the natural talents God had given her.

"Remember these things when you're tempted to get anxious about this tour," she muttered, her fingers moving back to the letter. "You are making your grandmother happy. And proud."

Reading the letter again, her fingers traced the words *hurt* and *suffering.* Just a few weeks ago, Dr. G had told her and Melanie of a story he'd read in *The Guardian* about Jews who were prisoners in concentration camps. What was the name . . . Her brow furrowed. Dachau. That was it. And numerous stories of Romanian Jews suffering persecution, driven from their homes without another place to go.

If the stories were true, there were many people who needed help. But how could she do anything? She was just a pianist.

The word *hope* rushed into her mind on a simple melody of four notes. One for each letter, it played over and over.

Perhaps that was what God wanted from her with this tour. People needed hope. Joy. What better way to lift the spirits of those who were weary than a night of music?

As her fingers finished reading the letter, she leaned back in the chair. Life hadn't been the same in England after Grandmother went back to Holland. To the land of her heritage and childhood. The Great War had devastated so much, it wasn't unusual for people to long for their roots and home. For a simpler time before the world had erupted in war.

Since Chaisley spent so much time on the road traveling, she encouraged her grandmother to follow her heart. As hard as that was to say aloud, it had been the right thing.

Celestia Frappier had a new mission in life after that. When she'd gone back to Holland and her ancestral home, the memories she shared with Chaisley multiplied. She found journals and clothing and all sorts of items that fortified the history that she'd clung to all her life. The rejuvenation, healing, and wonder had leapt off the pages of each of her grandmother's letters.

That wonder seemed to carry Grandmother in her new life in Holland. The woman was tireless. Each letter was filled with news about helping one charitable group or another. The memories of neighbor helping neighbor spurred her on to continue spreading and sharing her heritage. The tone was much like this letter, cheery and happy. But there was always a tinge of sadness. Of worry.

Most people didn't see the men, women, and children that poured into Holland from Germany and Austria as anything other than a nuisance. Refugees to be shuffled off to someone else. But not Grandmother. She had always seen those less fortunate than she and was willing to use the wealth and resources God had given her to help.

A tap at the door made Chaisley turn in her chair. "Come in."

Dr. Grafton's cologne. What a surprise.

"I was expecting Melanie"—she stood and held her arms open— "but you're always welcome too."

His steps drew near and then he hugged her and tapped her nose. "It always amazes me how you distinguish who is in front of you without seeing our faces or hearing our voices." He squeezed her arms. "Don't worry, Mel is coming, because I'd like to discuss a few things with you both while they are on my mind."

"Oh?" She reclaimed her seat. "That sounds serious," she teased.

He cleared his throat. "It is. But only because I want to take precautions."

Her smile slipped from her face. "Precautions?" She pleated her skirt in her fingers. Was the state of Europe so bad they needed such things?

"For your safety." His voice shifted slightly. He must have turned away. "Here's Melanie. Would you close the door?"

"Of course." The door clicked and Melanie's lighter footsteps approached.

A chair scratched across the floor, then another.

Chaisley wasn't ready for anything heavy yet. "Melanie"—she held out the other letter—"would you read this for me first, please?"

"Of course." Her friend took the letter. The paper crinkled. Mel cleared her throat. "It's in German, so I need to translate as I go. Forgive me if I'm a bit slow."

"Dear Miss Frappier,

"My name is Mary, I am eleven years old, and I live in Berlin. Several years ago, when I was only five years of age, my mother brought me to one of your concerts in Paris.

"It was the best night of my life. That night you opened up my heart and mind to music. It spoke to my very soul.

"You see, I was a difficult child. I constantly threw tantrums, struggling to figure out the world around me. I should probably tell you: I am blind."

Chaisley gasped and put a hand to her throat. Never had she received a fan letter from a blind child!

Melanie continued reading.

"The world calmed down as you played. That was the first time that had ever happened.

"I told my mother I wanted to be a pianist that night.

"After that, Mother arranged for me to take lessons until things became more difficult for us here. They took her away for a while, and my piano teacher hid me. When she returned, she was broken and not the same. They performed some kind of operation on her because she is also blind. Our house was taken away.

"Ever since, we have gone from home to home to stay with friends. My mother says we must hide so they don't take me away as well. She is afraid. My piano teacher tries to see me when he can, but I can tell by the sound of his voice that he is also afraid now. His visits have become quite rare.

"I do my best to give my mother hope by playing for her, but all she does is cry.

"I hear you are coming back here to tour, and my piano teacher is trying to get tickets for Mother and me. I think if she could just hear you again, she would once again have hope and remember what it did for me as a little girl.

46

"I am leaving you the address of my teacher in case you would like to write him or the two of us a note of encouragement.

"Please keep playing. I wanted you to know how much you inspired me and changed my life. We all need hope—and you gave that to me.

"I pray I get to hear you play again soon.

"Thank you for opening up the world of music to me.

Mary Beth Klein"

"Mary Beth"—Melanie whispered the name again—"just like my mother." Her voice cracked.

Chaisley swallowed back the emotions clogging her throat. What kind of operation would they have done on the mother just because she was blind? It didn't make sense. Still, what a brave young girl. In the midst of difficult times, she was encouraging her mother. "Mel, I need you to make sure we send tickets to that address. Multiple concerts if you can, so they can surely come to at least one."

"Of course." Her friend's response was strong and determined. "Just look at how you've affected this one life, Chaisley."

She shifted her face toward the window. "What is happening in Berlin? And why would they take Mary Beth's mother away and perform surgery?"

Dr. G cleared his throat and by the sound of his chair, he must have shuffled in his seat. Since he didn't answer right away, that meant it was something he didn't want to share with her. He cleared his throat again. "I have heard rumors that they have sterilized people whom they believe are imperfect. To protect the Aryan race."

"*What?*" While the news in Europe depressed her most of the time, Chaisley thought she had at least stayed informed. Apparently that wasn't true.

"This isn't common knowledge, Chais. That is why I wanted to speak to each of you today."

The weight of words from a young girl about her mother's plight penetrated deep into Chaisley's heart. Little wonder her grandmother had become so passionate about helping everyone she could. "Has Grandmother seen some of this in her work?"

"Yes." The answer was quick. "Chaisley . . . we've never wanted you to feel less of a person because of the effects of the accident. But there are many people being treated as less, whether blind, deaf, missing a limb, or simply of a different race. They're regarded by some as not even human—not deserving of life. Your grandmother asked me to keep all this to myself until she found the right way to speak with you about it."

"But why?" She swallowed hard. "We've never kept secrets before. And no one has ever treated me as lesser. Gracious, the majority of the world has no inkling that I've lost my sight." Heat raced up her neck into her cheeks, but she resisted the urge to duck her head. What did she have to be embarrassed about? It wasn't as if she chose to be blind.

But Dr. Grafton's words gnawed at her. Had she been wrong to refrain from telling people she was blind? She hadn't wanted anyone to feel sorry for her.

"I can tell by the look on your face that you are second-guessing your decisions to be independent and keep this to yourself. You've done nothing wrong." Melanie's fervent words touched Chaisley. "Not a thing. You haven't lied to anyone. You've lived your life and performed and blessed people the world over. Just look at what you've done for this little girl."

"Mel's correct. It's the Nazis who are doing the wrong. They are perpetrating this lie—spreading propaganda far and wide." Dr. G's tone held the tint of anger. And it took a great deal to anger her guardian and dear friend.

"But is there a way I can help? Something more than just playing the piano? Something to give people joy and hope?"

Dr. Grafton sighed. "Let's take this one step at a time—"

Chaisley nodded. "You're right. I need to write her back. Encourage her. And her mother as well." Her thoughts swirled.

"That's a wonderful idea." He cleared his throat again, a sign he wanted to change the subject. "But there's a great deal more that we need to discuss. I've had some ideas about the upcoming tour."

"Are you going to come along?" Melanie chimed in.

"No, I have quite a bit of traveling to do myself to check on colleagues in a few clinics and other friends, but this is about the amount of . . . disharmony I keep hearing about. It has led to violence and crime."

Another bit of news to Chaisley. How much had they kept from her? Or had she simply kept her head buried in the sand?

Dr. G continued, his tone sober. "In order to guard our correspondence, in case you need to convey something of importance to me or vice versa, I think we should go back to writing in the original form of braille, or perhaps something else."

Well. That wasn't what she was expecting. Were there thieves out to steal the mail? "You mean with the dashes and dots?"

"Yes." Papers rustled. "I took the liberty of making a sheet of the alphabet, numbers, and punctuation for each of you as a refresher. Memorize it and then burn them."

"That's a little extreme." The catch of apprehension in Melanie's voice set Chaisley's nerves on edge.

Dr. G's voice grew more firm. "Finding an original form of braille isn't easy. There are very few even familiar with it outside of perhaps some braille teachers who are fascinated with its history and the War of the Dots. So this should be a safe form of communication."

Oh dear. All the lessons she'd pushed him into teaching her over the years. He'd endured her fascination with braille and her insatiable hunger to understand everything behind the invention that allowed her to read books and music. "Why are these precautions necessary?" She raised her eyebrows. "Because of Hitler and his Nazis?"

His long breath told her he was choosing his words carefully. Which meant she'd struck the truth. He *was* worried about Hitler. "It's my job as your guardian to ensure your safety. No matter how far-fetched the rumors might be"—there was a catch in his voice, then that pause that proved he was coddling her—"I still want to be cautious."

Rather than call him out, she'd play along. "If these precautions are necessary, then perhaps we should memorize the Boston Line Type and New York Point versions as well. Just in case."

"Just in case . . . what?" Melanie's tone held fear.

Chaisley opened her mouth to say she was teasing, but Dr. Grafton's words halted her. "That's an even better idea. We can alternate each sentence. I will bring them to you tomorrow." A pencil scratched on paper—he was writing a note.

So this was more serious than she thought. "I believe I still have them in a book here."

"If you do, you should burn them as well after you memorize them. Just in case." His voice was clipped.

"What is it you're not saying?" The higher pitch of Melanie's voice clued in Chaisley about how much anxiety this was causing her.

She could relate. Dr. G never did anything without a purpose. If he thought they needed to guard their communications while on tour, there was good reason. She reached for Melanie's hand and turned her face toward the scent of lavender and lemon. "Mel, I believe our dear friend here is simply thinking about worst-case scenarios and making sure that we are able to safely communicate in case things escalate."

"Escalate?" Melanie's voice squeaked. "Why?"

"Because I'm blind," Chaisley stated as calmly as she could, even as the depth of the reality in Europe sank in. "Which means I could be seen as less than worthy. Unfit to live. That's what you mean, isn't it, Dr. G?"

BERLIN, GERMANY—SATURDAY, FEBRUARY 19, 1938

For the first time in a long time, he had hope.

That his country could make it through this depression stronger, larger, and wealthier than ever.

That with a powerful leader at the helm, his homeland would not be humiliated again.

The only way to erase any residual humiliation was to get rid of those who couldn't pull their weight. Those who were less than perfect. Those who couldn't make decisions for themselves. Those who weren't of the superior race.

In the past, weak leaders had exacerbated the mess that his country had inherited. But no longer.

If people would simply take the time to listen to the Führer's heartfelt words, they'd understand and agree with what was best for the world. And they *would* reach the world. He'd seen the plans. Hitler would start taking Europe little by little, and then his power would spread around the globe. It wasn't a matter of *if*. It was a matter of *when*.

His own family didn't understand. How could they? His mother had left eons ago, and his siblings were scattered all over Europe. They'd had no correspondence. Not since he'd returned home to Germany for his father's funeral had *he* understood. Five years ago, his eyes were finally opened. And now he would do anything—*anything*—to see things set to rights.

Hope was a wonderful thing.

chapter
TWO

LONDON, ENGLAND—WEDNESDAY, MARCH 16, 1938

Melanie looked at the half-packed cases on her bed and wiped her hands on her skirt. The trembling in them had grown worse the last hour. Why couldn't she quell her ridiculous nerves?

If only Mum were still alive. They could sit down, Melanie could pour out all her fear and worries, and her mother would say all the right things to calm her.

A knock sounded on her door, and she put a hand to her chest to steady the wild beating of her heart. She needed to pull herself together. "Come in."

The door opened and Dr. Grafton stood in the door frame. "I was wondering if you would take a walk with me in the garden. I have something of great import to discuss with you."

She blinked and glanced back at the cases. In only a day's time, they would be leaving England for the tour. Which would last the next eighteen months. It would be the longest time she'd been away from England since her mother passed. The first bit would be spent in Amsterdam visiting Chaisley's grandmother. But then it would be travel, travel, travel.

Dr. Grafton cleared his throat.

"A walk. Yes, of course." She grabbed her shawl and followed him out the door. Once they were outside, Melanie could still hear Chaisley playing the grand piano in the music wing.

Dr. Grafton shoved his hands into the pockets of his trousers, and they walked for several minutes in silence. When they reached the center of the garden and the circle of benches, he held out a hand, inviting her to take a seat.

She did and the shaking in her hands was more apparent. Clasping them in her lap, she watched him sit a couple feet away from her and stare out to the horizon. "As you know, your mother and I were very close."

A slight nod and a swallow were all she managed. She'd fully expected Dr. Grafton to become her stepfather, until the sickness hit her mum with a ferocity that took them all by surprise.

"She was very proud of you, Melanie, and asked me to keep an eye on you once she was gone."

Hot tears slipped from her eyes and down her cheeks. Mum had taken the world on as a single mother and had provided for her daughter while tutoring Chaisley. Raised by blind parents, Mum had convinced Chaisley that she didn't have limitations after losing her sight, that her exceptional gifts needed to be shared with the world.

Neither her mother nor Dr. Grafton could have foreseen where those gifts would take Chaisley, but her friend had faced life with a smile. And her music.

That amazing music.

"When I hired your mother to come teach Chais twenty years ago, I had no idea she would become my best friend and how I would adore you as my own daughter—just like Chaisley." His voice caught as he gazed down at her.

Why was his smile so sad?

"Melanie, I know you're scared. Especially since you know who your father was—and because you have family in Germany."

At the mention of her father, her stomach lurched, and she placed a hand over her mouth. She didn't have any good memories of the man, and the few stories her mother shared when she was older were enough to reinforce in Melanie's mind that he'd been an evil man.

"Frankly, after reading that little girl's letter and hearing about what the Nazis are doing, I would be terrified to go back myself. But I know Almighty God. No matter the evil those sinful people are perpetrating, He is still a loving God—waiting for hearts to turn to Him. For five years we've watched the Nazis escalate Hitler's plan. He might have fooled a great deal of the world during the Olympics, but his actions ever since have only convinced me that we are headed toward another world war. And many more lives are at stake. I fear the more power he attains, the more people he will eliminate. Especially the Jews."

He shook his head and looked back at her with a sad smile. "My apologies, Mel." He covered her shaking hands with one of his. "I tend to get worked up as I understand more about what is happening. I don't want you or Chaisley to worry, but that's why I've done a great deal of traveling the past couple years and will be doing much more. My practice here will be run by others while I continue my work abroad. I need to help."

"Help?" She swallowed hard. "With what?" It was awful enough to know she'd have to go back to Germany, but why did dear Dr. Grafton have to go? He was supposed to stay back in England where it was safe.

He patted her hands and looked straight ahead. "It is our duty as believers to do everything we can to stand against evil and speak truth. Share the gospel. For me, that means helping the hurting. Just like God has given Chais the gift of music, He gave me the gift of healing others. In that, I've made connections all over Europe. Many of us have been meeting in secret for some time now to help—and not just the sick and dying." He waved a hand. "The details right now don't matter. In due time, you'll understand. But I do have something very important to give you. Well, two very important somethings." He grinned and pulled out a well-worn envelope and a clean and crisp one. "The older one is from your mother. She asked me to give it to you after your twenty-fifth birthday, whenever you needed it most. Since I don't know what it says, that made it difficult for me to decide on the when part, but this is the first time I've seen you need it. That must mean it is time.

"If you'd like to read it in private, that's fine, I simply wanted you to have it. Things haven't been the same since we lost your mother, but I'm here for you." He released the envelope into her grasp.

"Thank you." Her mother's loopy script spelled out her name. Melanie ran her hand over it and let out a shaky breath. She gazed up at him, willing the tears to melt away. "And the other?"

Dr. Grafton sat up a little straighter. "This next one must be kept secret. Only you, Chaisley, Celestia, and I can know about the contents."

Her eyes widened. What could it be?

He held out the envelope but kept a grip on it. "In this envelope is a list of contacts. An established network across Europe that I have been building for years. These people are willing to lay down their lives to help others. I ask you to guard this with your life. Memorize it if you can."

"But . . ." She laid the envelope in her lap and stared at it.

"Melanie . . ."

She met his gaze. What she saw there haunted her. Then like the weight of a heavy blanket, the gravity of the situation settled on her shoulders.

"Let me be blunt. Hitler and the Nazis took control of Austria a few days ago. I know that information hasn't been widespread here yet, and you have probably been too busy preparing for the trip to keep up with the news. While Hitler has not kept it secret that he wants to rule the world, his propaganda has kept secret what he *really* wants to do. He's trying to convince people that what the Nazis are doing is good—that they have no ill intentions. That he can turn the economy around and make life abundant again. But things are happening across Europe that are pure evil. Most people don't want to acknowledge that they are true because we're all still recovering from the Great War and this awful financial depression."

Melanie pressed a hand to her chest. The last time Dr. G's face was this grim was when her mother passed away. The heaviness pressed harder on her, making it difficult to breathe.

"There are those who see the truth of what is going on. If the world stands up to Hitler and his Nazis, then war will be upon us. I believe we are a long way off from that—most likely years away—but I simply want you to be prepared. Your safety, and Chaisley's, is of utmost importance." He tapped the envelope. "Fear will want to be our constant companion in the coming days, but we have the Lord. Remind yourself that fear is not from Him. Trust in that and in God. You contact whoever is closest to you in time of need, understood?"

She studied him. Could things really be as dire as he made it sound? She hoped and prayed it wasn't. Not just for their safety, but for her own sanity. Then it hit her. "When you said help the hurting, you said more than just the sick and dying. You're not just going to check on clinics and work with colleagues, are you?"

A slow shake of his head accompanied the softening of his eyes. "I've got to help."

Help whom? Why was he being vague? Was he putting himself in danger?

"If you see anything that can be done to help, you let me know."

There it was again. "Help? Help whom?" Her mind swirled. What was Dr. Grafton expecting of them while on a continental tour?

He held up a hand. "You and Chaisley can have that conversation if the need arises. Right now, it's best if you two don't know everything."

"Is she aware of any of this?" She waved the envelope around.

He shook his head. "No. There was much I didn't even understand until her grandmother opened my eyes the past year or so. It was then that I solidified this"—he tapped the envelope again—"and we—fellow medical workers and I—agreed to do what we can. We all took an oath as doctors to the sanctity of life, and as believers in Almighty God, we have a calling. I don't know what God might ask us to do, but we can't pretend we don't know what we know. You two have an opportunity to minister to people and see and hear what is really going on across Europe. I'm sure if the need becomes more urgent, Celestia will keep you informed. She will probably share more when you see her anyway."

Her stomach flipped over itself and she stared out at the garden.

"For such a time as this . . ."

Melanie frowned. What?

"For such a time as this . . ."

Her favorite story when she was a young girl was that of Queen Esther. Mordecai called on Queen Esther to save her people, though it put her own life at risk.

"If the need becomes more urgent . . ." Was she being called? Was this *her* time?

If only she had Mum's courage! But she didn't. She'd grown so . . . fearful. Timid.

When did that happen?

Chaisley was *always* ready to take on the world. She often challenged Melanie to step out of her comfortable, predictable life.

Dr. Grafton's eyes softened. "I understand that this is a lot for you, but I've seen how fiercely protective you are of Chaisley. I've seen how passionate you are about bringing people hope."

He tapped the letter from Mum.

"Maybe this will help more than I ever could. Just know that I will always be there for you. Always. If I need to travel across Europe to help you in some way, just say the word."

Her heart swelled. She loved this man like a father. "Thank you, Dr. Grafton."

"I'm sure we'll talk much more before you leave so I'm going to go check on Chais now. The piece she's been writing sounds like it takes at least ten hands to play." He shook his head as he stood. "I'm sure God has an amazing plan for this trip, Melanie. He's going to use you both in mighty ways."

He tipped his hat and walked back toward the house.

Once he was out of sight, she looked down at the envelopes in her hands. Mum's called to her with such a longing that she shoved the other into her pocket and ripped into the worn envelope. How long had Dr. Grafton carried this around with him?

She unfolded the paper and read.

Dearest Daughter,

You have been the light of my life. I have mourned the fact that I will not see the day you get married, or get to hold my grandchildren. But . . . I am rejoicing in a way that you cannot fathom. Soon and very soon I will get to see Jesus' face.

When we left Germany, I saw you retreat into yourself. You became afraid of a new life—a new country, new people, and a new language. It took almost two years for me to see my brave little girl again. Please, my darling . . . don't retreat into fear when I'm gone. You are older and so much wiser now. You have a wonderful job working with Chaisley. I asked Dr. Grafton to hold this for a while so you could grieve and find your footing again, but if, by chance, you find yourself afraid of life without me, go and read the book of Esther.

Melanie's heart fluttered. Esther.

She closed her eyes. *Father God . . . I don't know what You're doing, but I'm listening.*

She inhaled the sweet fragrance of the garden long and deep, then lifted her shoulders and read on.

> *It was your favorite Bible story when you were little, and I believe it helped you to finally move past whatever held you back.*

Melanie blinked back more tears. Mum never pushed her to get over her grief and was always right there whenever she was afraid. But Mum was also a great encourager. How many times had Melanie requested to read the story of Esther? And her mother had told her she was just as brave as Esther.

Funny, as a child, she hadn't understood the depth of the story, but she clung to another girl swallowing her fear. Now, it resonated and thrummed within her chest.

What was God asking of her?

She had no idea. Other than to step forward in faith and let go of her fear.

But fear had become a bit comfortable. She thought of herself as the voice of reason. Keeping a realistic view of the world. Not pessimistic. Not optimistic.

Shaking her head, she cleared her mind and went back to her mother's letter.

> *You have the potential to change the world, my sweet Mel. I don't know how the good Lord will use you, but in my mother's heart, I know He will. Don't be afraid, precious daughter. I pray you cling to Him and seek to know Him more and more each day.*
>
> *I don't have much energy to write all that I long to say, but I pray we have the chance for many conversations in the coming days.*

Since this is now after your twenty-fifth birthday, I am gifting you the last of what I had on this earth. Dr. Grafton knows how to contact Mr. Abelman, and he will give you the money I saved up for you, as well as the house left to me by my parents.

Use it for whatever God lays on your heart.

My energy is depleted but I love you, my darling daughter. Forever and always.

Remember . . . "For such a time as this . . ." Be willing to step out in faith and courage.

Mum

She looked to the sky and watched the white clouds move and shift across the blue expanse. A slight breeze picked up and the smells of the garden intensified.

As she breathed deep, the oxygen seemed to stoke the small flame alight in her soul. She stilled, her eyes fluttering shut as warmth flooded her, from the top of her head to the tips of her toes.

All right, God, You have my attention. What do You have for me to do?

CHAISLEY SIPPED HER TEA, the warmth coating her throat. There wasn't anything left to do in preparation for the tour. Her trunks were packed and downstairs ready to be loaded into the car tomorrow. Melanie was somewhere in the massive house, checking off the last few tasks on her to-do list.

Chaisley took another sip, relishing the quiet of the room. The fire crackled in the hearth, its heat soothing. There were no other sounds in the room. Savoring the peace of the moment, Chaisley leaned back into the plush chair and kept her hands wrapped around her teacup. This was the last time she would be alone for a long time. Best to tuck away the memory of what peace felt like.

She'd need it when she was being shuffled from venue to hotel to venue.

A frown tugged at her lips. Gracious. They hadn't left yet and already she was dreading the travel and tight schedule. Not good. She needed an adjustment in her attitude before they began their journey. A ribbon of anxiety wrapped around her ribs. It was more than her attitude that was the issue. This whole tour had her on edge.

But why? It didn't make sense. This is what she'd been preparing for—for months and months on end. Every time the creativity flowed and new music formed in her mind, she couldn't wait to play it, finish it, *share* it.

She should be thrilled that she could travel Europe and play her music. But instead? She'd rather stay right where she was.

Her fingers trembled, sloshing warm tea onto her hand.

Chaisley wiped at it with the linen serviette in her lap, leaned forward, and finished her drink, her fingertips feeling for the cool china saucer. She slid her cup onto the small plate with a clink.

Her thoughts pecked at her like the geese at bread morsels by the pond on the back of her property. She'd never been afraid to travel and perform. The thrill of her fingers slipping over cool piano keys . . . the surprised gasps from the audience as she played difficult pieces . . . the roar of the crowd when she finished with flair a piece played to perfection . . .

Those things had inspired her. Refreshed her. Invigorated her. Her playing prowess was not in question. So why this hesitancy? Why was she reticent about leaving?

Have you prayed about it?

Heat warmed her cheeks. How many times had Grandmother asked her that question when life perplexed Chaisley?

Too many to count.

But she hadn't prayed about it or anything else the last few months. Other than her prayers at meals and bedtime for her grandmother, she'd become stiff and reclusive. It happened before any of her big tours and she promised herself each time not to let it happen again. But it did.

Tears pricked her eyes. The Lord felt so distant. But she'd been the one to stop communicating. Stopped her excited study of Scripture each day. Her mind was consumed with the tour during church. At home, she was at the piano most every spare moment.

She dropped her head in her hands. "I'm sorry, Lord." Her hands muffled the words.

The door burst open. "Chaisley! You have—" Melanie's slippers slid across the wood plank floor as her words fell off. "Are you all right?"

She waved a hand. "Fine. Just thinking. Praying."

Melanie's steps became muffled as she crossed the rug. "Okaaaay. Do you want to talk about it?"

"Not right now. But I'll be fine." Chaisley straightened and pasted on a smile. "You sounded excited when you opened the door."

Her friend was silent for a moment. Then the cool weight of paper touched Chaisley's hands. "Here. I was going through the mail and found another letter from Mary Beth. Did you write to her?"

Chaisley loved the idea that her letter had reached the young girl. "I wrote her in braille and encouraged her to respond in kind."

"Did you tell her?"

The question hung in the air.

Over the years, Chaisley never wanted any special treatment because she couldn't see. In fact, she'd done her best to keep it hidden from everyone except those closest to her. She didn't want or need anyone's pity. She simply wanted to be herself. Being a famous concert pianist drew enough attention as it was.

"No." She whispered the word then lifted her chin. "I haven't told her."

"Hm." Melanie didn't expand on that but settled into the couch. "So why tell her to write to you in braille?"

Silence fell as Chaisley's fingers traced the lip of the envelope. "Nothing is wrong, Mel. I'll read my letter and then come down for dinner."

Her companion didn't respond with words, but came close and gave Chaisley's shoulders a squeeze.

She bit her lip, covering Melanie's hand with her own. It wasn't her intention to worry her friend. But she wasn't sure she could explain all the swirling emotions inside her right now.

Soft footsteps were followed by the click of the door.

Tugging the letter free of the envelope, she found two pages. With practiced movements, she ran her fingers over the raised dots.

Dear Miss Chaisley,

I have been floating in the clouds ever since we received your letter. And you wrote it in braille! That was very thoughtful of you.

My piano teacher told me that you arranged tickets for all of us to several of your concerts. My mother cried happy tears.

My mom is the best, though she is very sad right now. We help each other, but ever since we had to move from our house in Berlin, she hasn't been the same. Mom said bad men were trying to hurt us. So we have to hide in this new place. I think we are still in Germany, but I don't know for sure. But my teacher knows where we are.

I try to be encouraging and positive, even though it is smelly. And we can't play our records.

I miss my records. I used to listen to your records all the time. Music makes me happy and helps me when I try to do math. I don't like math, but Mom says I have to learn it.

Thank you for making beautiful music.

Thank you for writing me, please write back.

Mary Beth

Tears ran down Chaisley's cheeks. The paper shook in her hands. Bad men were after Mary Beth and her mum? Whatever for? She fished her handkerchief out of her skirt pocket. Wiping her face, she sniffed back the rest of her tears. She shuffled Mary Beth's letter with the other page and started reading.

Dear Miss Frappier,

I don't know if you will read this letter. Mary Beth was so excited to write you. Thank you for giving my daughter the gift of a lifetime by writing her back. I know she told you many times how much she loves your music. It is lovely and inspirational. God has gifted you. I am thankful that you share that gift with our world.

It is a world that is so dark right now.

Your letter encouraged me to lift my face out of the darkness I've been living in. Mary Beth told me that she wrote you of what was done to me. Apparently, I am less than human in the Nazi way of thinking, and so I shouldn't be allowed to bring another life into this world. I have heard horrible stories about others who have been taken away to special schools and hospitals, but I don't know what is true anymore.

Chaisley had to stop reading for a moment and clear her thoughts. So what Dr. Grafton had said was true. Who else was having to endure such atrocities?

I don't know if you are a God-fearing woman, but if you are, would you pray for us, Miss Frappier? We have had to escape our home and are currently in hiding. Germany has become a horrible place to live. Especially for the Jews and others like us.

Many friends of mine, who also have disabilities, have been arrested or taken from their homes. It has become a sin in Germany to be disabled. We are marked as unworthy. Of love. Of family. Even of life.

But that is not the truth. It does not matter if we are born blind or seeing, able to walk or in need of a wheelchair, hearing or deaf. I firmly believe we are all born for the glory of God. But there are those who see us as a scourge on the earth.

Please pray, Miss Frappier. That God would have mercy on us and get us to safety.

Thank you for the generous gift of tickets to your concerts. It will be the highlight of our year.

God bless you,
Geraldine Klein

Chaisley pressed the letter against her heart. Sobs shook her frame.

If she lived in Germany—would they have done the same to her?

The thought sobered her. Did others know about these horrors being done to innocent people?

Why, God? The cry ripped from her heart toward the heavens. Hiccups rattled her diaphragm, and she tried to slow her breathing. Her fingers scanned over the text again. This time, questions assailed her.

How were they living in hiding?

Who was helping them?

She chewed on the corner of her lip. The date of the letter was almost two weeks ago. Had they moved from wherever they were since then?

Folding the letters back together, Chaisley slid them into the envelope and then put it in her pocket.

A new purpose behind this European tour was before her.

She would find Mary Beth and her mother and get them to safety. No matter what.

AMSTERDAM, NETHERLANDS—FRIDAY, MARCH 18, 1938

Rick sat in his new employer's office and stared out the window. He was supposed to start his cover assignment as a driver days ago but was sent home after the news of Germany taking over Austria reached them. This morning, he'd been called back in.

Prayerfully, he still had a job. He hadn't heard from his contact in Amsterdam—who was supposed to relay news from headquarters—for two weeks, and each day more and more people sought refuge in Holland.

Most of them Jews.

How could the world be ignorant to what was happening? Newspapers and the radio kept them up-to-date. Or . . . was no one reporting the truth?

He raked a hand through his hair, fighting the frustration swelling in his stomach. His work with SIS gave him an inside look at what was happening in Germany, Britain, and other parts of Europe. Without this job, he would be like so many others. Head down. Working to feed a family and keep a roof overhead. Struggling to live one day at a time.

It was difficult to see the hardships of others when survival was foremost in the mind. When fear ruled every decision made for the safety of loved ones. He understood that. He did.

He rested his elbows on his knees, head in his hands. It wasn't just the Germans listening to Nazi propaganda. His own government's disposition of appeasement was suffering more and more disapproval from the British people. Germany's manipulation of British media was weakening, thanks to brave diplomatic correspondents.

But the Führer's propaganda machine had done a fair amount of damage. They seemed to say something different to whatever group of people they were speaking to, placating the whims and longings of the crowds.

Especially the young men.

Rick stood and walked to a large window looking over an industrial part of Amsterdam. It was cloudy today, which matched his mood as memories from years ago swam to the surface.

Young men, looking sharp in their crisp Nazi uniforms, marching in unison in a parade for Hitler.

Bonfires of books, furniture, and other goods lighting the night sky in Berlin.

The glee and joy as the Nazi youth harassed Jewish citizens.

Then the Olympics happened, and all the while, behind the scenes, the man was planning to take over as a world power and do abominable things to people he deemed unworthy of life.

Some were willing to give Hitler the benefit of the doubt. He was making them strong again. He was helping the economy. They didn't have to pay attention to what he was doing in Germany.

Then Hitler invaded Austria.

Anyone paying attention knew how desperately Hitler wanted his home country to return to the German motherland. *Real* Austrians were German speaking and of German blood. Rick had heard that too many times.

Gratitude welled in his soul that he'd gotten out of Germany before the Anschluss, when Hitler annexed the smaller country into his. But when Rick heard that many of the Austrians had celebrated Hitler's takeover of their country, he'd felt sick. Heartbroken. Austria thought it was gaining freedom. They must have had no idea what could be coming.

And if they did, shame on them.

Shame on them *all* for allowing hatred and discrimination to continue.

He swiped a hand down his face and glanced at the clock. Thirty minutes had passed. Maybe he wouldn't receive this new job today. Even though it was his assignment. If not, he should track down his contact and see if he should get a different job. Was the assignment gone? Had something changed? He stood and walked to the door—

It opened in a whoosh.

"Mr. Zimmerman, my apologies." The thick Dutch accent matched the man's thick belly. "I have exciting news for you, but it was tedious to confirm and then double-check on your credentials before I could offer you the job."

"Oh?" This sounded promising. The higher-up the client he was assigned to drive around, the better the information he could obtain. Not that the man in front of him would know why he was *really* working here.

The man slid a folder across the desk as he took his seat. "It would mean a great deal of travel for you, but if you are amenable, the job will be generally easy and prestigious as well."

Easy? Prestigious? Rick opened the folder and read the top page, his shoulders stiffening. He scanned the paper, rubbed his chin, then read it again. No. He wasn't misreading things.

He wouldn't be driving for a diplomat. Or even some mid-level government official somewhere. He laid the folder down and looked at the man. "You wish me to drive for a *concert pianist*?" It was impossible to keep the derision out of his words.

The man grinned from ear to ear. "Haven't you heard of Chaisley Frappier? The world's most renowned concert pianist? She is said to be the very best of the best. She can play the most complicated of Liszt pieces with the panache and flair of Chopin."

Irritation grated his chest, and he wanted to bolt out of the chair and march out of the office. He didn't care if she could play Tchaikovsky with her toes. Why would he be assigned here? This was a job for an entry-level agent.

Okay. Deep breath. He was supposed to be a highly qualified man looking for work, not a disgruntled British spy upset that he'd been pulled out of the thick of things in Berlin. With his cover, he had no right to be turning down a job during these times.

He couldn't let his pride get in the way of doing a job his contact had chosen for him. After all, he was out of Germany for a while, and that was a relief. He schooled his features, scooted forward on his chair, and grabbed the folder again. "She sounds fascinating."

"She is. And who wouldn't appreciate getting to chauffeur the greatest pianist in the world?"

Thank heaven the man studied some other papers on his desk and wasn't watching Rick's reaction. The piles of papers were each a foot high, and Rick counted eight that he could see.

"Indeed."

Perhaps there was significance to some of the locations of the concerts? Or to the pianist herself? She was from England, but there had to be something more if they were putting an agent on her. Wait. His new boss just said she was the most renowned concert pianist—which meant she would be playing for big audiences . . . prestigious audiences. That must be the key.

He took a deep breath—no way to find out except taking the job and listening in. Time to do what he was trained to do. "I can't say that I know much about famous musicians, sir. But I'll take the job. And do whatever is necessary to ensure that she gets to where she needs to go on time."

"Good, good." His new "boss" steepled his fingers together. The man seemed completely unaware that his new driver was an SIS agent.

Rick had to keep it that way.

In addition to the other elements of his cover, he was also supposed to lack higher education. Being a driver made him non-threatening, since most people got into the car and ignored the person behind the wheel. This hoity-toity musician wouldn't be any different.

The man behind the desk pulled his thick glasses from his bulbous nose and cleaned them with his tie. "Your references were impressive, so don't let me down. One of the owners said you would be the man for the job." He waved at a fly buzzing around his head. "Isn't it exciting to be a part of something so grand?"

"Grand?"

"This tour is to bring unity and hope across war-torn Europe. Almost all of the concerts have been sold out for weeks, and the tour lasts for eighteen months."

"Eighteen months?" Surely he wouldn't have to drive this woman around for a year and a half! He'd be bored out of his mind. His skills were needed elsewhere, weren't they? Why him? "Is that normal for a . . . pianist?"

Now his boss looked more than a little miffed. "Isn't that acceptable to you? With unemployment rates skyrocketing across Europe, most men would love to have a job that gave them peace of mind for that long."

The jab hit its mark. Agents were supposed to be shadows. Not perceptible to the average citizen. He couldn't afford to make this man take undue note of him. "Of course, it's acceptable. Thank you *very* much. I was simply shocked to hear that a pianist could tour for that long."

The man sniffed. "Not many government officials and leaders will pass up the opportunity to hear her play." He settled his glasses back on his face and folded his arms over his belly. "Word is, Queen Wilhelmina herself will be graced with a private concert."

Ah. That was the point of this assignment. Driving the pianist would give him access to all the concertgoers. Would she be playing for the Nazis? This might give him an opportunity to gain access into otherwise off-limit places.

He'd done it before, picking up more information than any of the others by pretending he didn't understand when they'd infiltrated the offices of the Nazis.

"You will be her exclusive driver for the next eighteen months. She also has an assistant traveling with her." He reached for a pen, his movements stiff as he eyed Rick. All signs of his former exuberance gone. "Perhaps I've made a hasty decision. I was excited to have a man of your qualifications to assign to Miss Frappier. But now I'm—"

"No, no. Please." Why had he allowed his emotions to show? He knew better. "I'm sorry. I haven't gotten a lot of sleep the past few days, and I don't know what came over me. I apologize. I'm extremely grateful for the job."

The man's eyes narrowed, and he stared at Rick for several seconds. "All right then." He scratched something on a slip of paper and handed it to Rick. "They arrive tomorrow, the address was confirmed this morning. You will take the Rolls Royce Phantom III Limousine. It's our best car and the most luxurious. I expect you to return it in pristine condition."

"Yes, sir." Rick stuck the slip of paper into his pocket and kept his head down. "Thank you for believing in me, sir."

"If I didn't have a family at home to take care of, I would've taken the job myself." The man relaxed in his chair. "But you're young and unattached so that makes you perfect for the job." He leaned forward. "You will also be offering protection of sorts since your passengers are women. Do your best to be clean and in uniform at all times. Make sure you bring a knife with you. Just in case. We can't have thieves or vagabonds attacking such a notable luminary on our watch."

"Yes, sir. I will not let you down." No point in telling the man he had several pistols with him. Which were illegal in Nazi territory, but necessary for an agent.

"See to it that you don't." The man dismissed him with a wave.

Rick left the building and jogged down the steps—

He frowned. He'd caught sight of someone out of the corner of his eye. Who . . . ?

His contact.

Finally.

The man ducked into an alleyway. The man was a lot thinner

and had more gray hair than the last time they'd seen each other. Rick strolled in the same direction then ducked into the alley.

Charles handed him a folder. "Read the file and memorize it. To the last detail. Then destroy it. Your languages will come in handy for the travel and give you opportunities to listen in. The highest-profile targets all across Europe have tickets for this woman's concerts, which leads us to believe that Miss Frappier is more than just a pianist. Who knows what kinds of meetings you might encounter. Be ready for anything, at any time. We will have contacts reach out to you as additional assignments arise. But for now, learn what you can by listening."

Rick nodded and grabbed the folder. If there were opportunities to help further SIS operations in Eastern Europe and stop the Nazis, he would find them.

His contact slipped away into the alley, and Rick opened the folder and found a picture of a lovely woman on top.

Chaisley Frappier.

The pianist.

Closing the folder, he tucked the file inside his jacket and headed back to his hotel. He would have to spend the evening studying up on Miss Frappier and music terminology.

The biggest question on his mind, though, had nothing to do with music.

Was Miss Frappier a Nazi sympathizer or not?

chapter
THREE

AMSTERDAM, NETHERLANDS—MONDAY, MARCH 21, 1938

Chaisley ached from the voyage. How could she be tired of it already? Granted, their ship had troubles early on, and they sat in the port of Dover for three days. Although now they'd made the short trip by sea to Amsterdam. The first leg to the continent was done, but she was already dreading more travel, and the tour hadn't even started yet.

"It's bone-wearying, isn't it?" Melanie moaned. "I don't know about you, but I'm tired of traveling already."

Chaisley laughed and then yawned as she stretched her limbs and stood. "You took the words right out of my mind."

"Well, at least we are finally done with our journey by boat for a while." Her friend let out a breath. "Going by car is much more enjoyable. The water always makes me queasy."

The sounds of travel cases being moved around their room joined in with the cacophony from the dock.

"Our new driver is supposed to come to the stateroom and get our bags. I'll assess him and determine if he is acceptable by the time we reach your grandmother's." Melanie had become much more direct and protective as they'd journeyed.

It reminded Chaisley of the years before Melanie's mother died. Melanie had been quite the force to be reckoned with back then. After her mother was gone, though, it was a different story. So to hear confidence back in her voice now was more than encouraging.

Perhaps this journey was giving her friend a new purpose as well.

Purpose. The word washed over her, leaving renewed resolve in its wake. Her thoughts hadn't stopped spinning in the last week and a half with partially formed plans and ideas that led to more ideas.

And then she remembered Dr. G's contact list.

At first, Chaisley feared what might arise to put them in a position to *need* the list, but now? Giving hope to those suffering overpowered her fears. More than anything, she wanted to give hope to Mary Beth and Geraldine. There had to be more like them as well.

Using music to inspire and lift spirits was a gift. Twelve new pieces written in musical braille sat in her music folder, their themes all reflecting brighter futures.

Hope.

She ran her fingers over the buttons of her dress, smoothing the fabric.

This tour would be different. *She* would be different. Ready to do anything within her power to help those in dire straits.

Exactly what God was calling her to do wasn't clear. Yet. But she was back in the Bible, praying, and seeking Him. And in time, she would talk to Melanie about all her ideas. She needed a bit more time to think through details.

A knock sounded at the door, and she turned her face in that direction.

"Come in."

Melanie's take-charge tone almost made Chaisley giggle. She lifted a hand to her mouth and covered her mirth.

The door creaked open.

"*Ik ben de chauffeur van mevrouw Frappier.*" The male voice was a bit hesitant. Was the man nervous?

"This is Miss Frappier. I am her assistant, Miss Brigman," Melanie replied in perfect Dutch.

"Friederich Zimmerman."

The slight rustle of something—his uniform? He must have bowed.

"But I prefer to go by Rick."

Chaisley raised a brow. A bit too familiar for a driver, but she didn't have the opportunity to comment as Melanie continued her inquisition.

"Do you speak other languages, Mr. Zimmerman?"

"German, Miss, if that is more comfortable?" The man's soft voice held kindness. Humility.

Chaisley liked it, which made her like the man. So far. A lot could be heard in the intonations of a person's voice.

"We can do either. Do you speak English as well?" Melanie continued, her tone no-nonsense.

"Very little."

Chaisley restrained a frown. His response was . . . different. Was he embarrassed that he didn't speak much English, or was it something else? She'd have to hear him speak a bit more to ascertain what she'd picked up.

Chaisley stood and turned her face toward the sound of his voice. "It is a pleasure to have you as our driver."

His shoes shuffled a bit on the floor. "It is my honor."

Had he noticed anything? "I guess we should be off. My grandmother will be anxious to see us." And *she'd* counted down the hours until she could hug her grandmother again.

"Of course. Allow me to load the bags into the auto. It shouldn't take too long."

Cases clunked against one another, and his heavy footsteps moved away. Chaisley waited for Melanie to be at her side.

Melanie took her elbow. "He'll need to make one more trip for the rest of the luggage. Are you ready?"

"I am." She pinched her lips together. "But I don't wish to use the cane right now. It calls too much attention to me."

"I understand. I'll just whisper directions as we go." The clicking of the wood as Melanie folded up Chaisley's long walking stick was a familiar sound. "I'll tuck it into my bag and have it, just in case."

"Thank you." When she'd first heard of the foldable cane, Chaisley had contacted Dr. Grafton to find out if she could order one made to her specifications. The long stick had been a lifesaver to her on many occasions, serving as her eyes when she was in a new location.

A whoosh of air blew through the room. Chaisley paused. The driver's steps were different this time. Quicker. Lighter. Brass buckles clacked against one another. Ah, he was gathering the rest of the luggage.

"If you'll follow me." His voice was a baritone. Smooth and rich.

Melanie's palm slipped beneath Chaisley's elbow and navigated her toward the door. "It's narrow and then a sharp right turn down the hallway. That will be familiar. Until we get to the gangplank."

Chaisley nodded and walked beside her friend, hearing the sounds of other passengers preparing to leave the echoing ship.

"Left. At least ten steps straight. Stay close to me, the gangplank is much narrower than in England. A bit steeper as well."

Chaisley had learned to navigate the world quite well on her own, but situations like this, where a misstep could mean a fall—or worse—she accepted assistance. "I'll hold onto the belt of your dress and walk directly behind you. No need for me to call more attention to myself by falling off the gangplank."

"Just play like you are afraid of heights. No one will think a thing of it."

Chaisley took hold of her friend's belt. The leather was smooth and firm under her fingers. "I'm ready."

"Here we go. Slight step up to the ramp and then a steep decline toward the dock. It's at least two hundred feet in length." Melanie moved forward.

With a deep breath, Chaisley stepped up and felt the decline of the ramp under her feet. She put a hand over her brow acting like she couldn't bear to look down. They moved at an *adagio* pace down the gangplank. Their slow tempo was easy, their steps rhythmic. Chaisley listened to each step Melanie took before she took her own. She scrunched her nose at the salty sea air, thick with the aroma of fish. Thank goodness a stiff wind kept the air moving past.

The clanging of metal against metal evoked a picture of the buoys around the lighthouse near her childhood summer home. It was the same sound now, but multiplied. How many ships were in the harbor? There were enough voices for a crowd of several hundred. The voices—accompanied by the horns of the ships, all at different pitches, and the lapping of the waves against the dock below—were a veritable symphony.

After her ninety-fifth step, Chaisley felt Melanie come to a stop.

Her companion's rushed whisper reached her ears. "Take a large step forward. There's a gap."

She did as instructed and then Melanie took her elbow again and they fell into step, side by side.

"The car is straight ahead. Nothing between us and it, about forty paces."

At the vehicle, Melanie gently tugged her to a stop. "It's a Phantom limousine, just like the one at home." The words were so soft they barely reached Chaisley's ear.

A door released an almost silent creak as it opened, and she reached forward to feel the auto's frame. She lowered her head as she ducked into the car's interior. "Thank you, Mr. Zimmerman."

She slid across the seat to allow Melanie entrance. The soft velvet beneath her moved a bit as her friend sat and then the door clicked closed.

"That wasn't so bad." Melanie switched to English. "But I think you need to tell our driver at some point."

"I will in time. If we are fortunate to have the same driver for the extent of the tour, I'm sure we will get to know him quite well." The auto shifted—a shift she was used to. The driver was in his seat now.

The engine purred to life, and they moved forward.

Papers shuffled beside her. "According to the information from the service, we are supposed to have the same driver for the entire tour." Melanie patted her arm.

Chaisley leaned her head back and closed her eyes. "Good."

There was something about the man's voice . . . the warmth in it.

So far, she liked what she'd heard.

Chaisley leaned toward Melanie. "Once we arrive, you go on in and see Grandmother. I need to speak with Mr. Zimmerman."

Her friend stiffened beside her. "I'm not sure that's a good idea. We've just met this man."

She released a tiny huff. "Fine. If you wish, you and Grandmother can watch out the window for our every move and have her butler come out and stand in front of the car as a guard. But I'm going to speak with him. Alone."

A measured exhale slipped from Melanie, but no words for several seconds. "I can agree to that. But I'll return when I see you exit the car."

The limousine went around a curve, and Chaisley was shifted toward the door. Anticipation shivered up her spine as the car slowed and went up a slight incline.

They'd arrived.

As the car pulled to a stop, she leaned forward on the edge of her seat, found the driver's shoulder, and tapped on it. It was firmer than she'd expected. Then again, her drivers were normally older . . . rounder gentlemen. Mr. Zimmerman's voice and movements seemed closer to her own age. Switching back to Dutch, she began, "Mr. Zimmerman, I'd like to have a word."

"Certainly, Miss Frappier."

Melanie gripped Chaisley's right hand, squeezed, then released it. Her dress rustled a bit as she slid on the velvet seat to exit the vehicle.

Once Chaisley heard the firm latch of the door, she continued. "I'd like to know a bit more about you since we will be spending so much time together."

"Yes, ma'am. What would you like to know?"

Now was not the time to mince words. Melanie had been so protective of her, it was *her* turn to make sure her friend and confidante was in good care as well. With a deep breath, she clasped her hands tight in her lap. "How old are you? Do you have a family? Where are you from? And most important, do you align yourself with the Nazis?"

RICK STUDIED THE WOMAN in the rearview mirror while a tall gentleman walked in front of the car and stood there. To stand guard?

An extra precaution, no doubt, since Miss Frappier's assistant had gone inside. Most of their conversation had been in English, so he'd been right to say he didn't speak it well. A lie that would serve him well on this assignment.

Was she about to tell him whatever her secret was?

He studied the woman again. She was beautiful, with blonde hair and light blue eyes that sparkled as she spoke. In the light outside the ship, those eyes appeared almost silver. But now, inside the vehicle with the deep blue velvet interior, they were darker.

She didn't meet his gaze in the mirror. It appeared she was focused on the back of his head. He had better answer her questions. "Well, first, I am thirty years old. My father was killed in the Great War, and my mother died soon after. I'm the only one of my family left. I am not married, so if you are concerned about me being away from anyone, don't be. My parents were both born in Germany but met in Switzerland. I was raised here in Amsterdam." All true. Now came the part he didn't like.

He took a breath. "I do not align myself with any political party. I am a simple, uneducated man seeking to do good work and make an honest wage." He watched her face. No reaction.

"Mr. Zimmerman, you just lied to me."

His eyebrows shot up. How on earth . . . ? "Pardon me?"

She continued to stare at the back of his head. "Your age is true, as is the information about your family and where you are from. But the last part wasn't. Just like earlier when you said you didn't speak much English." She leaned back against the seat, her jaw firm and set. "Now, let's try again, or I shall have to find another driver for the next eighteen months."

How did she know? Without even looking him in the eye? He cleared his throat. *Please, Lord, don't let my next words get me fired.* "Do *you* align with the Nazis, Miss Frappier?"

A wry laugh softened her face for a moment. He shifted his gaze away from the mirror. It wouldn't do to be caught staring when he was trying to keep his job. "Nice try. Do you often seek to appease whomever you work for by siding with them?"

"It's gotten me this far."

"I don't believe it has." She leaned forward again. "You see, I can hear it in the tone of your voice. You are not an uneducated man at all. And I believe that you *do* have very strong feelings about the political climate in this world. So why don't you just tell me the truth now? It would save us a great deal of time and trouble."

So. She wanted an answer, or he would be fired. She was from

England. Her grandmother was from Amsterdam. Her last name was clearly French. His best guess was that she was not a Nazi sympathizer. But what if he was wrong? His job was to spy. On her. And whomever she came into contact with.

Lord, please let that be the right choice.

"I indeed went to university."

"Aha, I knew it!" Her smile lit up her face. "Now about the other thing?"

Apparently, she would know if he lied so he had better just get it out there. "I do not align myself with the Nazis."

She drummed her fingers upon her knee for several seconds. "Finally. The truth. Which now makes me wonder, why did you lie?"

He needed to be careful. Her ability to guess when he was lying was . . . disconcerting. "Most of the people who have hired me as a driver prefer to have a non-threatening person behind the wheel. Someone without opinions. Someone uneducated, who they can command or walk all over, if they are so inclined."

"Another honest answer. Thank you."

She didn't move to leave the car, but also didn't say anything else.

"Might I ask what you heard in my voice that told you I lied?" It was far too forward to ask such a question, but *she* opened that door.

Her fingers drummed a fast rhythm again, and her face tilted toward the roof of the car. "I am an expert at hearing things."

Not really an explanation. He took a breath to say so, but held his tongue.

"For instance. Just now, you wanted to say something else, but you decided against it. Are you worried about losing your job?"

Good grief. He wasn't going to get anything past this woman, so he better just spill the truth. "Yes, I was worried about losing this job. I was also not convinced with your explanation."

She laughed, and it was almost musical. Which made sense for this woman surrounded by melodies.

"I appreciate your bluntness."

"Thank you, ma'am."

Leaning forward again, she dipped her chin, tilted it back and forth as if she was weighing a decision, and then reached a hand forward to the back of his seat. Her fingers tapped out another fast rhythm.

Rick held his breath. Would she learn all his secrets with her strange ability to suss out the truth? Her dossier said she was a prodigy, but was she also an agent? A spy? But for whom?

Her tapping stopped. "I don't think you have noticed quite yet, but I'm sure eventually you would since we will be spending so much time together, and you seem to be an observant man." The nearness of her voice startled him from his thoughts.

He waited.

The rhythm of her fingers began in earnest. Then stopped. "Mr. Zimmerman, I am blind."

Everything slowed for a moment, as if his head was stuffed with cotton wool. Then the day's events zipped through his mind's eye.

The whispers between her and her assistant.

The assistant's discreet hand beneath the pianist's elbow.

How Miss Brigman hovered close when Miss Frappier entered or exited a room.

His gaze went back to the rearview mirror.

She wasn't staring at the back of his head on purpose. She didn't know he was looking at her in the mirror.

"Well, this is embarrassing." Miss Frappier leaned back against the leather seat. "I've had a few reactions to my disability, but instant inability to speak is not generally one."

Nice job, Rick. He gripped the steering wheel. "I apologize, Miss Frappier. I didn't even . . . That is to say, it wasn't . . ."

That musical laughter filled the car again. Was she laughing at him? He couldn't blame her.

"You don't have to feel sorry for me, Mr. Zimmerman. Or find the right words to say. I wanted you to know because you'll be with me on the tour."

Scarlet burned his cheeks, but he couldn't stop the grin tugging at his lips. "Thank you, miss. Forgive me for my delayed response."

Miss Frappier's hand reached toward the armrest of the door, her slim fingers wrapped around the handle. "No forgiveness necessary. However I would ask that you not say anything to anyone outside my circle. It's not something I necessarily hide. Yet I have also chosen not to advertise it. There is no sense in calling attention to myself. I manage just fine. I'm sure you can appreciate my desire for discretion."

"Of course, Miss Frappier."

"Thank you, Mr. Zimmerman." She opened her car door. "Bastiaan—my grandmother's butler—will tell you where to park the car and show you to your quarters."

The butler scurried toward her door, holding it open as she exited, and slammed it shut when she was gone.

Rick watched her take measured steps to the massive oak front door, which was flung open to reveal Miss Brigman and an older woman with a cane. They embraced the pianist and all entered the manor house.

A sharp rap on his window startled his gaze away. The butler stared at him, his face dark with a fierce frown. Rick rolled down his window and opened his mouth to greet the man, but he was cut off.

"Continue on the drive and turn right at the curve of the road. Garage is on the right. I will meet you up there to unload the luggage and then I will show you to your room."

Rick nodded and turned the key, the engine roaring to life.

So . . . the world didn't know that their most famous musician was blind. Did the SIS know?

If so, what else had they not told him about the pianist?

chapter
FOUR

AMSTERDAM, NETHERLANDS—FRIDAY, MARCH 25, 1938

Celestia made her way up the fourth flight of stairs to the attic space she'd prepared. The girls would join her shortly. Was she ready? The question resounded time and again in her head.

Once she was in the room, she put a pillow on the floor and knelt.

Heavenly Father, direct my words, my steps, my actions. I don't wish to scare my granddaughter, but she needs to know. Melanie too. Her fear has been so great since her mother died. Give us all courage in the coming days. Please stop the atrocities. Stop the evil behind all this.

Tears burned her eyes. No person who had a family and loved them wanted to share news that was life-altering and potentially devastating. Nor would they want their family to have to live in this kind of world. But could one person—or even a handful of people—make a difference? If they were caught . . . they would surely face the horrors whispered behind hands. Being made an example as a political prisoner would be horrendous. Being forced to labor in one of the camps made her shiver.

But wasn't that what laying down one's life meant in this day and age?

Footsteps approached so she pulled herself up to stand and lifted her shoulders. Fear wasn't of the Lord.

Chaisley and Melanie entered.

"Please, close the door." Celestia kept her voice soft and calm. But she wanted to blurt out everything all at once and send her granddaughter far away where she'd be out of danger.

Melanie did as she asked. "There's a table in front of you and a chair to your left, Chaisley."

Her granddaughter sat down, and Celestia stood in front of them. "I asked you up here because I don't wish anyone else to hear."

Chaisley leaned forward, her blue eyes steady. It had been two decades since Celestia had been able to look into her granddaughter's eyes and find recognition. But God, in His infinite wisdom, had blessed them abundantly with a wonderful tutor who gave Chaisley the tools to navigate life. And now, her granddaughter's talent had brought her around the world. An amazing accomplishment, but one that could put her in danger.

She would be in the spotlight as she traveled.

Hitler most assuredly already knew about her. Especially since she was touted as the best. He did love being at the top and surrounding himself with others at the same level. He would want her to play for him. That was a given.

Celestia drew a breath. "This last year, we've heard many murmurings, and we all knew that there was something below the surface. . . simmering. I haven't wanted either of you to worry, but I have been working with a group of people preparing for the worst."

Chaisley's chin lifted. "The worst? You mean war? Dr. G spoke of this as well. It's been quite unsettling."

Celestia took her seat and shook her head. With her cane in front of her, she placed her hands atop it and braced for a long, hard conversation. "This is much more than war, my dearest." She swallowed against the lump in her throat. "It has been so lovely the past few days to have you here and to catch up that I haven't wanted to ruin it by going into the ugliness of the world's affairs, but I cannot wait any longer."

Chaisley's hand reached forward and Celestia took it. "Grandmother, our time together has been wonderful, but before we retired last night, Melanie and I spoke. A sense of urgency is upon us both. I told you about the little blind girl and her mother. I want to help."

Such a wise woman, her granddaughter. "I was ignorant to what was happening for too long. In fact, I'm ashamed to admit that I was so glad to be in my homeland that when I first heard rumors, I convinced myself it had to be gossip. It couldn't truly be happening. Not here. But over time, I could no longer ignore the truth. What the Nazis are doing is shameful. It's been going on for years, and Hitler has been in power for five. That's too long in my opinion."

Tears choked her for a moment, but her granddaughter's strong grip gave her courage to continue. "It's no secret that Hitler despises the Jews and any that are not of his so-called master race. I have many Jewish friends here who are worried that staying in Europe will put their lives at risk. They left Germany hoping to find sanctuary here, but after the Nazis took Austria as well, those who can afford to do so are planning to leave. Since I started to dig deeper, I was horrified to learn that there has been a law the past *five* years in Germany that orders the Germans to sterilize anyone they deem unworthy of creating life."

Melanie gasped and put a hand over her stomach. "What do you mean? It's a law?" The young woman began to shake. Her mouth dropped open. "The letter . . . it wasn't just Mary Beth's mother . . ." She stood to her feet and paced the room. "No . . . it can't be. I think I'm going to be sick." Her hand went to her mouth.

86

Celestia bolted from her chair and wrapped Melanie in her arms. "It is sickening, yes, but we don't have the luxury of waiting or crying over this situation." She gripped the young woman's arms in her hands. "Your mother was one of the strongest women I knew—leaving the atrocities and hatred that she did—and so are you, Mel. You need to swallow this fear. What the Lord has set before us is a mighty task indeed."

Melanie's trembling calmed, and she lifted her chin. Once she was back in her chair, Celestia took the time to study how her granddaughter was taking the news.

Face ashen, her lips in a tight line, Chaisley barely moved.

All right then, she'd continue. "This law means that they have forcibly sterilized people with disabilities, with mental issues, even those they believe are alcoholics by heredity. And it goes further than that. We have someone within Germany—inside the Nazis—who has told us a plan will soon begin to send away children who have any of these afflictions."

"For what purpose?" Chaisley's brows drew tight together as color filled her face.

"Under the guise of special schooling—" Celestia allowed the words to hang for a moment while she willed her own stomach's contents to stay in place. "But the rumblings are that these children will be . . . eliminated . . . to ease the burden of their care on society."

Her granddaughter rose to her feet with such force that the chair behind her toppled. "When?"

Celestia shook her head, though her granddaughter couldn't see it. "I don't know. According to our informant, the talks about it have just started. He has put his life at risk to give us information. He mentioned the tensions in Germany are rising each day. More and more political prisoners are being arrested and taken straight to camps. No trials. No way to defend themselves. All while Hitler's propaganda is being spread about how Germany is thriving and overcoming the awful unemployment and sad economy. I hope I never meet the man." She wanted to spit the words but refrained. "What he has done to my mother's country is despicable."

The more she said, the more the fire inside her grew. She longed to take vengeance herself. Every day she had to pray for the Lord to quell her anger, to remind her this was about saving people, not killing the enemy. "They want to purge Germany and Austria—and eventually everywhere that Hitler takes control—of anyone and everyone that they deem not good enough. The longer Hitler is in power, and the longer the world tries to appease him to keep him at bay, the worse this is going to get. Our informant told us these things so we could help whomever we could—but we haven't heard from him in a week, so I pray daily for his safety."

Melanie's complexion had turned from green to gray as she went to pick up the chair and touched Chaisley's arm. After they retook their seats, she put her forehead in her hands.

Celestia's hands shook as she gripped her cane even tighter. "I know this isn't easy to hear. But it's better to be prepared and to understand what you might be walking into as you travel on this tour. It's also best that you don't know too many specifics of what I am planning here. My hope is to use the wealth the good Lord has gifted me with to help whomever I can."

She glanced at Chaisley. Tears slid down her granddaughter's cheeks. Melanie still had her head in her hands. Had she shared too much?

Chaisley turned her head toward the group again, her shoulders rounded tight. "Grandmother? Are you all right?"

Oh. She had trailed off, hadn't she? "Yes, my dear. Just gathering my thoughts. As I was saying, I wish I'd never seen the Great War, but I fear what is coming is so much worse. I can't sit by and do nothing or pretend it isn't happening. But each time you return for a bit of respite here, know that things will be different.

We won't talk about it. I'll keep the details to myself unless a time comes when you must know for your own safety."

Chaisley stood again, walked over to the window, and placed her hand on the pane. "That's why Dr. Grafton gave us the list of his contacts. He already knew. I often wondered why he chose to travel so much the last few years."

"Every single one of the people on that list can be trusted. Timothy ensured it." Celestia's voice cracked, and she pressed a fist into her hip. She would have to have a soak after this. Her body simply wasn't what it used to be. But now was not the time to get emotional or fall apart. Both girls in front of her understood that if she used the good doctor's first name it was either because she was about to cry or to let her temper reign. She coughed into her hand and raised her chin. "Grafton has organized a network across Europe. They aren't simply contacts, they are people in key places, situated across Europe, ready to mobilize resources as soon as we need them. Again, we can't predict what is going to happen, but we can watch, prepare, and be ready. We are praying that other groups like ours will rise up and heed the call. But because of the eyes and ears of the Nazis, trust is hard to come by. We may only be a few in the face of a great enemy, but I think of what God did through Gideon, and I am encouraged."

Chaisley leaned her forehead against the glass. "Mary Beth, the little girl who wrote to me, said bad men were looking for them and they had to go into hiding. And her mother, Geraldine, said that being blind shouldn't be a crime. This is really happening, isn't it?"

Celestia's throat clogged once again with tears. Why was it so hard to hold herself together? "Oh, my dear. I am so sorry to hear of their situation. But yes, it *is* happening." She choked on the words.

Her granddaughter made her way back to the table and sat down, sliding her hand palm up on the table. Celestia took it, giving her a pat.

Chaisley cleared her throat, but then sobs overtook her for several seconds. Then she lifted her chin and shook her head. "I'm sorry. It's just overwhelming to realize that it's not simply a bad dream."

Celestia squeezed Chaisley's hand. The hands that could bring audiences to their feet.

Her granddaughter sputtered and then swallowed hard, her face turning to flint. "They've already sterilized Geraldine. Since I read that letter, there's been a prodding in my soul. I knew I need to help but I . . ." Chaisley pressed a hand to her heart. "I haven't known what God was asking me to do. So when the first letter came, I was determined to find this girl and her mother. I don't even know if it's possible—but I need to try. We've been corresponding, and I gave them this address as a way to reach me as I travel."

"There will always be a place for them here if you do find them. How long it will be safe, I don't know. Who knows which countries Hitler will go after next."

"What else can I do to help?"

Shame wound around Celestia's heart, squeezing it. The good Lord was probably tired of hearing how sorry she was for not acting sooner. But the regret was almost suffocating at times. "Don't be like me and ignore things or try to reason them away. It took me far too long to get to this place, and I regret it more than you know. I could have helped so many had I not buried my head in the sand. There are still many that you can help. I don't know how. But . . . do the tour."

Oh, how she longed to take back everything she'd just said! To tell her precious granddaughter to run. Far away. But no. If no one fought the evil, it would win. "Give people an evening of beauty and hope. Make contacts and listen to everything around you. You not only have a gift with your music, you have an incredible gift of discernment with your ears. This might force you to act a part at some point, but remember how the Lord used Rahab, how He used Joseph and Esther."

Melanie stood and joined Chaisley. The set to the young woman's jaw was as fierce as the look in her eyes. "I didn't want to come, and frankly, I'm so scared I'm surprised my legs aren't shaking. But at least I know why we're here."

Her granddaughter nodded and let go of Celestia's hand. She crossed her arms over her chest. "Dr. G spoke with us about using the old form of braille to communicate. We're also going to use the other two from the United States as well."

Celestia smiled. Chaisley's determination was magnificent to behold when she wielded it. She was so like her father in that respect. A pang accompanied that thought, but she pushed it away. "Yes. That's probably the best way for us to send notes to one another right now. But a time may come when we will have to use something else. Some form of code. Especially once you travel into Germany. I don't trust our correspondence to remain private."

Chaisley stood and paced the space between the window and her chair. "I already have an idea. Let me work it out before we leave, and I will somehow get word to Dr. G as well." She turned her face to the window. "It's no coincidence that we decided to start the tour in Austria, is it?"

Celestia caught Melanie's gaze, her brows arched together, waiting for an answer. There was a new strength in the set of Melanie's shoulders, a boldness Celestia hadn't seen from the young woman in a long while.

Good.

Please sustain this boldness in her, Lord. In both of them. I commit these precious ones to Your will.

"No. It isn't a coincidence."

The room was silent for a moment before Melanie grabbed Chaisley's and Celestia's hands. "Wherever He leads . . . I'll go."

The words wrapped around Celestia, infusing her with courage. "Yes, dear hearts. If we are called into the lion's den, then we will go."

AMSTERDAM, NETHERLANDS—MONDAY, APRIL 4, 1938

Watching her friend say good-bye to her grandmother was harder than Melanie thought it would be. Probably because of the knowledge they now carried. And Mrs. Frappier had been like a grandmother to Melanie as well.

The past few days had been filled with lots of short, intense conversations. Chaisley was like a dog with a bone. Once she got hold of an idea, she couldn't let it go. So she'd pushed and prodded Celestia for information and worked with her childhood braille writing tools in her room in the quiet times.

No telling what Chaisley would come up with, but her friend had a brilliant mind.

It gave Melanie time to think and prepare for the upcoming tour, too. Quiet times at the manor had always been Melanie's favorite thing. Reading. Drinking tea. Resting. The manor in Amsterdam was so peaceful. But the recent developments had changed it all. Would they have peace again in Europe . . . ever?

Some moments she wished to be back in England in the safety of what had been comfortable. Honestly, paying attention to the newspapers and radio broadcasts upset her, so it was easier to ignore it.

Then there were other moments where she tired of hiding.

Tired of hiding the knowledge of who her father was.

Tired of fearing she had family members within the Nazi Party.

Tired of pretending it would all go away if she ignored it.

Truth be told, she'd always been afraid of someone from her family finding her and her mother.

She pushed the thoughts aside. She had no control over what happened. Fear was getting her nowhere.

Everyone around the manor seemed to have a task. Something they were doing to help this network of Dr. G's.

Except her.

She winced. Good heavens. Such self-pity. She had her part,

helping Chaisley on this tour. Perhaps they'd be able to find the Kleins and get them to safety. That was enough, wasn't it?

Should she pray harder? Longer? She toyed with the small fringe fob on her purse, a familiar ache sweeping through her.

Mother would know what to do too. She always had such a serene peace about her, even after her husband demanded she leave if she wouldn't obey. Not once had Melanie seen her mother anything other than calm.

With such a mother, why did she struggle so with frustration, fear, and her swinging emotions? She'd felt so brave, bold even, when they were talking about being alert on the tour to people who might need this network's help. But now, doubt filled her, which let the fear creep back in.

Inhaling a sharp breath through her nose, she let it out and swallowed all her thoughts.

Her gaze flitted to the Frappier women. Both inspired her. Why couldn't she be more like them?

The quiet conversation between Chaisley and Celestia ended, and they hugged once more.

Mrs. Frappier waved Melanie over. "My dear, I will be praying for you every day. Call or write or send a telegram whenever you need to. I will be here."

"Thank you." Melanie swallowed back the sudden tears clawing at her throat. Would they see one another again? She leaned in and wrapped the woman in a hug. "I love you and will be praying for you as well." *Lord, please protect her from danger.*

"Don't you worry about me. I'm in good hands." She winked.

"Yes." She forced a smile, which sent a couple of rogue tears racing down her face. "You are." Melanie swiped them away.

"Grafton is coming to visit in a few days. I'll write with any news." Celestia stepped back and grabbed one of each of their hands.

Melanie grabbed Chaisley's free one, and they made a circle.

"The LORD bless thee, and keep thee: The LORD make his face shine upon thee, and be gracious unto thee: The LORD lift up his countenance upon thee, and give thee peace."

"Amen." Chaisley's strong voice accompanied the squeezing of Melanie's hand.

She forced oomph she didn't feel into her own response. "Amen."

They walked down the steps toward the car with Chaisley's hand on her shoulder. She gazed out at the road ahead.

A road of challenges.

A road fraught with unknowns.

A road of . . . darkness.

IN THE DAYS since bringing Miss Frappier and her assistant to her grandmother's home in Amsterdam, Rick had done everything he could to track down his last known contact and update him on what he'd learned about the pianist. But the man was nowhere to be found. A fact that was a bit more than unsettling.

He'd risked sending a coded telegram as instructed in case of emergency to the agency in London and received a response that they'd lost several agents, communication was sparse, and to stay the course.

That would be difficult when the course was vague at best.

And then there was Miss Chaisley Frappier. With the tour beginning, he would have much more proximity to her. For days he'd wondered if her questions to him and the revelation of her disability were meant to distract him. It *was* a popular tactic.

Still, he had to admit he liked the woman. She seemed strong, forthright, observant. And apparently gifted at the piano, although he hadn't seen her play yet. The anticipation was killing him. Though he was by no means a music aficionado, he wanted to understand how a blind woman could be the world's foremost pianist.

The past several days he hadn't been needed, so Chaisley told him to take the time to relax and run any errands he might need to tackle before they hit the road.

Mrs. Frappier had been generous with his quarters, and the food was the best he'd eaten in months—possibly even years. It would be easy to relax and let down his guard here, but he'd made use of the time searching for his contact and making himself useful around the estate as much as possible. He watched from a distance as the three women spent a great deal of time with their heads together in quiet discussions or as they headed up to the attic.

Twice, he'd followed them and done his best to listen in—to no avail.

Too bad he hadn't been able to overhear them. His curiosity was piqued.

Movement out front of the estate brought him to attention. The women were headed to the car, and he reached for the rear passenger door. Over time, he was certain Miss Frappier would be useful. Even if it was just to get him into places where powerful people gathered.

"Thank you, Mr. Zimmerman." Miss Frappier got into the car first, followed by Miss Brigman. "Since we are headed to Austria first, I'd like to hear your plan for the trip." Her perfect Dutch didn't even hold the slightest hint of her English accent. Fascinating. Had she spoken Dutch as a child as well?

Most of the time the people he drove didn't care about details. It was his job to figure it out and then to get them from point A to point B. Her question only gained her more respect. "I was thinking it would be best to avoid driving through Germany, so we will go around and then into Austria." He shrugged his shoulders. "Which is now part of Germany, but I think you understand my initial plan and why."

"That sounds like a good idea." She nodded and leaned back against the seat.

Her companion, however, sat with her back straight and her shoulders stiff. "Two days of travel, correct?" Another perfect Dutch accent. Who were these women?

"Yes." He glanced again at Miss Brigman in the rearview mirror. She hadn't stopped studying him, her eyes narrowed and brow dipped. He offered her a smile. "We will be stopping at one of the hotels in France that was on the approved list."

"Wonderful. Thank you." Miss Frappier's head was down as she listened to something her assistant whispered to her. "Mr. Zimmerman, another question, if you don't mind?"

"Not at all."

"I like to count things. How many steps. How many people I hear around me. How many days, months, hours, etc. I think you get the point." That musical laughter of hers accompanied the last sentence.

He liked her even more and didn't mind laughing along with her. "I do."

"So if you aren't too bothered by it, I'd like for you to inform us each day how many hours we can expect in the car on the road."

"I can do that." He glanced at Miss Brigman who still wouldn't soften her gaze to him. "But be forewarned that some of the borders take a bit longer than they used to. Your papers will get quite a looking over." He sent another smile to Miss Brigman, hoping to put her at ease and stop that continuous frown in his direction.

She didn't smile in return, but her gaze softened . . . maybe? Or perhaps that was wishful thinking on his part.

"Are you both ready to depart?" He hoped they were. Getting on the road meant his assignment was underway. His hands tightened on the steering wheel. It was best if they didn't know how eager he really was.

"Yes, Mr. Zimmerman." Miss Frappier nodded.

Relief spiraled through him. At last. "Excellent. Also, I know 'Mr. Zimmerman' is quite the mouthful. Please, feel free to call me

Rick when we are in the car. It's easier." He caught a slight lift of her lips in the rearview mirror. A little thrill danced up his spine—

What was he doing? He wasn't here to make friends. Or to find the client attractive.

Miss Frappier inclined her head toward him. "Then I insist you call me Chaisley—at least while we are in the car and not surrounded by others." Her Dutch was consistently perfect. How had she learned to speak with a flawless accent? Suspicion replaced the earlier spark of intrigue.

"Call me Melanie." This time the assistant did offer a slight smile. "At some point during our time on the road, I should like to speak to you about ways we can aid Miss Fr—Chaisley. Since we are in a secure space, I can answer questions you might have."

"I'm not sure I understand?" He pulled out of the long drive and onto the road. Was there more to the story?

"Chaisley told me she shared with you that she is blind. There are many ways I help her to navigate when we are in unfamiliar locations."

"Oh! Of course." He shook his head. Not what he'd been thinking. "I will do anything and everything I can—"

"Hold on." Chaisley held up a hand. "First, you need to know that most of the time, I don't need help. I *never* wish to draw attention to myself. Which means I try to do things as normally as possible. I don't want to be coddled. While I haven't intentionally kept this a secret, as I mentioned previously, we don't go around announcing it. There's no need."

A glance in the rearview mirror revealed her jaw had tensed. Clearly a sore spot there.

"Yes, Miss Frappier—I mean, Chaisley. No coddling."

"Second, you must be exact. Every time. It will be harder for you because Melanie is the same height as I, so her stride is the same length as mine and she has developed an accurate sense of distance. That's why most of this will fall to Melanie, but as my driver—and in case she becomes ill or something of the sort—you need to be able to do the same things."

"And is that why you didn't use the cane I saw in your stateroom on the ship?" He might as well ask the question while they were having this discussion. When he'd first spotted it, he'd thought one of them was injured.

"Very astute, Mr. Zimmerman."

He straightened a bit. Had Miss Brig—Melanie just praised him?

"Rick," he offered again.

She lifted an eyebrow at him. "All right, Rick. I'm impressed you noticed. In all honesty, Chaisley can get around just as well as I can when she's by herself and she uses the walking stick, but that is neither here nor there. There will be crowds clamoring to see her perform, all of whom have no idea that she's blind. As well-meaning as some fans can be, they can also be a hindrance, and that is where we might need to enlist your help."

Hmm. Had he underestimated the magnitude of Chaisley Frappier's fame? He'd assumed only the wealthy or royalty indulged in concerts these days. But masses of fans? That would be a sight to see. "Yes, miss. I can do that."

"Good." Melanie relaxed into the seat. "But let's save that chat for a stop for luncheon."

He nodded as the two women whispered between themselves.

Curious. They switched from Dutch to French. And again . . . flawless. His own couldn't even compare, and he'd studied for a decade with an expert linguist.

Why wouldn't they speak in English—wasn't it their native tongue? His mind swirled back to his discussion with Chaisley that first day in the car. Ah, that's right. She'd discovered that he'd lied about not understanding English even though she hadn't forced him to tell the truth on that score.

Which meant that whatever they spoke of, they wished to keep secret. Good thing he spoke French as well. The bad thing was that their voices were low and hard to distinguish over the sound of the engine.

His mind raced. Was Chaisley so private a person that she didn't want to say anything about her schedule or concerts in front of her own driver? Or did she have something to hide? Was that even a possibility? Someone of her fame and clout . . . it wasn't out of the question.

He listened as he drove several kilometers, but nothing stood out. They spoke of her grandmother, a doctor friend, and looking forward to seeing them both again.

Voices lowered—

Wait. What did she just say? He eased off the gas pedal so the engine sound would soften for a moment.

Something about . . . contacts . . .

His stomach dropped as a previous question barreled to the forefront of his mind.

Who *were* these women?

chapter FIVE

GERMANY

If his mother could see him now. In his Nazi uniform. Polished boots. Rising through the ranks to work directly under the Führer.

Wouldn't she be proud? Perhaps she wouldn't have divorced his father and left had she known what was coming. He could have grown up with parents who loved each other and doted on him.

No matter. He gazed into the mirror to check that everything was perfect. Spotless. Herr Hitler had summoned him this morning, saying he was the perfect Aryan specimen. The perfect officer. The perfect example of a man loyal to the cause.

Maybe another promotion was coming.

After all, he had single-handedly rounded up those Polish Jews trying to start an uprising.

He smiled into the mirror, showing his white and straight teeth.

He deserved another promotion.

He would be loyal to the end. Because he believed.

Hitler would change the world, and he would be right by his side.

BELGIUM

"If there is any change in elevation whatsoever, even as tiny as half an inch, make sure you tell her. Give her specific directions left, right, forward, backward. If you can do it accurately, give her the turn in degrees if it's not exactly ninety degrees. And give her an approximate distance from the next door or turn as in so many feet." Melanie was pointing a finger at him, and he did his best to hold back his laughter. She reminded him of a teacher he had when he was a child.

"Meters okay? I know you British like feet, but I'm more familiar with meters." Rick scribbled notes as fast as he could on a notepad while they sat in the car and ate their lunch. He glanced back at them. Was his cover holding?

Melanie nudged Chaisley just as she was about to speak.

Chaisley's mouth snapped closed and then she nodded. "Yes, meters are fine. Just be clear which you're using."

Interesting. What was that about? "What else?" Rick shoved a bite of sandwich into his mouth and held his pencil at the ready.

"When we arrive at places, get as close to the curb as you can if there is one. It's easier to navigate stepping directly onto the curb. It eliminates a stumbling hazard if you're too close or too far away. When you open the door, whisper any directions she'll need immediately. Then wait for her to place both feet on the ground before moving. She needs her balance." Melanie took a slice of apple and bit into it. "Are you overwhelmed with all the information?"

Yes. But he would not let on for a moment. "Not a bit. I admit that I enjoy numbers and the preciseness of this little project."

Chaisley laughed. And not just a little laugh, this was full-on laughter.

"What did I say?" He stared at Melanie in the mirror, but she had begun to laugh with her friend.

"I simply find it funny that you think of me as a project."

Oh boy. "I'm sorry, I didn't mean it in any way to be an insult."

"Not at all." Chaisley's smile brightened the entire interior of the vehicle. "My Mum and Dad always had to give me *projects* to do when I was young, to keep me occupied. Especially while my father was having the music wing built. I pestered him over and over about that."

That smile was dangerous. Her laughter was a threat. In training, his superiors had drilled the stupidity of entertaining a *tendre* for an asset or target. He'd always been so sure he was immune to such things. Now . . .

Here he was, turned to mush by a smile of all things. It wouldn't do. However, it *would* serve his purpose to keep the camaraderie flowing. So he returned her smile with a small one of his own. Not that she could see it. But Melanie could. "They sound like wonderful people. I'd love to meet them someday."

Her eyes lost their sparkle, and her smile faded.

Uh-oh. Perhaps he'd pushed too far. But that was what he did. He was good at it. As an agent, it was easy to be unattached and emotionless.

Her chin trembled the tiniest bit. "They were killed on my birthday twenty years ago."

Sudden silence seemed to suck all the air out of the vehicle. Now he'd done it. "I'm so sorry. I—"

Melanie shook her head at him, and he clamped his mouth shut.

He took a sip of water out of his canteen, and it felt like his swallow echoed inside the small space of the vehicle, which seemed to grow smaller by the second. The death of her parents had been in Chaisley's file. Bringing them up was exactly what he should have done. To test her. Find out everything he could.

So why did he feel like a terrible man now? Like he'd betrayed her.

Melanie began to put away things in the picnic basket while Chaisley's face was turned toward the window. The ever-proper assistant cleared her throat. "We should probably get back on the road so we don't arrive too late. I know we will need our rest tonight."

Rick tidied up the front seat, glancing back at the pianist. Her profile was still lovely . . . but so sad. Then she leaned her forehead against the window and closed her eyes.

She'd lost her parents twenty years ago, so she'd been just a child. How had she endured that loss at such a young age? And being blind on top of it all? He dusted crumbs off his slacks. It was hard to imagine.

He'd been in his early twenties when he lost his parents. It hadn't been easy to survive without them. He rubbed his chest, trying to erase the ache.

It didn't work. He did a mental shake of his thoughts. This wasn't personal. He was doing his job. That was all.

Still, he couldn't dislodge the feeling that he'd purposefully opened a wound and poured salt into it.

"Don't feel sorry for me, Rick." Chaisley's tone was sharp. "I can practically feel it oozing off of you. I don't need your pity."

He jerked back, her words ringing through him as if she'd slapped him. Who'd said anything about pity? "I'm sorry. I was thinking how hard it was to lose my own parents and thought of you and—"

"I had two wonderful parents who God gave me for a short time. Then two incredible people stepped in as my guardians. One, you've met. My grandmother. And then I had Mary Beth—Melanie's mother—and my dear friend here. I've been blessed by so much more than others who are less fortunate that it is insulting to have you feel sorry for me." Her face was still aimed toward the window, but her words were firm.

"My apologies. Please forgive me."

"You are forgiven."

He frowned. It sure didn't sound like it. He looked in the rear-view mirror.

Chaisley relaxed and leaned back against the seat. "I'm a bit tired, so I'll think I'll try to rest now."

Rick didn't respond—he put the car in gear and steered them back onto the road.

It was going to be a long ride in the silence.

AUSTRIA—WEDNESDAY, APRIL 6, 1938

The crowd burst to applause after her opening piece—her latest composition. Warmth uncurled in her chest. It didn't matter how long she played and performed, the anticipation of premiering a new piece ate at her until she finished playing it for the first time.

The cheers erased weeks of fretting. Their adoration washed over her, and she reveled in it. But only for a moment. Then she stood, gripping the rounded edge of the piano, and took a deep bow. It was impossible to take in all of the cheering. The roar of the crowd with thousands of voices on different pitches and high, shrill whistles.

Thank You, Lord, for a successful evening.

Yes, this crowd loved her talent. Praised it to the skies. But it meant nothing without the One who gave it to her. He deserved the praise. That reminder helped to keep her pride in check.

Most of the time.

The thought cooled some of her excitement. She needed to focus. Get back on task. She held up a hand, and the crowd began to quiet as she took her seat on the bench once again.

"Enchant us again, Fräulein!"

The crowd chuckled at the exuberant audience member. But his outburst felt like ice-cold water had been dumped on her.

Fräulein.

Astonishing how one innocuous word could change everything in an instant. Reminding her of where they were.

The *Anschluss* that had taken place.

104

Were some of these people calling her name now the same ones who cheered for Hitler when he invaded a few weeks ago? She suppressed a shiver.

It was pointless to let her mind wander to anything but music right now.

When it was silent in the great hall, she lifted her hands and went into her tribute to Franz Liszt with *Mephisto Waltz No. 1*. Liszt was touted—especially in Germany and Austria—as the greatest pianist of all time. His exceptional skill, both as a pianist and composer, was unmatched. Which was why she had chosen several of his pieces to wow this Austrian crowd.

The piece was vibrant and fast, which always thrilled her audiences. As soon as she played the last note, she didn't wait for applause but went directly into Liszt's *Hungarian Rhapsody No. 2*.

The showy piece was instantly recognized, and applause rounded the concert hall like waves building on a shore.

The audience quieted again as her fingers and arms fully engaged with the keys on the Steinway concert grand.

The instrument resonated and vibrated beneath her hands. The music filled her ears, but didn't excite her like usual. It felt more like a battle. The notes seemed to burst from her fingertips, almost like bullets. But what was she trying to destroy? To kill?

She closed her eyes. She needed to sync her body with the music again. Not one part of this piece could sound discordant to the audience. But the thought of Mary Beth and Geraldine, their situation, and the lives of countless others hung heavy on her. How did one digest the kind of evil that desired to snuff out beautiful lives like theirs?

Like hers?

Tears burned the edges of her eyes, and she swallowed hard. That was it. What she couldn't shake.

Her life was an anathema to people like Hitler.

Invaluable. Unworthy.

She picked up the tempo of the piece feeding the anger now simmering in her soul.

This was just a performance. Just a performance. Just a performance. She could play the part. Do her work and bring awe to the crowd.

She focused her mind on the piece at hand, though she could probably play it in her sleep.

If she was going to do anything to help during these times, she needed to be the famous concert pianist who astounded her audiences everywhere she went. Perhaps, behind the scenes, she could save lives. Was that what God was calling her to do?

Yes. She could use her tour, her fame, whatever it took . . .

She allowed the smile that filled her heart to fill her face.

From one flamboyant piece to another, she played and poured her heart out onto the keyboard.

Heat built within her, and she felt the rush of it in her face. Every time the audience rose to their feet or took their seats once again, the stage around her brimmed with the scents of their colognes and perfumes.

When she started a new piece, the hush that fell over the great auditorium echoed upon itself, making the room feel bigger and bigger . . . like a giant bubble growing until it was about to burst.

Her fingers rippled over the keys once more. Then stilled.

Breathe, Chaisley. The thought flipped a switch in her lungs and she inhaled a full breath as she finished the piece.

The final note rang through the auditorium, as if suspended in the air between her and the crowd.

"Zugabe!"

The cry pierced the air. The crowd's rowdy stomps and applause became a tidal wave of sound rushing over her.

She stood, held the edge of the piano, and bowed. She took two steps to the right, bowed again, and turned around. Melanie was at her elbow immediately and offered her a glass of water as they walked offstage.

The roar of the crowd's applause, their cries for an encore, continued for two minutes and then shifted into a roar of conversation, footsteps, and rustling of clothing.

"Whatever spurred you on this evening, my friend, keep at it," Melanie gushed. "I mean . . . wow. You had everyone entranced."

But Chaisley shook her head. The applause was wonderful, but she couldn't escape her thoughts about the Nazis' goals. "I played for all of those who are helpless against what is coming. I'm still not sure how God is calling me to help, but—"

Melanie's insistent poking in the side stopped her short.

"I'm sure Almighty God will use your talent for His purpose."

Rick. How much had he overheard?

"The fact that you are a willing vessel is huge, Miss Frappier."

In the overflow of her adrenaline as she'd walked offstage, she hadn't paid attention to the sounds of anyone other than Mel. A costly mistake. While Rick's words sounded sincere, she hadn't been tuned in to listen. Her guard had been down. Had he overheard everything she said? Was he now saying only what he thought she wanted to hear?

With her faculties now tuned in to his presence, she swallowed and took several sips of water. Might as well push to see where the man really stood. These were not times of easy trust and she couldn't bear the thought that she would put anyone in danger. "How do you see this playing out for the Lord's will, Mr. Zimmerman?"

He didn't answer right away, and the sounds in the auditorium and from backstage kept her from hearing his breathing or any other slight movement.

Melanie squeezed her elbow. Her friend seemed strong and unafraid. Had she and Rick spoken?

"I am in awe of your talent, Miss Frappier. I've never heard a pianist with such skill, such passion."

There was no guile, no dishonesty, no empty flattery. She took another sip and raised her eyebrows in his direction. "While you didn't answer the question, I'm going to pose a new one. Are you a believer, Rick?" She hesitated using his given name, but perhaps God had placed him in her path for a reason. If so, she wanted to know that *now*.

"I am." His response was short and to the point. No hesitation in his voice. Either he was telling the truth or he was a masterful liar, honing his skills since he now knew her listening skills were sharper than most.

Melanie patted her arm and moved closer. "We would love to hear more about that this evening, Mr. Zimmerman. That is, if you are willing?"

"I am." Again, nothing but warmth and honesty.

"Good. Because I really should get Miss Frappier a few moments alone so she can mentally prepare for the rest of the concert." Melanie tugged at her arm.

"Of course. I'll wait right here. Let me know if there is anything I can do to be of assistance."

"Thank you." Chaisley followed Melanie's guiding arm to the dressing room she'd warmed up in earlier that evening. Once the door was clicked shut behind her, she let out a long breath. "Thank goodness he's a man of faith. At least he claims to be."

"What did you hear in his voice?" Melanie eased her down into a chair and pulled another close and sat so that their knees were touching. "Can we trust him? I *want* to trust him from what I see, but you are a much better judge of character." The huff she released held exasperation. "How sad that we live in a time where we don't know who we can trust! What has this world come to?"

Chaisley reached forward and patted her friend's knee. "I was just thinking the same thing. But you are right to keep your guard up. What I hear from him is trustworthy. Right now, at least. The more time we spend with him, the more we can ascertain." She took several more sips of cool water and a long, deep breath. "Grandmother had someone watching him at her house. He was very helpful and easygoing with everyone there. But he did leave several times, and he sent a telegram."

"Does she know where it went?"

"London. But I think it's wise to reserve judgment." Chaisley pursed her lips and pinched the bridge of her nose. "The fact that he jumped into a conversation about God is encouraging."

Melanie bumped knees with her. "We certainly know that Hitler doesn't believe in an Almighty God or His will. Nor would the man's followers."

"I've already confronted Rick about aligning with the Nazis. He told me he did not."

"You believe him?"

Chaisley chewed on that for a moment. "I do. But until we know for *certain* that he can be trusted, we should continue to speak in French when we need to speak privately."

"Agreed." Melanie shifted. "What about the code you were working on for us to communicate with your grandmother and Dr. Grafton? I haven't wanted to pester you about it, but I have this feeling—"

"Me too." She bit the inside of her cheek. "No one else is around, correct?"

"No one."

"I've finished it. I'll teach you over the next few days and somehow get word to Grandmother. I don't like the way it feels here. It's not just oppression . . . I can't put my finger on it, but I don't like it." She shivered and wiped her hands on her gown. The long silk number was a deep shade of navy that brought out her eyes. At least, that's what her seamstress told her. Right now, it seemed too thin to provide her warmth.

"Me neither." Melanie's trembling vibrated into Chaisley's knees. "Why does it feel cold in here all of a sudden?"

"I don't know, but I don't like it." She rubbed her arms. If only she could play the piano in the long silk gloves that matched the dress. Melanie always did a fabulous job describing every piece of clothing to her so that Chaisley could picture it in her mind. Over the years, colors lost their brilliance in her imagination, but she looked forward to heaven when she could see them all again in full glory.

"It's time to get back out there. But first, you need to know that there is a newspaper man who wishes to speak with you afterward. I didn't tell him that you don't do interviews, I told him I would need to ask you first." She scooted her chair away. "So do you want me to give our standard answer?"

She opened her mouth to say yes, but paused. Why did she feel hesitant? Quieting her heart and mind, Chaisley closed her eyes. *Are You trying to get my attention, Lord?* An interview was a daunting prospect. Uncertainty gnawed at her. Was it time to reveal her blindness to the world?

Where did *that* thought come from?

Her mind turned to Mary Beth and other children like her. How encouraged would they be to hear she had a disability, but it didn't stop her from dreaming. From living life.

Still, was that the right message to send when it was their physical struggles that made them targets of such venom?

Perhaps telling the world about her lack of sight was exactly what she needed to do to alert people that she was willing to use her fame to help them. Could she get that across? It certainly would bring more attention to her.

Another serious thing to consider. If she went public, it might gain the attention of the Nazis. Not the good kind. Wouldn't that lead to all sorts of scrutiny and dangers for her and Melanie?

What is Your will, Lord?

"*My peace I give unto you . . . Be of good cheer; I have overcome the world.*" The verses from John cut through her, the peace Jesus promised right on its heels.

God wasn't ashamed of her blindness. Her family had never been ashamed of it. And she hadn't either. It *was* time to tell the truth. This was not the time for her to cower in fear. "I'll speak with him."

"All right." Melanie's shock was obvious in her voice. "I should be used to you doing things outside the norm. You're terrific at it." She tugged at Chaisley's hand. "Ready to head back out there and impress the audience some more? You still have several of your new creations to share."

Chaisley laughed. "Yes, I'm ready." She stood up and followed Melanie's lead out the door. As soon as they climbed the stairs to the backstage area, the thick smell of the velvet curtains assaulted her senses, and she sneezed. "I think these curtains are due for a cleaning."

A handkerchief was placed in her hand. "Here, use this."

After blowing her nose and brushing stray tendrils of hair that tickled her face, she straightened her shoulders. "All right. Ready."

Melanie guided her to the edge of the curtain and shifted her aim just a bit to the right. "Twenty-two steps to the left edge of the piano."

Chaisley gave a brief nod and lifted her shoulders back. Stepping out from behind the curtains, the warmth from the lights hit her face and the audience erupted into applause. Lots of foot stomping and whistling accompanied it.

Reaching the edge of the piano, she gripped it for a moment and did her pretend scan of the auditorium by taking her head from the left to the right and even up to the ceiling. The whistles and applause rang in her ears, but the adoration didn't overwhelm her like earlier.

The peace she'd felt in her dressing room still blanketed her. The first half of her performance had been for these people. But this half . . . she swallowed the tears burning her throat.

This performance would be for the Lord alone.

She bowed and slid her right leg under her long evening gown to find the bench with her knee. She waved and nodded to the crowd as they continued to cheer. Then turned her body to the left and lowered herself to the leather bench.

As always, the crowd's applause let her take her time getting settled. She skimmed her fingers over the keys without pressing any of them down.

The crowd hushed, and she counted to ten. Anticipation built in the auditorium.

Then she dove into the rest of her concert.

While she played, gratitude to the Lord flowed through her, infusing her performance with a rightness she hadn't felt in ages.

She lost herself in the music, in the love of God that He had showered upon her. It was as if she'd stepped into a beautiful painting, where the colors were vibrant and bright and sunshine was being poured out on her.

When the concert was all done, shouts of *Zugabe! Zugabe!* echoed throughout the concert hall. With a wide smile, Chaisley bowed and headed backstage. Melanie was at her elbow before she reached the velvet curtains and escorted her back toward her dressing room.

"No matter how many times they shout for an encore or just one more, you leave them wanting more."

Chaisley stilled. Who was this stranger whose voice greeted her?

Her senses went on high alert. "It's a little something I learned touring in America."

Melanie's grip tightened on Chaisley's arm. A sure sign that this was someone unexpected but quite important.

"It is ingenious." The man's smooth words didn't stop the chill that started at the base of her neck.

This man wasn't to be trusted. "Thank you."

"I am here to inform you, Miss Frappier, that the Führer himself will be in attendance for your concert in four days' time. I'm sure you wouldn't mind adding a few of his favorites to your repertoire since you will have someone so prestigious in your audience? I would be happy to provide you an extensive list."

Slick words with no heart or feeling behind them. They were empty. Shallow. Dull.

"I will see what I can do." She kept a neutral expression. No sense trying to even pretend she wanted to look at the man. She stepped forward to her dressing room, praying Melanie would help her since she'd lost count of steps with the interruption. Something she never did.

Melanie had hold of her arm in an instant. "Excuse us, sir. Miss Frappier is exhausted after her performance, and I must insist that she rest." Her tone was firm, yet courteous.

"Yes, yes, of course."

Her friend led her into the room and closed the door. Chaisley held her arms out in front of her to find the chair she had vacated just an hour or so prior. She leaned on it. Her breaths came in great gasps.

Melanie's breathing didn't sound much better. "I don't think my heart has beat that fast in quite some time." Her voice betrayed a hint of fear.

Neither of them spoke for several moments as the weight of what they just learned hit full force.

Chaisley collapsed in the chair, her legs barely able to hold her up. She placed her elbows on her knees. "So. It would seem that the man who wants to control the world will be coming to one of my concerts."

chapter
SIX

As he drove the car back to the hotel, Rick did his best to appear focused on the road and not give any sign that he was listening to Chaisley and Melanie talk in French.

Hitler was coming to one of her concerts? Just the thought of seeing the man made his skin crawl. And his outrage burn.

Should he wire London? Ask if there's something they wished for him to do? He'd never been close to the man himself before.

And he would be in the front row, watching Chaisley perform. His pulse tripped.

Hitler was going to see *Chaisley* play the piano. Not knowing she was blind. What would happen if that madman found out? Rick rubbed a hand over his mouth. Well, he'd have to ensure no one found out.

There was no way he'd let Adolf Hitler get within six feet of Chaisley Frappier.

Barely two weeks had passed since he'd started his job as her driver, and he'd done everything in his power to dig up everything he could on his employer. While he was still in the dark about what

Miss Frappier, her grandmother, and Miss Brigman were up to, he was certain of one thing.

Chaisley was an amazing person. A *good* person.

They were on the same side. They had to be. He felt it deep in his gut. And if he couldn't trust his instincts? He shouldn't be a spy.

Wait a minute. What did Melanie just say about a code? A code for what? First contacts, now a code. What *were* they up to?

Chaisley switched back to Dutch. "Rick, I need to ask a favor."

Her soft, cultured voice cut through his frantic thoughts. How did she make his name sound like an endearment? He pushed the thought away, raised his eyebrows as if startled to attention, and glanced in the mirror. "Ask away, Miss Frappier."

She chewed on her bottom lip for a moment then lifted her chin. "The concert on Sunday?"

Melanie's eyes caught his, her concern evident.

He flicked his eyes back to the road. People were still filling the streets after the concert tonight. A petite woman in a fine mink coat clutched the arm of a lanky man in a tuxedo. He said something, and she tossed her head back with a laugh, slapping his arm.

Rick tapped his thumb on the steering wheel. How was that type of joy possible when their country had just been invaded by a rogue government?

Once the road was clear, he eased the gas pedal down, making a left turn and then a right. Finally they were away from the thick of the crowds. He rolled his shoulders, trying to work some of the tense ache from them. "Sorry, ma'am. You asked about Sunday. It's the last concert here, correct?"

"Yes." She leaned back against the seat again with her arm propped up on the door. Her fingers drumming. "It seems that we will have none other than Herr Hitler in our audience that evening. This concert has been sold out for months, so I'm wondering who he stole the tickets from. I suppose some of his wealthy supporters would be willing to give theirs up—but nevertheless, he will be in attendance. Which means there will be many of his men and guards with him. Which in turn makes me wish for a bit more . . . show of protection for myself."

Ah, their minds had been on the same thing. "Yes, ma'am. What is it that you need me to do?"

"I would like you to don a different uniform that evening. Not that of a driver, but something a bit different . . . perhaps." Her brow furrowed. "Something that is a bit more imposing. You need to have the appearance of . . . ."

"A bodyguard?"

She nodded. "Yes. Perfect. A bodyguard. I will gladly pay whatever is needed for your new attire. How tall are you?"

"In British measurements, I'm a couple inches over six feet."

"I thought you were about that height. That helps. An intimidating figure is what I need." She whispered something to Melanie.

A prick of unease needled him. Those whispered conversations had increased in the last few days. "If you don't need me first thing in the morning, I will get what I need then and make sure that it meets your approval."

"Thank you, Rick." She leaned forward this time. "I would like you by my side at all times that evening. Even when I am playing the piano. No farther than six feet away. Melanie will show you where to stand, and I will need to practice a few times with you standing there because it might take some getting used to."

"Whatever you need." He wiped a sweaty palm against his pant leg. Part of what he loved about being a spy was being unnoticed. Melting into shadows. Just another face in the crowd. Now he would stand on a stage.

In front of thousands of people.

In front of Hitler.

He wouldn't be blending into the background or hiding in a crowd.

At least everyone would be focused on her and the magical

116

sounds coming out of her piano. He turned left into the hotel parking lot, relief washing over him. He needed to get alone. Fast. How did he tell his bosses he was going to be only fifty feet away from the biggest threat to peace in Europe?

"Also," Chaisley said, oblivious to his distress, "I delayed speaking with a newspaperman after the news came about our . . . guest. But I will have to speak with the man tomorrow. There is sure to be an article out by the time the tenth rolls around."

Rick eased the limousine to a stop in front of the hotel's front doors, killing the engine. Why was she telling him this? Did he need to make an appearance? "All right. You just tell me if there's anything else you need me to do." He pulled the key out of the ignition and grasped it in his palm.

The two women went back to whispering.

The metal of the key pressed into his skin as he clenched and unclenched his fist. He needed to send a carefully worded telegram to his bosses. Surely, with this kind of access, they would give him some sort of assignment. The prospect was terrifying.

And a little thrilling to think he could be a part of taking Hitler down.

"I think it's a bad idea!" Melanie's harsh whisper caught his ear. Were they talking about the newspaperman? From what they'd told him, Chaisley didn't do interviews. So why had she chosen to do *this* one? His eyes narrowed as he exited the car, walking toward the back passenger door.

What did Chaisley have up her sleeve?

And why did he have a sinking feeling in his gut?

FRIDAY, APRIL 8, 1938

"You can't possibly do a concert in front of Hitler. Not after this." Melanie tossed the newspaper onto the table. Her anger was so hot right now, she would strangle Hitler if he were in the

117

room. She paced in front of the table while Chaisley sat drinking her tea.

Oh sure. It was fine for Chaisley to be calm. She didn't have to deal with all of the chaos from this interview. She just had to go on stage and play the piano. Chaisley didn't have to worry about the reporters clamoring for another interview, another comment, another . . . another . . . another.

No, that was Melanie's job. To clean up her friend's bombshell.

Melanie pressed the heels of her hands to her eyes. Complaining wouldn't take care of the stack of telegrams in her satchel. Or the gaggle of reporters stationed at every available exit in the hotel. She chewed her thumbnail for a moment, her anger ebbing for a moment.

Chaisley was not a reckless woman. The opposite, in fact. That's what made this all so mind-boggling. Why was she telling the world she was blind *now*?

Melanie flopped into a soft armchair, her head slamming against the plush headrest.

"Are you done with your tantrum?" Chaisley brushed her fingers over a lemon square on her plate. She picked up the pastry and nibbled on the corner.

The barb stung. "I don't know how you can act so nonchalant about this." Melanie wanted to grab Chaisley by the shoulders and shake some sense into her. Instead, she leaned forward and picked up the paper, smoothing it to read the front page.

Chais shrugged. "Probably because I can't undo anything. God gave me peace about what to say, and I said it. Read it to me." She took another sip of her tea.

Melanie took a breath. The paper shook in her hands. Chais was right about one thing, this couldn't be undone. "'World's Most Renowned Concert Pianist Scheduled to Play for the Führer on Sunday.'"

"Gotta love how they twisted the words to say I am playing *for* the Führer. Ugh. As if this wasn't a last minute charade." Chaisley half-laughed. "It's really not that bad. So far."

Melanie groaned. "I'm rolling my eyes at you."

"Oh, believe me, I could feel it. Go on." Her smile grew.

"'Miss Chaisley Frappier, touted as the world's greatest pianist for many years, is on a hope-filled tour of Europe, which is set to last about eighteen months. During this time, she will spend a good deal of time in Austria, France, Belgium, Hungary, Italy, Germany, and Holland.'

"'Miss Frappier spoke with us after one of her concerts and said she has been thrilled to share music with the world. Critics over the years have spoken of her "uncanny accuracy," her "speed and ability to play the most daunting of pieces," and most recently, "her unparalleled gift at composing music." But what many do not know is that Miss Frappier is, in fact, crippled. She is blind.'"

Melanie's stomach curdled. Crippled! How dare that man . . .

She took another inhale to try and calm herself. It didn't work because she'd already read what was coming. "'She lost her sight in a tragic accident outside London on the same evening her parents were killed.'" That sentence made her blood boil. "No mention of the fact that it was a *German* bomb that caused the accident in the first place." She flicked the paper with a loud *thwack*.

"Probably because I made sure I didn't say that." Chaisley dabbed at her mouth with her linen serviette. She looked calm. Peaceful, even. How? "Please continue. So far, it's not horrendous. Other than the word *crippled*—which is complete rubbish."

Fine. She'd read the rest and just see how Chaisley felt about it then. "'While Miss Frappier's loss is tragic, it should come as no surprise that her *German ancestry*'"—she nearly spat the words— "'is a testament to her overcoming all obstacles and shining as the best of the best.'"

"They make it sound as if I'm one of Hitler's Aryan purebloods . . . and oh, she wasn't born this way, it was a horrible accident.

Someone else's fault." Chaisley wrinkled her nose but then chuckled. "My grandmother's parents were German. That's a bit far removed to make such a statement, don't you think? And what difference does it make whether a person is born blind or becomes blind?"

Now she sounded riled. Good.

Melanie shook the paper. "What message does this article send? Do you think people will assume that you align yourself with the Nazis since you're playing in front of Hitler? I mean, the headline says you're playing *for* him."

Chaisley frowned. "I can't worry about that right now. I've decided to make contacts like Dr. G suggested. There are plenty of schools and universities for me to play at as well as concert halls on this tour. That will give us more opportunities to connect with people if the prospects arise. While I don't relish the thought of playing in front of Hitler, there are people in Germany who might need us more than we know. We must move forward as planned and see what we can do to stop the evil."

Melanie sat down beside her and grabbed her hand. "I know. And I want to help too . . . but I don't like how this has made me feel. I'm worried." Which, in all honesty, was too tame a word for her feelings right now. They were in a tempest.

The facade of peace she had crafted over the last few weeks lay shattered. It was one thing to try to figure out how to help people in need. But now that everyone knew Chaisley was blind . . . what would happen?

It was a nightmare. And what did Chaisley's grandmother think? Did she even know? Did Dr. Grafton? Was this a threat to the network in any way? Her friend said she felt the Lord's prompting to share about her disability, but how was that helpful when she was about to perform before a man who hated anyone who was less than perfect? This didn't feel brave.

It felt stupid.

Dangerous.

Melanie glanced at Chaisley. Her friend's shoulders were rigid. Her chin tilted up. It would be no use to voice her concerns at the moment, but perhaps she should reach out to Dr. Grafton. Make sure he knew what Chaisley was up to.

"Mel . . ." Her friend leaned forward. "I'm worried too. I'm sorry I've put you in the middle of this, but I just found out this morning that any Jew with a Polish passport who has been living in Germany for more than five years has had their passport suspended. With this economy, Poland can't support tens of thousands of people returning. Which means those in Germany are stuck in a country where they are despised and at risk." Her friend's hands were clenched tight in her lap, knuckles white. "I fear this is just the beginning of what is to come for them. And with the forced sterilizations and what the Nazis might do to disabled children in the future? I can't stand by and do nothing."

Melanie blinked. Chaisley trembled, bright red spots blooming in her pale cheeks. All signs of calm and equanimity had disappeared. Her friend's shoulders curved inward, almost as if she were collapsing in on herself.

Oh.

Oh.

Melanie's cheeks warmed as blood flooded her face, the heat of it almost unbearable. If anyone was blind in this friendship, it was she. How had she not guessed Chaisley's true motive?

She closed her eyes. Because she had been so tied up in her own emotions, her need to do something *more*, that she missed how afraid Chaisley was.

She sat down in her chair again and reached for her friend's hand, prying her fingers apart.

Chaisley carried herself with such poise and grace it was easy to forget that she was ever afraid.

She smoothed her friend's hand with her fingers. "Oh, Chais. I'm so sorry."

A choked sob rattled Chaisley's chest. "It could have been me, Mel. If my family stayed in Germany all those years ago . . . I could be one of the pour souls caught in this evil." She put her other hand on top of Melanie's, clinging to it. "How can I hide what God has given to me . . . what has turned out to be a gift? I can't stay in the shadows any longer. Not while I have a voice and can do something about this."

Their clasped hands blurred as unshed tears filled Melanie's eyes. "Why didn't you tell me how you were feeling?"

Chaisley turned toward the sound of her voice. "Why haven't you told me about your anxiety?"

She should have known she couldn't keep anything from her all-too-perceptive friend. "We're a pair, aren't we?" Melanie huffed out a laugh and let go of Chaisley's hand to blow her nose.

"You didn't answer my question."

"And you didn't answer mine."

Chaisley tapped her fingers on the arm of her chair.

"What are we going to do?"

Chaisley's jaw set. "I'm going to keep my ears open, make contacts, and pray that God shows us. Besides that, I'm not really sure. But one thing seems certain. On Sunday, I'm going to play the piano in front of Adolf Hitler."

VIENNA, AUSTRIA—SUNDAY, APRIL 10, 1938
THE GOLDEN HALL OF THE MUSIKVEREIN

Chaisley tuned out everything around her until the silence engulfed her. Not a sound existed in the great hall until she allowed a long exhale to escape her lips. Her fingers found the keys, and she began Chopin's *Fantasie Impromptu* to warm up her fingers.

Memories washed over her. Grandmother sitting at her side while she practiced this, her favorite piece. Grandmother's pride when, at the age of twelve, Chaisley mastered the difficult rhythm of four against three in a matter of days. As soon as Chaisley heard the beautiful song, she knew she had to learn it and begged her teacher for a braille copy. She'd had the entire score memorized in the span of an afternoon.

Another memory surfaced as her fingers flew over the keys—Grandmother asking her, just before Chaisley headed out on her first worldwide tour, to play *Fantasie* for her one last time on the piano her parents gave her. The smells and sounds of her childhood home flooded her senses . . .

Cinnamon and orange from her favorite scones baking in the kitchen. The clinking of the china tea service on the rolling tray as Cook brought it in, Grandmother's tender voice: *"No matter what, my dear, always use your gift for the Lord. He gave it to you."*

Chaisley could almost feel the strong yet weathered hand on her face as the memory rushed over her.

"And maybe, one day, when there is no more threat of another Great War, you may return to my homeland, and play for the people there . . . I know England has been your home, but you are also a child of Holland. Promise me you will go and play for my people someday . . ."

Chaisley shook her head as her fingers found the last E flat. She was fulfilling that promise on this trip. But was it enough?

The braille letter she'd received from Dr. G had been eye-opening. Challenging. The man was using the fortune he'd inherited from his family to help people escape the Nazis. He expressed time and again that he didn't want her to worry. What he was doing was what God had called him to do, and he encouraged her to pray about how God could use her on this tour.

She'd smiled at that. How like the Lord to send her the encouragement she needed, to fan the spark He'd already lit into a flame. Now it was just a matter of *what*.

Chaisley rubbed her fingers on the keys for a moment, the

smooth ivory comforting and familiar. *Show me, Lord.* Everything around her stilled as she waited.

Then one idea.

And another.

Her hand rose to her chest, pressing against the deep ache gnawing at her. But in the midst of the swirl of her thoughts, a wild plan formed in her mind.

Could she pull it off?

Grandmother had made it clear that she was using her final years on this earth—and whatever financial resources she had—to help others. What would the Nazis do to Grandmother if they knew she was helping the Jews? Germany had already taken Austria, what if they went after Holland next?

In her mind she could hear the soldiers marching into Amsterdam, whistles blowing, people screaming, as the Gestapo arrested anyone they desired.

Clamping her eyelids shut, Chaisley willed the horrific thoughts away. There was no turning back now. The wheels had been set in motion. And nothing could make her grandmother give up her cause.

Chaisley had that same determination with her music. But now . . . Now the Lord was asking her if she would use that tenacity and drive in a different way.

The time to act was upon her. *Yes, Lord.* A settled feeling swept over her. Almighty God would guide her steps. And she would follow Him.

She stretched her arms above her head and rotated her neck in circles. Melanie and Rick would be done securing her dressing room at any moment. Whatever they had planned, she trusted them. She was here to warm up on the piano and test it out. It was time to play the part.

Scales flowed from her fingertips. First, all the major keys. Then all the minors. Natural, harmonic, and melodic. Arpeggios were next.

In the middle of C# minor, the unmistakable throat clearing of the conductor she'd met when they arrived sounded to her right. "I'm sorry for the interruption, Fräulein Frappier. Is the instrument satisfactory?"

Chaisley turned her head toward his voice. "Yes, it is, but the tuning in the eighth octave is off, and the tension is a little loose there as well. I'm sure you can rectify that before tonight's concert."

Another clearing of the throat. She imagined his face turning red, lips tightening. Most conductors didn't like to hear that their nine-foot concert grand wasn't in the best of condition when it had probably been tuned that very afternoon. "We are honored to have you here, Fräulein. The Führer asked for everything to be the very best for you, so I will call the tuner back immediately." Feet shuffled away toward stage front. His voice was stronger now but held an edge. "We are overjoyed to have such honored guests with us this evening. We've never had the world's best pianist *and* the world leader of our day."

He sounded so smug. Well, two could play at that. "It should be quite an evening."

"I must say, Fräulein, I've never heard a woman play with your skill and . . . um . . ."

"Lack of sight?" When the man had called months ago to schedule this date on the tour, he'd practically begged her to come. Now? His tone of condescension stiffened her spine. She would not give him the upper hand. Difficult enough for the great conductors of the world to accept her gender and superior skills. Now that they knew about her blindness, they would be all-too-inclined to dismiss her.

The quick footsteps approaching from the left were definitely Melanie. And by her stride, she wasn't happy. *"Guten abend."* Her tone held a chill. "I must insist that we allow Fräulein Frappier to finish her preparations for this evening's concert. The world's best pianist shouldn't have to accept interruption from a common conductor."

The haughty words grated over Chaisley. Whatever was her friend up to?

Fingers snapped. "Friederich!"

The next set of footsteps was heavier. Purposeful. Rick. "Yes, miss?"

A tug at her elbow pulled Chaisley to stand and then into motion.

"That will be all." Melanie's dismissive command followed them offstage.

Once they were safely inside the vehicle once again, Rick spoke from the front of the car. "Well done, Miss Brigman."

"I couldn't have done it without you, Mr. Zimmerman. I couldn't believe the gall of that man. Some of these Germans are downright insulting."

Chaisley agreed. The conversations she'd overheard since the newspaper came out were like little knives stabbing at her heart. As if she were suddenly less of a person.

But word had also reached her that newspapers around the world had reported that there was no match to her talent. Even more so now that they knew she was blind.

Melanie and Rick were still chatting about what they'd over-heard. Mel was riled up. "That sniveling little conductor can just pack up his Nazi views and try them on someone else. Don't let it get to you, Chais." Her friend squeezed her arm tight.

"I know."

"You handled yourself very well, I might add." Mel still sounded like she was about to punch someone.

For any of this to work, Chaisley had to keep her wits about her. And even though parts of the newspaper article weren't what she would have written herself, she could use it to her advantage. Her great-grandparents were the purest of Germans—almost royalty to Hitler's Pan-Germanist Nazis. She could show the same air of confidence and condescension that Hitler portrayed and expected from his master race.

Since he was coming to the concert—and by now he surely knew the truth about her—what did that mean? He wouldn't harm her, would he? No. She'd gained even more acclaim overnight when everyone found out she was blind. To be honest, Hitler was probably coming because he always wanted the best of everything, and *she* had been touted as the best. It didn't hurt that she was of German descent. But now that the article was out, his presence tonight could mean any number of things.

Would he come after her? Melanie and Rick?

Her stomach plummeted. Every shred of confidence from earlier evaporated.

Had she signed her own death warrant by sharing with the world that she could no longer see?

THUNDEROUS APPLAUSE RESONATED throughout the large concert hall. Chaisley stood, gripped the edge of the Steinway with her left hand, and bowed deep at the waist. She imagined the gold statues Melanie had described, which acted as pillars to hold up the slim balconies surrounding the hall. The stage was relatively small, with no curtains, simply doors leading off the stage and to the back under the pipes of the massive organ.

She bowed again, taking her time. The margin for error was zero. A bead of sweat slipped down her neck and onto the collar of her evening gown. When was the last time she had been this nervous?

Not in years.

Stop it. Thinking about being nervous would reflect in her playing. And she couldn't afford that.

Now was the time to play her trump card.

She nodded in the direction she knew Hitler sat, took her seat on the padded bench, and started into Liszt's piano transposition of Wagner's *Song of the Evening Star*.

Wagner was a favorite of the Führer. So much depended on her impressing him . . .

Chaisley allowed the music to take over, pouring everything she had into the piece. She didn't need to see the faces of her audience to know that she had them enraptured. The great hall was devoid of sound other than what emanated from the piano.

Thank You, Lord, for this gift. Please guide me.

Even though her face portrayed the confident, accomplished musician, she feared the fierce pounding of her heart might give her away. Or the slight tremor in her legs. The plan *had* to work. But if it did, it meant a more difficult path lay ahead. Was she capable of seeing this through?

She must. Just like Esther.

Lives were at stake.

Two minutes before she was to be onstage, one of the Führer's men came to tell her that the nobility—almost royalty—of her German lineage, accompanied by her recognition as a great pianist, had caught the attention of the leader of *Deutschland*.

He also made sure to mention that since her blindness had been caused by an accident, it hadn't "marred" her in any other way.

Hadn't marred her.

Insufferable man!

"But it makes you impossible for Hitler to resist." Rick's words after the little meeting echoed in her brain.

No pressure.

Well, whatever they had intended by insisting to speak with her right before the concert was for naught. She'd prayed the whole walk onto the stage and as she took her seat.

Now as the last notes resounded from the heart of the great instrument, Chaisley slowly lifted her hands and rose again to the crowd's resounding appreciation. Keeping her head lowered, she bowed and placed her hand over her heart, acknowledging her gratitude.

Hurried footsteps ascended the steps to her right, and she breathed deep as they marched toward center stage. Rick's steps from behind brought him closer. Guarding her. Giving her strength. When she'd been introduced at the beginning of the evening, she'd almost turned around. Run away. Hid. The enormity of her revelation to that newspaper felt like a boulder crushing her into the ground.

But she'd stood firm. Barely.

Now was the moment she'd dreaded.

The Führer was onstage. She heard him speak briefly to the crowd, and the very sound of his voice, so full of self-righteous passion, sent a shiver racing up Chaisley's spine. She hated his voice but had studied it for hours in preparation for tonight. With all her senses heightened, she could recognize his voice with just one syllable.

More applause and shouts of adoration forced her smile.

Then steady steps approached her.

Chaisley kept her head bowed and waited for the steps to stop. Then she lifted her chin, every inch the famous pianist. She was the best. Adolf Hitler always wanted the best.

The reminders kept resonating in her brain.

Rumbles of applause still echoed across the room, and the steps halted to her left with a click—his heels snapping together?

"Fräulein."

She bowed again. "Führer Hitler."

"Your mastery was brilliant. Thank you for coming to Austria, the land of my birth, and blessing us with your talent."

"Thank you." She raised her chin and nodded. Tried to portray the proud artist he wished to see. "It has been my pleasure."

"I greatly appreciate your chosen piece for the finale in acknowledgment of me."

"You are most welcome." It was impossible to breathe with him so close.

He cleared his throat and sniffed. "We want to show the world the superior quality we aim for here in Deutschland. I want the finest, Fräulein. And you are that. How grateful you must be for your German blood."

Dipping her head once, Chaisley gritted her teeth. Would he keep her here on display all night? When she was playing, the thought of thousands of eyes on her didn't matter. But without the security of her instrument, Chaisley felt exposed. The urge to shrink back was overwhelming.

Give me strength, Jesus. I need Your courage. Straightening her shoulders, she offered a smile and lifted her chin. "I thank you for the honor of your compliment." The words tasted like chalk on her tongue.

Another haughty sniff preceded his words. "I hope you will play for me again."

Chaisley could imagine the man before her from the descriptions Melanie had given. But she replaced it with the picture she'd created in her mind to help her be confident in his presence.

A short, middle-aged man sprouted in her imagination. He was slightly balding, with thick jowls and a paunch belly. The urge to laugh was inappropriate. The situation was dangerous. *He* was dangerous. But she would not fear him. "Perhaps that could be arranged."

"You have spirit." It sounded like his lips were in a smile, but his tone had changed. "I have many visitors coming here as well who will appreciate a fine concert."

"My schedule is quite full, but I'm sure we can discuss the details at a later date."

"Indeed."

She lowered her chin again and dropped into a slight curtsy. His commanding footsteps sounded close to her and then moved away, back toward the stairs.

"Deutschland's own virtuoso. The finest in the world!" The Führer's voice shouted to the crowd.

Thunderous applause sounded, and Chaisley bowed again, letting her smile brighten.

Adolf Hitler had just played into her hand.

"What did you just do?" Rick's whispered words behind her sounded as though he spoke through clenched teeth.

Melanie gave her a tap on the elbow on her right side. "I was wondering the same thing."

Chaisley bowed once more as the crowd continued to clap and cheer. She kept a smile pasted on her face as she turned around and walked with her two companions offstage. "I've left a door open in case we might need it."

"I wish you would have discussed that with me first." Was that hurt in Mel's voice?

"What is it you two aren't telling me?" Rick pulled on her left arm.

"Not here." Chaisley kept her hand on Melanie. "Let's discuss it in the car."

Melanie led her to the dressing room, and she sat, taking in the quiet. Chaisley nodded toward her friend. "Thank you. I wasn't sure I would make it." Her hands shook almost as much as her voice.

"This is only the beginning, but I'll be here every step of the way."

More tremors coursed through Chaisley's body. *Dear Lord, help me.*

The Führer's manipulative words made her stomach roil. And it wasn't just his putrid breath.

She was a trophy to him. For now. Which meant it was time.

Let the finest concerto of her life begin . . .

chapter
SEVEN

Why on earth would the Führer want to applaud that woman? She was blind. *Blind!*

It had been torture to sit through an entire concert where everyone cheered and clapped. It didn't matter that she could play the piano. It didn't matter that she was beautiful. It didn't even matter that she had German blood in her.

She was imperfect. Flawed.

Crippled.

Just like the paper said.

But when the Führer came back to his seat after speaking to the woman onstage, he'd told him to find a way to bring her to play for his inner circle back in Berlin.

Why?

It made his skin crawl.

It didn't help that the pianist's man—whoever he was—kept looking in his direction. And that woman who came out at the end. Who was she? Why did she look familiar?

The whole thing irritated him.

If they were going to purify the world, their focus needed to be sharp and on target.

It was a good thing he'd been promoted.

Hitler needed him.

To stay the course. To weed out the imperfect. To cleanse the scourge from this earth once and for all.

RICK DROVE AWAY from the concert hall biting his tongue as Melanie and Chaisley spoke in hushed French in the back seat.

It didn't matter that Chaisley thought pretending to be on Hitler's good side might give her some kind of advantage along the way. Yes, she'd left the door open to be invited to play for him again. Yes, that might give Rick an opportunity to gain valuable intel. But this was dangerous. Every hair on the back of his neck stood up when the man approached her.

Pure. Evil.

As a spy, he wanted to applaud her and think about all the ways they could gather information. But since he'd gotten to know her a little better, he wanted to protect her. Not spy on her. Not help her play concerts for Hitler.

He wanted to shake some sense into her.

It didn't sound like Melanie was all that pleased with Chaisley either. Especially since this had apparently been a decision she'd made on her own.

Everything he picked up now from their conversation told him the women had been informed that something much worse was coming. Chaisley was talking of preparing for it.

Her tone changed as she talked about someone named Mary Beth? A child? Wasn't Melanie's mother also named Mary Beth? But that couldn't be her—Melanie's mother had died. These women were determined to find and help someone else with that name.

It was so frustrating not knowing the whole story. But how could he find out?

Melanie would fight tooth and nail for her friend—that much was all too apparent.

Rick understood it. He felt like a heel for eavesdropping. He needed to earn their complete trust so they would voluntarily share these things with him. But how could he do that?

"Rick, do you think Chaisley has put herself in unnecessary danger?" Melanie's sharp Dutch echoed from the back seat.

One glance in the mirror showed him that Chaisley wasn't a bit pleased with Melanie's question.

He'd better choose his words carefully. "There's a part of me that cheered her on for standing up to him and doing what she did. Then there's another part of me that wanted to rush her offstage and away from him because my senses kept screaming, danger, danger, danger!"

"Don't you think *my* senses were screaming the same thing?" Chaisley wrapped her arms around her middle. "But staying in Hitler's good graces right now might help us assist those in danger from him and his Third Reich."

Her words told him that he *had* gained Chaisley's trust—otherwise she wouldn't be so blunt.

"What has gotten into you?" Melanie shook her head. "I will support you no matter what, but it would have been nice to know ahead of time to what lengths you were willing to go."

"I wasn't expecting him to come onstage and speak to me personally about playing for him."

"But you thought it could happen."

Chaisley pursed her lips at Melanie's assertion. "Yes, I did."

Rick needed to defuse the moment and fast. He pulled over onto the side of the road, placed the car in park, and then turned around in his seat. "I don't think the best use of our time is to squabble about how things unfolded. What we should be talking about is what we do from here. My job is to drive you and protect you. I can't do that very well if you don't tell me everything that is going on."

Chaisley chewed on her bottom lip again. "Agreed."

"Agreed." Melanie didn't look too happy about it, but dove into telling him about a letter Chaisley received before they left England. It was deplorable what had been done to this little girl and her mother. Rick's respect for both the women in the back seat surged as he listened to them share their hearts about being challenged to find these two—and possibly others—to help them escape Hitler's clutches.

So maybe he'd jumped to conclusions about their code and contacts. These women couldn't be spies.

But then Chaisley mentioned her guardian. A doctor. Someone with contacts across Europe. Both women were vague. The only key factor was that they knew they had people that could help them should they need it.

Who was this doctor? Another agent? Someone Rick might know?

The other possibility was one he hated to consider. What if these two women were being used—by double agents?

Would Rick be able to save them before it was too late?

TWO HOURS LATER, Rick waited on an informant in an alley that smelled worse than it looked. Which was saying a lot. He'd already spotted a dead rat, two dead birds, and what appeared to be a dead cat.

HQ had put him in touch with their last known informant who was still free, and the choice of meeting spots was looking worse by the second.

Why was the man late?

Rick shoved his hands deeper into his pockets. He'd give him five more minutes, but it wouldn't be safe to hang around much longer. Someone would surely notice him, and whether it was someone from this seedy side of town or the Gestapo, neither one would have pleasant results.

Shuffling from the other end of the alley made him turn around.

Sure enough, a man—way too skinny for his height—headed straight for him.

"G2586." The man whispered into Rick's ear.

"Eggs are good with toast." Rick shoved out a hand.

But as they shook hands, nothing was passed between them.

The informant smiled wide and spoke through clenched teeth. "Nothing written." He spoke English with an American accent. "Too risky."

"Okay." Rick nodded and smiled like they were old friends simply running into each other.

The man stepped closer. "Things are escalating at a rapid pace. They are growing their troops every day. Watching more and more people. Closing in on everyone they suspect. Arrests have grown in number, so I am leaving. Tell your boss or whoever needs to know. I haven't seen my wife and kids in over a year. You need to focus on communications. The enemy is confiscating more and more each day and listening in on whatever they can access to try and stop any leaks." His words were clipped and fast. "Word is anyone they find colluding with any country against Germany will be executed."

AMSTERDAM—TUESDAY, APRIL 19, 1938

Celestia was certain that the last letter she'd received from Chaisley had been opened before it was delivered here. The edges had the appearance of being steamed.

Since it came from Austria, and since the Anschluss where Nazi Germany took control of the country, she was convinced they were checking people's mail. She couldn't prove it, but what other explanation could there be?

Tensions among the network ran high. Much higher the last week.

The question was, could anyone read the original braille code they were using to communicate?

Was Chaisley able to come up with a new code? Perhaps she'd

discovered an even more obscure form of braille they could use. Celestia couldn't remember how many there were—but hopefully they'd have something soon.

She sat at her desk with her braille slate, ready to compose a letter to her granddaughter, but the words would not come. How could she let her granddaughter know it was time for a new way to communicate and not arouse suspicion? Her fingers brushed the slate, the bumps now so familiar to her touch, but her mind would not settle. If Chaisley had finished whatever she was working on, how could they all learn it if they weren't together in the same place? She'd have to send a telegram to Grafton.

Since he was always on the move, he could go to Chaisley and then bring word to her.

As she stared out the window at the beautiful gardens beginning to bloom, a tear slipped out of the corner of her eye.

Chaisley used to love to go into the gardens with her back in England. Back when she could see and her childlike excitement over every color and shape of flower excited her.

Now that same excitement was evident in every note Chaisley composed. Every concert. Grafton had been right, and Celestia was not too proud to admit it.

Her granddaughter had needed the freedom to be a child again. To laugh and play and live her life. What would Chaisley's life have become had Celestia fully given over to her fear? She shivered. It didn't bear thinking about.

God carried them all through the tragedy of loss and made it something beautiful. Each of them, not just Chaisley, but Grafton, Melanie . . . even she had been given fresh purpose.

And now He was doing it again. But this time on a bigger scale.

It seemed every newspaper in the world now wanted to talk about the world's greatest pianist, who was blind. Some were probably wanting something positive to talk about rather than the depressing facts of the economy or the slow recovery of the war-torn continent of Europe. Others, no doubt, wanted to stir up controversy. One even mentioned that it had been a lie for her to perform all these years and not let her audiences know.

Why would people care? Wouldn't they be even more mesmerized by her skill and talent now that they knew? Celestia shook her head. What a sad world they lived in.

She glanced back down at the paper, slate, and punch tool. Writing in braille was tedious. Everything had to be punched precisely and written from right to left so that the raised dots would be in the correct order when the paper was flipped over for the recipient to read it. Whatever code Chaisley concocted was surely even more intricate.

So the practice was good for her.

Hitler was on the move. Celestia's gut told her he wouldn't be satisfied with just Austria. And since so many in Austria had celebrated the annexation, his confidence was probably bolstered even higher.

Thousands of Jewish refugees had made it into Holland and all of the Netherlands since 1933 and Hitler coming to power. It was no secret he wanted Poland, Czechoslovakia, the Netherlands, and Belgium. That was just to start. Which meant all the Jews and other refugees who weren't of the Nazis' master race and had fled Germany would now also be at risk.

It was already difficult to find countries that could take more refugees. Visas were hard to come by unless you knew someone in the government and it still wasn't easy. While the Netherlands had allowed many in, they also encouraged the refugees to go to a country much farther away.

People knew. They could feel it. Those against the Jews were spreading hatred and it was growing.

Now that six hidden rooms capable of housing ten people apiece were built in here at the manor, she had been gathering supplies, a little at a time.

It was time to let Chaisley know. Everything. In case something happened to her, or if the war didn't come until after she had left this earth for her heavenly home. Someone would need to be here, someone who knew how to help. The access to the rooms must be kept secret. Even her most trusted staff didn't know how to get into them. Celestia was the only one who knew how to find and open the hidden doors. That information had to be safeguarded.

Chaisley could handle it. She'd seen the determination in her granddaughter's features.

Time was short.

Knock! Knock!

The door to her sitting room was locked so Celestia rose from her chair and went to answer it.

The look on her butler's face was pure agony. "Mrs. Frappier, I'm so sorry to disturb you, but there's a family from Berlin at the gate requesting assistance. They said Dr. Grafton sent them."

She exited her room and locked the door. "Take me to them, Bastiaan. Have they told you anything?"

His shoulders were stiff as they walked the long corridor. "I should warn you, the wife is bruised, the children too thin. She said Dr. Grafton told them you could be trusted and offer them safety."

"And the rest of the story?" she prodded. Her butler was normally composed and seldom revealed much emotion. Today, the tall man was obviously disturbed.

"Her husband was taken away by the Gestapo. She said he was an informant for the British SIS and doesn't know whether he's dead or in one of the work camps."

"Oh my." She picked up her pace and passed up Bastiaan as they headed for the stairs.

But his hand on her arm halted her. "Ma'am, is this really happening?"

She glanced back and caught the sheen in his eyes before he blinked it away. It shook her to her core to see the man so unsettled. "I'm afraid so." With a hand to her forehead, she willed herself to stay strong. "And I fear it will get much worse."

chapter
EIGHT

BUDAPEST, HUNGARY—SATURDAY, APRIL 30, 1938
HUNGARIAN STATE OPERA HOUSE

Chaisley longed for a nap. Not just any old nap would do, either. It would have to rival Rip Van Winkle to erase her exhaustion.

Two concerts a day for the last two weeks was a grueling pace. All the days seemed to blur together.

Another concert was before her tonight, so she'd lain on the couch in her dressing room to tame her thoughts and rest her mind. But the voices of the hungry wouldn't leave her alone.

After hearing of the poverty and people struggling along the way, her heart had broken. So she talked to Melanie and Rick and they devised a new plan of action. On the morning of her concerts, they went to the market and purchased breads, fruits, and cheeses to give people on the streets. Melanie and Rick did all the disbursing since she didn't navigate the crowds as well as they did. But she sat in the car with the window cracked so she could hear people's responses.

It was those voices that she heard on repeat. Gratitude that someone cared. Crying out for them to return tomorrow.

If only she could help everyone—fix the world. But she was only one person.

Hitler's plan was no longer just a whispered secret. She'd heard many rumblings in the towns they'd visited so far. But most people chose to go on with their lives and do their best. Not that she could blame them. Food had to be put on the table. Provisions had to be earned for roofs over their heads. No one wanted to be gathered up and taken to a work camp.

Many Jews had fled Germany already. From what she'd heard, those who'd had the money and the way to obtain the correct papers and visas had started to leave as early as 1933. Then there were those who saved up for it and left—going as far as their money would take them. But they were hard-pressed to find work, and many looked down their noses at them. Because some countries—like Hungary—were beginning to side with Germany and taking on the same rules and beliefs.

What had this world come to?

"Chaisley." Melanie's voice preceded a touch to her shoulder. "Fifteen minutes until you need to be onstage, but Dr. Grafton is here to see you."

She bolted to a sitting position. "Goodness. I must look a mess. Please send him in."

"You don't look a mess at all. He's right outside, so I'll get him." A few steps sounded, then the door opened.

Gracious, she must have been deep in her thoughts. She hadn't even heard Melanie enter the room. Chaisley swiped at her face. "Dr. G," she held out her arms. "I'm so glad you're here."

He wrapped her in a hug. "I know there's not much time, and I must get back on the road, but your grandmother asked me to stop in and find out if you'd finished the code you were working on. She suspects that your last letter to her was opened by the Nazis."

They hadn't wasted any time, had they? Sweat flushed across her body. Of all the scenarios she'd run through in her head, her mail being surveilled so soon hadn't been one. A foolish mistake. "Yes, I finished it. But it's complicated."

"Complicated is good. Less chance for them to know what we're communicating." He touched her cheek. "It's so good to see you."

The warmth in his words squeezed her heart. "I've missed you." She leaned into his hand. If only they could go back to simpler times. "I'm so grateful for your help. How do I teach you and Grandmother the new code?"

"I'll come see you in one week's time. Make sure Melanie knows the code by then. The four of us will be the only ones who know it. At least for now and until we are confident in it."

She nodded. Now was not the time to tell him about her conversation with Hitler. He needed his focus, and she didn't need another person hovering and telling her it had been reckless. "I'll have everything ready for you in a week."

"Stay vigilant, you two. Your driver seems to be an honorable man as well. I'm glad he's around to keep you safe. I better let you get to your performance. I love you."

"I love you too."

And with quick footsteps, he was gone.

Melanie grabbed her hand. "The place is packed—again. With lots of young students as well as plenty of other people from the community it would seem." She tugged at Chaisley's shoulders and led her over to the chair. "Let me brush out your hair and you'll be ready to go."

Melanie pulled the brush through her hair in long, gentle strokes, and Chaisley breathed deep, held it for a count of four, then exhaled and held it again. It was good to get her focus back on the task at hand. Having Dr. G close again made her heart ache for home.

Lord, if there is just one person that we need to meet or help tonight, please guide us.

The new melody that had started in her heart and mind over the last few weeks wouldn't leave her alone. It was the saddest melody she'd ever composed, and it had grown exponentially as she worked on it. There was no ending yet, but perhaps over time there would be a resolve from minor to major. Something to leave the listener with hope.

"I've been praying for you and will be there right beside you. Rick is also going to be onstage again, just in case."

"Oh?"

"We were talking before Dr. Grafton arrived, and Rick thinks it's best for your protection to have a 'show of strength,' I think is how he put it. You aren't a weak blind female. You are the world's best pianist, and you are confident and well-protected."

She could agree to that. In these tenuous times, it was best to stay ahead of things. "I'll have to thank him for thinking of that."

Five minutes later, she was standing at the edge of the curtains on the stage of the Hungarian State Opera House.

She pasted on a smile and lifted her shoulders as she walked out onto the stage to deafening applause. Rick's footsteps matched her own, bolstering her confidence, making her feel strong and courageous for whatever lay ahead.

Reaching the left edge of the piano, she ran her hand over the smooth surface and gripped it tight as she found the bench with her leg.

Once she was seated and comfortable, she launched into her favorite piece to the wild cheers of the audience. She'd forgotten how boisterous young people could be. It made her smile widen and energized her.

Two and a half hours later, she stood from the piano and bowed.

"*Bis!*"

"*Bis!*"

"*Zugabe!*"

"*Encore!*"

Shouts echoed from throughout the crowd.

But even as the audience expressed their hopes for more, she bowed a final time, waved to them, and exited the stage with Rick at her elbow.

Back in the dressing room, she changed out of her formal gown—this time a green satin that was Melanie's favorite—and put on her comfortable travel dress before they headed back to their hotel for the evening. Melanie and Rick had gone to keep an eye on the crowd of young people and would return when it was a good time to leave. Places like this, it was best for her to take her time so the crowds could disperse. It helped her to exit without being mobbed.

A knock sounded at her door, and she went to it. "Who is it?"

"Rick and Melanie." A familiar, rich, deep timbre greeted her.

She unlocked and opened the door and felt both of them brush past her. A new scent wafted over her. "What's the new smell? Rick, is that you?"

A small chuckle. "I ran out of shaving cream and had to try something new. Sorry."

"Don't apologize, it suits you." To be honest, she liked it. A lot.

"We have someone waiting outside who wishes to speak with you." Melanie's words weren't in her usual cadence. Tension laced the rhythm now. "Someone who could use our help."

Chaisley's heart leapt. This is what she'd prayed about. That God would use her however He saw fit. Her nerves got the best of her though and she felt a tremble in her arms. What if she didn't know what to do? What if she couldn't help them?

Rick cleared his throat. "We've heard the basics of their story, and we believe they are who they say they are. It's a mother and daughter."

"Good." She swallowed. It had to be the exhaustion that overwhelmed her at the moment. Now was the time to be strong. Lifting her chin, she went to the chair over by the dressing table and found her seat. "Is there still a crowd outside?"

"Yes. Many of the young people are waiting to see if they can catch a glimpse of you as you leave."

"Well then, bring the visitors in here. They can sit on the couch. I'm assuming we will need the privacy."

"You're right. I can go get them, but let me pack up our things first." Melanie shuffled around the room.

"I'll go get them," Rick volunteered. "That way I can check around and make sure no one else is lurking about. I'll find the manager and find out when we need to be out."

LEANING UP AGAINST the door to the dressing room to guard against anyone who dared to enter, Rick crossed his arms over his chest and listened as Irene and her daughter Helen shared their story with Chaisley. Their clothes were ragged, their faces grim.

Melanie's face was filled with caution. Chaisley's—

With compassion.

"Up until November of last year, we lived in Germany. My husband was taken to one of the camps six months ago." The mother's frown deepened. She was gaunt and feeble looking. Even though she was still quite young, perhaps only thirty-five or so, the woman's appearance was that of someone twice her age. "We searched for him but were told we would be imprisoned as well if we didn't go away." She sniffed and put a worn hankie to her face.

The daughter spoke up, her voice stronger, angry, and yet full of fear. "They came for me at school since I am blind. Said they were going to put me in a special school, that I wouldn't live at home anymore. I couldn't bear to not be with my mother. I still don't know how I got away, but I just knew they were going to do unthinkable things . . . perform that awful surgery. We've all heard the rumors."

"How old are you, Helen?" Chaisley's soothing voice calmed the room.

The young woman deflated. Her shoulders sagged and tears spilled onto her cheeks. "Sixteen."

Rick fisted his hands at his side. She was just a kid!

Melanie sucked in a quick breath.

Chaisley frowned. "I'm glad you escaped."

"My mother found me hiding in the sewers behind the school and we have been running ever since."

Irene sat up straighter and found her voice again. "When I saw the newspaper talking about you, I felt the Lord was giving me direction and that I must find you. No matter what. Please . . . is there any way you can help us? We have no money. We have no clothes. We have nothing. We haven't eaten in days—but we will do whatever you ask of us if you can just get my daughter safely away from Hitler and the Nazis. I can stay and wait for my husband."

Helen began to sob. "No! Mama, you must come with me! I can't do this alone. I'm scared . . . I won't go without you."

Melanie wrapped her arms around the girl as Chaisley reached for the mother's hands. She grabbed them and then knelt before Irene. "You must listen to me, Irene. I'll make sure you have clothing and food, but as for getting your daughter to safety, I don't know what I can do, but I will contact some friends. If we find a way for you to safely leave, you *must* go with your daughter. Give me your husband's name, and I will get it into the hands of whomever I can to help, but you've got to trust me. Your daughter needs you. You must go."

Now the mother began to sob in earnest. "I can't leave him here."

"Promise me." Chaisley found the woman's face and held it in her hands. "Promise me you will go if we find a way."

Irene nodded and the mother and daughter then collapsed into each other's arms crying and whispering that they loved each other.

Rick left his post at the door and wiggled around the women until he was at Chaisley's side. "Here . . . let me help you." He assisted her from her kneeling position and leaned close to whisper in her ear. "You are doing a noble thing, but are you certain your contact will be able to help?"

She dipped her chin in a nod. "Whomever Dr. Grafton has on his list means they are willing and capable of doing just about anything."

He raised his eyebrows.

"Don't be so shocked, Mr. Zimmerman." She patted his chest. "If you knew Dr. G like I do, you'd be certain as well."

He wanted to laugh at how she knew what he'd been thinking. The woman was remarkable.

Shuffling back to his place at the door, he watched as the group of four women mopped up faces, shared whispered words of encouragement, and then all stood and hugged each other.

"Let me go check the exits." He left the room and scanned the rear of the building, where the limousine was parked. Satisfied, he went back to the dressing room. "I believe the crowds have all gone." He kept his voice soft so he wouldn't scare off the two women who didn't know him. "Perhaps we could go back to the hotel and feed everyone and make a plan from there."

"Excellent idea." Chaisley reached for her things, but they had moved with their guests.

"Let me get them." Melanie took their bags and coats in one arm and then reached for Chaisley's elbow. "Irene and Helen, there's plenty of room for you in our car. When we get to the hotel, I'll secure you a room, and you can get cleaned up. I'm sure I have some clothes that will fit you."

Rick peered into the hallway—no one was around. He led his group to the car and waited until everyone was safely ensconced inside before he closed all the doors, took his seat behind the wheel, and started the engine. Once he had everyone at the hotel, he was going to reach out to his superiors. They needed to know the truth of what was happening.

HANDS SHAKING, MELANIE left the hotel and went for a walk. Something had to calm her quaking nerves and sitting in her room wasn't helping.

Ever since the concert on April the tenth, she couldn't shake the feeling that something was off. Maybe it was the way Hitler's entourage adored him that sickened her the most, or the fact that Chaisley had agreed to possibly play for him again that had her on edge. Nothing had felt quite right until they helped Irene and Helen.

Even though she didn't want to be anywhere near the Nazis, her tiny fire of passion had been fueled into an all-out bonfire.

Yes, this intrigue made her uncomfortable. Yes, she'd rather be back home in England. But could she stay and help Chaisley with whatever God laid out for them?

Yes.

The posh neighborhood was quiet, and the stars twinkling in the night sky gave her spirit a feeling of peace and calm.

Exactly what she needed.

Irene's story was so powerful. So real. It put faces to those who were suffering, and the truth sank so deep into her soul that she felt like she carried a hundred pounds on her back as she led the woman and her daughter to the hotel and arranged a room for them.

How had people lived like this for years? How had the world not responded and stopped it?

Oh, sure, it was fine for those who had plenty of money, those who were Aryan, and those who went along with the Nazis. But there were so many who were hurt, starving, imprisoned, or dying.

Her steps quickened as she worked through her thoughts. Determination to help spurred on her steps until her legs protested that she'd gone too far. Perhaps it was time to turn back.

She focused on her surroundings and started. Gone was the lovely neighborhood surrounding the fancy hotel. Instead there were sagging brick buildings and flickering streetlamps. The scent of stale cigarette smoke lingered in the air. Shouts of laughter cut through the silence on the street as three men and two women stumbled out of a nightclub.

Definitely time to get back.

She turned on her heel and headed back the way she came. Her legs ached from the long walk, but she was at least a little more clear-headed than she'd—

Rough hands grabbed her and slammed her up against the brick wall of a building. A scream vaulted out of her throat, but a smelly hand pressed over her mouth. She bit at the hand, but it pressed her harder into the wall, her head hitting with a smack.

"You filthy Jew-loving woman." The man spat in her face, and it ran down her cheek. His German accent was thick and heavy. "I saw you with those refugees after the concert. Stinking Jews! If we were in Germany right now, I'd have the Gestapo take you to the camps." He lowered his hand and gripped her shoulders in what felt like a steel vise.

Something fiery surged inside her. "But we're not *in* Germany, are we?" She spat back at him, hitting him square in the eye.

The man's eyes narrowed as he swiped at his face and slammed her into the wall again. He called her terrible names as he ripped at her clothes. "Let's see how you feel wandering the streets naked and see what the vermin of the street will do to a filthy woman of no moral character!"

She screamed at the top of her lungs and kicked at his groin with all her might. Her shoe made a hard landing, and he grunted, his grip slackening for a moment. She turned to run, but he clutched her skirt, jerking her back toward him. The fabric ripped completely in two and fell to the ground. He clamped a hand on her arm and whipped her around to face him again.

Heat boiled from her legs up to her neck and she clawed at him with her nails and bashed her head into his chin.

He drew back and roared in pain. "You—"

But then he was gone. No . . . he was on the ground, another man on top of him, pummeling the monster's face.

Her knees buckled and she squatted to the ground. Her trembling fingers lifted the remnants of her skirt, wrapping it around herself as best she could. The hotel. If she could just make it back there . . .

But her legs wouldn't hold her up. Her heart pounded so hard that spots appeared before her eyes. No! She wouldn't be weak now. She *couldn't*. She put a hand to her chest and did her best to slow her breathing. She had to get out of there now!

Strong, gentle arms slid around her, lifted her, and carried her back to a waiting car.

Rick.

Everything was a blur as he brought her to safety.

Once they were in Chaisley's rooms, her whole body quaked so hard, her teeth chattered.

Rick wrapped her in a thick blanket and shoved a cup of coffee in her hands. "Drink."

She obeyed.

"What's happened?" Chaisley's panicked voice echoed across the hotel room.

Melanie listened as Rick explained in hushed tones.

"We're leaving Hungary. Tonight!"

Melanie had never seen such fury in Chaisley's face. She sounded ready to order an army into battle. But as furious as Chaisley was now, if she'd been able to see the devastated state Melanie was in . . .

Melanie closed her eyes. Forced a word past her trembling lips.

"No." It came out stronger than she'd thought it would. "We can't leave until we help—"

"Hush." Chaisley came closer and placed a hand on Melanie's head. "Dr. Grafton's contact has already come and gone with them. They are taken care of. We are not staying here, Melanie.

If you'd like a bath before we leave, that's fine. But we. Leave. Tonight."

She had no more strength to argue but peered up at Rick. It was a miracle that he'd rescued her. How had he been in the right place at the right time? She studied him for several seconds. "I didn't thank you for saving me. I'm sorry."

"Don't apologize to me, Melanie. I'm just thankful I was there."

She chewed on her lip. "How *were* you there? How did you find me, Rick? I'd walked a long way from the hotel."

The silence was overwhelming as she waited for his answer. But she could see the muscle in his jaw moving. What didn't he want to tell them?

"The answer is simple. I was following you."

chapter
NINE

Chaisley paced the hotel suite in front of the windows. Rick had moved furniture for her so she'd have a clear place to walk and think. Thirty paces one way, turn around, thirty paces back.

Dr. G was supposed to arrive this morning since he'd been delayed in France last week. She'd been trying to convince Melanie to tell him about the attack, but as of last night, she still refused to speak about it. She insisted she was fine—that Rick arrived just in time.

Rick.

He said he followed Melanie that night because he was worried about her leaving the hotel on her own. Chaisley wanted to believe him. But she'd heard that same tiny change in his voice when he'd told them that as when they first met. So it was part truth and part lie? But why?

Why would he lie to them?

Over their short time together, she'd come to enjoy his company and, dare she say . . . trust him. But should she? He already knew too much if she'd made a mistake on that account. She couldn't imagine him double-crossing her or putting her in harm's way.

With a shake of her head, she turned in her pacing once again. No. When she'd confronted him about not telling the full truth at the beginning, he'd conceded. Every instinct within her told her that Rick *was* trustworthy.

And that wasn't just because she *wanted* him to be trustworthy. Because she liked him. More than she probably should.

Was her judgment clouded?

If only Grandmother were here. She was always able to help when Chaisley started overthinking everything.

Tap, tap.

The simple sound put a smile on her face. She made her way to the door and pulled it open. "Dr. G!" She opened her arms.

"How is my favorite pianist doing today?" She could hear his smile through the words.

"Much better now that you're here." Moving back, she gave him room to enter and then closed the door. "I was worried when you were delayed."

"Nothing to worry about . . . yet. Several of my contacts asked to meet privately with news that things have been changing. Everyone sees it, but they don't quite know what to make of it." His steps moved toward the couch. "Shall we sit?"

She made her way to a chair that she'd instructed Rick to place facing the couch. "I'm glad you were able to meet with them. And thank you. Your network of contacts is truly astounding. We were able to find help immediately for a mother and daughter who came to us the night we last saw you."

"Just make sure that you keep that list safe. We don't want to put any of them in danger."

"I will." She put a hand to her heart. "I've memorized it, and so has Melanie." Rick came to mind again. Should she ask—

"You've got that look on your face where you want to bring up a touchy subject." His relaxed chuckle washed over her. "Go ahead. It's just us, and we've got time."

As she launched into the doubts she was having about Rick, her relief was almost overwhelming. Her shoulders relaxed, and the tightness in her stomach dissolved. It really was a beautiful thing to share one another's burdens. She went all the way back to when he'd first started and then left it on a question about his explanation for following Melanie.

The long sigh that escaped Dr. G after she finished put her even more at ease. "You can vanquish your doubts, my dear. I was afraid it was something much more serious."

"Oh? Really?" She leaned back against the chair's cushions, feeling better already.

"Yes. In fact, I should tell you that I had Rick fully checked out before he started as your driver. He might choose his words carefully at times, but that's only because he wishes to protect you, I'm sure."

She released her pent-up breath. "That *is* a relief."

"But your instincts are spot on, Chais. That's good. You must be careful who you trust in these times, so keep that guard up." He paused and the rustling sounded like he was shifting closer to her. "My dear"—his voice was low and soft—"I have prayed for a long time for a man worthy of you to catch your interest. And from what I see in your face . . . that is . . . I believe Rick has done exactly that."

She stiffened against the chair as her eyebrows shot up.

"Don't look so surprised. I delivered you when you were born, and I've been watching you ever since."

Blinking several times, she took the time to think over his statement fully. It was one thing to like a person. Another to be attracted to them. And another thing altogether to say that person had caught her interest. Was that true? Could she admit that? Opening her mouth, she was about to deny it when she realized she couldn't. "I think you might be—"

The door between her suite and Melanie's opened with a click and swish. "Knock, knock! Dr. Grafton!" The overly enthusiastic sing-song lilt of her friend's voice barely covered the edge Chaisley heard underneath.

When would Melanie deal with what happened?

"Melanie, it's so good to see you." Dr. G responded with equal enthusiasm. "You look lovelier than ever."

"Thank you. So is Chaisley teaching you the new code? It's quite brilliant."

"Not yet. We were just catching up."

"Good, I didn't miss anything." Melanie giggled. "I need plenty of practice on it myself."

"All right, well, I guess we better dive in. If I'm to teach Celestia, I better have a handle on it myself." A clap was followed by rubbing. "Let's see this code."

Chaisley didn't mind the shift in conversation. Examining her feelings for Rick was a bit too new anyway. Besides, her guardian already suspected, so they could talk about it another time. "I've chosen pages from ten of my favorite and most intricate piano pieces to hide our code in. . ."

She launched into the idea. Unless someone was an expert at reading musical braille and knew each piece backward and forward, they would never guess that within the music was their hidden communication.

TUESDAY, MAY 10, 1938

Chaisley inhaled deeply then pushed the breath out in short puffs, willing her body to relax. It was a rare day off. A day to rest. Recuperate. But sleep was elusive. She counted sheep. She lay as still as possible with her eyelids closed and breathed slow and steady. Relaxing thoughts. Lullaby music.

Another hour of sleep would be so lovely.

Nope.

Her brain wouldn't allow it.

Melanie was on her mind.

After working for hours with Melanie and Dr. G on the new code, the forced emotion she constantly heard in her friend wore on her. Enthusiasm, teasing about when she made a mistake, excitement when she got it correct. Each time it was all just a bit too . . . false and cheery.

It hadn't been even two weeks since the assault. Multiple times a day Chaisley asked Melanie how she was doing. Each response seemed calm and resolute.

But they weren't honest.

Mel should know that Chaisley could tell. But when was the right time to push?

It must have been awful to experience how deep the hatred for Jews had grown. Prejudice had crescendoed from *pianissimo* to *fortissimo* without people even realizing it.

Mel seemed even more eager to do whatever they could. But she wouldn't talk about what happened. When would the facade crumble? And would Chaisley be able to help her when it happened?

In the years prior to the tour—with all the planning and scheduling—another sonata had begun in Chaisley's heart. It was slow and melancholy. Its purpose had been unclear at the time, but her conviction to listen and be ready for whatever the Lord held in store increased like a chorus of timpani in a grand finale. Perhaps she would play it at her next concert. Unlike her most recent composition, this piece stayed somber.

She climbed out of bed and put on her robe. Settling onto a couch in front of the fireplace in her room, she tucked her feet up under her.

It sickened her to think of the extent the Nazis had gone through to erase the reality of what they were doing. Melanie and Rick described the posters and signs they'd seen everywhere in Austria. How quickly they had been posted. Others told them such things were worse and rampant within Germany. When she'd asked why people hadn't seen the propaganda during the Olympics in Germany, the response angered her. Hitler used his army and police and other loyal groups to take it all down when the world descended on Berlin.

They definitely put on a good show that stated, "Hey, we aren't trying to start a war, so pay no attention here." And for the most part, it worked.

Here in Switzerland, things didn't seem as dire, but then, people kept to themselves. The Swiss didn't want to side with anyone, but they didn't want to allow refugees in. Chaisley wasn't quite sure what to think of the country's neutrality. Of course, Switzerland shared a border with Germany, so tensions had to be high. Saying they were neutral must be how they survived.

She needed to understand what it could be like to walk in the Swiss peoples' shoes, even though she wanted to shout from the rooftops about the truth.

Funny. A few months ago, her thoughts had simply been to bring hope and entertainment to people through her music. But now? She prayed daily that God would let her be part of whatever it took to stop the Nazis.

She mentally went through the upcoming calendar. They would spend a couple weeks traveling around the country here and performing more than two dozen concerts, then they would head back to Austria for one more. It was one invitation she couldn't decline. To do a private concert at Mirabell Palace in the Marble Hall. She'd accepted at the last minute before they'd left London. Of course, if she'd had any idea then that the Anschluss was about to take place, she'd never have agreed. Even so, she'd return. Maybe she'd be able to speak to Dr. Grafton's contact in Salzburg one more time.

She'd been to the Mirabell Palace as a child with her parents and could still remember all the gold trim, inlays, and ornamentation in the room. Massive arched windows had giant circular windows above them. Even though she wouldn't *see* it again, she could picture it as it had been. It would be a delight to play the piano in a place with so many memories of Mum and Dad.

But . . . who would the private audience be?

A shiver made the hair on her arms stand up.

After Salzburg, they would head to France and Belgium, and then they would go into Germany.

Her stomach twisted. It really was the lion's den.

They were only scheduled to be in Germany for one week before heading into a lengthy tour in the Netherlands, then it would be back to France for a month, Spain a month after that. They had two weeks off and then dove right back into more concerts in Romania, Czechoslovakia, and Yugoslavia.

She was tired just thinking about it all.

A week in Germany wasn't much time to find Mary Beth and her mother. But it was also an eternity to spend in the lair of the beast.

Several taps sounded on the door to the room connected to hers. "Come in."

"Good morning. I've brought Rick with me and some pastries." Melanie's cheery voice still sounded a bit forced.

"Pastries sound great, but what's wrong? Don't even try to argue with me. I know your voice."

Melanie's huff was very unladylike. "Nothing's wrong, per se, just something we need to discuss. I hate it that you can hear every intonation. I simply wanted to start the morning off happy."

"Well, don't try so hard next time." Chaisley laughed along with her friend.

Rick sighed, and it sounded like he took a seat across from her. "Tell me, are you two like this all the time?"

"Yes."

"Yes."

More laughter.

"I've never had sisters, so this is a new experience for me."

"Have a pastry, Rick. And don't act like you haven't seen us like this before. You've observed us closely for the past few weeks." Melanie's voice had lightened. No forced cheeriness.

Something touched Chaisley's hand.

"Here."

The plate was cool against her skin.

"It's a croissant on the left with Swiss cheese at one o'clock, strawberries at three o'clock, and, of course, some Swiss chocolate at five o'clock."

"Perfect." A scritchy noise from Rick made her cringe. "What are you doing, Rick?"

A light chuckle floated toward her. "Sorry, I didn't realize my fork would squeak like that."

But it was Melanie's full-blown laughter that caused her to wrinkle her brow. "What's so funny?"

"You should see his plate. He's separating and arranging his food the same way." Her friend continued to giggle. "Don't shrug at me like that, Rick, it's sweet."

"Just trying to think about what it would be like to live with blindness. And it's good for me to practice these things so I can help her. Like you." He obviously shoved a bit of something into his mouth because he took a few seconds and then she heard him swallow. "Melanie, you arrange your plate the same way. I've watched you do it for weeks."

Chaisley's eyebrows arched as her heartbeat ticked upward. He was thinking about her? She plucked a strawberry from her plate and took a bite. It wouldn't do to start grinning like an idiot. And he probably didn't mean anything romantic by it. It's not like he was in love with her.

But that he would even think about what life was like for her spoke volumes about the kind of man he was.

Melanie cleared her throat. "Force of habit. I do everything the same way Chaisley would do it. You know by now that life with Chais is a precise art. Steps. Food. Directions. Descriptions."

"I'm learning and I'm always impressed." The deep timbre of Rick's voice warmed Chaisley's insides.

"Chaisley is more talented than I at everything—except, of course, driving. But you never know, she could very well be better at that too."

Their voices harmonized together in laughter. It was nice to feel a bit relaxed and . . . normal. This. This was why people tried to ignore the horrors of the world.

"Seriously, every meal I manage to get something on me. While she's always as pristine as can be. I haven't seen her bump into anything yet, and I tripped over my own feet this morning."

Rick's laughter was masculine and deep. Genuine and warm, like a cup of hot chocolate.

Enough. It was best to stop thinking about him. A blush rose up her neck and into her cheeks. "You haven't seen me on a bad day. Just wait."

"They're few and far between." Melanie's fake whisper only caused the blush to deepen.

A knock at the door brought a welcome reprieve.

"I'll get that." Rick's tone was steady. A plate clinked on something. He must have set it down and she listened closely to his footsteps. It only took him twelve to reach the door.

He opened the door. "Yes?"

"*Grüezi.* This came for Miss Frappier, sir." A man spoke in Swiss German.

"*Danke.*" Rick's tone was firm.

The door shut, and Chaisley heard the lock move into place as well. His footsteps came closer until she could smell the lingering scent of his shaving cream. "This is for you."

"Here, I'll read it for you." Melanie shifted beside her.

"I believe it's in braille. I could feel it through the envelope."

The seat across from her made a slight swishing sound as Rick sat.

Chaisley ripped into the envelope. It was indeed in braille. She set down her dish and smoothed out the paper on her lap. Then she read it. A smile grew as she continued toward the end. "It's from a small group of blind students at the music school we visited yesterday. They wanted to thank us." She paused and her smile slipped. "And to ask for our help. Their teacher is Jewish and is leaving soon. Within the week. She advised them and their parents that it would be best for them to leave the country as well."

Melanie placed a hand on Chaisley's shoulder. "How many are we talking about?"

Her fingers flew over the page and her heart clenched as the reality of what was happening sank in. "Twenty students. About half of them are Jewish. All are blind, some from birth and the others from sickness or accidents." Her breath left her in a whoosh. "Can we help that many?"

"How much longer are we here?"

Rick must be writing on paper. She could hear the scribbles of his pencil.

"Two weeks."

Melanie patted her shoulder. "I'll call Dr. Grafton right away."

She nodded. "That's probably best. Then we'll need to get in touch with his contact. They'll need visas and a safe place to go."

AMSTERDAM—MONDAY, MAY 23, 1938

"Celestia, I have an idea." Dr. Grafton removed his spectacles and rubbed the bridge of his nose.

"I'm listening." She studied him. The man was tired. They'd spent the last thirteen days doing everything in their power to get visas, travel arrangements, and accommodations for the blind students and their families. Many of those days, he'd stayed up well past when she'd given in to exhaustion and gone to bed. A couple of times, she'd found him still at it in the morning.

He rubbed his face and replaced his glasses. "I just received word from a friend in South Africa. I think he might be able to assist in getting these families visas there for a long-term option after the students and their families journey here. Afrikaans is another form of a West Germanic language. It's closer to Dutch than German, but the Swiss German is different anyway. If these students and their families know their language well, it will help them overcome a lot of the pronunciation differences."

"That's a great distance for these people to travel." She tapped her fingers on the desk. "Costly as well. It will most likely need to be a permanent relocation."

He held up the letters in his hands. "From the sounds of what the parents have written, most of them are hoping for something permanent. They haven't felt an immediate threat in Switzerland, but they've heard too much from Germany and feel it encroaching on them. They don't think they'll be safe in many places in Europe. If they're going to travel, they'd rather go farther from the threat while they can." He grimaced. "Which, I have to admit, I think is a smart idea."

She leaned back. "I hadn't thought about that. Tensions are high, and every diplomat I've spoken to here will give us a visa to get them here, but then they are pushing to make sure they move on once they arrive. I wonder if they're telling us everything, and I can *feel* the fear underlying their tones. I also have friends in the United States. Perhaps we should think about that as a destination as well?"

"We should. Make the inquiries to get us started. The more safe avenues we have, the better our chances as things escalate." His face was a bit haggard. The past few months had aged him.

Celestia reached out a hand and patted his shoulder as she stood. "God willing, everyone's eyes will soon be opened to what's really happening. Let's just do the best we can each day. As Chais-

162

ley travels, I'm sure there will be more and more who we will need to help. Especially when she heads into Germany."

His shoulder tensed under her hand. Had she laid another brick on his already heavy load? "Does that worry you as much as it does me?"

Her grimace—no matter how fast she covered it—couldn't be missed. "If I were still in England and not here? I would be far more worried and yet less concerned all at the same time." She couldn't bear to hold his gaze so she turned to the window. "There? I would be far away and hearing the rumblings with nothing to do but twiddle my thumbs and worry. Here . . . I know far more and am entrenched in my own work to help. But I also know that God has called us to this. I can't deny the work He has called Chaisley to and the hope she can share. But if anything happens to her—"

"I have to keep pushing those thoughts down because I tend to get too worked up and angry."

Bile rose in her throat, hearing her silent fear echoed in the doctor's voice. *Oh God, have we done the right thing, involving Chaisley? Melanie?* She glanced down at Dr. Grafton and sighed. "That is what keeps me up at night."

He remained silent for several moments. "If I think too much about the consequences, I want to whisk her away someplace safe and keep her there until all this is past. I'm not even sure we will all live through this, but I know that Jesus is waiting at the finish line so we must soldier on and do what we can." He nodded and took a sip of his tea. "I should probably take a short nap since I haven't been getting much sleep. Then I will make some more calls. But first . . ." He caught her gaze right before she refilled her own cup.

"But first, what?"

"When are we going to discuss your plan?"

"What plan?" The man was entirely too astute for his own safety.

"Celestia, you're going to need my help. So tell me about the hidden rooms."

chapter
TEN

The scent of cold stone was so familiar to her now. She'd never taken much notice of it as a child. Back then, it was the aroma of fresh baking bread or a sweet dessert that caught her attention.

But on this tour, she'd lost count of how many times the stone buildings had invaded her senses.

Stone tile gave her a dust-like taste in her mouth. Brick added a metallic note. Plaster walls and wood walls were in stark contrast to each other in how the sounds bounced or echoed off of them.

Then there were the scents. One reminded her of the outdoors, the other of paint.

Walking into the Marble Hall, the aroma assaulted her and brought back a swirl of memories from her childhood. The floors and walls had just been polished—she could smell the remnants of cleaners heavy with lemon oil.

Fresh flower bouquets must be every ten feet or so in the hall. Just like when she was a child, but now their fragrances were almost overwhelming they were so strong.

All the smells brought the pictures from her memory into vivid vision.

As her heels clicked on the marble floor, the sound echoed throughout the empty room. In a few hours, the room would be full.

The patron who'd asked her to come would attend with his family and a few friends, but she'd been informed that many high-ranking Nazi officers had demanded attendance as well.

Funny how it wasn't a request, but a demand. And they wanted it known.

With a sigh, she kept her left hand on the wall and made a full sweep of the circumference of Marble Hall. It wasn't a huge space and the acoustics from the high ceilings were incredibly rich. The number of people would help temper the echoes and absorb a bit of the sound so she could feel free to play the majestic grand at full volume.

Lord God, please help me to do this to the best of my ability. No matter the audience. Play through me. Thank You for this gift. Thank You for the blessing of music. And lead me to the people that need me or lead them to me. Show me Your will. Please.

Her heart settled into a relaxed and comfortable rhythm. She may not know what was to come, but He did.

Ever since she'd told that reporter she was blind, things had shifted. Not just in her heart, but in how she was received.

Both good and bad. All these years, she'd told herself that keeping her blindness a secret had kept her humble. No need to tell people the adversities she'd had to overcome.

She'd come to realize, though, that she'd kept it close so that people couldn't judge her. Or show pity. She'd never considered how much her pride was involved.

Things were different with the Nazis gaining power. There were those who didn't appreciate someone with a disability being praised and recognized. And many now ignored her. At least, that's what Melanie reported.

She wanted to say that was fine. She didn't mind being ignored. But deep down, she had to admit she wasn't used to it. For more than a decade she had been in great demand. Every time she walked out on stage, she knew that all eyes were on her. *That* was what she was used to.

Even though she performed in front of thousands of people on a regular basis, she'd stayed protected in a small bubble of valued friends. The more she pondered it, the more she came to realize that pride was a struggle she needed to face head-on.

From early childhood on, she'd gained praise from everyone around her for her exceptional gifts with music.

It became expected. God had given her something rare. Monsieur Beaufort called her a true prodigy. And after that term had been thrown around a few dozen times, she came to love the fact that she was special. And it had nothing to do with her being blind.

Or did it?

Oh . . .

Oh, God . . . forgive me.

She dropped to her knees in the middle of the great hall, bowed her head, and lifted her hands. *Father, forgive me for my pride. Forgive me for not understanding this sooner. Forgive me for all the times I haven't seen with my heart those I could have helped. Help me not to be blind to them anymore. Show me—with Your almighty sight—how I can help. Thank You for bringing us here. Even though this is the hardest thing I've ever done. Keep us all strong and courageous to do what You call us to do. No matter how difficult the task.*

She lifted her chin, stood, and then made her way back to the piano. She couldn't allow her pride to stand in the way any longer.

Earlier today, she'd visited a university, and the music students were fascinated by her. How long that would last in this new Nazi culture was yet to be seen. But hopefully seeds had been planted in their young minds. That *everyone* was useful—worthy. She would no longer just entertain or give people hope.

She would point them to this truth.

Dr. Grafton had two contacts in place here. One was a professor at the university who was keeping his eyes and ears open to how the Nazis were appealing to the young generation. Another was wealthy and being pressured by the Nazi Party. How long they would stay in Austria was a tough guess, but at least they had them in place for now.

Taking a seat on the bench before the piano, she closed her eyelids and did her best to imagine the room. While she couldn't remember the exact details of it from two decades ago, she could recall the massive gold scrolling on the walls and the cherubs at the top of the walls. There were a lot of gold accents, she remembered that much.

Accepting the invitation to do this private concert had been the right choice.

Before Germany took over Austria, the country was renowned for its musical history and concert halls. But it would most certainly change. More than it already had.

It had been less than two months since the *Anschluss*. Less than two months since she'd played in this country. But Austria felt different in that short amount of time. The air was different. Sadder. As if a thick fog of fear blanketed Salzburg. Even this concert hall.

Her shoulders curved inward. A darkness far worse than blindness was stretching its fingers into the hearts of men. Her hands shook against the piano keys. Pulling them back, Chaisley made fists then relaxed her fingers a few times.

Drowning in her thoughts of the darkness and what was happening—and what *could* happen—wasn't productive. Not right before a performance. Maybe she couldn't stop the whole Nazi Party, but she would play her part. And not let the fear threatening to choke her win. *Please help me, Lord. To be wise. And not be afraid.*

She sat up, straightening her spine and placing her fingers on the piano keys once more.

167

As she ran through her usual warm-up and practice session, her thoughts bounced all over the place. Focus was getting harder and harder to come by.

Three hours later, it wasn't much better.

The crowd had gathered at the Marble Hall, and Chaisley had to attend an invitation-only gathering before she performed.

That hadn't been part of the initial agreement, but apparently it had been another demand.

As she, Mel, and Rick walked into the building, the flurry of voices grew. She braced herself for the coming half hour and pasted on a smile.

Conversations died down as she entered the smaller room for this gathering.

"Our guest of honor has arrived." A nasally voice spoke in high German from the left of the room. It resonated above what voices were still engaged, and the room silenced.

"It is my privilege to introduce you all to the woman who has amazed me with her incomparable talent at the pianoforte . . . The greatest pianist the world has ever known . . . Miss Chaisley Frappier!" A beefy hand tugged at hers and brought her forward two steps.

The owner of the nasal voice must be the patron who'd invited her for this concert. He'd laid the compliments on a little heavy, but she would be grateful for the support.

Applause filled the room, and she curtsied. Then she held up a hand and waited for the room to quiet again. "Thank you for your gracious invitation. It is *my* honor to play for you all this evening."

Keeping her bearings would be difficult in a room filled with people who moved and meandered. She held her place, and as soon as conversations picked up again, she felt the presence of Mel and Rick move beside her again.

"Three couples are moving toward you." Mel's soft whisper gave her a moment's warning. "We are ten paces from the door behind us."

"Fräulein Frappier, we are looking forward to your concert." A woman on her right spoke. "My mother wanted me to be a pianist, but my fingers were not coordinated enough." Her light laughter was brittle and crackly. This woman smelled of rose water and . . . tobacco.

The two did not mix well.

Chaisley lifted a handkerchief to her nose that she kept for just this reason. She'd learned when she was young to keep her hankies in a bag with fresh peppermint leaves. The oil would rub off the leaves, and if a smell overwhelmed her, she could breathe in the fresh scent and clear her senses.

"I took lessons as a child"—a male voice on her left entered the conversation—"and my father dreamt of me being the next Beethoven, but I was terrible and my teacher slapped my hands with a ruler."

Chaisley drew back a bit and lowered her hankie. "Simply because you hit the wrong note?"

"No." The man guffawed and snuffed like a giant hog going after a corn cob. "Because I didn't listen to a word he said."

Several men joined in the harsh laughter. The man continued with horror stories of his teacher.

This was not the kind of crowd she was used to—or maybe it was because she didn't spend much time conversing with a wealthy audience before a concert. She much preferred listening to the stories from those who stayed afterward.

" . . . he continually yelled at me to stop banging on the keys, but it was much too fun. So I kept at it." The storyteller had the men in the crowd rolling with laughter.

It wasn't that funny.

In fact, it wasn't humorous at all. Granted, she might have missed the funny part of the story, but she couldn't bring herself to offer up a fake laugh.

A tug at her right elbow. "Ignore our *gentlemen*, Fräulein." A smooth and silky alto voice accompanied another tug. "Please, join the ladies over here for a more cultured discussion. The men have obviously enjoyed too much brandy already."

Forcing a cordial smile, Chaisley wished she didn't even have to be in this room at all. How had she gotten into this?

"I'm right beside you." Mel tapped her left arm. "She appears to be headed about twelve steps to your right."

Chaisley moved in that direction with her friend close beside her.

The women were in the middle of a lively chat about a new dress shop which seemed to be everyone's favorite.

" . . . they expected me to wait three months for the new gown."

"I was told four, so three isn't so bad. It's my own fault for not getting an appointment sooner."

"But everything I've seen come out of their shop has been divine. I don't mind waiting." The woman gasped. "Fräulein, *that* gown is stunning. Who is your designer?"

A slight nudge to her arm. Mel's signal that she needed to answer.

"I have one in London and one in Paris." Chaisley swallowed. At the moment she couldn't even remember who had designed the gown she was wearing.

"Well, that shade of mauve is absolutely lovely on you." Another voice.

"Thank you." Her head began to pound. Too many new voices, and an overwhelming bouquet of perfumes. "If you'll excuse me, I believe I need some water." She lifted her hankie once more.

She stepped back and then moved to her left with Melanie beside her.

"There's a large column over here that we can duck behind for a moment. Rick is still stuck with those men. Poor guy." Melanie led her and then pulled her to a stop. "I am so sorry. I don't know how to help you . . . I wish I knew a way out. It's terrible that they thrust this upon you without letting you know ahead of time." Her whispered words held a hint of panic.

"There's no way out, I'm afraid. I must continue on the best I can. But I won't be able to play if this headache intensifies." Chaisley squeezed her friend's hand.

"Here"—Mel shifted her until her back was to the massive column—"lean up against the column here and close your eyes. I've got a headache powder in my handbag. I'll get you a glass of water—or something to drink it down with."

"Don't leave me for long."

"I won't. There's no one headed toward you right now. I'll be quick."

Chaisley listened as Mel's steps moved away. She took a deep breath and prayed for the headache to be lifted so she could perform. But conversations swirled around her. For most people, it would simply be noise to be ignored. But every sound seemed magnified, especially with her head pounding.

"Word has come that several of the professors at the university will be arrested and taken to a work camp this week." The man speaking sounded . . . *pleased* about it.

She wasn't sure how far away the conversation was taking place, but Chaisley did her best to tune in to this specific one and block the others out so she could hear.

"It's about time. Our country needs to be cleansed of all the rabble and dissenters." This speaker's condescension was palpable.

She pictured a man with a smug face and a mustache like Hitler.

"I, for one, will be glad to see them fill the camps. If it comes to executions similar to the Night of Long Knives, I'm all for it."

"Hear, hear!"

The voices moved away as others agreed until she couldn't hear them.

Chaisley put a hand to her stomach. How could these men speak of eliminating people as if it were as simple and insignificant as scraping something off their shoes?

"What's wrong?" Mel gripped her shoulder and placed a glass in her hand.

"I've got to get in touch with Dr. G right away." She kept her voice as low as she could and relayed what she'd overheard.

If her friend's intake of breath was any indication, Mel was just as horrified as she—but could they alert people in time?

During the concert an hour later, her focus was still on what she'd overheard. It was a good thing her fingers, arms, and mind had muscle memory. The times when she tried to think of something else or keep her mind only on what she was playing, her thoughts went to the future, the Jews, and the young blind people she'd met. Which caused her emotions to overflow into the music, and the audience's applause was filled with even more exuberance.

At least she didn't have to see all the men who were surely there in their Nazi uniforms.

She ended a piece by Wagner, and her fingers took her straight into her grandmother's favorite piece. It hadn't originally been on her program for this evening, but she needed the furious three against four to help her through. Her beloved *Fantasie Impromptu* refreshed her spirit.

From there, she dove into her finale, which was a trio of pieces that she'd written especially for this tour. The heartbreaking emotion of the first piece in *adagio* usually had the audience enraptured as she built into the majestic and broad harmonies of the second. By the time she reached the third piece, many people stood to applaud and then were caused to hold their breath as the *vivace* section took over. Her fingers flew over the keys of the piano in a rapid succession of arpeggios and flourishes as the song built to the grand conclusion of harmonics moving from an array of dissonance and resolving from minor to major.

At the final notes, her chest heaved as if she'd run ten miles. She left her hands pressed down on the keys with her foot down on the sustain pedal. The music continued to echo throughout the room, and the applause began.

The noise of chairs moving from their position told her that the audience was coming to its feet.

As the roar of the crowd grew, she lifted her hands and stood from the bench. Taking the edge of the piano in her left hand, she bowed deep at her waist and held it.

Once. Twice. A third time.

Amid the cries of *Encore*! and *Bis*!, she turned on her heel and felt Melanie's hand on her elbow after a mere three steps.

Harsh footsteps marched behind her and then halted as a gruff voice resonated above the crowd's dying applause. In staccato German, the man cried, "*Heil* Hitler!"

"*Heil* Hitler!" rang out from the audience.

The man went on. "An amazing performance tonight from the greatest pianist in the world in honor of our leader."

As the applause swelled once again, Chaisley cringed. She did *not* play in honor of that deplorable man.

"Don't listen to him. It's more of the Nazi lies." Melanie's whisper helped. A little.

"But I don't want people to think I played for that man."

"Hush." Melanie squeezed her elbow. "One of the men in uniform is headed this way."

"Fräulein, Fräulein Frappier." Heels clicked together.

Chaisley lifted her chin and waited.

"The Führer sends his greetings."

She nodded.

"I will be reporting back about what a nice concert it was. The simplicity was greatly appreciated."

Nice? Simplicity? She opened her mouth but a squeeze at her elbow held her in check. "It was kind of you to attend." She forced the words out. The man was the equivalent of a heckler.

"While I prefer the concerts we host in the homeland with our superior musicians"—she could picture him looking down his nose at her—"it was a nice distraction from a long day's work."

"I will have to hear these *superior* musicians when I'm touring in Germany." Graciousness wasn't her forte, especially after an insult like that.

He cleared his throat. "Please, don't take offense, Fräulein. It was a lovely concert, and I've heard that the Führer enjoyed your piano-playing."

Her piano-playing. Wow.

She bit her tongue to keep from spewing anything back at him.

"It's a shame you lost your sight. You could have been a star."

Melanie squeezed a warning on her arm, but it wasn't necessary. Peace such as she had seldom felt overflowed her. It didn't matter what he thought. His words were meant to insult her and rile her up.

Funny. He'd almost succeeded. Thank goodness the Holy Spirit had intervened on her behalf.

All the anger and pride melted away, and she gave him a genuine smile. "It was lovely to perform in this magnificent hall and share a bit of music with the audience." She curtsied. "Now if you'll excuse me, I'd like to thank our host and hostess."

The man mumbled something harsh, but she ignored him and walked in the direction Melanie steered.

"They told me they would be in a private room in the palace, but I'm not certain where." Her friend spoke in a low tone.

Conversations swirled around Chaisley as she and Mel walked away. Then the voice from earlier pierced through the cacophony. The same man who spoke of the professors being arrested. The words she'd overheard earlier barreled to the forefront of her mind and made her stomach clench.

"Where are we? I'm disoriented." She *had* to stop allowing her emotions to get to her. She felt as though she'd fallen off the piano bench and into oblivion. If she wanted to help, she'd have to be stronger than this. To hold up against conversations she heard from Nazi allies, to deal with naysayers like the man at the end of her concert.

"We're heading for the private ladies' room to freshen up. It was next to the room we waited in before the concert."

"Thank you." Now that she could imagine it in her mind, she didn't feel as if the world were off kilter.

After a ten-minute break in the washroom to gather herself and do her best to wash the swirling words from her mind, she nodded at Melanie. "I'm afraid I've allowed my pride to get in the way, Mel."

"What do you mean?"

"Wanting to use this tour to help . . . thinking I was strong enough, famous enough—"she waved a hand and shook her head—"to withstand this. But hearing those men speak earlier? It shook me. To my very core. This is real. Lives are on the line. We are on the verge of war . . . And then that man at the end? I've been so accustomed to everyone's applause and praise. This gift God has given me is incredible—I know that—but I've taken it for granted."

"Don't let the words of that man—"

Chaisley held up a hand. "I'm not worried about what he said, although I'll admit he riled me up. I feel as if the Holy Spirit took over for me and calmed me. And then I had the most unusual thought. Jesus was praised in the streets a mere week before the crowds cried to crucify Him. At the concert where Hitler was present, I wondered if those cheering for me and singing my praises were the same who praised the Nazi leader. It makes me think of what our Lord must have gone through." She gave a sad laugh. "And yet, I know He didn't have His own pride standing in the way . . ." Letting the words linger for a moment, she bit her lip and then continued. "My prayer was to be more like Jesus. And I'm realizing I have such a long way to go."

"Oh, Chais . . ." Melanie sniffed. "I hadn't even thought about what that must be like for you." She sniffed again and then blew her nose. "You inspire me more and more each day to be more like Jesus. And even if we can help just one—that must be why we're here."

Chaisley opened her arms and leaned forward. Her friend moved into them, and they held each other for several seconds.

After a moment, she pulled back, giving Melanie's hands a squeeze. "All right, there's so much more I want to say, but I don't want to keep our hosts waiting."

"Why don't you sit here and collect yourself. There's a comfy-looking chair in the corner here. Seven steps to your right." Melanie led her to the chair and Chaisley sank into it with a sigh. "Good. Now how about I go find them and then I'll come and get you?"

"That's a good plan." She held up a hand. "Do we know if they are Nazi sympathizers?"

"No. Sorry."

Chaisley smoothed her hands over her dress. "That's all right. I just wanted to prepare myself."

"I'll be back as soon as I find them. Stay in here. I'll make sure Rick is outside the door."

"Thank you." She waited until she heard the door close and then lifted her face upward.

God, help me. I need Your armor more than ever. I wanted to punch that man in the face. Forgive me for my pride and my ugly thoughts toward him. Help me to honor You.

She recited the passage from Ephesians. "'. . . be strong in the Lord, and in the power of his might. Put on the whole armour of God, that ye may be able to stand against the wiles of the devil. For we wrestle not against flesh and blood, but against principalities, against powers, against the rulers of the darkness of this world, against spiritual wickedness in high places.

"'Wherefore take unto you the whole armour of God, that ye may be able to withstand in the evil day, and having done all, to stand. Stand therefore, having your loins girt about with truth, and having on the breastplate of righteousness; And your feet shod with the preparation of the gospel of peace; Above all, taking the shield of faith, wherewith ye shall be able to quench all the fiery darts of the wicked.

"'And take the helmet of salvation, and the sword of the Spirit, which is the word of God: Praying always with all prayer and supplication in the Spirit, and watching thereunto with all perseverance and supplication for all saints—'"

The door creaked, and she turned her face toward it.

"I've found them." The joy in Melanie's voice was indescribable. "You are going to love them. They are believers, Chais, and they need our help."

Chaisley closed her eyes. Fellow believers! Finally, some good news after a difficult evening. *Lord, thank You for the chance to help Your people.* Her throat was thick with tears, but she swallowed them. There would be time to process all her jumbled emotions later. "Let's go hear their story." She allowed her friend to lead her to the couple and heard a door click softly behind them.

"We shouldn't be disturbed here." A man's gentle voice greeted her ears. "And all the Nazi officers have left."

She nodded. This was *not* the man she'd assumed was the host from earlier. "You are our hosts? The ones who invited us for this concert?"

"Yes." This time it was a lady who spoke. "I'm Jacqueline, and this is my husband, Gustaf. We have been in awe of the talents God has given you."

"Thank you." She curtsied.

"We don't have much time." The woman's voice held an urgency. "I hate to be so blunt, but it's a necessity of the times."

Chaisley nodded. "I understand you are believers?"

"Yes. And we are of Jewish blood as well. Our granddaughter was born blind and is only six years old. We are afraid what the future will hold for us here in Austria, no matter how much money and influence we have at the moment. As soon as the Nazis find out we have Jewish blood, we will be scrutinized, and we can't risk that."

"Please." The man sounded like he was choked up. "Do you have any connections that might help us escape? We will leave everything behind if we must."

PARIS, FRANCE—MONDAY, JUNE 6, 1938

Rick took long steps back to the car. He opened the door and got in. But then he couldn't force himself to start it up. He sat there with his hands on the steering wheel and stared out at the street.

The news from London wasn't good. They hadn't heard from anyone until Rick contacted the SIS. The man directly above him had been taken as a political prisoner in Germany. Communications were to be ceased for at least three weeks. Maybe longer.

Much longer.

Too many informants and contacts for the SIS had been rounded up and sent to work camps. He didn't even know of any he could use anymore. On top of that, the handful of SIS operatives in Europe all seemed to be silent as well. Everyone except for him. How was that possible? How were the Nazis discovering them?

The head of the SIS—Laurence Grand—wasn't certain whether there was a leak, a double agent, or if Germany was spreading its wings and intercepting wires or listening in to phone calls. It didn't appear that they had the manpower or capability for that *across* Europe, but perhaps the SIS had underestimated their enemy. Just like they'd already underestimated Hitler and how far he was willing to go to put his plan into place.

Nevertheless, it was time for Rick and the others—if they weren't already captured—to clamp down and change their strategy. London was upping the urgency and manpower, but it would take some time to get people in place.

Section D was now in play. The group he'd been asked to be a part of by the leader himself. When the plans were still being laid out, the timeline seemed far off. But now? They had to be ready to implement at a moment's notice. And since Rick was in place undercover, a great deal might fall to him when the time came.

Section D. The details ran through his mind, and he gritted his teeth.

He started the engine and gripped the steering wheel until his fingers ached. The car felt like it was shrinking around him, suffocating him. He inhaled and pushed the air out in a burst. He couldn't afford to lose his nerve now. For three months, he'd kept his cover with Chaisley. He'd told her he'd be honest with her. But all-out war was coming.

Again.

If he buried the thoughts of Section D in his mind—and simply didn't think about it—then he could work on staying honest with her and keeping his voice steady so she wouldn't suspect. The problem was, she had no idea he worked for the SIS.

And it was a secret he *had* to keep.

It would be so much easier if he could tell Chaisley and Mel.

He'd listened in on their conversation in the car after the concert at the Marble Hall. Chaisley actually overheard a conversation about the Nazis' intent to arrest professors who didn't line up with their plan. The two brave ladies had made sure to get in touch with their friend—the doctor—and warn him. Surely, they had saved several lives that night.

They were on the same team. So was there harm in him telling them the truth?

Then he wouldn't have to run around in secret—always worrying if he would be caught. As Section D was implemented and he had to spy on and destroy Nazi communications and transportation, the women would understand what was going on.

But he'd made an oath to the SIS.

On the other hand, they could help him keep his cover. Although he'd developed such a great friendship as they traveled, he hated to jeopardize that.

Who was he kidding? He wasn't worried about the friendships. No matter how he'd tried to stop it from happening, he'd come to care for Chaisley a great deal more than he'd ever thought possible. Sometimes, late at night, he'd allowed his thoughts to wander. What it would be like to fall in love . . . have a family . . . live a normal life.

None of which could ever happen. Not now. On the precipice of war.

As he navigated back to the hotel, he prepared himself for what he would say to the ladies.

It was simple. They needed to know the truth. At least that he worked for the British government.

His grief over his friends and colleagues could certainly cover his stress over what he had to keep to himself.

At the hotel, he parked the limousine and braced for what he had to do.

Best to remember that they were all trying to help people. They were trying to save lives. An omission of part of the truth was necessary.

As he entered the suite, Melanie took his hat and coat.

Chaisley's face brimmed with a smile. "You're back."

It warmed him to see her delight. "I am." If only he could bottle the smile on her face and the sparkle in her eyes for just a few moments.

But her face turned serious. Drat that uncanny ability of hers. "Oh no! What's happened?"

"I'm not sure how to say this." Rick didn't want to make a mess of things. Especially since he'd come to respect these ladies so much. But now, he worried about telling them. How would they react?

Chaisley frowned. She moved her stockinged feet out from

under her and set them on the floor. Resting her elbows on her knees, she gripped her hands together. "Just tell us the truth."

His mind started to backpedal.

Would it be okay to go rogue *and* continue to do what was right to help the British against Germany?

The agency had told him to carry on with his job. Well, there were times when a man had to take matters into his own hands and make decisions.

Rick took a bolstering breath. "I'm not just a driver." He'd start small and go from there. "First, I speak multiple languages. French included."

No response from either of them, but he could practically see the wheels turning in their thoughts as they digested this information.

Melanie was first to show her understanding of what he'd just said. Her brow creased, her eyes narrowed. "You're telling us that you have listened in on our conversations? Without telling us."

But Chaisley laid a hand on her companion's arm. Her face serene. What was she feeling? "If you're not just a driver . . . then who are you?"

There. A slight tremble in her chin. What did she think of him at this moment? "I work for the British Secret Intelligence Service."

chapter
ELEVEN

So *that* was the secret he'd been keeping from them.

Rick was a spy for the British.

While in one sense it made Chaisley feel better to have him with her—especially after all the encounters she'd had with Nazi soldiers—on the other hand, the thought made her shiver.

She'd never known a spy before. Was there more he was hiding? With everything in her, she wanted to be able to trust this man. "Why didn't you tell us?" The question was silly, but she needed to hear his voice as he answered.

"I'm not authorized to. I'm not even supposed to tell you now, but I think it's the only safe way we can work together and accomplish our goals. I believe we are on the same team, and I trust you both. I can help protect you, and you can help protect my cover."

He was sincere. Gone was any perception that he kept something to himself. In fact, there were notes of relief in his tone. Like it was good to tell someone. To have someone to confide in.

"What goals do you believe we share?" It was important to push now and find out what he really thought. While she hated to put everything in jeopardy, she had to know without a shadow of a doubt that she could trust this man with her life. With Melanie's life.

The squeak and moan of leather gave her the picture that he was shifting in his chair. Perhaps leaning over his knees.

She leaned forward to show her full attention.

He released a sharp breath. "Goals? To stop Hitler. To keep another war from happening. To save people he wants to eliminate. I can't believe the filth and garbage that are part of the Nazis' propaganda and what they say about the Jews and others. It has gotten bolder and more insulting the past couple years."

"Where were you before Amsterdam?" Melanie zeroed in on a great question.

"Inside Germany. It was getting hard to be there and hear the constant propaganda each day. Our best informant was arrested the day I left." The sigh he released was almost a groan. "The Gestapo have been at full force the past few months. Rounding up what they call political prisoners and sending them to work camps. In all truth, they are also rounding up those they believe are informants and Jews who were outspoken or had any power whatsoever. A good friend of mine was taken several weeks before I met you. A Jew. A good man."

The slight crack in his voice was telling. He must be comfortable with them because there was far too much emotion for a man trained as a spy to portray.

"Is your friend all right?" Chaisley's heart went out to the man.

"I . . . I don't know. That's the difficult part. These work camps are terrible. I searched for him, but things escalated and I had to leave. There has been so much hate and prejudice stirred up that it feels like people have been brainwashed. No other country wants another war . . . except Hitler. He wants to rule the world and focus on his Aryan master race. Which means that eventually all people of a different race or color will be subject to whatever he has planned. And I think it's much worse than work camps. Although, how much do we really know about what is happening there?"

The air in the room seemed to get heavier the longer they talked. And the new melody running through her mind haunted her. Shaded her every waking moment, mingling with her grief. "Why were you assigned to drive for me?"

His hesitation troubled her.

"I'll admit, I wasn't excited about the job. I didn't understand why they thought it would be good to take me out of Berlin to drive a pianist around. But then I realized that you would have access to people the SIS were interested in."

"Is that so?" Was that all she was to him? A way to get close to people he could spy on? It hurt. More than she cared to acknowledge.

"But don't you see? This has helped all of us. I can help *you*." He pleaded—a tone she hadn't heard from him.

"I'm sorry, Mr. Zimmerman. I don't *see*. Frankly, I'm disturbed that you didn't tell us this right away. Especially after I was honest with you about everything from the very beginning." She didn't like the way her stomach tied up in knots. Nor the way she was reacting. But she couldn't stop the words from rushing out. "Was all of this fake to you? Pretend?"

"Wait a minute." Had he come to his feet? "No, this wasn't fake." His voice was above her now. "I've come to care for you and Melanie both. I thought we were all friends. All working together. All believers." Now his tone held a bitter tinge as it weighed down on her. "And you *haven't* been completely honest with me from the beginning. There have been plenty of conversations full of secrets which you have kept from me."

The words hit her like an arrow. They had done that. She had doubted him plenty of times. Shared only what she thought he needed to know. Yes, he had a right to throw it back at her.

But why did it have to hurt so much? Her emotions were worse than a pendulum out of control. "I think you need to leave now." She rubbed her forehead.

"Chaisley . . . I'm sorry." The words were cracked.

Like their friendship.

"Please. Go."

BERLIN, GERMANY—TUESDAY, JUNE 7, 1938

He woke up from the nightmare covered in sweat.

It was her! Up on that stage.

How long had it been since he'd seen her?

Fifteen . . . twenty years?

Sitting up on the edge of his bed, he mopped his face and neck with his shirt. He should have known she seemed too familiar.

Now, the question was . . . what was he going to do about it?

A lot had changed in all the time that had passed. He'd made something of himself. Was one of Hitler's right-hand men.

Of course, it appeared she'd made a good life for herself as well. Still, could they reconnect? Was that wise? Surely, she understood what was needed.

Perhaps she wasn't happy. She might even want to be a part of something as revolutionary as what he was doing.

He glanced at the clock. It was only two in the morning. He needed sleep and plenty of it. As he lay back down, his thoughts tumbled over one another.

He didn't need to make a decision right away, but it did seem prudent to keep an eye on her.

What if she desperately wanted to get away from what she was doing now but didn't know how? He could help.

One of his best skill sets was getting rid of those in his way.

PARIS, FRANCE—WEDNESDAY, JUNE 8, 1938

"Chaisley, we've got to talk." Melanie gripped her shoulder.

"I know." The past two days she'd kept her concert schedule but other than that, she'd hidden in her suite and cried. Then prayed. Then cried some more.

Why?

She wasn't sure—other than the fact that she'd felt more for Rick Zimmerman than she'd let on. But now what did she do? He was a spy. There were any number of things he probably had to keep from her.

"Tell me what you're thinking," Mel prodded. "Then I'll tell you what I'm thinking."

"We all have secrets, but I don't know what I think about Rick anymore. I trusted him."

"I know." Another squeeze to the shoulder. "I did too. And I still do."

Ever-protective Melanie couldn't have shocked her more if she'd slapped her. "You do?"

"Yes. He was there for me in a tough situation. His job demanded he keep a secret from us. I can accept that—I mean, we are fighting against the Nazis, right? And I believe he's been forthright with us about everything he could. Especially after you grilled him." Her light laugh pierced the dark mood in the room. "And I know you care for him."

Chaisley nodded. There wasn't any point keeping her feelings from her dearest friend. "Dr. G guessed as much as well. He said he thought Rick was an honorable man. But what would he say if he knew what we know now?"

"I think you are giving Timothy Grafton way too little credit. Why don't you talk to him about it next time you see him? It would be unusual for both of you to misjudge a person."

"Why are you on his side?"

"I'm not on anyone's side. Just trying to help you grasp the voice of reason." Melanie's voice traveled around the room accompanying the soft rhythm of her steps.

"What are you doing?" Chaisley didn't like this feeling of losing control.

"I'm picking up your things from last night. I know how you like things tidy and in their place. This is so unlike you, Chais. Maybe you should just forgive him and move on. This can't be good for your emotional well-being."

More proof of her sulking attitude the past couple days. She never left things out. They caused tripping hazards, and she'd have a hard time finding them again. "Have you talked to Rick?"

"Yes, just a little bit ago."

"Is he all right?" The fact that she cared enough to ask should tell her something. But her stubborn will was in the way of her own logic.

"He's pretty torn up about how things ended the other night. But he's trying to hide it." Melanie didn't stop her movements.

"Have I really left my things in that big of a mess?"

"For you, yes. But it's not that bad. I don't mind."

She needed to stop making messes. Of her things. Of her relationships. "Maybe we should ask Rick to come talk."

Her friend sighed. "*Finally.* I think that's a great idea." Quick footsteps were followed by the click of the door, giving her no chance to change her mind.

Lord, help me be discerning. I don't know what to think anymore.

The door opened again, and this time two sets of footsteps entered. As they came closer, Chaisley could smell the new shaving cream Rick used. It was oddly comforting.

"I'm sorry, Chaisley." The humility in his tone was her undoing. "Please know that I would never intentionally hurt you. But I *had* to follow my orders until I knew you and Melanie could be trusted. I will do whatever I can to gain back your trust."

Tears streamed down her face, and it took her a moment to gather her thoughts and calm the quivering in her chin. Words wouldn't come, so she nodded. And just like that, the peace she'd been so desperate for the past two days rolled back into her heart.

"Can we talk about it?" He cleared his throat, and the couch lowered next to her.

His presence beside her was like a warm hug. She swiped at her cheeks. "What would you like to talk about?"

"Well . . . now that you know I overheard you in the car, would you like to tell me more about your plans? I know it's not just to play concerts around Europe. That you have contacts and want to help people. There's something brewing in that brilliant mind of yours. I can almost see it."

A hand covered hers from the other side. Melanie. She squeezed and held on.

Might as well start at the beginning. "In all actuality, it did indeed start off as just a European tour. I'd thought to bring hope and music into people's lives and unify them in the bond of humanity and the struggle everyone has faced after the Great War." Chaisley swallowed. What had sounded so noble before the tour now sounded hollow in comparison to what people were suffering.

Melanie squeezed her hand again.

Chaisley put her other hand to her chest. "Before we left England, I felt this weight on my very soul. As if God was calling me to something bigger than myself. I had no idea what it was. Dr. Grafton said he had the same feeling, Melanie as well. When we made it to Amsterdam, Grandmother shared with us some of the awful things that are happening and that she too was being called to help. She didn't tell us the details at the time because she was trying to protect us, but I have a feeling I know what it is." She swallowed hard. Though proud of her grandmother for taking a stand and doing something, she also understood the consequences.

She blinked and the darkness that had become her constant

companion pressed in on her. This was no time to falter. "Now that I know what Hitler is doing to those who are disabled, and what else he plans, I have to do something about it."

A rush of air escaped her friend beside her. "That's why you gave that interview and told him outright what happened and that you are blind." She squeezed her hand again.

"Yes." She lifted her chin toward the man she longed to trust. "Rick, I *don't* give interviews. Never have. I've also never told any-one but those closest to me that I am blind. I felt like I was supposed to do the interview and use whatever standing I have to show the world how valuable a blind person can be. We're building a network to help people. That's another reason I've added more universities and schools to the schedule. Somehow, we need to let people know we are willing to help without showing our hand to the Nazis."

"That's wise." Rick's voice was soft. "I want to help in whatever way I can while I'm with you."

Oh. That made sense, didn't it? He would have to leave at some point. She bit the inside of her cheek against the sudden swell of sadness. To think there would be a day when he *wouldn't* be her driver . . . "But what are you here to do? Why is a spy working as a pianist's driver?" She needed answers now. Before they went any further.

"My job has always been to gather information. From whom-ever and wherever I can. But our informants were disappearing rapidly in Germany. There were only a handful of us agents left working in Europe. The Gestapo hunted us down and tortured people to get information. I was sent to Amsterdam to take a new position."

"Ah. For me."

"Yes. I didn't know who I would be assigned to. My superior hasn't been in contact, so I don't even know if he is still there. But the goal is the same. Chaisley, Melanie—we are on the same side. I don't believe it a coincidence that God brought us together."

"Do you trust us, Rick?" Melanie asked the question, her hand stiff in Chaisley's.

"I do."

Forthright. Solid. He sounded honest.

"And you are willing to put your life in our hands and hold our lives in yours?" she prodded.

"I am."

Melanie squeezed Chaisley's hand twice.

Chaisley leaned forward. "Then let there be no more secrets between us. I can't abide you keeping anything from us. I've detected from the beginning that you were hiding something. Now that you've told us, I need that honest connection. If I think you are not being truthful with me in the slightest—I won't be able to trust you and that would be disastrous."

"Agreed," Rick chimed in. "I vow to you right now that I will be honest with you. No more secrets."

"And we vow the same. Right, Melanie?"

"Right." Melanie released her hand. "So how many languages do you actually speak, Rick?"

"Fluently?"

"Yes." She tapped the seat of the couch.

"Seven."

"Well, Chaisley's got you beat. I believe she's up to eight now." Melanie's light laugh helped break up the seriousness of their discussion.

"You should tell us which languages you speak so we can compare." Chaisley pursed her lips. "I guess it's only fair that I start, since we asked the question. I speak English, French, German, Dutch, Italian, Spanish, Hungarian, and Russian . . . oh, and if you want to count it, I'm fluent in braille."

"Me too!" Melanie's tone was much more relaxed. "Although I only speak Dutch, German, French, and English."

"Add Romanian to my list, and subtract Russian and Hungarian.

Maybe I should have you teach me braille—that sounds like a brilliant way to send coded messages."

His voice was more relaxed than she'd ever heard it.

"Why on earth are we still speaking in Dutch?" Melanie laughed. "It takes a lot of effort to keep my accent up."

"Agreed." Chaisley switched to English and patted her friend's back. "But you do it quite well, I must say."

"You both do. It's impeccable." Rick's deep baritone washed over her. "I agree, English between us is much easier. Until we have need of a code."

"Funny that you should mention codes." She scrunched up her nose and chuckled. "We have something to teach you."

TOULOUSE, FRANCE—MONDAY, JUNE 20, 1938

The cool evening air outside the concert hall was a nice respite to the heat of the day. Rick paced the walkway and kept himself on the lookout for anyone suspicious while keeping a close eye on Chaisley and Melanie.

The past twelve days hadn't given Rick any time to breathe, much less get time alone with Chaisley to try and fix what he'd broken. Their last conversation had made great strides in the right direction, but it wasn't enough. They weren't in the same place anymore. More than anything, he longed to repair their relationship.

It had taken her telling him to go for him to come to his senses. He couldn't imagine life without her.

But how was he supposed to move forward?

Granted, the past two weeks had been fruitful as they'd connected with Dr. Grafton's contacts across France and helped build a network of people willing to help house and transport people escaping Hitler. The wealthy family they'd helped leave Austria had given them a great deal of money to assist in funding their rescue efforts, and Dr. Grafton's contacts were some of the most remarkable people Rick had ever met. If he didn't work for the SIS and have a job driving Chaisley, he'd march into the fire with those people.

It was a beautiful thing to see passion to stand up to the growing evil ignited.

If only more people were willing to rise up. So many cowered under fear—and he couldn't blame them one bit. It wasn't easy to simply survive right now.

But God was paving the way for them to continue in their rescue efforts, and it truly was miraculous to watch.

Rick couldn't change millions of minds overnight, but he could help reach one person at a time.

So far their little band of three had communicated with contacts by telephone or letter. They kept the messages light, using flowers as their code words. This helped them know how many people would be traveling or needing shelter. Any detailed communication went to Dr. Grafton in braille, which meant Chaisley handled all of that.

A few of Dr. Grafton's contacts wrote in braille when they needed to share details—but not regular braille. Each paragraph alternated between original braille with dashes, New York Point, and Boston Line Letter. Code words were also inserted into the text. It had worked well so far, and Rick had to dive into his crash course of braille headfirst to help out. Musical braille was a complete mystery to him since he didn't understand musical scores, but he was willing to learn.

It had been decided that any communications into or out of Germany would be done in Chaisley's detailed musical code. And that correspondence would remain between her, her guardian, and her grandmother.

Should a Nazi spy ever suspect any of their communications, the Nazis would do their best to decode them. Since Chaisley's grandmother already suspected her mail from Germany had been read, they were on high alert.

At least while they'd been in France, Rick and the two ladies hadn't seen any tampering with their letters. Everything they'd sent out had made it to the destinations. For now.

But deep in his bones, he could feel the time was coming when that wouldn't be the case.

Word had trickled to him from his own headquarters and encouraged him. The cease in communications had been lifted. They'd found two moles. One in Germany and one in London. Now that they were gone, things should improve. Even if just marginally. More officers and agents were being trained daily. That was a good sign.

He checked his watch as he scanned the remaining throng outside the concert hall.

People came in droves to see Chaisley perform. Crowds lined up outside the concert halls, universities, and opera houses to meet her. Word had spread like wildfire that the brilliant pianist was blind. Many people wanted to express their amazement at her talent and her ability to overcome. Some wanted to just get a glimpse of her and watch how she did it.

And, of course, there were those who frowned and criticized the masses for praising a "cripple" and an "invalid." Two words he despised.

But the people who mattered most were the quiet ones who waited until all the others left. Who wished to speak to them in private.

Tonight, they spent more than two hours outside as Chaisley and Melanie spoke to the ones who waited.

Melanie carried a small leather notebook tucked inside a pocket of her dress. Whenever she pulled it out, Rick's senses heightened, and he scanned the sidewalks and corners looking for anyone who might be watching with sinister motives.

He couldn't risk anything happening to Chaisley or Melanie.

Melanie was still writing information down, and Rick didn't see anyone nefarious around. But it was dark. Someone could be in the shadows.

Chaisley leaned forward and whispered something.

Her strength of late amazed him. Over the brief time he'd known her, he'd watched her bloom. Even under the pressure of all she poured into each performance. She indeed gave people hope and inspired them.

And then there was Section D. The order was simple: "to plan, prepare, and when necessary carry out sabotage and other clandestine operations, as opposed to the gathering of intelligence."

This addition to his job while he was Chaisley's driver complicated matters. When they were in Germany, he was to gather as much information as he could on how the Nazis were using the railways. And if he had a chance to plan sabotage of communications or electricity, he was to put things in place for that. Another agent was tasked with Germany's agriculture and food supplies.

The SIS scrambled to replace agents, contacts, and informants. But they needed more people on the front lines and fast. During the cease in communications—he'd felt completely in the dark. Now that information was flowing again, he prayed each day for the recent dwindling numbers to turn around and surge upward.

Hitler and his Nazi regime were growing exponentially. Any day could be the start of a new war.

His heart sank a little as he watched Chaisley. How could he leave her? In the months he'd spent with her and Melanie, their kindness and compassion had captivated him. Challenged his own faith. And only strengthened his resolve to help their cause. To do whatever he could to help the innocents she was quietly helping to escape. But he was still a spy. And he had an obligation to his country.

Was there a possibility he could help them through his job? He scratched the side of his jaw. *What is Your will here, Lord? I don't know what to do.*

When the women reached the last person waiting to speak with them, he moved closer and then escorted them back to the auto. The car was quiet as he drove them back to the hotel. It had been a full night. They had to be exhausted.

Once they were in their suite of rooms, which Chaisley insisted upon now to help Melanie feel safe and protected, Melanie excused herself for the night. Chaisley ensconced herself on the couch, her feet tucked up under her and a blanket over her lap.

He eyed her from his stance near the front door. "You should get some rest."

"You shouldn't worry overmuch. You know it takes me a bit to unwind after a concert." The soft smile on her face was relaxed. Comfortable. "If you've got some time to sit and chat, I'd like the company."

An invitation too tempting to refuse.

He took a seat across from her and propped his feet up on the coffee table.

"Please remove your shoes, Mr. Zimmerman. We don't want to scratch the fine wood."

He winced. Caught again. "Sorry."

"It's quite all right." Her smile broadened. "I have to give you a hard time. Everyone mother-hens me, it's about time I do the same."

After he removed his shoes and wiggled his toes around, it was amazing how much his body relaxed. He let out a sigh.

"See? Much better, isn't it?" Her voice was lighter than he'd heard it in days.

"Much." And it was. But his relief had everything to do with the beautiful woman opposite him.

Chaisley's smile was wide. "We haven't had a chance to talk lately, and I'm sorry for that. I didn't want you to think I was still upset with you."

The admission did his heart a world of good. "I've been worried that I'd ruined things between us."

"No. You didn't." Her face softened as she dipped her chin. "I don't want to lose your friendship."

That perked him up. And the pink that entered her cheeks made him smile. "Your friendship means a great deal to me as well."

She was silent for several moments. He loved the way her fingers delicately played on her lap whatever melody was in her mind. The way her long eyelashes brushed the top of her cheeks when she blinked. Did she have any idea what a stunning woman she was?

"So tell me, Rick . . . do you have dreams for your future?"

His eyebrows quirked upward. She wanted to know about *his* dreams? He plucked a thread off his pants. How could he express what he wasn't even sure about himself? "Well . . . at this point, my dreams are to survive whatever is coming. When I think of what we all went through during the Great War, the thought of another is awful. But I fear it will be much worse and that has squashed any thoughts of my own dreams."

She tipped her head to the side, a soft smile lifting one corner of her mouth. "Surely you must still have hopes for the future."

He did. What would her reaction be if he told her he wouldn't trade this time with her for anything. That he didn't care what the future held as long as she was in it in some way. But he couldn't dare admit that out loud. Best to turn the question back to her. "What about you and your dreams?"

Her profile was lovely as she faced the fireplace. "I do. But they have dimmed the past year or so—like you, it's hard to see past what might be coming. Still . . ." She hesitated, then tapped her knee with her fingers. "I'd love to marry and have a family someday. While my grandmother is still alive so she can be a part of my children's lives. She's been such an integral part of mine. But not many men are interested in marrying someone who isn't whole."

That last part made him jerk in his seat. Did she really see herself that way? He would have never guessed. She carried herself with such confidence and poise. "Not whole? Is that how you think people see you?"

She shrugged. "I've heard it quite a bit of late. My grandmother and Dr. G never allowed me to think less of myself after the accident. They made sure to give me the tools to thrive and told me I could accomplish whatever I wanted if I put in the time and effort. And frankly, I took a lot of pride in the fact that people were fascinated with me as a prodigy."

"But now you've chosen to listen to the naysayers?"

Another shrug. She still wouldn't turn her face toward him. How odd. Most of the time he felt as if she was looking straight at him. Or through him.

Several seconds passed before she dipped her chin, and her fingers began to tap again. "I know it's silly. But there are times I wonder how on earth I'm supposed to meet someone and get to know him as I'm touring the world playing the piano. There've been plenty of admirers from afar over the years, but I don't have any real friends other than Melanie. There's no time."

"Well, now you've got me, too." His superiors would scold him for saying it—and letting it happen in the first place. If only his job didn't still hold many secrets.

That smile of hers could melt an iceberg. "You're sweet, Rick. I greatly appreciate your friendship and have enjoyed getting to know you."

"But . . . ?"

She frowned. "But what?"

He laughed at the expression on her face. "Sorry. It sounded like there was a *but* in there, like you were about to tell me we couldn't be friends anymore."

She waved a hand toward him. "Heavens, no." Those lovely fingers were tapping at full speed now. "I think I wanted to tell you

197

that I'd love to get to know you better, but then I second-guessed myself because that would sound awfully forward and unladylike."

The uncertainty on her face twisted in his heart like a knife. "I'd like that too." But was it a good idea? How were they going to navigate the dangerous waters ahead?

"I hear the hesitation in your voice. You're concerned. Like I am." She pulled her knees up under the blanket and circled her arms around them. "I've never met anyone like you, Rick. And not just because you're a spy." Her laugh was light. "I love your heart. You've jumped in and helped every step of the way. You rescued Melanie. You protect me and encourage me and support me. But I'm scared. More than I care to admit. These times are so uncertain."

Oh, to keep her safe! To have that right because she belonged to him. But with who she was, and what they all were doing, was keeping her safe even possible? He didn't mind risking his own neck, but hers? "I'm scared too."

Because there was a very real chance that none of them would escape this alive.

MELANIE'S LEGS WERE STIFF. She'd been leaning up against the door to her room in the suite. She wasn't even sure how long she'd stood there. But she couldn't move.

In front of Chaisley and Rick, she'd done her level best to show that she was strong. The attack hadn't gotten to her. That the news of Rick working for the SIS didn't faze her. That the ever-growing danger around them didn't scare her.

But it was all a lie.

Everywhere they went, she saw Nazis ready to arrest them.

She worried every time Rick disappeared in the night.

And then . . . every night, the memories of the attack overwhelmed her.

Tonight had been harder to hide it than ever before. As soon as they'd returned to the hotel, her legs had started to shake, and her insides quivered.

They were safe. No one could get to her here.

But the memory of that night wouldn't leave her alone. It screamed in her mind that she was vulnerable. Weak. She shouldn't be there.

If anything good had come out of the attack, it had given her more resolve to help those less fortunate.

The bad often outweighed that good.

Then the voices inside her would start to fight.

This was Chaisley's battle, not hers. What business did she have trying to save people when she couldn't even save herself?

She shook her head. No. That wasn't the truth. She was just as passionate about this as Chaisley. She wanted to be a part.

This was the right thing to do.

But what if she was attacked again? She'd never have the strength to endure it twice. She'd fall apart. And everyone she was trying to help would suffer in the process.

Chaisley would be alone, and Melanie couldn't abandon her friend like that.

She was a worthless human being.

Slumping to the floor against the door, she buried her face in her hands.

Would she ever get past this? Or would it haunt her for the rest of her life? Why did it feel like her prayers had been useless?

Ever since the attack she'd read the book of Esther every day. Hoping to find the strength that she needed to continue on. It had helped, but moments like this made her doubt herself.

"God, help me. Please." She spoke to the ceiling. "I can't go on like this. Chaisley needs me. Lots of people need her. Give me Your strength . . . God, I'm begging You. Please. Take this burden from me."

As she choked out the last words, hot tears burned trails down her cheeks. The first time she'd allowed it since the attack.

Now the floodgate was open.

She moved to a crawling position and sobbed her way to the washroom where she splashed cold water on her face, but the tears continued. Grabbing a towel, she buried her face in it and wept. Lying on the cool floor, she sobbed and released it all into more capable hands.

She wasn't alone.

Her Father understood.

In that moment, she felt cocooned in His arms as she poured out her fear and grief.

chapter
TWELVE

The concert hall smelled . . . clean.

Melanie described the hall, with its pillars and rectangular windows, to Chaisley. The ornate architecture on the outside. The marble floors and statues. The lavish chandeliers draped in crystals hanging from the ceiling and the seats covered in velvet. Ordinarily, she would have loved every detail.

But it seemed empty and without life. Like all of Berlin. The weight of something dark and oppressive seemed heavier with every breath.

As they'd navigated the space where she would play, and she'd done an early practice this morning, something within Chaisley balked at doing a concert here.

In the realm of the Nazis.

But she desperately wanted to see Mary Beth and her mother. There had been tickets provided them for tonight. Would they show up?

She made her way down the twenty-nine steps out the front

201

entrance with Rick and Melanie at her side. "Let's go. But please drive us around for several minutes, Rick, before we reach our final destination."

"I have it all planned out." Rick chuckled. "If someone follows us they will simply think I'm describing the city and points of interest to you."

"Perfect." That would make it easier for them to visit the blind school Melanie had found.

Thirty minutes later, she exited the car. Taking a deep breath before entering the door, she put a hand to her stomach and did her best to quell the unease brewing inside.

She'd read the newspapers, heralding the so-called excellent work of the Gestapo in executing "Operation Work Shy." They had arrested almost ten thousand criminals, vagrants, and "anti-social" people. Whatever *that* meant.

But a letter from one of Dr. Grafton's contacts informed her that among those arrested had been almost eleven hundred Jews.

All of whom were sent to concentration camps.

The nausea hadn't left since she'd read the letter. The enormity of evil was almost impossible to comprehend. She pressed her shaking hand to her stomach again. She needed to calm down. Getting emotional would make her sloppy.

So many lives depended on her. On Melanie and Rick, Dr. G and Grandmother, and the plan they'd developed to rescue these precious people. "I'm right beside you." Mel's calm voice from the right soothed her frayed nerves.

"Me too," Rick chimed in from her left.

It was time. She gave a nod, and she heard the doors open. The plan was simple. Get in. Find a room to camp out in. Let the head of the school know they were present and ask to speak to the students. If they did it all as quickly as possible, perhaps the SS and Gestapo would never know they'd been there.

"Rick, it appears there's an empty classroom to your left. Take

Chaisley in there and stay with her. I'm going to find whoever is in charge." Melanie's firm order was quiet.

A tug at her left elbow, and Rick's deep voice cocooned her. "I'll walk with you. Only about six paces to the door."

"Thank you." As they entered the room, she smiled. "You were correct. Six on the nose."

"There's a chair over here behind a desk. Wait just a moment." His footsteps sounded all over the room. A door opened and closed. More steps. "Okay, I had to check it out first. Twelve steps over to the desk." He was at her elbow again, letting her step with confidence.

She found the desk and chair and took a seat. "Thank you, again."

His steps went back and forth in front of her.

"Are you nervous? Is that why you're pacing?"

"There's so much we don't know about this place. Do you have some sort of plan?"

She laced her fingers together, willing her heart to stop pounding in her ears. "Actually, I wanted to encourage the students first."

"And then?"

"I don't know. But they might need to know what's really coming so they can be prepared. And know that there are people willing to help."

He sucked in a breath. Loud and long. "They're just kids."

Yes, they were. But someone had to prepare them. "Keep your tone quiet, please, Mr. Zimmerman."

"Might I also remind you that we are in *Berlin.*" Rick's words were whisper soft but held a sharp edge.

"I know very well where we are." Footsteps—a great many of them—sounded in the hallway. She understood Rick's hesitation. Her own nerves seemed tighter than a piano string. But he would see. God was at work.

"Miss Frappier, I've brought you the students."

Chaisley restrained a frown. Why was Melanie's chipper voice so forced?

Chaisley stood. Was her friend trying too hard to be positive or was it because she was speaking in German? What had she seen? "Wonderful. Welcome." She clapped her hands together and prayed that if Melanie needed to warn her about something, she would do it soon.

Steps and shuffling were accompanied by soft commands from a couple of older-sounding people. Teachers?

Someone touched her elbow. The scent of Mel's hand cream gave her away. "There are only twenty-one students left." She'd switched to English. "The headmistress is gone, and there are two teachers."

"What happened to the headmistress and the rest of the students?" There should have been twice that many.

"The woman in charge was taken as a political prisoner last week for helping a Jewish family leave. At least, that's the rumor."

"If I may, Fräulein." A young voice that sounded as lyrical as Mozart's sonata in C Major spoke up. "Many of the families are finding a way to leave." Her voice was so beautiful and uplifting, even when conveying the words that weren't pleasant. "Especially after the older students were taken away to hospitals for forced sterilization."

Chaisley gasped. The blunt statement sounded so harsh coming from one so young. Like a slap in the face. What had they had to endure here?

"We have tried to be honest with our students here and their families," another voice chimed in. "My name is Freida, and I am one of the teachers."

"Where are the others?" Her voice sounded so strained. *Be calm.*

"We aren't certain. Some told us of their plans and left of their own accord. The others simply disappeared."

A warm hand covered hers. Rick. Chaisley held on for dear life. She needed all the strength she could muster to keep a positive outlook for these kids.

The teacher continued in German. "But the students have been thrilled to hear about your tour and are excited to meet you today."

The change in subject was forced but for the best. Chaisley listened to every sound in the room. The precious breaths of people surviving during uncertain times. Arms and legs shifting. The rustle of clothing. A tap here and there of a shoe on the tile floor.

She straightened in her chair, and a strength that was not her own filled her. "I'm so glad to meet each one of you today. I hope to learn your names and ages in a moment. But first, let me introduce myself. My name is Chaisley Frappier. I am a concert pianist." She said it with confidence. "And yes, I am completely blind. I have been since my tenth birthday." With a swallow, she surged on. "I don't know what you've been told by people, but you are *not* less of a person because you cannot see. You are just as worthy of life as anyone else on the planet. God made you just the way you are, and He has given you gifts to use."

Did she sound too preachy? She shook her head. No. What she said was the truth. Someone needed to tell these kids how wonderful they were. How valuable they were.

Several clicking noises sounded around the room.

"I can tell some of our students have questions. They are instructed to click their tongues and raise their hand. Would you mind, Miss Frappier?" The teacher who'd spoken before was on her right now.

"I'd love to hear them. Oh, and please, tell me your name and age when you ask a question."

After hearing from each student, ranging in age from seven to eighteen, and answering every question from her favorite color to why she loved the piano so much, she folded her hands in her lap. "I can feel a tension in the room. A sadness. What is it that you're not telling me?"

Several sighs reached her ears.

"It's our last day." Lydia—the young woman with the lyrical voice—answered. "They are shutting down the school tomorrow."

Chaisley leaned forward in her seat. "What will you do?"

"Most of our families are seeking refuge elsewhere. Some are even leaving tomorrow if they can." Lydia's voice moved closer to her. "But those of us who are on our own will have to figure something out. There's a man who has hired people like us before. He owns a brush factory. His name is Mr. Weidt. I'm hoping to find employment with him."

"Me too. My name is Anne, and I'm sixteen," a sweet voice piped up.

"And what about your teachers?" Chaisley aimed the question to her right, where both teachers had come to stand.

"We aren't sure what we will do, but we want to make sure all the students are safe first." The emotion behind the words gave Chaisley the idea that both women were crying.

There had to be something she could do to help. For the long term. But what? "I have an idea. What if you all could come to my concert this evening? There's plenty of space backstage for you to sit and listen."

"That's not possible, Fräulein Frappier," one of the teachers said, "but thank you for the invitation."

"Why not?" Melanie conveyed the same question Chaisley wanted to voice.

"The streets aren't safe for the students after about four o'clock."

"Why is that?" Rick's commanding presence filled the space next to her. His protective streak was out in full force.

"We aren't allowed to speak of it." The quieter of the two teachers answered. "Now . . . we do have a piano in the basement. It's probably out of tune, but I'm sure the students would love to hear you."

As the kids begged her to play, Chaisley's thoughts drifted to Mary Beth and her mother. Were they already gone? Would she ever find them?

Lord, protect them.

As much as she longed to find the mother and daughter, a new thought sank deep into her heart. Their sweet letters had been the

206

catalyst for Chaisley's new journey. God had used them to move her heart to a new place . . . to urge her into action. No matter what happened, she would continue to hope for a meeting but would leave them in the Almighty's hands.

"Follow us, please. Be careful on the steps."

Lots of shuffling followed the teacher's voice out the door.

Then a slight tap on her shoulder. Not Melanie's usual signal.

"Miss Frappier." The older teacher, speaking in a hushed tone. "We need help. Some of the students without families need to move to safer locations. Otherwise, they will certainly be taken away."

Chaisley swallowed hard. "To . . . ?" The words felt like thick porridge on her tongue. Impossible to speak or swallow.

"I don't wish to speak of what I've heard. Can you help?"

Her heart picked up its pace. "How soon?"

"As soon as tomorrow, if you can. There are four students, ages sixteen to eighteen. We had a friend who secured visas for them to the Netherlands, but we haven't had a way or funds to get them there. The visas expire at the end of the week."

"I'll do it." Rick's low voice edged in on her left. "I can take them tonight after the concert and be back in time to help you tomorrow afternoon." He squeezed Chaisley's hand. "This is what we're here for."

Chaisley nodded.

"You have a safe place to take them?" The woman sounded elated and skeptical all at the same time.

Chaisley smiled. "Yes. I know someone with a home in the Netherlands." Grandmother would love to have young people in her home.

The older woman was silent for a moment. Then she sniffed and Chaisley could hear the tears in her voice. "After you play for them, I'll help them pack their things and make sure they are ready to go."

"They've been living here at the school?" Chaisley's brow furrowed.

"No. They've been living with me." The woman stepped away. "Come. We should get you downstairs."

"God bless you for your generosity, miss. There aren't many willing to take such risks." Rick stayed at Chaisley's elbow as he spoke.

"Thank you, sir. It's been a challenge. But we've made do with what the good Lord has provided."

Chaisley couldn't imagine what these teachers and students had faced. As she allowed Rick to lead her down the stairs to the basement, she pondered the reality of what the teacher had sacrificed . . . what the students had endured. Did they have enough food?

The room was musty, but it couldn't cover the delight she felt radiating from the students. The old upright was indeed out of tune, and the bench creaked every time she moved, but she still played some of her favorite pieces for the kids, and their *oohs* and *aahs* nourished her soul. The younger students even squealed during the fast sections.

If these sweet students could endure such difficult times, she could as well.

When she finished, the teachers said their good-byes to the students and there were lots of sobs and questions about what would happen next. Once they were all back upstairs, Chaisley leaned against the wall to get her bearings for a moment.

"Miss Frappier . . . these are the four I was telling you about. Lydia, Anne, Charlie, and Grant."

Chaisley stepped forward and greeted each one with a handshake and placed her palm on each face. Hopefully she would learn much about these four over the coming months and hear how they were thriving, but first, she had to get them to Amsterdam.

Without being discovered by the Gestapo.

INSIDE THE BORDER OF GERMANY—SATURDAY, JULY 9, 1938

"Papiere!" The officer shouted, spittle landing on Rick's coat. "Who. Are. These. Children?"

He couldn't answer. Why couldn't he speak? He gripped the steering wheel and stared at the red-faced man.

Hatred seeped out of the man's glare. "Take them away! They don't deserve to live!"

Rick leapt out of the car and fought against the horde of guards that surrounded him. But he was no match. They would take the children. No!

He punched and kicked—

Kicking at whatever restrained him, Rick opened his eyes and got his bearings. His breaths came in short, hard gasps. He fisted the thin blanket that had covered him in the backseat and threw it on the floor.

It had seemed so real.

He rubbed both hands up and down his face. The full morning sun heated up the interior of the auto.

The kids were safe. He'd dropped them at Celestia Frappier's home after a stress-filled eight hours in the car and then drove back over the border into Germany.

The guards at the German border had questioned him for a long time since the kids' visas were expiring soon but eventually let him through. It was a miracle.

What would he have done if they had refused him? What would have happened to those four incredible young people who had so much to offer to the world?

Shaking off the remnants of the nightmare, Rick climbed out of the rear seat and back into the driver's seat. The drive had given him a good view of several places to investigate for the SIS.

Now, more than ever—after getting to know those kids and hearing their stories—he wanted to help stop the Nazi machine that seemed to gain steam at every turn. He didn't care if he got caught or lost his life in the process, he would do everything in his power to make sure *everyone* was seen worthy of life.

BERLIN

Melanie opened the door to the suite. "Shh." Hopefully the surprise would help Chaisley's melancholy after the tough day yesterday.

"Why are you shushing, Mel? I haven't said anything." Chaisley's voice floated from one of the bedrooms.

Goodness, so much for being stealthy. The woman could hear a hippo sneeze all the way in Africa! "I have a surprise for you, so why don't you come out." She suppressed her excitement and led her guests in.

Chaisley walked into the sitting room from the bedroom, her eyes red-rimmed as if she'd been crying, but she pasted on a smile. *"Guten morgen."*

"Good morning, to you too, my friend." Melanie put a hand to the back of each of her visitors. "I'd like to introduce you to Mary Beth and Geraldine Klein."

Chaisley squealed, threw out her arms, and rushed toward them. "Mary Beth, where are you, my dear?" Her hands searched the air until Melanie positioned the young girl within her reach.

"Fräulein . . ." The girl burst into tears.

Chaisley pulled her into her arms, and they sobbed together.

Melanie wrapped an arm around Geraldine's shoulders as the other woman cried silent tears. "I told you everything would be all right."

"It's not a dream?" The woman's German was broken up by gulping sobs.

"No, ma'am. It isn't."

"Fräulein Frappier is an *angel*."

Chaisley laughed as she held Mary Beth. "Not in the least . . . all credit goes to Melanie here and the good Lord." She moved toward Geraldine and Melanie helped them all navigate into a three-person hug.

After several minutes of tears and laughter, Chaisley released their guests. "Please, you must tell me how this happened. I was so hoping you'd be able to come to the concert."

Mary Beth bounced on the settee and crossed her ankles in front of her. "Oh, Mama was afraid to try. My teacher was taken to one of the work camps."

Melanie watched Chaisley's face turn fierce as she responded. "Why?"

"They said he was an informant against the Nazis." Mrs. Klein wiped at her nose.

Melanie barely restrained a scoff. A piano teacher? An informant? But wait. Hadn't Rick told them that the Gestapo had rounded up a lot of informants? *Dear God, help us all.* Even with all she'd heard from the students, Dr. Grafton's connections, and the newspapers, it was difficult to comprehend what was happening here in Germany.

". . . listening to phone calls. The Nazis will stop at nothing to achieve what they want."

Melanie wanted to get out of this country as soon as possible. They were supposed to be leaving for Amsterdam in the morning, but it wasn't soon enough. Perhaps they should leave as soon as Rick returned with the auto.

"We have nowhere to go now." Mrs. Klein continued to wipe the tears from her face. "No one will hire me, and I can't risk them taking my sweet Mary Beth away."

Chaisley stood. "Give me just a moment, please. I'll get us some refreshments." She walked to her bedroom. "Mel?"

Melanie followed her into the room. "You're going to call Dr. Grafton, aren't you?"

"Yes. There's got to be a way to get them visas. If there *was* a way, I'd take them with us tomorrow."

There wasn't any chance they could obtain visas that fast.

A loud banging on the door to the suite jolted Melanie. "Who could that be?"

Another loud round of knocks.

"Message from the Führer, Herr Hitler!" resonated through the door.

Mary Beth and her mother both trembled, then the tears started in earnest.

Melanie ran to their guests and grabbed their hands. "I'm going to take you into the other room with Miss Frappier. But you must be very quiet. Don't worry."

Mary Beth's hand trembled in hers, but they followed her instructions, making no noise as she settled them in chairs and shut the connecting door.

Melanie took deep breaths as she rushed back to the door just as another loud round of knocks began. She schooled her features to portray her annoyance at the loud interruption and opened the door a couple of inches.

"What *is* it?" Jaw set, shoulders rigid, she hoped to give off an air of confident irritation.

"An important message from the Führer himself." The man's bellow could surely be heard down the street.

"Must you disturb the entire hotel? Hush now." How she dared to speak to an officer this way was beyond her.

The man scowled. "You will deliver this message to Fräulein Frappier immediately." He thrust an envelope at her, raised his arm in salute, and clicked his heels together. "Heil Hitler!"

She closed the door before he could expect a response. Then she locked it and put the chain on for good measure.

For several minutes, she leaned against the door, the envelope feeling like it got warmer every second she held it. She wanted to throw it into the fire immediately, but that could have disastrous consequences for them all.

"Mel?" Chaisley had snuck up beside her. "Are you all right?"

Her hands shook. "I'm fine."

"You handled yourself quite well." Chaisley touched her arm. "I don't know if I could have held myself together like that."

Melanie flopped down into a chair, her nervousness escaping in a wry laugh. "I can't believe I scolded him!" She smacked a hand to her forehead.

Geraldine and her daughter huddled by the bedroom door, obviously shaken by the man's harsh interruption.

"But you played the part. That's what you had to do." Chaisley sat across from her. "Geraldine, Mary Beth. Please, come sit. It's all right. He's gone."

Melanie rushed to her feet and guided them over to the sitting area. The mother still trembled as she held her daughter close.

"I'm so sorry about that." Melanie did her best to comfort them. "Would some tea help?"

"Thank you, but no." Geraldine's head shook back and forth. "The only thing that will help is getting out of Germany and going far, far away. But I don't know if that's even possible anymore."

Chaisley straightened in her chair, a determined look on her face. "I will get you out of Germany, my friends. I don't know how or when. But I *will* get you out."

Melanie cringed and shifted in her seat. Chaisley meant well. And probably *would* figure out a way to save this mother and daughter. But sometimes her friend's sweeping declarations made her uncomfortable. Especially when her own bravery was nowhere to be found.

And then there were the practical details of the situation. Where could they hide them in the meantime?

"I will get you a hotel room somewhere safe for the time being." Chaisley patted Geraldine's arm. "With plenty of food for a few weeks until we can arrange something else."

It was as if she'd read Melanie's mind. "Yes. I'll work on that right away."

"Now." Chaisley lifted her chin. "I guess you better read me the message."

Melanie opened the envelope and scanned the one page. "It

appears," she huffed, "that Hitler is demanding your attendance at a private concert for his most distinguished supporters on August the fifth."

AMSTERDAM, NETHERLANDS—WEDNESDAY, JULY 27, 1938

Celestia sat in the third-floor parlor with the blind students Rick had brought from Berlin. They were all such sweet children. Many nights since they'd arrived, she'd cried herself to sleep.

In each precious face, she saw her granddaughter. Had her family not left Germany, Chaisley could have ended up being just like them. Hunted simply because they were blind. Irreparably flawed in the eyes of a madman.

Of course, if her family hadn't left Germany, Chaisley wouldn't have been blinded in London by a bomb. Celestia's precious son and his wife might still be alive as well. She resisted the urge to thump her cane on the floor. These thoughts were taking her nowhere good.

Almighty God was in control—even though He had no part of evil. It was only because of sin in this world that things were as they were.

"Mrs. Frappier?" Lydia's musical voice jolted her. "Are you all right?"

"I'm fine, dear." Amazing how these children could sense her feelings without her saying a word. She must be more cautious from now on. No use in unsettling these sweet ones. Not when they'd already been through so much.

No child—no *person*—should ever be treated as less than human. Over the years, the overprotectiveness of her granddaughter had melted away as she'd watched Chaisley blossom and grow.

As much as she hated for Chaisley to put herself in harm's way now, Celestia was praising God for what He'd done through her.

These young people were proof of that.

It had been almost three weeks since their arrival, and they'd begged and pleaded to have jobs to do to help others find their way to freedom.

Immediately, Celestia went to work teaching them all the different forms of braille. The young people were quick to learn. They'd already mastered New York Point version of writing and reading and also the Boston Line Letter. It had taken all of one day for them to master the original braille from 1829.

Today, she had them in the parlor with their braille slates to start on the work of learning Chaisley's more intricate code embedded in braille music. With four extra sets of hands, she'd be able to get messages out quicker to her granddaughter and Grafton. And since she'd become the hub here, Celestia needed the help.

The music form of braille was similar to what the students already knew, but they had to learn all the musical terminology on top of understanding paragraph form, bar-by-bar form, and bar-over-bar form.

Since the musical alphabet only contained A–G, Chaisley had come up with a way to show all twenty-six letters of the alphabet for sending missives. Depending on the octave designation, the letter could change. A–G in one octave were the actual letters. One octave up would represent H–N. Two octaves up represented O–U. Three octaves up represented U–Z.

Numbers were easy to incorporate and a dash at the end of a line indicated a change in form for the next.

Changing between paragraph form, bar-by-bar form, and bar-over-bar form should confuse anyone trying to read their communications.

The fact that they had to even think of such a thing made Celestia's stomach churn. But Grafton reported that two of his letters never made it through, which meant she'd been correct.

The Germans were reading—or at least attempting to read—their mail.

Perhaps more of the network should learn the code. But it was tedious. Especially for anyone who didn't already understand and read braille and music. Maybe she should at least give the idea to Grafton.

They were preparing for the worst and still hoping for the best. Some in their circle of connections believed that Hitler would take over all of Europe and Asia, and then woe to anyone who disagreed with him or who he deemed unworthy.

Then there were others who believed Hitler would start a war, but they could stop him before he killed too many people or did too much damage. While Celestia had always been a pessimist in nature, she wanted to be an optimist when it came to this. It was much easier to think that all this work they were doing was simply worst-case scenario and wouldn't be necessary.

But something deep down inside her told her that wasn't to be.

Yes, she would do whatever she could to help people.

Yes, she would buck up and not sweep the reality of what was happening under the rug.

Yes, she would pray every chance she had that they could help as many as possible.

Right now, it was beautiful to have everyone here. Chaisley, Melanie, Timothy, and Rick needed the rest and refreshment before heading back into the fray. She would revel in every moment she had with them.

"How are you this morning, Mrs. Frappier?"

Grafton caught her by surprise. Especially since he never used such formal speech with her.

He waggled his eyebrows at her. "Have you been on your best behavior?"

The students giggled, and she joined them as she walked over to hug him. "You best remember who is your elder, Timothy Grafton. I could still take you over my knee if I had to."

The kids' laughter echoed throughout the room. He waved her toward the door. Oh dear, it must be serious.

She turned her face toward the young people. "All right. Work on writing the phrases I gave you earlier in braille music using the octave designations we've discussed. I'll be back in a few minutes."

"Yes, ma'am," the four youngsters replied in unison.

Celestia moved toward the door and followed Grafton down the hall. He motioned to a small bedroom, she entered, and he closed the door behind them.

"You're teaching them Chaisley's code, aren't you?"

"I am." She folded her arms over her chest. "They're old enough to understand what's going on and they are all smart as whips. I thought it would be wise to have others who can help."

He nodded, his face grim. "That is wise. We really don't know what's coming and communication is getting difficult with all the moving pieces and people spread out over Europe. I've taught all of my contacts the New York Point and Boston line, but I haven't had the chance to teach them the rest. I should make that a priority." He rubbed at the stubble on his chin and sat in one of the chairs beside the large bay window. The sun caught the grey flecking his hair. Celestia's heart broke a little. It hadn't been there a few months ago.

"Celestia, I need to ask for your assistance. There's a family downstairs that needs a place to stay for a while."

She sat in the chair opposite him, resting the hook of her cane on her wrist. "That's not a problem, I've got plenty of room."

The shadow in his eyes darkened. "They're Jewish."

"As I stated before, it's not a problem." *Thank You, Lord, for preparing me for such at time as this. To help Your people.*

One of his eyebrows lifted. "In time, it might become a problem, and you know that. Otherwise you wouldn't have built those rooms. But before I introduce them to you, you need to prepare yourself." He picked at his thumbnail for a moment before meeting her gaze. "They have been mistreated. I'm not sure by whom, but they are malnourished and haven't had a decent meal in who knows how long. The father has been out of work for months, and no one in Germany would hire him. It took me weeks to get visas for all of them."

She patted his arm. Grafton had done an amazing job convincing government officials he'd connected with in five different countries to help with visas. But at the rate people were fleeing, legitimate visas were becoming increasingly difficult to procure. And even with legitimate ones, sometimes the Nazis still chose not to allow people to cross borders and instead shipped people off to the work camps. "We will thank the Lord for His provision and do whatever we can to help." She moved toward the door. "Please, introduce me to our new friends and I'll get them settled."

But he stopped her with a hand on her arm. "Celestia. There are more coming. Are you prepared for that?"

She stiffened. "Of course. Are you insinuating I cannot handle what is coming, Grafton?"

He appeared to weigh his words before speaking. "I don't think you fully understand what is happening in Germany. It's much worse than we ever thought. Far beyond what happened in the Great War, and it will only get worse from here." He reached out and covered her hand with his, his tone softening. "I know you have the heart for this and the room . . . but eventually, the people coming and going won't go unnoticed."

In the back of her mind, she'd known that. Which was why she'd felt prompted to prepare the hidden rooms. "I know. But let's take one day at a time. Are you still able to find transport for people? Especially the children?"

"Yes. For now. Our best options are still England, the United States, and South Africa. But the latter two cost a great deal more money. Word is spreading, but many are too scared to leave. Especially those who still have family here. Chaisley alerted me to the students Rick drove here and started sending word to blind schools across Europe about what is being done in Germany to those who

218

are disabled. I don't know what it will take to get people to rise and help before it's too late."

He rubbed his jaw and stood, staring out the window that overlooked the back gardens. "I made a vow to help people. To heal the sick. To save lives." He turned back to her, his eyes so very sad. "And now we are fighting a monster who wants to snuff out life with a snap of his fingers."

Celestia lifted her shoulders and clamped her jaw against the anger swelling inside her. "That's just it. We're fighting. We're doing everything we can and we're trying to let other people know."

"I feel like I should be doing more." His face fell, and he looked at the floor and shook his head. "But maybe that's just the Lord preparing my heart for what He has in store." He took a long breath and straightened his shoulders. "Let's go meet this family."

Her heart broke at the expression on his face. Determination and a soft smile had attempted to cover the defeat she'd glimpsed. "You need some rest."

"This is also true." He opened the door, and they journeyed down the stairs together.

In the large parlor, a family of six huddled together in front of the fireplace. It wasn't chilly today, but they shivered. Little wonder.

They were skin and bones.

"Welcome to my home." Celestia sent them a warm smile and stepped closer as she spoke to them in German.

"Thank you." The father had his hat in his hands.

"Let's get you settled in a couple of rooms"—she stopped abruptly and changed her mind—"Actually, why don't we get something to eat."

The children's eyes lit up. Yes. That was what they needed first. She motioned them to follow her to the dining room, and she left Grafton with them to chat at the table as she headed into the kitchen to speak with her cook.

"Mrs. Werner?" she called to the woman.

The plump lady came around the corner with a large pot in hand. "Yes, ma'am?"

"Do you still have the vegetable soup simmering?"

"Yes, ma'am." She looked puzzled.

"I know it's early, but we have some guests that need food. Could we perhaps get bowls of soup along with some bread? Let's start with small pieces and a small bowl since I don't know when they last ate. I'm sure we will still be down for luncheon if their stomachs can tolerate that."

"Of course. I'll bring it out straightaway."

"Thank you." Celestia left the kitchen and headed back to the dining room where the father was speaking to Grafton about the work camps. Not a pleasant subject. She walked up to the mother. "Some soup will be here in just a moment. Then we can get you settled and we can come back down for luncheon."

"Thank you, ma'am." The woman's gaunt face beamed a smile at her. "That sounds lovely."

Celestia took her seat and caught the doctor's gaze.

But it was the father who spoke, his voice cracking. "You need to know this. Hear me well. The work camps are death camps."

His mouth twisted into a hard line for a moment before he spoke again. "The more power Hitler gains, the faster he will implement his plan and come after us all. It won't take the Führer long to kill every single Jew left on the earth. That is his plan. Don't fool yourself into thinking anything different. It doesn't matter how far we run. He will hunt us down. There is no hope for us."

Such weariness, such pain in his eyes. Celestia fought back the urge to weep as the man shook his head.

"No hope for anyone"—he caught and held Celestia's gaze—"who defies this devil."

chapter
THIRTEEN

Chaisley walked through the foyer of her grandmother's large manor house and into the dining room. The laughter and conversations around the table had turned into joyous times for most everyone at the manor.

A sweet blessing in the midst of such adversity.

Now, if only they could reach Klaus.

The father's bitterness and despair had lessened a fraction seeing his family cared for, fed, and happy. But he always left the room when anyone dared to be positive in the midst of their circumstances. He just couldn't see any hope.

So she, Mel, and her grandmother had started praying for the man three times a day. Just him. For several minutes, they would meet in private and pray for God to reach his heart, soften it, and show him that there was still life. Still joy.

Listening to all the voices now, Chaisley navigated her way to her seat at the table so she could be surrounded by the joyous chatter.

Grandmother insisted that every guest take great care to leave

221

the furniture where it was, to pick up after themselves, and to keep an eye out for anything dropped on the floor that could pose a hazard to any of the blind people inhabiting the house.

For the most part, it worked wonders. But whenever there were small children about, there was a chance for a stray toy or shoe here and there.

Caution was her new best friend as she roamed the house. More often than not now, she ended up carrying her foldable cane.

Grandmother kept her up-to-date on all the guests. They prayed for each one daily in the early morning hours before anyone else awoke.

As she left the dining room and made her way to the sunroom, her heart cinched. Grabbing onto the joy of these moments kept them going, yes. But the other conversations and the reality of what she'd experienced and heard made the time difficult. The sorrow and fear she heard in their guests' voices were forever engraved on her heart.

There was no escaping or covering the horrors for even the children any longer. The truth was better for all of them to be prepared.

The rumblings that Hitler wanted Czechoslovakia couldn't be ignored.

Every day she prayed for leaders around the world to stop the insanity.

This evening, she'd play another concert at the Amsterdam Royal Concert-Gebouw to another sold-out crowd. Oh, how she longed to share what she knew in front of the entire crowd. But that would surely draw unwanted attention to her, which would risk the good they were doing.

That couldn't happen. They were just getting started—the groundwork had barely been laid for their vast network to continue helping people escape.

"A penny for your thoughts." Rick's low timbre greeted her from the direction of the door in the adjoining parlor.

She smiled toward him, her heart doing a tiny leap. "Would you like to join me? I'm reminiscing over our time here."

Soft footfalls made their way closer. "It's been harder than you hoped, hasn't it?" The cushion beside her sank.

How did he know?

"By the furrow in your brow, I'm guessing that my words are correct?" The smile in his tone made her feel warm. Safe. Protected. Something Rick always managed to do.

"Exactly. I'm not as good at hiding my feelings as I thought I was." She drew in a breath.

"I've come to know you pretty well, Chaisley. Your facade is impeccable, but you forget what I've been trained to do. I'm also a bit partial to studying my favorite subject."

Warmth bloomed in her face. She shifted on the settee so her body faced him. "I just realized I don't know what you look like, Mr. Zimmerman."

He chuckled. "Oh, we're back to formality now?"

"Only because you have been studying me and know what I look like—late at night, early in the morning, even all dressed up for a concert—but I only have what I picture in my mind from what I hear and smell and . . . touch." She dipped her chin and swallowed. "Would you mind if I study your face?"

His breaths quickened. "I don't mind. But how—?"

"With my hands." She lifted them. "You'll have to scoot closer though. My arms aren't that long."

The cushion shifted and she felt his weight move until their legs touched. The tingles that shot up her spine spread throughout her limbs.

He put a hand on each of her wrists and pulled her hands to his face.

Her palms conformed to the planes of his face, and she held it for a long time. Then, with slow movements, she moved her right hand over the left side of his face.

Thick hair, the ridges of his brow, a straight nose, and the rugged edges of his jawline all took shape in her mind.

"Sorry." He whispered. "I need to shave."

Heat worked its way up her neck. "I don't mind." She moved her left hand the same way she'd moved her right and then did another pass with both hands at the same time. She imagined her hands were like those of a sculptor as he worked with clay. She could see every bit of his face and it was even better than she imagined. "What color are your eyes?"

"Brown." His hands were on her wrists again as she held his face.

"And your hair?"

"Blond. Although it has been darkening over time." His voice was so soft, but she felt his breath on her face. "It probably looks a little bit like dirt now."

She laughed. "You are a very handsome man, Rick. Even with hair the color of dirt." She dreaded removing her hands, but it was only proper. As she pulled them away, his hands snatched them back and held on.

"Not really. Especially in comparison to you." His breaths were quick, like staccato notes played on a drum. "You are truly the most beautiful person I've ever met. Inside and out."

She held her breath. They were so close she could feel the space between them diminishing with each second.

When his breath touched her lips, she anticipated his kiss. She'd never been kissed by a man before. Not in a romantic way or on the lips. "Rick," she whispered and put her right hand back on his cheek. They were only an inch or so apart. "You've come to mean a great deal to me." She should kick herself for spilling her heart so easily, but she trusted this man. With her whole heart.

"I care about you more than you know, Chaisley."

Her heart beat so fast it could outrun her fingers on the piano.

The squeaky turn of the doorknob caused them both to jerk away.

"You won't believe the request that just came in from Queen Wilhelmina for you to play this evening!"

Melanie's voice didn't indicate that she'd seen anything. Her quick steps approached the settee. "I know you won't have any problem working them into the concert, but she's apparently a very big fan of yours." Papers shuffled. Her footsteps stopped. "Oh. Is everything all right? What did I interrupt?"

OUTSIDE BERLIN, GERMANY

The cool night breeze wafted through the cracked windows of the Rolls-Royce, soothing his flushed skin and unsettled heart.

He was an idiot. No doubt about it. A complete dolt.

How could he have been so stupid? All it took was the brush of Chaisley's fingers against his skin and he lost all composure.

Nothing had prepared him for the feel of her "seeing" him for the first time. Her touch had been gentle but sure. It had taken every ounce of restraint within him to not touch her face in the same way. And the fact that she returned any sort of feeling for him was almost too much to comprehend.

But what could they do about these feelings? The whole world teetered on the edge of war. They were transporting children with disabilities out of Germany almost every week. And he was still under the orders of Section D which put him in danger every step of the way. Which could put her in more danger.

Any kind of relationship other than friendship should be the furthest thing from either of their minds. But after months together, they needed one another.

He let out a long breath. He needed to focus. Tonight's mission was tricky, and he would need all his wits about him.

His superior had contacted him yesterday after weeks of silence.

A couple other officers had intercepted intelligence regarding a flurry of activity at different German railway depots. He, and any other operatives close by, were to discover and report on what was happening.

And to sabotage the event, if they deemed it necessary.

Twenty miles east of Berlin, his first mark came into view. A lone depot nestled in a large copse of trees. Rick slowed his vehicle. No light shone out of the building and, from what he could see, there were no vehicles near it. But that didn't mean much. He spotted a small open patch on the side of the road and pulled over.

He grabbed his notebook and the chart of scheduled trains. This was a ghost stop for German soldiers to switch out while riding with supplies. The trains here veered south into Czechoslovakia, with several more ghost stops along the way before reaching Dresden, the last stop before the Czech border.

He looked at the map—

Wait. Was that another line going east? Grabbing his torch, he clicked it on, covering it so only a bit of light shone on the map, and dragged his finger along the line, following it across the border into Poland.

Now why would Hitler want supply trains rolling into Poland? The Führer had made his desire for the Sudetenland clear, threatening the world with war if the part of Czechoslovakia was not given to Germany.

But *Poland?*

Rick shook his head. Focus. Tonight was about understanding where the SIS could infiltrate and sabotage railroad lines. He tapped his pencil against the map. What was wisdom in a situation like this? On one hand, being able to derail large sections of Germany's railway would halt the Nazis' ability to spread troops, supplies, and weapons. It would give Britain, France, and any other allies the opportunity to pounce on—and perhaps subdue—the Wehrmacht. The Nazis would be in trouble without their powerful armed forces.

However, the train was also the main way Jewish families were fleeing Germany into surrounding nations. He clicked off the torch and rubbed his eyes. He needed sleep. Everything was beginning to blur together. He grabbed his small Thermos and poured a cup of black coffee. Perhaps a jolt of caffeine would do the trick.

A few minutes later, he pulled his cap on and grabbed his small notebook, pencil, and torch. Time to inspect the area.

Grass whispered under his feet as he followed a small dirt path toward the single building. It was simply constructed. No platform, only three stairs to the door. But the moonlight illuminated a worn path from the door to the tracks. So this depot was well used.

He waited five minutes, listening for the rustling of grass. The crunch of boots on gravel. Anything that might alert him to the presence of someone on the premises. When all he could hear was the whisper of wind, he clicked on his torch again and made some notes about the size of the building, the number of windows, and access points. He rounded the corner to the west side of the building and spotted another building deeper in the woods. It was at least two times the size of the depot.

Rick glanced over his shoulder, then back to where the building was. The depot seemed to block the view of it from the road.

He slid his notebook into his pocket and turned off his torch. It looked like there was another slim, well-worn path from the back of the depot into the trees. A warm breeze rustled the trees, and Rick paused. Was that the snap of a branch? He made it a few more paces when all the hair on his arms stood up.

Someone was behind him.

Slowing his breaths, Rick slipped his hand into his jacket and pulled his gun from the holster.

The footsteps weren't hurried, but purposeful. Rick counted to five and then whirled around. "Drop any weapon you have, or I will shoot to kill."

The figure paused, both hands going up. Rick locked his gaze on the shadow, his fingers tight on the handle of his gun. *Please help, Lord. I don't want to have to shoot this man.*

"A blessing on the fallen brave!"

The figure's words were a whisper on the wind. Yet Rick caught the smooth and cultured British accent.

And the code phrase.

The tension eased from Rick's shoulders. "Those who fought with Wellington." He lowered his weapon as the man came forward.

"Agent Zimmerman, you are a difficult man to track down. I commend you." He held out a hand. "I am Agent Fairsworth, and I've been sent by Trumble."

Rick holstered his gun and gave him a handshake. "I just heard from him yesterday. Has something changed?"

Fairsworth folded his arms over his chest, his expression difficult to discern in the darkness. "A great many things. You and I were sent on the same mission to determine which railways and depots to sabotage, yes?"

At Rick's nod, the man continued.

"The prime minister, with support of the cabinet, has now decided to work with Hitler and allow him to annex the Sudetenland. The deal should come to fruition in the next few months. We are two of only a few agents outside of the cabinet who know it's coming."

What? Rick rocked back on his heels, trying to absorb what he was hearing. His government, the British prime minister, was capitulating to Hitler? "Why?"

"From what I understand, there is great hope that if Hitler gets what he wants with Czechoslovakia, he will stop throwing a temper tantrum and allow the rest of the world to live in peace."

The scoff escaped his lips before he could stop it. "You know that's not true. Just look at what he's done to this country. To its most vulnerable people!" He shoved his hand through his hair, knocking his cap to the ground. He snatched it up and smashed it back on his head. "What on earth is Chamberlain thinking?"

Fairsworth straightened and poked Rick in the chest. "It is not for us to question what the prime minister chooses to do. Right now we have a new mission vital to ensuring Hitler sticks to his word. Are you in, or are you out?"

Rick's face burned. Spending time with Chaisley and Melanie had made him too bold in his opinions. Good soldiers, good *spies,* only had one purpose—to serve the good of their king, country, and government. "I am in. Forgive my lapse of judgment."

"No forgiveness needed. Now. Listen closely. We know that Germany did not abide under the restraints of the Treaty of Versailles. They've rebuilt their military power, munitions, and communications. While other agents are working on deciphering how the Germans are using wireless communications, we've discovered they are running thousands of miles of cable across the country."

Thousands of miles of cable? Rick closed his eyes. How on earth were they supposed to track that?

Fairsworth must have sensed his exasperation because he let out a laugh. "Daunting, I know. However, I have worked a source— mid-level in the *Heer.* He is looking to escape Germany in the next few months. I'm trying to talk him out of it. His information has been excellent thus far."

He leaned against a tree. "There are communication clusters in railways and depots like these, where they center telecommunications. If those clusters are tampered with or cut, it impacts huge areas throughout the country."

Ah. Well, that was certainly more doable than what he'd been imagining. "So what is my assignment?"

"When you can, escape the pianist in the middle of the night. I have a coded list of several railway depots where these communication clusters might be. My contact was certain that at least seventy-five percent of these depots are hubs." He handed Rick an envelope. "I've decoded half of them for you—find and examine, then sabotage whatever you can. I'll take the other half."

Rick took the packet and slipped it into his jacket pocket. "When do we start?"

Fairsworth smoothed his hair back and glanced at the sky. The clouds were clearing, moonlight streaming through the branches of the trees. "As soon as possible. I've already disabled the communications in the big building behind us. So one down. Hundreds to go. We know that Frappier is slated for another concert in Berlin. It appears Hitler has taken quite a shine to her. Perhaps that distraction can play in our favor. We have a man on the inside there as well, so you would be free to slip away."

Rick's throat went dry. The thought of Chaisley becoming a pawn in Hitler's hands . . .

But he couldn't object. He'd already crossed the line once. If Fairsworth found out he had feelings for his assignment, who knew what would happen to him. Being pulled from his mission would be the least of his worries. "Sounds good."

As Fairsworth pushed away from his nonchalant position, his features were illuminated for the first time since he'd surprised Rick in the woods. He looked every inch the British aristocrat. Older than Rick, fine featured, thin nose, pale skin. Arrogant twist of the lips.

Rick had met his fair share of Fairsworth's kind during training.

"I've heard excellent things about you, Zimmerman. Despite your unfortunate German heritage, you are an exemplary agent."

Nice backhanded compliment. Almost sounded sincere. "I appreciate it, sir."

Fairsworth clapped Rick's shoulder. "Take heart. If all goes as it should, Hitler will have his land. Chamberlain will have a victory. And the world will have peace." He gave Rick a lazy salute and then turned on his heel, melting back into the woods.

Rick fell back against a tree, trying to process everything the other agent had revealed. He loved being a spy. He loved Britain. Supported his government.

Usually.

But his original question came back to haunt him. What was the British government thinking? Did the prime minister truly think that Hitler would lie down and play nice if they gave him another piece of the world?

Everything Rick witnessed in the last few months suggested otherwise. The thousands and thousands of families who had their children ripped from their arms would also disagree. And German Jews, who loved their country but were losing their homes and livelihoods with increasing rapidity, knew better than anyone that Hitler wouldn't be appeased with *some* power.

He wanted it all.

Rick pushed away from the tree and made his way back to the car. Tossing his supplies back in his sack, he sat for a moment, hands on the steering wheel. He would look at the list of sites when he made it back to the hotel. Hopefully he could integrate a few of the locations into delivering children to Chaisley's grandmother.

Chaisley.

He let out a groan and rested his forehead on the wheel, resisting the urge to bang it against the hard metal.

How on earth could he keep news such as this from her?

chapter
FOURTEEN

BERLIN, GERMANY—FRIDAY, AUGUST 5, 1938
PRIVATE CONCERT HALL OF THE FÜHRER

The day she dreaded was here.

The request—no, the *demand*—to return to the concert hall in Berlin for Hitler's special concert had put her on edge for weeks.

When the demand came, Melanie protested. Grandmother protested. Rick protested.

But they all knew she had to do it.

Chaisley had burned the handwritten note after sending her reply. She didn't want any trace of the man in her possession. Somehow burning it felt a little cleansing.

But now? She'd have to face him again.

There was always the chance she was being double-crossed. Had Hitler invited her to make her an example in front of his high-ranking officers?

So far, her facade had held. And she needed it for a little longer. Her fingers trailed across the cool glass of the car window. *Lord, I need Your wisdom. Thank You for Your protection. Please continue to keep us safe.* They'd received contact from several others in Germany who were trying to get children out. Children who were born deaf, blind, missing a limb, or suffering from epilepsy.

All conditions which would put them at risk with the Führer's purification plans. Thank heaven the use of braille in their communications was holding up so far. No one seemed the wiser. Grandmother was certain that mail had been intercepted, but if that were true, the enemy hadn't cracked the code. Otherwise, they'd all be in work camps—or worse—by now.

Her mind went back to the concert where she'd met Adolf Hitler. Leaving the door of his invitation open seemed brave at the time. As if she were capable of doing something so impressive that she would have an opportunity to stop him and his mad plan to take over the world killing millions along the way. How foolish she'd been to put them all at risk. Now that she knew so much more? She wished she could take it back and never agree to it.

But there was no chance of that wish ever coming true. The things she heard each day sickened her.

The news from France and Spain—where they would be headed next—was also grim. Many families knew they couldn't wait to take action. And everyone feared they would hear of Germany attacking Czechoslovakia at any moment.

Who would be next?

Grandmother now had fifteen Jewish people staying with her until she could secure them passage elsewhere.

The four blind students staying with Grandmother refused to leave. Instead, they helped to read the letters that came in from their contacts. Chaisley couldn't blame them for wanting to help. Feeling useful at a time like this was paramount.

As the car rounded a turn, Melanie grabbed onto Chaisley's hand. "We're almost there. Promise me this will be the last concert here? I'm afraid of what will happen to us if we come back."

With a nod, she squeezed her friend's hand. "I promise. I don't like it either. But this seemed necessary to keep up appearances and, hopefully, keep Hitler distracted from our work." She pinched the bridge of her nose. "I only wish I could have met Mr. Otto Weidt, the man with the brush factory, and thank him for what he's doing. But I wouldn't wish to put him or those he employs in danger."

The auto pulled to a stop and Rick's clear voice was aimed at them. "I'm going to park the car and then I will be right beside you the whole time. Both of you." He cleared his throat. "Please wait and take your time going up the steps. I want to catch up with you before you go inside."

Chaisley nodded.

"You don't have to tell me twice." Melanie groaned. "The last thing I want to do is face all those officers without you beside us."

Chaisley took a sharp inhale. "I guess we better go. The sooner I get this over with, the sooner we can leave." She heard the door open, and she scooted toward Melanie's side of the car.

Once they were out and the door was closed, the noise of the engine moved away.

"All right," Melanie whispered close to her. "Rick's almost to the parking lot. If we pretend we're just chatting here for a moment, then take the steps slow, I bet he'll catch up to us before we reach the top."

"Sounds like a great plan." Chaisley shifted her bag containing her music.

"Wait. Don't move. Someone is coming."

She stilled at Melanie's hushed warning, then pretended to smile. "Keep your appearance up. We're just standing here chatting, remember? Perhaps they will simply pass by."

But as the footsteps came closer, Chaisley's insides began to shake.

"Miss Frappier." A man whispered her name. "Please help."

Something crinkled and then footsteps began again, but running away.

Quick steps toward them accompanied those moving away. "Hey, who was that?" Rick's concerned tone was accented by a deep breath.

"I'm not sure." Melanie sounded as confused as Chaisley felt. "But he gave me an envelope."

Chaisley took it and turned around. "Let's go back to the car, where we can read it and then lock it up in the auto if we need to. We've got plenty of time before the concert begins."

"But Herr Hitler is expecting you in less than twenty minutes." Melanie's voice quavered.

"If we're late, we're late. Let him think me a diva. I don't care." She took long strides in the direction she assumed was the parking lot.

"Watch out." Rick gripped her elbow. "There's a step coming up."

The three of them walked to the car side by side, and once they were all inside, they each locked their doors. Chaisley wasted no time opening the envelope. Just like she suspected, it was written in braille. And not just braille—but their code. Which meant that Grandmother or one of Dr. Grafton's contacts must have helped this man reach out to her.

Her fingers quickly scanned the letter and tears burned at the corners of her eyes. She swallowed against the lump growing in her throat. "That man was a teacher. He's hidden twenty-seven young children that are deaf or blind and needs help getting them out of Germany. They've been threatened, and he's afraid they have run out of time. Three sets of the parents went to the Nazi leaders to protest the order that they be sent away to special schools. Those parents were taken to the camps."

"Oh no." Melanie's words came out on a sad sigh. "What about the others?"

"A few of the parents have completely abandoned their children.

Some are trying to get extra jobs to earn enough money to leave. Then there are a few that are Jewish, and the teacher doesn't know where they are or what has happened to them." Bile rose up her throat and Chaisley hated repeating what was on the page. "After the concert this evening, I'll call Dr. G and get his advice." She tapped the paper against her palm. "But we *are* helping those children."

"Give me the letter." Rick's command was soft. "I need to hide it."

She folded it and placed it back in the envelope and then handed it over.

"We better hurry and get inside." Mel's voice sounded much more anxious than it had before. "Like you said, the sooner you perform, the sooner we can leave."

With a nod, she opened her door and waited for her companions to be on each side of her. This time, there was no chatter, just their footsteps as they moved in quick silence to the concert hall.

"Wait here," Melanie instructed, and Chaisley listened to the click of her heels across the floor. Sticking to routine was best. Her assistant would go speak to whomever was in charge and find the place they were to use as a dressing room. Then she would ask about Chaisley warming up on the piano. After that, they would hide out until the concert began.

Except this time, a wrench was thrown in the works.

Hitler demanded to speak to her.

They'd barely made it into the room when the rhythmic thumps of marching boots echoed down the hall.

As it grew louder, she reached for Rick's hand and then Melanie's. "Lord, help us!" The words rushed out.

"Amen." Rick squeezed her hand.

"Quick. Sit in the chair and look like I'm about to do your hair." Mel practically shoved her into the seat.

The rhythm had now turned into thundering steps. They were close. Why had she agreed to this? Her heart pounded so hard she thought for sure it must be visible through her evening gown.

"Breathe, Chais." Rick's lips touched her cheek after his quiet words.

Taking his advice, she breathed deep. Then again. And again.

The marching stopped. "Heil Hitler!" The loud shouts were almost enough to bust down the door.

Why such a racket to simply speak to her? To show his power? To intimidate them?

The loud single knock was superfluous at this point.

"Here we go," Melanie whispered. Three steps to the door. The turn of the knob. "Good evening. How may I help you?"

"Miss Frappier is expecting the Führer." The voice was high-pitched for a man and sounded far too young to be serving as a soldier. "Heil Hitler!"

"We are short on time, Herr Hitler, so I must insist that you don't take up all of Miss Frappier's time."

Where that bravado came from in Melanie, Chaisley wasn't sure, but she wanted to cheer her friend on.

"Fräulein Frappier." The voice of Hitler. A man she'd come to despise. Hate even. "It is wonderful to see you again."

Every word grated on her skin. But she lifted a hand to him, knuckles up. "Good evening." She couldn't even bring herself to speak his name.

And then . . . he touched her. Took her hand in his and kissed the back of it.

At least the man could pretend he had the manners of good society. Old society. Before war had torn up the world. She pulled her hand back.

"Thank you for coming to perform for us tonight. This will be a gift to my men and most trusted supporters. There are intense days ahead, and I know this will be a boost to them."

Intense days? She couldn't thank him for inviting her. Couldn't say she was excited to be here. What *could* she say? "It will be a privilege to play the impeccable instrument I hear you have acquired."

"The best of the best." Pride oozed from his tone, and she imagined the tiny mustache above his lip doing a little dance as he congratulated himself for taking it.

"Fräulein." He stepped closer, and she could once again smell his putrid breath. "In a few months, we will have much to celebrate. I wish you to return the middle of November for that." It wasn't a question. It wasn't a request. Hitler wished it and she was supposed to acquiesce.

She snapped her fingers and turned her head away from the man. "Melanie! Check my schedule, please." Pretending she was a diva gave her a moment to stall.

Always quick on her feet, especially these last few weeks, Melanie sounded like she was digging in a bag and going over papers. "Miss Frappier will be in Amsterdam the middle of November."

"Plans can be changed. She will play for me again on the fifteenth of November." His voice turned away from Chaisley. Then steps. "Please play my favorites tonight, Fräulein."

Shuffling, steps. Then the marching started down the hall again. The door clicked shut. Then locked.

"I don't like it." Rick squeezed Chaisley's shoulders. "I don't like it at all. Celebration? What does he have planned?"

She didn't like it either. "I guess that's the reason he demanded to speak to me today? At this point, he won't take no for an answer, so we will simply pretend to go along with it. Somehow."

"Chais, I think it's time we discuss ending the tour early. You can pretend all you want that you'll return, but I don't think we should come back."

Melanie's firm words resonated within her. She was right.

To come back here would be foolish.

Maybe even fatal.

Four hours later, she'd performed and then endured Hitler's long-winded speech about the best of the best and the pride of Germany.

He even went so far as to explain to the entire audience that she was born perfect and was of *superior* German lineage. Her injuries were the cause of an accident and were the proof that people of the *superior* race were better than everyone else. Look what she had overcome, and look at how her talent was incomparable.

It sickened her. But as the roar of the crowd grew with every *superior*, she kept a smile pasted in place and resolved that she would not let this man win. No matter what she had to do.

When Melanie and Rick finally escorted her offstage to the dressing room, Chaisley vomited. Ten showers wouldn't wash away how disgusting it was to be in Adolf Hitler's presence.

The man emanated pure evil.

Melanie lifted the wet towel from her neck. "We need to get back to the hotel as soon as possible. I can't stand to be here."

"Me neither."

"I'll go get the car." Rick didn't sound too happy either. And why would he be? The entire evening had kept them all on edge. "Will you be okay here by yourselves? We could always walk out together."

"It'll be fine. I can help Chaisley change, and we'll be out in a jiffy." Mel wiped down Chaisley's face again. "I'm so sorry about all this. I wish I could fix it."

As the door opened and closed, Chaisley slumped in her chair. "That first time I played with him in the audience, I'd been so arrogant to think that I could do something big to stop him. Now that—"

Slam!

Was that the door busted open?

"Give me your bag. It must be searched before you leave here."

Who on earth? That forceful, arrogant voice had to belong to a Nazi.

Melanie stomped over toward the voice. "Excuse me, but you have *no* right to be in here."

"I am a Nazi officer with orders. You will do as I say!"

Shuffling. Then more footsteps.

"How *dare* you? Get your hands off me!" No fear in Melanie's tone, only rage.

Smack!

Had Mel slapped him?

"Get out of my way, woman." The man hissed the command. Had *he* hit Melanie?

It sounded like he was turning over furniture as he stormed toward Chaisley. "Is this all you have with you?"

"She's a concert pianist. It's her *music,* you fool."

Chaisley restrained a full-on laugh. Melanie had become a roaring lion!

Papers rustled as he apparently dug in Chaisley's bag.

Her breath hitched, but she willed herself to stay cal—

Oh no! She'd left a partially composed letter to Grandmother in that bag! It gave details about the last group of children they'd rescued. It was in braille code, but . . . what if . . . ? Bounding to her feet, she placed her hands on her hips. "I demand that you return my music to me at once. I will speak to Herr Hitler about this intrusion! Your behavior is atrocious."

Her bag was shoved into her hands. "You don't fool me, pianist. We know you're up to something. My superior works for the Führer, and he doesn't trust you. So neither do I!" Quick stomps and then the door slammed.

"We've got to get out of here, *now!*" Melanie grabbed her hand and dragged her out the door.

Chaisley stumbled behind her trying to keep up. When they made it to the car, she practically fell into it.

"What's happened?" Rick sounded panicked.

"Drive. *Hurry.*" Melanie wrapped an arm around her shoulder and pulled her close.

Back at the hotel, Chaisley couldn't stop shaking. Did that

Nazi know where they were? Would he come after them here? She grabbed Rick's hand. "Let's drive away from the city. Find a small hotel somewhere else. And make sure we aren't followed."

The exhaustion in them all was palpable, but they agreed her plan was the best. When they reached a quaint hotel and checked in with two adjoining rooms, Chaisley was beyond anxious to speak to Dr. Grafton. She picked up the telephone in her room. "Rick, would you stay with Mel and me for a moment? Just until I finish this call?"

"Of course." It sounded like he hadn't left the door. Was he guarding it?

She put the call through to her grandmother's. She hated waking the house, but she needed to ask about the visas for Mary Beth and Geraldine. Because she couldn't stand to stay here much longer. Not after tonight. It was a risk to ask about the visas over the phone, but maybe if she switched up languages, she could throw off anyone listening in.

Were the mother and daughter all right? It was too risky to visit them at their hotel. Chaisley drew too much attention, but to know she was in the same city and couldn't do anything to help them yet broke her heart.

When Dr. G answered, she spoke as vaguely as she could. A sentence or two in Dutch, then switched to Hungarian, then to French, then to English. Using a few code words along the way.

"I'll be there tomorrow." Dr. G's voice was gravelly in his French response. "The flowers older than a fortnight need to be exchanged."

So. Those old enough to be sterilized needed to leave immediately. The Gestapo were only growing bolder in their arrests. There was no way they would stop searching for them. "I'll ask the driver if he can make a trip tonight."

"Good. No need to wait for me. I'd love to visit the hotel where you are staying."

In other words, get out as soon as she could, and leave a coded letter at the hotel with details.

He switched to Hungarian. "I've learned there are many new groceries I'd like to pick up. I may stay several weeks, but will try to be back by the time you return at the beginning of November."

She longed to tell him about what happened. To pour out her worries and fears. But she couldn't. It wasn't safe.

For any of them.

"God be with you," she whispered in English.

"And you, my child. I love you and how brave you are."

She hung up the phone and sucked in a breath. *Was* she brave enough to keep going? As her whole body shook, she couldn't stop the tears.

RICK GRIPPED THE STEERING WHEEL and rounded a sharp curve. The towering forest on either side of the road kept any moonlight from hitting the pavement. His palms were slick with sweat. All of his training was to extract information. Get in and out of buildings without detection. Blend in and hear things people thought were secret.

But this mission had become so much more than spying for Britain. God, in His wisdom, had given him a greater purpose in helping those the enemy wanted to destroy. He glanced in the rearview mirror. The weight of responsibility for these six young people with him tonight put his nerves at a level he hadn't experienced since his first mission. But that was nothing compared to the tension that gripped him when he thought about Chaisley. His most precious cargo was in the grip of the Nazi regime.

His chest tightened.

Was Chaisley safe? Was Mel? Would that Nazi officer come looking for them again? Rick's throat tightened and he cleared it. No use asking questions when he had no answers. Right now, the best thing he could do was pray for them, as he knew they were doing for him. *Please, Lord, protect them. Give them wisdom. Keep them safe.*

It was the same prayer he prayed every time he left. With so many around them losing their livelihood, homes, and even their lives, it was difficult to know the right words to ask the Lord to intervene. That was the beauty of prayer, though. God knew, even if he couldn't articulate it well.

He drove up a small hill and caught a white marker on the side of the road. Some of the tension left his shoulders. Only two miles to the Netherlands. Celestia should be at their meeting point, seven miles past the border.

"We're almost there." His voice was hoarse from lack of use.

"Praise God!" One of the young women breathed the words out in a prayer.

The teenaged boy in the front seat reached out and touched his arm. "You're a good driver, Mr. Rick. I haven't gotten sick one time."

Rick smiled. "Thank you, George. I'm glad to hear it."

The car fell silent once more, and he maneuvered the vehicle around the last corner before the border.

Bright headlights blinded his vision. In the distance, he could make out the shadows of a blockade and two large military vehicles.

A new checkpoint was blocking their path to freedom.

Oh, Lord, please help us. The plan had been to cross where there wasn't one, so he hadn't prepared the kids. This could be disastrous.

Rick looked at his passengers in the rearview mirror. "All of you, listen to me. There is a checkpoint here. They are going to ask us questions and want to see papers. I have the papers Miss Melanie gave us and will talk to the officers. I need you all to pretend like you are asleep." He licked his lips and took a deep breath, trying to keep any hint of fear from his voice. "If they talk loud or touch you, act like you're waking up from a deep sleep. Do you understand?"

"Yes, sir," the kids responded in unison.

"Good. Do not talk to them unless I tell you to. I'll call you by name if you need to respond." Rick tapped his finger on the steering wheel and slowed. "I'm approaching now. Let's ask the Lord to give us wisdom."

The kids all bowed their heads and prayed.

The teens settled and Rick rolled toward the checkpoint, stopping just short of the German officer in front of Rick's vehicle.

A young man came to the driver's door and tapped the window. "Heil Hitler. Show me your papers."

Rick leaned over and opened the glove box. He grabbed the envelope with the papers. The children had falsified passports and names, but after much debate, the group decided to keep his papers the same for this trip.

He handed the envelope to the soldier, who pulled them out, the envelope fluttering away in the breeze. He took his time, reading each passport, each document with care. After an eternity, he folded the papers and passed them back to Rick.

"Why are you going to the Netherlands at this time of night?" His eyes looked black in the shadows.

Rick lowered his voice. "Please, keep your voice low. The children are sleeping. We are driving home from Berlin. The children have lost their parents, and I am driving them to their grandmother. We have been traveling all day."

The soldier looked across Rick at the boy and then glanced to the back seat. He said nothing, but his gaze was relentless. Rick knew the tactic well. Glare. Say nothing. Make your mark nervous. Most civilians couldn't stand the silence and would begin blabbering.

Rick stayed calm. He began to tap a rhythm on the steering wheel. "Is there a problem?"

The light caught the young man's eyes, and Rick suppressed a shudder. They were the coldest eyes he'd encountered in a long while.

They narrowed as they locked on his face. "Do I know you?"

244

Had his cover been blown? He affected a lazy shrug. "I don't know. I do get that a lot. Must be a common face." Rick let out a chuckle.

"No." The word hung between them. "What is this uniform you are wearing?" His torch beamed into the car, up and down Rick's clothing. "You are a chauffeur."

He said it like Rick had a disease.

"I am."

The soldier stepped back. "Out of the vehicle. Now."

Rick clenched his jaw and turned off the car. Slowly he eased out of the auto, feeling the press of his firearm against the small of his back. The last thing he wanted was to have to use it. These children deserved more than a Nazi hospital of horrors or listening to a shootout in the middle of nowhere. Though considering what had happened to some of their friends, he knew they'd already experienced some of the terrors of the impending war.

But he would do everything in his power not to add to it.

"Now. Tell me again why you are traveling to the Netherlands at night." The man couldn't have been more than twenty-one years old, but he was the epitome of a Nazi soldier. Fit. Strong. Unyielding.

Rick held his hands up, palms facing his interrogator. "I am driving these children to their grandmother. Their parents passed away just a few days ago. I—"

"Christoph! Have you finished? We are needed at—" The soldier skidded to a stop beside the other young man, his eyes wide. "Hey. Aren't you with that pianist? I saw you in Berlin. Aren't you her bodyguard?"

Rick tamped down the surprise that shot through him. "I am her chauffeur. But tonight, I am doing a personal favor for her while she plays for the Führer. As I was telling your fellow guard here, these children are being delivered to their grandmother. They've just lost their parents. Miss Frappier has asked me to see to this matter. *Personally.*"

The soldier named Christoph looked at Rick. "Ah. You work

for Germany's pride. The pianist. Why did you not say so in the beginning?"

His comrade shoved his shoulder, stopping any response Rick might have made. "Christoph, leave him be, and let him pass. The general needs you now. We are being sent back to Berlin. Trouble is brewing."

The young man nodded and glanced at Rick. "You may cross the border."

The two men left, and Rick hopped in the car and twisted the key, the vehicle roaring to life. Jerking the gear stick into drive, he drove through the now open border, holding his breath until they were on the other side and out of sight of the soldiers.

"Thank You, Jesus." The words burst out of him once the dark enshrouded them again.

Hannah's hand landed on his shoulder, and he started.

"Oh. I am sorry. I only meant to say you were wonderful back there. And the Lord was watching out for us."

George nodded. "I was praying so hard. And God heard!"

Rick let out a breathy chuckle. "Indeed He did."

Fifteen minutes later, the children were ensconced in Celestia's car, ready to head back to her home. Ready for a chance at a new life.

As was their protocol, they exchanged letters of information but did not speak above a whisper. Rick filled Chaisley's grandmother in on the new checkpoint.

"When I get back to Berlin, I will talk with Chais and Mel. We will have to find another way into the Netherlands. One that isn't such a main road." He gave Celestia a grim smile. "I pray your trip home is a safe one."

Celestia patted Rick's cheek, her hand warm against his skin. How long had it been since he'd felt the warm touch of a mother or a grandmother?

His eyes burned.

Too long.

"May God continue to protect you, Rick. Give the girls my love."

He gave her a short nod and strode back to his car. At least it was dark, so no one could see the tears streaming down his face. He pulled out his kerchief and wiped away the moisture.

Oh, if his friends saw him now, the ribbing he would take. The thought sobered him. Where were all of his friends? Those he'd trained with had spread across Europe, filling out their intelligence network. Were any of them still alive?

Swiping a hand across his face, Rick pushed the thoughts away. Now that the kids were safely across the border, Rick had one more mission.

He drove back toward the border, relieved to see the checkpoint was still open. No soldiers stood about, and the two military vehicles that had been there half an hour ago were gone.

A single soldier walked out as Rick drove to the border and must have recognized the vehicle and waved him through.

Thanking the Lord for His mercy, Rick sped back into Germany.

Another half an hour into his journey, he turned toward a railway station. Killing the headlights, he rolled slowly forward, his gaze darting over it.

Though the intelligence wasn't clear on exactly which communication hubs were permanent and which were moving, Rick's recent source had been adamant that this station had recently been outfitted as a permanent hub.

Parking his car a block from the station and away from any streetlights, he slipped out of his chauffeur uniform and pulled a black sweater on. A dark cap covered his blond hair. He grabbed his rucksack and exited the car, darting in and out of shadows to the depot. Nearing the east wall, he crouched and settled his breathing, listening for any sounds of disturbance.

Nothing. No sound at all.

He slipped to the back of the building and paused again. There was no light back there, and it took some time for his eyes to adjust. Shadows began to form, and soon he could make out the shape of a generator at the back of the building.

He slid his hand along the rough siding of the building, inching his way toward the power source. If his intel was correct, there was a box on the other side of this generator containing a mass of wires. All he had to do was cut and shred the lines and then get out.

The grass swished around his feet as he rounded the generator and spotted the large metal box. A silver lock glinted in the small shaft of moonlight. Rick set his pack down and fished out his lock-picking kit. Within a minute, the soft *snick* of metal releasing from metal let him know he'd succeeded.

Removing the lock, Rick lifted the metal lid, wincing at the groaning of the hinges. He paused and waited again. When he heard no footsteps, he put the lid to the side. He fished the small torch out of the side pocket of his sack and held it low over the box. The soft glow illuminated the cluster of telephone wires, and a shiver raced down his arms.

He'd found it.

Rick unsheathed the small, sharp knife he kept hidden in his boot and sliced through the wires. He grinned. There was nothing like the satisfaction of a sharp knife slicing through wires and ultimately scrambling German communications. He removed large chunks of the wires and then lit a match and tossed it in. He could revel later. Right now, he needed to get this box back together and get on the road.

Five minutes later, he made it back to the car. He slid in, tossed his rucksack on the passenger seat, turned on the car, and headed back to the main highway to Berlin. When no lights flashed in his mirror and no German military vehicles came speeding up behind him, Rick released a long breath, and a smile turned up the corner of his lips.

Mission accomplished.

For tonight, anyway.

But it wouldn't stop the Nazis for long.

SO SOMEONE WAS RESCUING disabled children and sending them away. The irony.

It was almost laughable. The Führer *wanted* to rid Germany of the infestation of the Jews and the inferiority of those who were a drain on society. This so-called rescue helped their cause. Let them take the little rats away.

Twice, he'd been informed of the border crossings. Twice, it had been after one of the pianist's concerts in Berlin. And twice, it had been her driver with the disgusting little refugees.

It wasn't that hard to put two and two together.

At this point, he didn't care about those fleeing. Let them leave. It would make his job easier later.

But if Miss Chaisley Frappier—who'd played at the Führer's request and been his guest—was involved . . . he would humiliate her, strip away her fame, and use her as an example for the future.

Soon the time would come to bring her to her knees. When all the world was watching.

The Führer would applaud him taking the initiative.

Once Hitler took over in Europe, they'd dispose of those unworthy of life properly. Preparations were already being made.

For now he had a different job to do.

But he'd be watching the pianist.

chapter
FIFTEEN

What used to be one of her favorite cities was now another re-minder that Hitler was on the prowl. Chaisley had hoped for an escape, but no matter how much they tried for normal, reality followed them.

She sat in the auto listening to the sounds of the evening as she and Melanie waited for Dr. Grafton. Since they'd been here, they'd helped care and transport for more than fifty blind and deaf children. Some, their parents had abandoned. Some, their parents had been taken away. And some had been trying to live on their own for months.

Since she and Melanie were relatively safe in France, Rick had asked for a couple days off to take care of some of his SIS work. He'd said he didn't want to put them in danger—which only meant that what he set out to do for the SIS *was* dangerous. It wasn't her favorite idea, but they could manage. Melanie could drive. And Dr. G was bringing the children to them so they'd have his help as well.

Still, it didn't feel right without Rick here.

What that said about her feelings for him was something she'd have to examine at another time. The crunch of wheels on gravel reached her ears.

A car door shut, then footsteps. "It's good to see you, Chais." Dr. G's rich voice through the open window calmed her insides.

She got out of the car and gave him a big hug. "It's good to be seen."

He released her but held her shoulders. "You look weary, my dear."

"I fear this has taken a toll on me, but we must soldier on and do what we can."

"Are you certain you are all right?" He was good at prodding.

"I'll be fine. The work we are doing is more important."

"Mmhm"—he cleared his throat—"when I see you again in a few days, we're going to talk about it. Whether you like it or not."

"I had a feeling you would say that. But for now, we need to get the children to their new home."

"You win. For now." His steps accompanied the light laughter she heard from him.

Several moments later, five children were loaded into their car. None of them had any belongings with them whatsoever. They must have had the clothes on their back and nothing else.

"Everyone ready?"

Melanie's voice came from the driver's seat.

*Yes*es echoed through the vehicle, and it slowly moved forward.

When they reached the farm on the outskirts of Paris, Chaisley said a brief hello to the farmer and his wife and hugged each of the kids.

Back in the car, she felt relief that another group was sheltered, but her heart still ached that this was necessary in the first place.

How long could they keep this up?

Leaning her head against the cool glass of the window, she sighed. That was her exhaustion speaking. Not her heart.

Back at their hotel, Melanie parked the car.

"I need some fresh air, Mel."

"Me too. Want to take a short walk before retiring for the night?"

"That sounds lovely." Chaisley exited the vehicle and stretched in the cool night air.

They kept a leisurely pace down the sidewalk for a couple of minutes. Mel was probably lost in her own thoughts like Chaisley. The past few weeks had a different feel than ever before. Heavy. Burdensome.

"We're coming to a corner. Let's head to the right."

"Sounds good." Chaisley nodded.

Thick hands grabbed her arms and slammed her up against a wall.

"Mel?" she squeaked, but a large hand covered her mouth.

"We know who you are." The voice was gravelly.

Chaisley writhed against her captor, and she could feel Melanie doing the same beside her. Mel's hand grabbed hers.

"Where did you take those children?"

She was pushed harder into the wall, but with a hand covering her face, she couldn't have responded even if she wanted to. Were these Gestapo? In France? Certainly they had no power here . . . did they?

"Well?"

Whoever held Mel must have removed their hand from her mouth because it was her voice next. "What children? I don't know what you're talking about."

"Don't play innocent with me." *Smack!* "We've been watching you for two days."

"I'm not playing innocent. I sincerely don't know what you're talking about. Perhaps you have us confused with someone else." How could Mel keep her voice so calm?

The one holding Chaisley loosened his grip. Just a little more and she could cry out for help. She'd heard other footsteps close, surely someone would come to their aid.

When the hand over her mouth relaxed a tiny bit, she bit him. Hard.

Then she screamed for all she was worth.

Whistles blew, and running footsteps approached.

In seconds, her captor was no longer holding her.

Chaisley's arms ached from the intense grip he'd had on her.

"What's happening?" she whispered toward Mel.

"The French police are arresting them."

"*Vous allez bien, mesdemoiselles?*"

"*Merci.* A little bruised, but I think we are fine." Melanie had ahold of her arm. "Let's get back."

"Wait. Who were they?"

"Disgusting Nazis," one of the policemen explained. "They do not belong in our fine city."

As the two of them walked back to their flat, Chaisley couldn't stop the shaking that took over. "You don't think those Nazi spies told their superiors yet, do you?"

"No. You should have seen them. Too eager and wanting to impress. No. Their goal was to parade us into Germany and gain applause. I'm sure of it. We're almost there." Mel's arm around her shoulder was the only thing holding her upright, and the confidence in her words bolstered Chaisley.

"I'm fine. It just shook me up, that's all." She straightened. As long as her secret work was safe.

"Don't lie to me. It scared at least ten years off my life."

"What on earth were those Nazis doing here?"

"Spying on us, that's what. They obviously have a presence here, even though most people probably don't know that. I think we need to tell Dr. G that he needs to be on his guard."

FRIDAY, SEPTEMBER 2, 1938

Melanie took a deep breath, the morning's conversation running through her mind.

"You ladies need some fresh air. How about a picnic?" Rick's words had still held tension, even through his forced smile.

"No." She'd snapped. "Can't the world see what's going on? I'm not going to risk Chaisley's life for a stupid picnic."

Not only had she practically yelled the words across the room, but she'd said them with such venom that no one said a word for several minutes.

"First, we're going to have a long overdue chat." Chaisley moved over and sat closer. "Second, we're going to go on a stupid picnic. Fresh air and a bit of normalcy will be good for all of us."

She'd balked. But Chais won. And she'd been correct. They'd spent two hours hashing out their feelings about all that happened, all they'd seen, and the toll it was taking on them emotionally. It had been cleansing.

Mel came to the conclusion that bottling it all up didn't make her stronger, it didn't help her ignore it better. It made her hurt worse.

A smile stretched across her face now. Their little trio had gone through a lot together the past months. They'd come to trust one another in a way she'd never trusted anyone else.

Lives were on the line. That changed everything.

They decided to enjoy some time at a café instead of a picnic and made new promises to each other and new routines. The weight of their underground work and what they faced had bogged them all down until melancholy moods prevailed. Starting each day with prayer was a wonderful thing, but when the requests were all so dire, it was hard to be positive.

Chaisley suggested they pray together as a team and then sing some uplifting hymns of praise. It had lifted all of their spirits.

Out in the fresh air, Melanie could think straight again. "I can't think of anything that smells better than freshly baked bread. Unless it's a freshly baked croissant." She bit into the aforementioned bakery item, flakes falling to her plate. She closed her eyes, savoring the layers of butter and pastry.

"I agree with you." Chaisley sighed, dabbing her lips with her linen napkin. "England has many wonderful things about it. But no one does pastries like the French."

"Or coffee." Rick took a long sip from his mug.

Melanie let out a chuckle and lifted her cup. "Hear, hear." She sipped her café au lait. Why did everything taste better in Paris? It wasn't her first time in the famed city, but each visit seemed to unlock more beauty. More delights. More delicious foods.

Her eyes drifted from their table in the small sidewalk café to the street. People greeted friends and hailed taxis. A large flower cart was situated on the corner, filling the air with the scent of hydrangeas and roses. A trio of women walked past, their chatter and laughter filling the café. Chaisley must be having a field day hearing French spoken properly. The language was like a song, lilting and rolling with fabulous flourishes. While Melanie was fluent, at times the appropriate emphasis on certain vowels and *r*s in the back of the throat were still a challenge.

"That was a happy sigh."

Chaisley's voice drew Melanie from her thoughts. She took another sip before responding. "There's just something about Paris. The food, the culture, the museums. It's my favorite city outside of London."

Chaisley gave her a grin. "It's good to hear the smile in your voice again, my friend."

It *felt* good to smile again. The last few months had taken a toll on all of them. Story after story. Face after face. Though a few had found freedom from Nazi terror, there were still so many who needed their help.

"For such a time as this . . ."

The verse echoed through her again, now a part of the fabric of her heart. Her prayers. Never had she felt so honored to walk alongside others as she did in the work they were doing with Chaisley's grandmother and Dr. Grafton. The Lord had been so good to them in the midst of danger and uncertainty.

And though He would undoubtedly bring others to them, the brief respite from logistics and Chaisley's performances was a welcome one.

She drained the last of her coffee and settled the cup on the saucer. Looking at her friends with a smile, she leaned forward. "I think we should visit a few fun sites before going to the *Palais Garnier*. What do you think?"

Chaisley nodded. "It's been so long since I've been here. It would be lovely to walk in a park or go to the Louvre. Even to walk around the base of the Eiffel Tower. I feel like it would do all of us some good."

Rick tossed his napkin on the table and stood. "I agree. I'm sorry for my tense attitude of late—I know, it can't be helped, but I do apologize for pestering you, Melanie."

"I'm sorry, too. I shouldn't have snapped like I did. The stress of it all has just been a bit too much, I guess."

Chaisley's grin was lovely to see. "It's wonderful to hear my two favorite people getting along again." She dipped her chin and leaned in over the table. "I know this hasn't been easy. But thank you both for all you've done."

Melanie winked at Rick and mouthed *favorite* as she pointed to him.

Rick's eyes sparkled as he bounced his eyebrows up and down. "I'll pull the car around. You ladies figure out where you want to go first."

Melanie glanced at her best friend. A soft smile played at Chaisley's lips and Melanie resisted the urge to chuckle.

"I can feel you staring at me." Chaisley wiped at her chin. "Do I have croissant on my face?"

"Oh no. You just look . . . besotted. That's all."

A rosy flush crept into Chaisley's cheeks. "I do not."

Melanie let her laughter out in full force. Her friend looked so bashful and adorable. "You do. And that is perfectly acceptable!"

She grabbed Chaisley's hand and gave it a squeeze. "If it makes you feel any better, Rick looks the exact same way when he thinks no one is watching."

The dreamy look was back. "Really?"

"Would I lie to you? Oh, let's talk about it later. Rick just pulled up." Melanie stood and helped Chaisley stand from the table. "Fifteen paces to the curb. Then the same four-inch drop to the street to get in the car."

They made their way to the waiting vehicle. Rick held the door open, aiding both women down the curb and into the car. Once everyone was situated, he turned and looked at them, his eyebrows high on his forehead. "Well. Where are we headed?"

Melanie bit her lip. "I liked Chais's idea of walking around the Eiffel Tower. There are so many pretty spots with sidewalks, and that reflecting pool is lovely."

Chaisley nodded, and Rick pulled into traffic.

Paris sped past her window, people and landmarks blurring as they navigated a roundabout. And then, there it was.

The Eiffel Tower, drawing closer and closer.

She leaned back in her seat, closing her eyes for just a moment. When was the last time she felt this much peace? Wouldn't it be lovely if she could capture this moment in a bottle, like one of those fancy perfumes sold in the high-end shops in their hotel?

It would be in a pale pink bottle, the color of a pink rose just as it blooms. It would have a crystal stopper and when she opened it, the fragrance of croissants and café au laits and roses would waft over her.

Her brow furrowed. Probably not the best combination of smells. And what a strange thought anyway.

She smiled and shook her head. Flights of fancy about sweet memories in pretty bottles . . . goodness, it was like she was eleven years old all over again.

"Mel, we're here."

Melanie's eyes popped open and she lifted her head. "I must have dozed for just a minute."

Chaisley patted her hand. "At least you didn't snore."

"I do *not* snore." She gave Chaisley's hand a soft pinch.

They exited the car, giggling.

"I'll park the car and join you in a few." Rick tossed Mel a light salute from the brim of his hat.

"Now"—Melanie released the word on a sigh and pulled Chaisley's arm through her own—"back to Rick."

Chaisley smacked her arm as she laughed. "Stop. He'll be back any moment."

"He's good for you."

"I think so too." Her smile diminished. "But these aren't exactly easy times. I—"

"Don't. Don't worry about bad timing, or how he works for the SIS and you're a concert pianist, or any other excuse. Don't doubt what you two feel. Just promise me you'll tell me the minute you're completely in love with him. Okay?" As if it wasn't obvious that her best friend was already halfway there.

Chaisley paused her steps. She bit her lip. "All right. I promise."

"Good. Now, do you remember anything about our first visit here?"

Chaisley lifted her face toward the sun, closing her eyes. "Only that it was heavenly. Describe it for me."

Melanie let her eyes take in the scene before her. Large walkways framed a shallow reflecting pool and on this warm September day, the tower was perfectly reflected in the water. On the outskirts of the walkways were large swaths of grass that led to the groves of trees shrouding the small park. One particular pathway led under the tower, and Melanie could see the large field of grass where families were picnicking.

As she described the scene to Chaisley, Rick approached.

An idea struck Melanie, and she gave her friend a sweet grin.

"Rick, would you mind walking with Chaisley for a bit? I see a street vendor and would like to get some postcards to send back to the manor."

Rick's eyes twinkled in the sunlight. "It would be my pleasure." He tucked Chaisley's hand in the crook of his arm and led her down one of the walkways. It wasn't long before their heads were drawn together in conversation. Good. Perhaps this would be one more friendly shove toward accepting that they belonged together.

Melanie bought her postcards but took her time catching up to the couple. The chance to stroll and take everything in was too tempting to pass up. Oh, she loved being with Chaisley. Helping her navigate each new situation, building, and city had taught Melanie so much. What an honor to help her friend not only share her talent with the world, but also simply live her life as unhindered as possible by her blindness.

But now that Rick knew how to help Chaisley and took great pleasure in doing so, Melanie relaxed. She had time to stroll. To pray. And she had so much to thank the Lord for. Thus far their travels had been good, relatively free from danger and invasive German checkpoints. Especially once they recognized the world-famous pianist in the car. But after the Nazi soldier burst into the dressing room at Hitler's private concert, and then the two that had been watching them here in France, they were all prepared for much worse in the near future. *Please continue to strengthen us. And lead us in Your will.*

Mel stayed twenty to thirty paces behind her friends, letting the sun warm her skin. She hadn't felt this good since—

Her stomach dropped.

No. Please, Lord. Please keep the memories of that horrible night at bay.

But they rolled through her mind like a film strip. She shivered and fought the tears gathering in her eyes. She would not let those horrid memories ruin a perfect day. She was fine. Unharmed. Rick had gotten there just in time.

But Melanie couldn't stop her eyes from darting to the left and right as she hurried to catch up with Rick and Chaisley.

"Are you all having a good time?" She prayed the note of cheer in her voice slipped past Chaisley's internal lie detector.

Rick raised an eyebrow at her, but Melanie shook her head and slipped her arm around Chaisley's.

"It's been wonderful. I feel so refreshed." Chaisley tipped her face toward Melanie. "Did you get your postcards?"

"I did. I'm sure your grandmother will love the picture I found of the Arc de Triomphe. And an update as to how we're all doing."

Chaisley nodded as the trio came to a stop in front of the Eiffel Tower. The sight of it took Melanie's breath away. As she described it to her friend, Rick shifted beside Chaisley and Melanie saw his gaze fixed on something in the distance. She tried to follow where he was looking but saw nothing.

"Are you ladies all right here for a bit? I need to run a quick errand before I forget."

An errand? Now? Melanie's brows drew together, and she opened her mouth to protest, but Chaisley spoke up first.

"Of course. We can walk the green and meet back in a half hour. By then we'll probably need lunch."

Rick smiled and pulled the keys from his pocket. "Perfect." He strode away from them.

Melanie frowned. Where was he off to? And why was he still looking back and forth like someone was following him? He'd promised to tell them the truth, but she had the distinct impression he'd just broken that promise.

"Mel? Are you ready to walk?"

She looked at Chaisley. Wait. Had she not heard the discomfort in Rick's voice? Or sensed how quickly his demeanor had changed? Melanie licked her lips and forced a smile. "I'm ready if you are.

While we walk, let's discuss which of your new pieces you want to debut at the Palais Garnier."

Chaisley's face lit up, and she began discussing her ideas. Melanie cast one last glance over her shoulder.

Rick was gone.

Well, when he got back, she would make sure he answered every question she had about what was happening.

And if he'd just broken his promise to them.

THURSDAY, SEPTEMBER 29, 1938

Minister Chamberlain was still trying for peace. Rick shook his head. Why the world thought they could negotiate with a man like Hitler was beyond him. Mussolini and Count Ciano from Italy had joined the prime minister in Munich along with the French Premier Monsieur Daladier for meetings to discuss how to move forward and keep the world from another war.

Everyone knew Hitler had been rearming Germany—which was in clear violation of the Treaty of Versailles. He'd occupied the Rhineland and taken Austria. He wasn't keeping it a secret that he wanted Czechoslovakia. Could these other leaders actually accomplish peace with such a man? Who said he wouldn't defy another treaty?

Rick didn't think peace was possible at this point. But after a coded phone call with his superiors back in England, Rick walked back to the flats where he was staying along with Melanie and Chaisley. They'd been able to secure an entire floor of apartments, which gave them a bit of security and privacy.

His shoulders felt weighed down. For several weeks, Melanie had pestered him in private about what he was up to. Reminded him that he'd promised to be honest with them. And he had been. Even assuring Melanie that it was his work and that was all he could share.

So he hadn't told them everything. Surely they would understand that being a spy for the British government meant he had to keep some secrets. It wasn't like he could go blabbing about the plans in place to stop the Nazis.

But Melanie continued to be suspicious of him. Every time he left them. Not that he could blame her.

He hated negative thoughts. Pessimism. And yet, here he was, a cynic. Worried that Chaisley was thinking the worst of him. Dreading the outcome of these meetings.

Mr. Grand had put Section D in motion—which was the right thing to do—and Rick worked his part with others across the continent. Which meant the possibility that he would be pulled from his job as Chaisley's driver grew into a bigger possibility every day. And where would that leave them?

The men he spoke with today seemed optimistic that all would be right with the world after these negotiations in Munich and they wouldn't need to implement anything else.

Rick found that hard to believe. Although God was in the business of doing impossible things.

When the elevator reached the top floor, he pulled out the key to his flat.

"Rick!" Chaisley called from down the hall. "Come have dinner with us."

His stomach rumbled and he smiled. "Dinner sounds great." Maybe it would help him get rid of this mood. "Let me get cleaned up and I'll be right there."

When he walked back out of his flat a quarter of an hour later, the smells in the hallway made his mouth water.

He knocked on Chaisley's door, and it opened almost immediately.

"Come on in." Melanie pointed toward the table. "We ordered a veritable feast."

"It smells like it." He spotted Chaisley and he couldn't contain his smile. What that woman did to him . . . wow.

But instead of greeting him with a smile, deep lines creased her forehead, and her mouth turned down.

"What's wrong?" He was at her side in an instant.

"While we were waiting for you, I was checking up on all the letters we've sent. There are a number of contacts who haven't responded."

That was odd. He studied the stacks in front of her. "Haven't we always received a response?"

"Yes. That's what bothers me." She ran her fingers over the braille on the sheet to her right. "As of right now, there are five who haven't written back. One, I worry about their safety. Two, what happened to the letters or what kept them from responding?"

He placed his hands on his hips and shook his head. "It was too good to be true to think that the Nazis weren't paying attention to our correspondence. But at this point, I think it's best to assume that someone has caught on and those letters have been intercepted."

Melanie's eyes widened as she sat at the table. "That's an awful thought." She shivered. "No offense, Rick, but I don't like the idea of spies. Well, the bad guys having spies."

"Me neither." He took the chair next to Chaisley. "All right, so let's hash this out. How easy would it be for them to read what you've sent out?"

She leaned back in her chair. "They'd have to have someone who was an expert in braille. Someone who had studied all the different dot languages from the beginning. Frankly, now that I'm saying it out loud again, I don't think there are very many that could do that. Especially not those who would willingly help the Nazis."

"What you're saying is that they probably can't decode anything. Right? At best, they might have a few snippets of information?"

She nodded. "I think it's time we switched all correspondence to all contacts over to only using the musical braille code I developed. It's much harder to decipher, and they'd have to have not only someone who understood braille, but someone who has a working knowledge of all the facets of music, and musical braille on top of that. Then that person would have to figure out my system." With a shrug, she leaned forward. "In my estimation, that could take months."

"I think it's time I master this more complicated code." Rick studied the braille sheet in front of Chaisley. "What do we have to do to inform everyone that we've switched? Are they aware of it?"

"Yes, Dr. G visited each contact personally over the last few months. He said it was paramount to plan ahead. He has a code word that he will use to call everyone, and they will know to switch."

"Sounds like it's time." He tapped the paper. "I should probably fill you in on what is happening right now." After he relayed what he knew about the meetings in Munich, they dug into the now lukewarm food.

But the company was great. The food was better than anything he could cook for himself. And Melanie was no longer eyeing him with suspicion.

Rick took the moment to study Chaisley. The woman fascinated him more each day. And she took his breath away any time she turned her face toward him. He blinked and forced himself to focus on his food. Time to face facts, he was head over heels. Not that he could do anything about it.

When he looked up from his plate, Melanie pinned him with a stare and quirked an eyebrow up.

Most likely with the same question that was on his mind.

When would he tell Chaisley that she'd stolen his heart?

FRIDAY, SEPTEMBER 30, 1938

The next morning dawned drizzly and gloomy—Chaisley didn't need her sight to recognize that.

Rain pelted the windows, and the wind blew in angry *sforzando* bursts throughout a tranquil melody.

She shuffled her way to the breakfast nook and yawned. "Good morning."

"Good morning." Mel's tone was a bit like the weather. Gloomy. "Your tea is steeping on the table."

"Thank you." She found her seat and reached for the china cup that her friend always placed in the two o'clock position. Wrapping her hands around it, she allowed her fingers to warm on the sides. "I smell toast."

"That you do." Her friend's laugh was light. "And there should be great rejoicing, because this time it isn't burnt."

"Aw . . ." She did her best to cover her giggle. "But I was just beginning to like it burnt. Although, I'd always prefer a croissant."

A knock sounded at the door—a rhythm she recognized. Rick.

"I'll get that." Melanie moved from the table. The door opened. "Come on in. I made toast."

"And it isn't burnt!" Chaisley tossed over her shoulder.

"Well, will wonders never cease?" Rick's warm baritone floated over to her.

Chairs moved and plates clinked as her friends took their seats.

"I've got news." A crunch followed the words. Rick must have bitten into his toast.

"Do tell." Chaisley leaned back in her chair. "Does it have something to do with the meetings you told us about yesterday?"

"It does." His cup clinked against the saucer. "I received a wire just a few minutes ago that they've granted the Führer Sudetenland."

She gasped. "They gave him what he wanted? Don't they realize that could be disastrous?"

"I tend to agree with you, but my superiors are hopeful. As is the rest of the world. They believe this will bring peace in Europe." The scrape of a knife followed his statement. He must be buttering another slice of toast. "Granted, most people don't know about this yet, but it will soon be on the front of every newspaper."

"Wow." It was hard to believe that they'd come to any kind of agreement. Could this truly be the beginning of the end? After all this time building a network across Europe . . . communications came in almost every day. People had been seeking help to flee their homes. Would all of that come to a stop if there was peace?

And what about Hitler and his Nazis? Just because they gave him part of Czechoslovakia didn't mean that he would stop spreading hate.

The silence surrounding her was somber. They were thinking it too. She could feel it. She gripped the edge of the table. "This isn't over, is it?"

chapter
SIXTEEN

Celestia coughed into her handkerchief and rolled over onto her side. It had been many years since a sickness had caused her to be bedridden. But here she was.

Movement over in the chair caught her eye. "You're still here," she rasped.

"Of course I am." Grafton leaned forward and placed his elbows on his knees. "You've got to take better care of yourself, Celestia."

"Posh. If it's the Lord's time for me to go, it's time." She coughed again. "You did get ahold of Chaisley, didn't you?"

"Yes. They are on their way back. Should be here soon, I suspect."

"Good. Thank you. There's much I need to tell her . . . ask her . . . just in case."

His head drooped a bit but he didn't argue with her.

"You also spoke with my lawyer?"

"You know I did. He was here, yesterday."

That's right. She'd forgotten. Which wasn't like her. Maybe the good Lord truly was calling her home. A thought she loved and

267

yet didn't love . . . all at the same time. There were still so many people to help.

"Grandmother?" Chaisley's voice from the doorway brought a sigh to her lips.

"Come in, child." She was seized by coughing before she could sit up properly.

Grafton stood and lifted her, patted her back, and offered her a glass of water. Always proper, that boy. Always caring. Always in his black suit. "I'll give you two some time to catch up."

"Thank you." Celestia wiped at her mouth with her lace hand-kerchief and then waved her granddaughter closer. Oh, she was losing it. Chaisley couldn't see the motion. "Come sit with me for a while."

For the next hour, her granddaughter showered her with questions about her health and then shared about all she'd seen and heard the past few weeks. Great sobs seemed to overcome her. "I can't bear what is happening, Grandmother. No matter how strong I am or how many we try and help . . . the evil just seems overwhelming."

Celestia didn't have words. Oh, how she understood what her granddaughter felt. There were now more than fifty Jewish people taking refuge in her own home. A number that would surely continue to grow.

"What about the Kleins? Grafton told me he secured them visas, but they are about to expire."

Chaisley's gulping sobs grew. "We can't find them. Apparently they were frightened and left the hotel, but they haven't returned."

"Oh, child. I'm so sorry. From what you told me, Mary Beth is a strong, resilient child. She'll help her mother get in touch."

"I pray they do." Chaisley mopped up her face with a hankie and straightened her shoulders. She laid a hand close to Celestia's and found her fingers. "I've rescheduled several concerts in Spain so that I could stay with you awhile. Perhaps you'll be back on your feet by the time I need to leave."

Celestia covered her granddaughter's hand with her own. "As much as I would love for that to be true, the infection is still in my lungs. Grafton has been honest with me—if my body can continue to fight it off, that's great. But there's also a good chance that I will soon be joining my precious husband and your parents in Jesus's presence."

"Please don't talk like that." Chaisley sniffed and swiped a hand at her tear-stained cheek.

"My child, I'm in the Lord's hands, and that's the best place to be." She coughed several times, and her granddaughter handed her the glass of water again. "Thank you." After a few sips, she handed it back, and Chaisley set it down on the side table without spilling a drop. "Now . . . let's talk about something happier."

Chaisley blew her nose. "Like what?"

"Like how beautiful you are. I've seen how you've taken the world by storm and have stood firm in the face of the enemy."

"And then I come in here and feel like a little girl and sob all over the place." She shook her head.

"Only because you feel safe here with me. I love that. But don't give up that strength or tenacious streak even as you grieve, my dear."

"I can't bear to lose you."

"You won't lose me. You know that. I simply will gain heaven, and you'll meet me there one day." She shifted in the bed as another coughing fit overtook her and she worked her way to sit up a bit more. "Now . . . if my time is short, I have a request."

"Anything."

"I was hoping you'd say that." Grinning to herself, she launched into her plan. "I've seen how you are with Rick, and there's no denying the way he looks at you. You two care for one another . . . dare I say, you love each other?"

"Love?" Chaisley cleared her throat. "Um, well, I guess, that is . . . we do care for each other. We've become close friends."

"Oh, don't beat around the bush. I can see it clearly on your face this very moment. Don't deny it. The world is in dire straits. There's no time to waste."

Chaisley's mouth clamped closed.

Yes. She was correct. "All right, then. Here is my request. I am asking you to promise me that you will marry him before the year is out. I would love to see you married before I pass on, but we don't know how much longer I have. That's why a promise will have to do." All this talking made her cough even more. "I'm so thankful that God has brought you love, Chaisley. I want to be able to take my last breath knowing that you are loved and taken care of."

Her granddaughter's mouth opened and then shut. Opened one more time and then shut again.

If it wasn't such a serious moment, Celestia would want to laugh at all the expressions passing over Chaisley's face. "Do you promise?"

"Well . . . don't you think this is something I should discuss with Rick?"

"Sure. Go get him right now. Let's get this settled today."

BERLIN, GERMANY—WEDNESDAY, OCTOBER 19, 1938

The man at the table in front of him was worthless.

"I thought you taught this to your students, Mr. Wolf?"

The man's hands shook over the paper. "I teach braille, yes. But this isn't that."

"Then what, pray tell, *is* it?" He smacked the paper with the back of his hand.

The man lifted his bound hands to his eyes and rubbed at them. "If I remember my schooling from university, this might be a form of the original braille from the early 1800s. These other forms seem to be some of the inventions from the United States."

He slapped the table. "You're telling me you don't know what it says?"

"No. That is . . . not all of it. Here are the words that I was able to decipher." The frail man slid a piece of paper across to him. "That's all I can do." He licked his lips. "Please, may I have a glass of water now?"

He walked across the room and grabbed a glass and the pitcher. He poured the water into the cup in front of the dirty little man at the table and then threw it in his face.

"Next time, I expect answers."

AMSTERDAM, NETHERLANDS

After being gone most of the day yesterday and into the night, Rick wasn't prepared to be woken up at six in the morning by the butler urging him to get dressed and go see Celestia.

But here he was, with gritty eyes, mussed hair, and dressed at ten past six knocking on Celestia's door. He suppressed a yawn.

Chaisley opened the door looking fresh and clean and . . . happy. She was beautiful. It was a good thing she couldn't see his state. "Good morning."

"Good morning." He leaned in and kissed her cheek.

"I see Grandmother had you summoned first thing." She giggled. "She called for you yesterday, but we found out you were away from the manor." Chaisley leaned closer and whispered. "She's not the best at patience."

"Come here, young man. We have much to discuss." Celestia coughed and waved her hand at him.

He did as he was told.

"Now. I'm not going to mince words because talking too much makes me cough. You love my granddaughter, don't you?"

He swallowed as he met her compassionate stare and nodded. There was no denying it. "I do." He shifted his gaze to Chaisley and watched for her reaction.

Pink swept into her cheeks, the corners of her lips turned up, and her eyes sparkled.

Rick couldn't tear his eyes away from her face. Dare he believe that she felt the same?

"Chaisley, my dear, Rick is staring at you like a lovesick school-boy." Celestia coughed again and then continued. "You better tell him."

Chaisley beamed at him. "I love you, too."

In two quick strides, he was by her side, pulling her into his arms. No other words were needed. Her hands roamed his face as his lips found hers.

All the horrors of the world around them melted away as he kissed the woman he wanted to spend the rest of his life with. No matter how much time God granted him, he wanted it to be with Chaisley.

Lost in each other's arms.

"Ahem."

Rick chuckled against Chaisley's lips and pulled back a few inches.

Celestia shifted in her bed. "Now that that is settled, I'd like to set a wedding date. Our work won't wait for such a thing, so I think it should be a simple ceremony. And soon."

"Yes," Chaisley agreed. "Very soon."

chapter
SEVENTEEN

Rick smiled as he watched Melanie hold another swatch of fabric out to Chaisley. The ivory satin glowed in the warm firelight.

"This one looks lovely with your skin tone." Melanie had taken charge of all things wedding and glowed almost as much as his bride-to-be.

The grin that split his fiancée's face was a sight to behold. How had he become so blessed? The most wonderful woman in the world was going to be his wife. And to have her grandmother's blessing *and* encouragement was more than Rick had thought possible.

It all happened so fast, and yet, it was perfect.

The butler appeared at the door of the large drawing room, clearing his throat. "Mr. Rick, you have a visitor."

"Oh?" He scratched the side of his face. Who would come to see him here? No one knew he was here except his senior office—

Oh.

His heart skittered to a stop then picked up double time. If Fairsworth was here, then . . . what had happened? He kept his tone light so he wouldn't upset Chaisley. "Where is my visitor, good man?"

273

"In the parlor, sir."

Rick glanced at the girls. Their heads were together as Chaisley felt the fabric in her hands. Well, he wouldn't interrupt them. Best to see whoever this was and send them on their way before the ladies even knew he was gone.

He slipped out and followed the butler down the hallway. With a bow, the older gentleman left him at the closed door.

Lord . . . help. Please don't let us be at war. He took a long breath then opened the door.

Fairsworth sat on a couch, his hands folded in front of him.

Rick frowned and strode across the small room to stand by the couch. "The news can't be good if you came here in person." He crossed his arms and arched a brow. "Well?"

The older gentleman's face softened. "Hello to you, too, Friederich. I'm well. Thank you for asking."

Why was he always so... contrary? Like he wanted to start an argument. Just because he was on edge and *really* wanted to get married didn't mean that he should be such a bear. "My apologies. But your visit is . . . unexpected."

Fairsworth clapped his hands on his thighs and stood. "Command thought I should give you this news face-to-face. Especially under the circumstances of your upcoming nuptials."

A sensation he didn't like prickled up Rick's spine. Not war. Please, not war. The world wasn't ready. *He* wasn't ready. "What news?"

Fairsworth's expression changed from his usual indecipherable Cheshire cat imitation to something more serious. "All agents are to escalate their efforts regarding section D. The Munich Agreement has not only given Hitler what he wants, it has apparently inflamed his hunger for power. The reports we have received are disheartening. The world will be at war before we know it. Hitler is unstable, at best."

Rick bit the inside of his cheek. Of course the Munich Agreement would fail. He saw that coming from a mile away. "What exactly do you mean by *escalate?* I'm supposed to get married on Saturday."

"That's what I'm trying to tell you, mate. You need to talk to your fiancée about the very real possibility that you won't be here on Saturday. Every single target on each of our lists must be hit. Now. We cannot delay. The faster we knock out their communications the more time we buy for the prime minister and other leaders to figure out what they want the next united step to be."

He was going to be sick. How was this going to work? He'd have to tell Chaisley everything he'd been doing the last few months and postpone the wedding. He rubbed his face.

She was going to be upset. But more than that, she would be hurt that he hadn't told her. Especially once they were engaged.

Fairsworth grabbed Rick's shoulder. "I know you love her. And while many agents would call you a fool for getting involved with someone during wartime, I won't do that." His voice was low. Kind, even. "But you better make this right with that girl before you have to leave. And you need to leave within the hour. Orders are orders."

He swallowed hard. "Thank you for coming."

"I'll slip out now. I hope all goes well with your fiancée. And that God protects you."

"He's protected me from the Germans so far."

Fairsworth gave him a wink. "I'm talking about the wrath of a woman having to postpone her wedding." With that, the agent slipped out of the room and out the front door without a sound.

Rick stood in the parlor, staring at the empty hearth for a long moment. All the joy had been sucked from him. He'd been a fool to not tell Chaisley everything and to get caught up in the dream of a future at a time like this. More than anything, he wanted to marry her. Maybe he should start with that. He inhaled sharply and then let out the breath as he counted to five.

Making his way back to the large drawing room, he made his way toward the women, who were now enjoying cakes and cups of tea.

"There you are!" Chaisley put her cup in the saucer and slowly slid it onto the table in front of her. "Where did you disappear to?"

Her senses were uncanny. Rick licked his lips and glanced at Melanie. She tilted her head, an eyebrow arched in question. He shook his head with a frown.

This was a conversation he had to have in private. He owed Melanie an explanation as well, but after he talked to Chaisley. "Mel, would you mind giving Chais and me a few minutes?"

Her gaze flicked from Rick to her friend. "Of course. I need to see the housekeeper about a matter anyway."

The click of the door echoed through the now-silent room. Rick took Mel's empty seat and reached for Chaisley's hand.

"You're making me nervous." Chaisley's voice shook. "Are you about to tell me you want to call off the wedding? I know this was sudden, but . . ."

Rick closed his eyes. Her vulnerability sliced through his heart. "Never!" The fierce whisper burst from him as he squeezed her hand. "But I do have something to tell you, and I pray you'll give me time to explain everything before you ask questions."

He cleared his throat and began telling her about that night outside of Berlin when he met Agent Fairsworth. He explained what he had been doing for his superiors as an agent of Section D and the news Fairsworth shared about Hitler.

Chaisley withdrew her hands from his and grew still. She was scared. It was written all over her face.

Father, I hate hurting her. "I have to leave within the hour to finish my part of the mission. I'm sorry I didn't tell you all of this once we were engaged. Frankly"—he rubbed his sweaty palms on his pants—"I didn't want to put a damper on the sweet time we were having. But . . . we need to postpone the wedding."

Her brow was etched with a deep V, her eyes dark. "You should have told me."

Never had he seen her so hurt. Never. And he'd done that. He wanted to wrench his own heart from his chest. Why had he kept it from her? "My reasoning at the time doesn't make sense to me even now. I'm so sorry. I've been a fool."

Her face turned toward the window. "I never asked you to divulge the secrets of your work, Rick. I only asked you to tell me the truth. Why was it so hard to tell me that you had a mission but you couldn't give me the details? I would have understood."

Tears streamed down her cheeks and the sight of them was a knife slicing through him.

She placed a hand over her heart, as though trying to press the pain away. "You've had almost two weeks to tell me. Did you not trust me enough to let me carry this burden with you? Even if I didn't know the details, I could still walk with you in it. Pray with you. That's what hurts."

He moved to sit beside her and pulled her into his arms. Her shoulders shook with soft sobs. "I was wrong. I'm so sorry. I thought we had more time . . ."

Why had he ever thought there would be more time? They were in the middle of watching a dictator spin out of control. "I'm so sorry." The words sounded inadequate and stupid to his own ears.

Her sobs stopped, and her breathing calmed. After a few moments, she sat up and pulled away. One thing she was definitely good at—composing herself for an audience. "You have to leave right away?"

Something inside him felt snapped in two as she put on the brave show for him. "Yes."

She patted his chest. "You have no idea when you will return?"

"No. I'm sorry." Watching her pull herself together and knowing the inward struggle it was made him want to volunteer for a good flogging.

Her face grew stoic.

But blank.

"We will pray for you, Rick. Every day."

He'd crushed her. "Thank you. Chaisley, I—"

"No more apologies. I will look forward to your safe return, and we will have the wedding then. Grandmother has been rallying, so that is good news. The end of my two-week hiatus is almost up. So I will find another driver and go back on tour." Her words were all business. No emotion.

He placed his hands on her shoulders and drew her close. Kissing her gently, slowly, he trailed a few kisses along her jawline and whispered, "I love you."

Her eyes closed and a single tear slipped out. "I love you, too. Please . . ." She choked back a sob. "Please come back to me."

GERMANY—FRIDAY, NOVEMBER 4, 1938

It had been twenty-one hours since Rick last slept and fourteen hours since his last meal. Hunger and exhaustion were now the least of his worries though.

As soon as the SIS implemented their plan in earnest, the Germans had been quick to get on the defensive.

He'd had to set out on foot to stay off roads, paths, trails, and any other detectable way to hit his targets. So far, he'd sabotaged or destroyed every target on his list except for two. And if what he'd overheard from the last German checkpoint was true, his fellow agents had succeeded as well.

But the Germans were a strong force. With additions to their army every day, it wouldn't take them long to rebuild. Which meant the SIS would have to continuously attack if they wanted to accomplish anything. How long could they keep this up?

Rick crouched in the low brush and checked his map.

This next hub was significant. Which meant it would be heavily guarded by now.

He checked his backpack. Only four sticks of dynamite left. It wouldn't do a lot, but it could be enough if he hit the right spot. But then he'd have to make it out in time.

Without getting caught.

He leaned up against a tree and let his mind wander back to Chaisley. If only they'd met at a different time. When the world wasn't in the tumultuous state it was in now. Perhaps they'd be living back in London with a couple of kids.

That thought put a smile on his face.

Noise from the road a hundred meters below him caused his senses to go on high alert. Who was coming?

He pulled out the binoculars and studied the officers in the German vehicle. The one in the back appeared to be high-ranking.

Rick glanced back at the dynamite.

His timing would have to be perfect.

But was he ready to kill?

With a shake of his head, he gathered his things and made his way closer to the target. They had to stop this growing threat. Which meant he had to do his part.

Twenty meters to the target.

He tried to stay hidden in the trees. So far, so good.

Click.

The unmistakable sound of the hammer of a revolver.

"*Halt! Wer bist du?*" Whoever was behind him sounded young. Way too young to be wielding a weapon.

Rick slowly turned around with his hands up.

The hatred in the young Nazi's eyes in front of him made him want to be sick. How had they hardened this young man? He couldn't be more than sixteen.

The soldier put the gun to Rick's forehead and narrowed his eyes.

In that split second, Rick watched as the boy's finger on the trigger began to pull. He ducked right before the shot rang out and punched the young man in the gut, grabbing for the gun with his other hand.

They fell to the ground, wrestling with the gun between them. Rick's experience, strength, and age gave him an upper hand. The kid was underneath him but held onto the gun with both hands.

Rick slammed his opponent into the ground hoping to knock the wind out of him, but the wiry boy was stronger than he looked as he yelled obscenities at him and screamed for help.

It wouldn't be long before other soldiers descended upon them.

With everything in him, Rick wrenched the gun from the Nazi's hands.

But the kid pulled out a knife.

Rick didn't have a choice. He slammed the butt of the gun into the young soldier's head.

The kid's head hit the ground hard. Blood pooled underneath. His eyes went blank.

"Halt!"

Voices came from the station.

Running footsteps headed toward him.

There was no time to catch his breath. Rick grabbed the gun, shoved it into his pack, grabbed the dynamite and matches.

He worked his way around to the east, knowing he only had a few seconds before the other soldiers found the kid.

Rick spotted the target. At this point, this was the best he could do. He lit the match, ignited the dynamite, threw it at the hub, and then took off running for all he was worth.

He couldn't think about how many soldiers might come after him.

He couldn't think about the kid he might've killed.

All he could think about was Chaisley and if he'd ever see her again.

AMSTERDAM, NETHERLANDS—MONDAY, NOVEMBER 7, 1938

Sleep had been replaced with tears each night since Rick left, until Chaisley couldn't cry any longer. She'd rescheduled as many dates as she could, hoping that he would return here at any moment. But she couldn't hide and postpone things forever.

He'd written her a beautiful letter in braille that she had read every day. But to not hear his voice . . . not feel his presence. Her heart ached with missing him.

Chaisley paced her bedroom and shook away the thoughts. They'd been through a lot the past six months together. They'd shared meals, conversations, hours upon hours in a vehicle together. They'd shared life. Real life. They could get through this time apart.

Oh, God, please keep him safe.

As she started the prayer, she made her way over to the window and knelt at the sill. She poured out her heart. For healing for her grandmother, safety for Rick, and to find Mary Beth and her mother and bring them to safety. Then she went down the list of the names of each person they housed at the manor. So many beautiful lives. And there were still more to help.

She got to her feet and headed toward the hall. If Rick didn't return today, she'd simply have to go back on tour without him. A thought she despised. But she and Mel had prayed for strength.

God would supply.

It was time.

She passed an open window and heard the engine of an auto rumble closer to the house. As it came up the drive, she recognized the engine's sound. That *was* Rick.

She made her way down the stairs and waited for him inside the foyer. She wanted to be the first thing he saw when he walked into the house.

The door creaked.

"Chaisley."

Her name on his lips couldn't have sounded sweeter.

She rushed toward him with her arms outstretched and prayed they wouldn't smash their heads together when she reached him.

He pulled her into his arms. "I love you."

"I love you too." She laid her head on his chest. "I'm so thankful you are safe!"

"It has been a harrowing few days, but I'm glad to be back in time to keep my cover as your driver. I was afraid you would already be on tour without me."

"What every lady wishes to hear." Melanie's comment accompanied her light laugh. "It's good to have you back, Rick."

"Oh, leave him alone, Mel. He's got plenty of time to practice what he should say later." Chaisley could feel the heat in her cheeks, but she was so grateful to have him back. She tugged on his hand. "Let's go sit and chat for a bit."

"I'd love to."

She led him toward the sitting room.

"How is your grandmother?"

"She rallied again yesterday. Dr. G says it still might be a few days before we know if she's going to get rid of the infection for good." She walked beside him and moved them in a different direction toward the music room.

"Ah. I was hoping you'd bring me here." They sat on the bench side by side. "Will you teach me how to play one day?"

"I'd love to." She touched several keys, then tilted her head toward him, and their lips met in a soft kiss.

When he pulled back, he ran a finger over her cheek. "I might not have expected God to work like this, but marrying you is exactly what I want."

"Me too." Heat continued to fill her chest and neck.

"I'm sorry to interrupt, but it's good to see you two happy." Melanie's no-nonsense greeting came from the door. "Looks like we still have work to do. Rick, you just received a wire."

Chaisley relished his closeness as she listened to Mel's steps and then heard the envelope rip open.

"Oh no," Rick breathed.

She felt him stiffen. "What is it?"

"Ernst vom Rath—a German embassy official in Paris—was shot by a young Jewish man. The SIS is certain Germany will retaliate." He kissed Chaisley's cheek. "Do you mind if I head into town?"

"Not at all." Every time a new report came, it never seemed to be good. As things spiraled, her hope that Hitler could be stopped waned. Would they be at war soon? Would it be the war to end all wars?

"I'll be back as soon as I can with news." He moved from the bench and his quick steps made her heart ache with his absence. How long could she keep touring Europe when such atrocities kept happening? But how else could she continue to help?

Her mind felt like a pendulum swinging one way and then the other. Wanting to hope. Spurred on to action. And then discouraged that they couldn't possibly do enough. Or afraid that the Nazis would come after them next.

"Everything okay?" Mel replaced Rick on the cushioned piano bench.

She nodded, then shook her head.

"I had a feeling." Mel nudged her with a shoulder. "Want to talk about it?"

Chaisley played an A-minor chord *fortissimo*, followed by an arpeggio of the same chord *pianissimo*. "Did you know why the piano has its name?"

Melanie tinkered with a few notes above her. "Tell me."

"The piano's predecessor was the harpsichord, but there was no volume control. Only so much that could be conveyed. No dynamics. No emotion, really. The piano was first called a *pianoforte* because it can be played both loud and soft. With all variations of dynamics. Over time, most people simply called it a piano."

She ran her fingers down the white keys. "I never understood what was missing in my life—but now I do. My life before Rick was like the harpsichord. Full of beautiful music, but there was only one volume. Now that I know love, my life is like the piano-forte." She lifted her hands and placed them in her lap. "I don't want to lose that, Mel. I don't want to lose *him*. And this world keeps getting scarier each day."

THURSDAY, NOVEMBER 10, 1938—KRISTALLNACHT

Rick stood outside Chaisley's bedroom door before sunrise, doing his best to calm his breathing from running up two flights of stairs. It was awful enough to have to wake her at this atrocious hour, but the news he had to deliver would shake them all. No, it would be worse than that. They would be devastated. Heartbroken.

He lifted his hand and knocked.

A minute later, the door opened. "What is it? Is it Grandmother?"

Even with her hair disheveled and tired eyes, Chaisley was beautiful.

"Your grandmother is fine. Please, we have to talk immediately. I'll be down in the parlor after I wake Melanie."

She nodded. "I'll be right there."

Within five minutes, the three of them were huddled in the parlor.

There was no way to say this gently. He leaned his elbows on his knees and fisted his hands. "I'll get right to it. The Nazis have done something unthinkable throughout all of Germany and its territories."

Melanie straightened beside Chaisley and wrapped an arm around her. "Go on."

Rick breathed deep. Best to just get it out. "Last night I couldn't sleep, and so I went to see a contact. I had a bad feeling about vom Rath's shooting. A wire came through about an hour ago that the Nazis have destroyed synagogues, arrested tens of thousands of Jewish men, destroyed and plundered Jewish businesses, and des-ecrated Jewish cemeteries. They had apparently been waiting for the perfect time to do all of this, because it happened in hundreds of towns across all German territories at the same time. The Nazis' excuse was the young Polish Jew who murdered the ambassador. Word now is that they will go after Jews full force."

Tears filled each woman's eyes, and their expressions held fire.

"Do we need to postpone the wedding again? You're needed, aren't you?" Chaisley's voice was steady. Firm.

Now that Celestia had rallied, they'd rescheduled the wedding. "I hate to do that, but yes. I need to go for a few days and see what I can do to help—what *we* can do to help." He reached over and squeezed Chaisley's hand. "Perhaps we can wait until Christmas to marry, since your grandmother seems to be recovering?"

She nodded. "But there's more bad news, isn't there? I can hear it in your tone."

He took a breath. *God, help us all.* "Not only are they trying to get rid of the Jews, but word is that they will soon be rounding up anyone who doesn't meet their criteria. I don't know if this is true, but one of our informants states that Schloss Hartheim will be used to . . . exterminate all of those deemed unworthy of life."

chapter
EIGHTEEN

BERLIN, GERMANY—FRIDAY, NOVEMBER 11, 1938

No need to hide Germany's intentions any longer. The world knew not to tangle with them—and if they didn't?

They'd learn soon enough.

If only the fools he brought in could decipher the braille communications they'd intercepted traveling around Germany and Europe.

Several originated in Amsterdam. Several, Berlin. The rest—coincidentally—followed the travels of Miss Frappier.

He tapped a missive in his hand. It was no coincidence.

If the communications had simply been in braille, he would have no interest in them. Those were easily translated.

But these were not.

What was the woman hiding? Why the need to communicate in some sort of code?

The answer was obvious. She was betraying the Führer.

Now was the time to expose that pianist for the disgusting vermin that she was. She loved Jews. She loved cripples. She loved the diseased and the scum of the earth. He'd had people watching her. Every concert, she spoke to *those* people afterward.

Well, she could just be exterminated with the rest of them. All he had to do was bring the proof to the Führer and show him what that traitor was doing right under his nose.

The shuffling of feet brought his attention back up.

"Here's the ones you requested." A lower-ranking officer led a shackled group of scrawny and filthy men into the room. "Heil Hitler."

"Heil Hitler." He shooed the man away and stepped up to the prisoners. "Do you all read braille?"

Nods were slow to come, but they affirmed that they did.

"Good. If you want to live to see tomorrow, you'll decipher this for me." He set the paper on the table. "You have one hour."

GERMANY—WEDNESDAY, NOVEMBER 30, 1938

The devastation across Germany, Austria, and the Sudetenland was the worst that Rick had seen since the Great War.

The Nazis claimed each attack and every bit of devastation was the public outrage over the assassination of vom Rath. And yet nothing of this caliber could have been simple public outrage. Not on this scale. Not across the continent.

No. Kristallnacht was planned. Probably weeks or months in advance. And the Nazis themselves carried it out.

The Jews who hadn't been able to leave yet were now in a fight for their lives.

Rick had snuck around to several of the so-called *work camps*. The conditions were hideous, and the purpose for them was all too clear.

Vernichtung. Extermination. He'd heard it from Nazi officers' lips too many times. Even so, it was hard to believe it was true.

He'd lost the contents of his stomach multiple times as he'd spied on what was happening. It was all too real.

He gripped the steering wheel tighter and took slow, deep breaths to keep his stomach from roiling again.

How could he help the world see the Nazis' true actions and intent? No way would the Nazis allow anyone close enough to take pictures and document their atrocities. The press were under Nazi control in Germany. Any reporters from other countries weren't allowed around.

No one was.

At least the night of broken glass had gotten the world's attention. There was far too much destruction to keep from the press. He pressed his lips tight. The Nazis seemed to enjoy the notoriety. Of course, they wanted their own spin on the story, but they were proud of what they'd done.

If the world powers didn't believe they were in an all-out war yet, they were sadly mistaken.

As he drove back to Amsterdam, his gaze went to the box on the floor. It was full of missives he'd found buried underneath rubble of several synagogues, and a few trinkets from businesses. If the guards wanted to rummage through it at the border, he'd have to put on his best acting and convince them he was a German just bringing back a few trophies for his family.

The urgency to rescue the children still left in Germany who needed them had raced to a fever pace, so he had to risk bringing the letters of those seeking help back himself. There were hundreds of children hidden across Germany with little to no food or supplies. And how long they could hold out shrank by the minute.

He'd destroyed a dozen communication lines in the past few days and had sent detailed sketches back to London of railway hubs and larger communication lines he hadn't been able to touch. He hid the sketches in pairs of his socks that he shipped home and kept copies with him in case they got confiscated somewhere along the way.

He'd gathered what information he could on Germany's power industry, but the Nazis were smart. They'd kept everything hidden and under close watch.

But as much as he wanted in his flesh to take Hitler down with his own hands, Rick now felt a deeper purpose. A stronger conviction. He'd done what he could as an operative for SIS. Now, he wanted to help Chaisley, Melanie, Celestia, and Dr. Grafton as they rescued as many as they could out of the clutches of evil. He'd prayed about it all last night and felt peace about his decision. His superiors would have to understand the importance of what they were doing.

At the moment, though, his focus had to be getting their little group safely back to London. And that might be harder than any of them imagined.

AMSTERDAM, NETHERLANDS—THURSDAY, DECEMBER 8, 1938

Snowflakes floated from the sky, some sticking to her bedroom window, most landing on the ground without a sound. They were giant, fluffy flakes that reminded her of the stiff tutus some of the ballet dancers wore in *The Nutcracker*. Melanie pressed her hand to the cold glass, her fingers following the path of the flakes.

Goodness, was it only four years ago when she went to the ballet? When life had been happy and normal?

She wrapped her arms around her middle and continued to stare. The world had upended itself in so many ways in such a short amount of time. Joy and peace seemed in short supply for everyone.

Her breath created a cloud on the glass, and she turned away. If she continued to stand there, chances were high she'd catch a chill.

Padding across the room, Melanie glanced at the clock. 11:13 a.m. Good. She still had time before meeting Chaisley and Rick in the front foyer of Celestia's home. She sat in an overstuffed chair and curled her feet beneath her.

Melanie chewed the corner of her lip, staring at her hands. Kristallnacht had changed everything. It was no longer safe to travel through Germany. The country's borders were locking up tighter than she'd ever seen.

Little wonder Chaisley had paused the tour indefinitely.

Führer Hitler was no doubt furious that his prized pianist hadn't shown up for his celebration. Every day for the first two weeks after Kristallnacht, Melanie had expected Nazis to pound on the doors and attempt to drag them all away. Time alone had calmed that anxiety inside her.

Standing up and blowing a stray hair off her forehead, she walked over to her closet. She tugged warm winter boots with thick rubber soles on over her heaviest wool socks. Plucking her coat off the back of another chair, she slipped her arms into it and buttoned it tight. She wrapped a navy-blue scarf around her head and neck, ready to face the winter weather.

Descending the stairs, she spotted Rick and Chaisley together. They were also bundled up for the cold, but standing as close as they could, hushed whispers passing between them.

Melanie smiled and approached them. "All right, you lovebirds, let's brave this crazy weather and go get some lunch."

The pair turned toward her, both of their grins wide.

"I just pulled the car up." Rick held his elbows out for both women. "Shall we?"

The drive into Amsterdam's downtown was quiet. There weren't many people out and about, which allowed them to enter Melanie's favorite café and get a table with relative ease. Once their orders of soups, sandwiches, and hot chocolate were placed, the trio relaxed into the booth.

"Thank you for driving in this snow so we could have lunch." Melanie nodded at Rick. "If I had to spend one more day in that beautiful mansion, I might have gone cuckoo."

Rick laughed and slipped his arm around Chaisley's shoulders. "I understand. The house is wonderful. And enormous. But I guess one can get cabin fever anywhere."

Chaisley smoothed her hands across the tabletop. "I was not thrilled to be out in the cold. But I confess a bowl of *mosterdsoep* sounds like just the thing. Not even Grandmother's chef can make it like the cook here."

It was true. The traditional Dutch soup was filled with flavors. Butter, stock, cream, leeks, mustard, and if the cook had it available, bacon. Judging from the smells wafting into the small dining area, bacon was definitely in it today.

Melanie cleared her throat and leaned forward to her friend, her voice low. "Have you come to a final decision about the tour?"

Chaisley turned her head toward Rick, who pressed a kiss to her temple. "We have. And I know you won't be surprised. Both Rick and I think it's wise to end the tour with a hopeful promise to return . . . when things settle. Most of Europe is reeling from all that has transpired, and no one balked when we paused a year's worth of concerts. Except the Germans.

"But Hitler's boldness against the Jewish population, his cruelty, and the way his armies are now controlling almost every inch of Germany in a vise grip have made me uneasy. More than that—I fear for my life. After that officer burst into the dressing room, what does the Führer know about us? I just don't know what he would do to me if I stepped foot back in Berlin." She shuddered. "I think now he would be bold. My fame and talent wouldn't matter one whit. He's shown he will be accountable to no one."

Rick caught Melanie's eye. "We're still working out plans, but I know that Chaisley would like to go back to England. Back to the manor for a while. At least until we see where things truly stand. From there, she can help to acquire visas for those traveling from Amsterdam and other areas of Europe while I finish up my work for the SIS, give them the information I gathered, and put in my resignation. Then I'll assist her in the rescue work she's doing.

"Dr. Grafton already has his small team in England working on the visas, but it's getting harder and harder every day. He will still have a base here at the manor, but we are unsure how long Amsterdam will stay safe. Celestia will return to England with us until she is fully strong again. Two trusted staff members will look after all those who stay. They know how to hide people if necessary."

Melanie nodded and leaned back as the waitress slid three steaming mugs of hot chocolate in front of them. She cupped her hands around her mug, her cold fingers thawing beneath its warmth. Chaisley was right. She wasn't surprised. Her friend was being wise and thoughtful.

A chill tripped up her arms, scattering goosebumps across her skin. She couldn't imagine the pressure. Yet her dearest friend had handled it with grace and poise.

Hopefully, she would respond in the same way when Melanie shared her own news.

"I can practically hear your wheels turning from here," Chaisley teased. "What has you in such deep thought, Mel?"

Well, Lord. That couldn't be a clearer sign to share my news, could it?

Melanie took a long sip of the rich, hot drink, and gathered her thoughts. "I am glad to hear you're ending the tour. I think it's smart. And I know that you and Rick are both seeking the Lord as to what He wants you to do with the work we've started these last several months. The network is in place, and I have no doubt Dr. Grafton will keep it running. Because people will need it now more than ever." Her nose stung as tears rushed to her eyes. Oh, this was going to be more difficult than she anticipated.

Chaisley slid her hands across the table, palms up. "Spill it, Mel. It's all right."

Melanie laughed, set her cup down, and grabbed her friend's hands. "You've always been able to read me like a book without your sight. Which is incredible." She sniffed, then plunged ahead. "I think I want to stay in Amsterdam. At least for now. Help with the families that are in the house. Work with the transportation team, or even get travel documents. This work—with these children and families—has changed me. My heart breaks for them. And while I know I can't save everyone, I don't think I can stop trying to help anyone I can. Besides, Mary Beth and Geraldine are still out there. I aim to find them."

With a big swallow over the lump in her throat, she glanced at Rick. "You told me about the *Kindertransport*. I hate the thought of separating Jewish children from their parents, but I think the best thing we can do for these children is get them out of Germany. And, with God's help, we can get their parents out as well."

A tear slipped down Chaisley's cheek. "As soon as Rick shared that news, I wondered how we could assist."

"I'm German. I could get back into Germany and help those children. I just wish . . ." She left the sentence unfinished.

Silence surrounded their little table. They were all thinking the same thing. When the Jewish and Quaker community leaders met with the British government to discuss the innocent Jewish children, it felt like a small victory within their small team. If only they could convince *their* government to think of all the endangered children. The ones being hunted down because they were considered less than, the poor young people being sterilized against their will, and worse.

One of their contacts had recently shared what Hitler said to the Nazi Party in Nuremberg back in 1929: *"If Germany was to get a million children a year and was to remove 700-800,000 of the weakest people then the final result might even be an increase in strength."*

More tears spilled down Chaisley's cheeks, which made Melanie's eyes water and burn. Oh, how she longed to be stoic and keep the tears at bay. She wanted her anger to fuel her, to keep her strong. "I guess I'm saying that we need to part ways for a while. You'll be in good hands with Rick by your side." She tightened her grip around Chaisley's hands.

"I'm not surprised to hear you say this. I will confess I worry about your safety. Yet if this is truly how you feel the Lord is leading you . . . ?" Her friend closed her eyes, her lips trembling in a thin line.

"It is." Melanie made her assurance firm and clear. "For now, my friend. I hope to return as your beloved assistant one day."

"Then—" Chaisley sniffed and gave her a watery smile—"you have my full blessing. Not that you need it."

Melanie tightened her grip once again around Chaisley's fingers. "But I *want* it. I never would have left you alone, Chaisley. Never. You are my dearest friend. The sister I always wanted. But the Lord started to change my heart when I realized you and Rick had feelings for each other. I knew Jesus was showing me that He had other work for me to do. Just like He called you to it before we ever left on the tour." She smiled at Rick. "You are in the best hands now."

Rick's hand covered theirs and he patted Melanie's wrist. "Thank you for trusting me with your sister."

Melanie pulled back and grabbed her napkin, wiping at her face. She cleared her throat and looked back up at her friends. "There is one more thing." Her throat felt thick and she coughed again. Perhaps a sip of hot chocolate would help. Or was it just nerves?

She sipped her drink anyway, then jumped in. "My brother is a Nazi."

Chaisley's jaw dropped open.

Rick straightened, his brown eyes wide. "What?"

Melanie nodded, looking down into her drink. "When Mum and I left, I was seven, I think? Maybe eight. Dad was horrible to my mother. Violent. Abusive. The day she gathered the courage to leave him was the day she first told me the story of Esther. We were brave princesses escaping an evil man who sought to harm us. But the Lord stepped in and saved us."

Sweat beaded on her forehead. Why was it so hot in this room?

"Oh, Mel." Chaisley appeared miserable as she shook her head. "No wonder your mother was so kind and so brave. Her courage helped me find my own."

Melanie managed a smile, but felt it slip as she went on. "I think after we escaped my dad, she felt like nothing could ever hurt her again. But it shattered her heart to leave my brothers with him. My older brothers I don't even remember, they were grown and gone by the time I had any memories. But my other brother, Randall, was only a couple years older than me. And oh, how he adored our father. He followed him around and became just as mean and ugly with his words as him. So I avoided him, and it didn't bother me one bit when we left him behind."

Burning clawed up her throat. "I know, it's awful to say, but I loved having Mum to myself and not dealing with any more yelling . . . or hitting."

She turned her face toward the window. What would they think of her now, knowing all this? "I was too young to understand how it all happened—my mother didn't share the details with me when I was little—and by the time I was grown enough to understand . . . she was gone." Melanie leaned back against the stiff plastic of the booth.

The table fell silent again. She used the moment to collect herself, her emotions, and her scattered and disjointed thoughts. "I believed my father was dead, because Mum told me he was. But when we were touring in Germany, I kept thinking I saw him. The same angry, stern face that frightened me as a child and haunted my dreams. He was a horrible monster of a man." She shredded her soggy napkin into tiny pieces. "It turns out . . . the face I kept seeing was my brother's. The first concert that Hitler attended, there he was, by the Führer's side. It appears that he is now a high-ranking Nazi official, part of Hitler's inner circle."

Chaisley let out a squeaky gasp. "Are you sure? Perhaps it's just someone who looks like—"

"It's him. I inquired about his name. And then . . . and then I sent him a letter."

Rick leaned forward. "You sent him a letter? That's awfully dangerous, Mel. Didn't you just say he's part of Hitler's inner circle?" His voice had turned hard, his eyes like steel.

Of course, he had a right to be angry. She'd risked putting them all in terrible danger. Not to mention, she had done exactly what she'd accused Rick of earlier. Mum always warned her not to point out the splinter in someone else's eye when she had an entire tree trunk in her own. Yes, she'd been hypocritical. Something else to apologize for. "I'm sorry. I didn't give him any information—not that he couldn't find me. But that concert on August the fifth? I was horrified because hatred was written all over his face. But then he responded to my letter. He wants to see me."

"See you?" Chaisley slapped a hand over her mouth. After a moment she spoke again, this time in a hushed tone. "Melanie, you can*not* be thinking of seeing him in person! He could hurt you!"

"She's right, Mel. This puts you in much greater danger. Especially with the work you want to do. How on earth do you think you can meet him, and risk him discovering you help the very people he is sworn to not only hate but destroy?" Rick's brown eyes were dark and intense.

She understood their shock and horror. More than they knew. Who wanted to accept that someone in their family was a part of one of the most abhorrent political parties in the world? "I don't know. But I have to try and share the truth with him while I can."

Deep within her soul, she knew the Lord was prompting her to watch for His will and an opportunity to at least meet her brother one time. "I know this comes as a shock. And I promise you I will not do anything stupid. I don't even know if he'll ever want to see me again after our first meeting. All I know is I have this urging from the Lord about him. I can't ignore that. Even if right now, I don't understand what it means. I'll keep helping with the group here until you all leave for England. But then I'll head back to Berlin."

The waitress appeared with their soups and sandwiches. But the savory aromas that had tantalized her stomach ten minutes ago now made it roil.

No one said anything for a long while. They made a show of eating, and finally Rick threw some bills on the table and they piled back into the car.

Once they were settled in the back seat, Chaisley reached out and tugged Melanie close to her in a hug. Melanie could feel the wetness of her friend's tears dampening her hair.

"I don't want to lose you."

The words were muffled against her winter hat. And they warmed her all the way down to her toes.

"I don't want to be lost." She hugged Chaisley hard before drawing back. "But I have to do this, Chais. I need to try to reach my brother."

Yes, the road before her was dangerous, and could possibly end in her losing her life, but she trusted Jesus above all things. "If I perish, I perish." The words eased from her on a whisper. "Your will be done, Lord. For such a time as this."

chapter
NINETEEN

Smack!

His hand stung from the slap. But these stupid people couldn't figure out the code. Every one of them deserved the firing squad.

How hard could it be to decipher a blind woman's message?

He should have followed Melanie after the concert and just grabbed her. If anyone understood what that pianist was up to, it was his long-lost sister who had been by the woman's side for years.

The traitor. She'd left with their mother all those years ago by choice.

Her sugary letter had played right into his plan. Of course, he'd responded, telling her everything she wanted to hear. All he had to do was get her back on German soil, and he would pounce.

Whatever information she had would be his.

And once the pianist's treachery was revealed, the Führer would want to promote him again.

Tempted to allow a grin to grow on his face, he swiped a hand over his mouth instead. Right now, though, he needed to know what that pianist was up to. Why on earth had she been carrying all her music in braille when she memorized everything? They'd searched her bag. The officer said he had sensed they were hiding something. But what?

He spun on his heel and headed to the door. He needed fresh air to think. He'd disposed of too many of these worthless blind people who couldn't decipher the code the past few weeks.

There *had* to be another way to catch the traitor.

Once the Führer knew about Miss Frappier's defiance of the Nazis, he would want to take matter into his own hands. He was already upset that she didn't show for the demanded performance on November fifteenth. Now that the world was watching with bated breath for Germany's Supreme Commander-in-Chief to make his next move, he could make an example out of her.

Walking out of his office to his car, he lit a cigarette and scanned the trees.

Wait a minute.

He squinted his eyes.

There—in the park. That man. Where had he seen him?

He snapped his fingers. The man had spoken with Melanie weeks ago. Was it after one of the concerts? He did his best to picture the exact location.

At the moment, the man was surrounded by children. He sat in the snow in his black suit while the children laughed.

Of course! He might not have to use his pathetic little sister after all.

He strode through the snow, staying out of sight as long as possible.

Ten feet away from his target, the man snapped his gaze up.

Gotcha.

ON A BACK ROAD IN GERMANY—TUESDAY, DECEMBER 13, 1938

Thank you, Lord, for a cloudy night.

Melanie's hands gripped the steering wheel. Having driven the route from Berlin to Amsterdam several times in the last month since Kristallnacht, each time the clouds covered the heavens she breathed a grateful prayer. It made it harder to see, but it also gave them more cover.

There were only three vehicles their little team could use, and she filled in as a driver whenever one of the others couldn't.

The job helped her to feel useful even though it caused her great stress every time. Not that she would tell any of the others that. But at the moment, the pounding of her heart was so loud in her ears that it drowned out any other sound.

Breathe deep, Mel. Even as she was thinking that, it was her mother's voice she heard.

She took several long, deep breaths and the pounding in her ears quieted. Her heart still raced, but that wouldn't stop. At least not until her cargo was delivered and safe.

Three young children huddled together in the back seat, a thick blanket draped over them. One—only ten years of age and yet the oldest by several years—suffered from epilepsy. One was born with a cleft palate, and the last child only had two fingers on her right hand.

It had been more than an hour since any of them had made a sound. Perhaps they'd fallen asleep. The rest would be good for them, the poor dears. They were so malnourished, worse than any she'd seen so far. Which made her concerned that things were only going to get worse. Sad, how that thought echoed every time. And every time it was worse.

The little ones devoured the sandwiches and water she'd brought so fast, Melanie hoped they didn't get sick.

But the food stayed down, and the children settled in for their long drive.

Melanie suppressed a yawn. With only a few hours' sleep the last few days, her exhaustion and the warmth of the car made an unsafe combination. She knew this route, the curves and slopes. The soothing sway of the car was enough to put anyone to sleep.

She smacked her cheek. *None of that! Stay alert!*

Only thirty-five kilometers stood between them and freedom now.

She cracked the window, the bitterly cold air whipping along the side of her head. Hopefully the kids wouldn't wake up, but she needed the stinging in her face to keep her awake. It wouldn't do to crash on her last mission.

Her last mission.

The thought was bittersweet. The horrors in Germany reached a horrific peak much quicker than anyone anticipated. Arrests grew in number every day as people were sent to work camps. She'd done her best to keep her chin up. Keep a positive attitude and take one step at a time. But she had to excuse herself often, find a quiet place, and cry.

The tiny little network started by Celestia and Dr. Grafton had been able to rescue hundreds more children since Kristallnacht, but now it was going dark, fleeing underground as Hitler's influence spread across Eastern Europe like a spider web.

She was proud of her work. She'd written her brother another letter, but with no response, her heart had changed. Especially during the planning of this last rescue. Each day, the urging she'd felt so strongly to see her brother waned like a candle about to sputter out the last of its light.

If her brother was in Hitler's inner circle, his heart had to be full of hate. How else could he be a part of the atrocities happening?

She had to let him go. Seeing him was too dangerous, and she couldn't risk putting anyone else in peril.

Her brother had chosen his path.

And she chose hers.

She lifted her chin. She would do whatever she could to save as many as she could. Just like Chaisley. Rick. Celestia and Dr. G.

She left the road for the hidden path which barely fit an automobile, maneuvering the car up a steep hill, then slowing to a stop for a moment. Below her the lights of small towns blinked and winked. Just half a kilometer before her was one of the last hidden areas where people could pass in and out of Germany without a checkpoint. She glanced at her wristwatch, squinting to read the time in the darkness. 2:12 in the morning.

They had made it. Well. Almost. The wide meadow was just ahead. She pressed the gas pedal and sped down the narrow, rutted path, eager to be reunited with her friends again.

A kilometer past the border, her friends were watching for them and waiting with a different car and papers for these children to board a boat from Amsterdam to London.

Not far now. There. She'd made i—

Harsh lights exploded through the driver's window.

No! She couldn't stop now, they were almost over the border!

But someone moved into the road—

Dragging Dr. Grafton! A gun at the older man's head.

Holding the gun was none other than her brother.

She slammed on the brakes and skidded in the snowy ruts. The car bounced and jostled, and she placed her other foot on top of the brake as well.

Gripping the steering wheel for all she was worth, she clenched her jaw. *Oh, God, please don't let me hit them!*

The car bounced out of the right rut and slid into a tree trunk, coming to a stop with a soft thump.

Her head snapped to the driver window. They were mere inches from hitting the men.

She slumped against the seat and fought the shaking in her limbs. What could she do?

Well, she couldn't fall apart. That was for certain.

"Melanie!" Her brother's harsh German accent sent a shiver up her spine.

She looked over her shoulder at the children in the seat behind her. They were her first priority. They'd been instructed to stay quiet, no matter what. How scared they must be!

God, give me wisdom. And fast.

Bleary eyes and tousled hair greeted her.

"Don't be afraid," she whispered to them. "Just stay down." She opened her door, and her mind spun. The terrain around her wasn't exactly conducive for them to try to run on foot. How far were they from their friends? It couldn't be that far. They were at the border which meant only a kilometer—a short thousand meters away. Perhaps Rick could see them even now. Could she signal them somehow?

And yet, it was too far.

Too far for her to get help.

A wet, frigid breeze cut through her coat.

The click of a gun hammer echoed across the open space.

"Hands up."

Her brother's voice was low as he aimed the weapon at her.

The nasty smirk on his face chilled her to the bone. More than the snow falling and adding to the drifts on the ground ever could. Melanie raised her arms, palms facing forward.

Her brother pointed the gun back at Dr. Grafton's temple.

"No! Don't hurt him!"

Her brother laughed. "So this man means something to you? More than your own flesh and blood?"

"My own flesh and blood pointed a gun at me and is now pointing it at my friend." Oh, he made her so angry! She resisted the urge to lunge at him and bit the inside of her cheek.

He sneered. "You're angry with me? What is it, exactly, that you and your friend do?"

The faces of hundreds of children flooded her mind in a millisecond.

Jesus . . . Jesus . . .

The tension in her body eased. All fear left her.

She angled a look at her brother and lifted her chin. "You know what I do. I work for Miss Frappier." She took a slight step closer to Dr. G.

"Don't. Move." Her brother jerked his chin toward the car. "Now, I suspect Miss Frappier is not in support of the Führer and the Nazi Party, which makes her an enemy. I also believe that she is up to something. Why is it, my dear *sister*"—he spat the word—"that we have discovered a great deal of communication traveling across Europe *in braille*?"

She was not going to be baited. "Probably because she reads and writes in braille and her fans—which include your Führer—want to communicate with her. She *is* on a European tour, as I'm sure you've heard. You were even at one of her performances."

His dry laugh sounded . . . evil. "You think I'm a fool, don't you?"

"Not at all." Think fast. She needed to keep him occupied until she figured out what to do. "But I do think your work for the Nazis has made you suspicious of everyone. You see an enemy in every person around you."

His eyes narrowed, lips thinned. "That's because most of them are. The Führer is a great man with the only solution for this world, and I aim to make sure that he succeeds."

Solution? Bile rose up her throat. She swallowed it down.

"Your face says it all, dear sister. You don't have what it takes to do what has to be done." He pointed the gun at her again. "Get in the car. And if you do anything stupid, I will shoot this man. When you get in the car, put the keys in the ignition and then put your hands on the steering wheel."

Melanie looked between her brother and Dr. Grafton.

He dipped his chin in a slight nod, but didn't say a word.

Oh, Lord, please help. I don't know what to do.

After another second's pause, her brother yelled. "Get. In. The. *Car*!"

She did as he instructed. Slowly. She closed the door and, through clenched teeth, whispered to the children, "Not a sound. Keep low." As she stared out the window at the sibling she'd so hoped to save, her thoughts spun. How had he found them? And what was he planning to d—

Oh! Dr. Grafton spun and punched her brother in the jaw! That threw Randall off balance. But not for long. He leveled a punch at his attacker that knocked Dr. G back.

"No . . . *No!*" Her screams fogged up the window with her breath, and all she could see was a tangle of the two men.

She wiped at it with her hand and saw blood on both men's faces.

Then her brother brought the gun down on top of Dr. Grafton's head.

The older man fell to the ground.

chapter TWENTY

The thump of a body on the ground shook her out of her stupor.

No. Get up. Please be all right.

But Dr. G didn't move.

Randall dragged him off the narrow makeshift road and into the trees.

The front passenger door opened, and her brother slid into the seat. The gun in his hand was now trained directly at her.

"What did you do? Did you kill him? He *is* still alive, isn't he?" If he'd taken the life of the only father who had ever truly loved her, they weren't moving an inch.

His eyes gleamed in the dim light. "Maybe for now. But he won't be for long in this cold. Now drive." He jammed the gun into her temple. "If you don't, I will shoot you. And each of the children hiding in the backseat."

Melanie took one last glance at Dr. G's motionless body. She fumbled with the keys three times before getting the key in the ignition and starting it. She'd come back after she dealt with her brother. And she *would* deal with her brother. Anger burned so hot in her now that she was ready to spit fire at him. "Where are we going?"

"Back to Berlin, dear sister. And on the way, you are going to tell me the key to the pianist's code."

"WHAT'S WRONG?" Chaisley cringed at Rick's sharp intake of breath. "What do you see, Rick? Tell me." The intensity of the moment made her heart race. The situation was bad. She could feel it.

"Keep your voice low. We're going to get closer."

"Where are Melanie and the children? Dr. Grafton? You were watching them through the binoculars. Tell me, please."

The car rolled forward.

She reached out and touched Rick's arm. "I have to know what's going on. They're my family."

He took a slow breath. "A Nazi just forced her back into the car. He had Dr. Grafton at gunpoint, hit him over the head with the gun, and left him in the snow." Rick's voice was calm and low. "We've got to do something. We can*not* let Melanie and those children be taken by him. We can't. God help us."

"Is Dr. Grafton all right?"

"I don't know, Chais. He's on the ground. Wait. He just moved. And the car is stuck. Melanie hit a tree when that madman stepped out into the road. Looks like the Nazi is forcing her to turn around. But the space is too narrow. Between the tree and the ruts in the road, their tires are spinning in the snow. That's good. It'll buy us time to close the distance." They rolled ever closer toward the enemy that had Mel.

"Can you go any faster?"

"We're about to go downhill, so we will pick up some speed. Right now, I'm praying he doesn't see us. Our headlights are off, but we're about to lose the cover of the trees."

Chaisley swallowed and, for the first time in many years, wished she could see. Her lack of sight hadn't made her feel helpless since she was a child. She clamped her eyes shut and clenched her jaw. *God, take this fear away. Show us what to do.*

Rick grabbed her hand. "Here we go. Get down. Just in case."

She leaned toward him as their vehicle went down an incline.

"We're in the open now, so he might see us."

"What is your plan?"

"I can see Melanie, her hands are waving around. That man better not hurt her." The words sounded like they'd been forced through clenched teeth. "Maybe she's stalling, because she hasn't made much progress getting the car out. She's been shimmying it back and forth but she's still at an angle in the narrow road. At least her captor would have to look over his shoulder now to see us."

Chaisley felt their vehicle come to a slow stop.

Rick grabbed her shoulders and lifted her to sit up again. "We don't have much time. I don't think the Nazi knows we are here, which is a miracle." He pulled her over to the driver's seat and she felt him slide out.

"What are you doing? You do realize I don't know how to drive, don't you?"

"Yep. But you're going to today. It's only about 100 meters. If that." His voice was a hushed whisper.

She heard the crank of the window and then the door softly clicked shut beside her. She could hear the other vehicle. The spinning of its tires. Over and over.

Rick's warmth came through the open window. "Our only hope here is for me to disable the car. It can only go a foot or so forward or back until she gets it straightened out. This is our chance, so I need you to listen close. You can do this."

She nodded. "Of course I can." She straightened her shoulders. She could do anything with God's help. Right? For Melanie and the children. To keep them from being taken.

"All you have to do is shift and work the pedals."

She could handle piano pedals—it couldn't be that much different, right? "Okay."

"Place your foot on the left pedal—that's the clutch. It has to be pressed all the way in to shift. Middle pedal is the brake. Righthand pedal is smaller—it's the one that makes the car go."

She found all three with her feet. "That's not so hard."

"Good. Now press in the clutch, and keep your left foot pressed in until I tell you to shift. When I tell you to go—" he moved her right hand and placed it on a handle—"crank this down a notch, press down on the right pedal, and ease up on the clutch. They have to work together, so feel the engine. You'll probably be able to do it better than anyone else. But in case you stall, press the clutch back in—" he placed her right hand on the dash—"You have to push this button to start the vehicle again. It's the ignition. Then shift and go. Got it?"

His confidence in her made her nervousness fade a little. "A blind woman driving, it makes complete sense. What are you going to do?" She gripped the steering wheel.

"Pray this works and very carefully shoot out a tire or two. It's a good thing I'm an excellent shot. But I can't drive and take careful aim at the same time. You're the distraction. And if I miss, you'll hopefully catch them and ram them. That's plan B."

"Let's hope plan A works then." She sat a little straighter.

"Once I've shot out a tire or two to disable their vehicle, I'll shout—that's your signal to hit the brakes and duck down onto the seat." A metallic click followed his words.

God, please make his aim true. "Okay." Her pulse throbbed in her temples. "Be careful."

"You ready?"

She pressed in the left pedal. "Yes." But it was amazing how the pictures of Father's car from her childhood sprang to mind. She could see it. Feel it.

The other engine across the way roared, then sputtered.

"Perfect. They've stalled and she's managed to get the back tire in a pretty good drift. As soon as Mel starts the car up again, I want you to go, all right? Just keep the steering wheel straight, don't deviate."

"All right."

She held the gear shift in her right hand, the steering wheel in her left. Her left foot was pressed on the clutch as the engine purred, and her right foot stayed on the brake.

The other engine roared to life again.

A shot rang out.

"Go!"

Chaisley blew out her breath, shifted, and pressed into the right pedal while she lifted the left, feeling the engine engage. She gripped the steering wheel with both hands as the car moved forward.

Another shot rang out. Then another.

But she didn't hear a shout. Had it not worked?

All she could do was continue ahead and pray that was correct. The wind whipped through the open window and strands of her hair wrapped around her face. But she refused to let go of the steering wheel.

She pressed the gas pedal all the way down and heard the engine whine at a higher pitch. Was she supposed to do something else? Shift? But how?

No. She was supposed to brake. No. That was only if Rick shouted. Had he?

"Chais!"

That was her cue. She stiffened her body, bracing for whatever was coming, and pressed the brake.

But the car slid into something in front of her, and she smacked her head on the steering wheel as the limousine came to a stop. The engine hissed and sputtered.

Whatever she hit caused her to lift her feet off the pedals, and she released the steering wheel. Her mind swam for several seconds, and a pounding grew in her forehead.

She put a hand to it and forced her mind to clear.

Where was Mel? The children? And Dr. G?

Were they all right?

Scuffling sounded in the snow in front of her.

"Chaisley?" Mel's voice.

Her door opened, and warm arms lifted her up as the brisk air greeted her face.

"Are you all right?"

Rick. He pulled her into his arms.

"I conked my head pretty hard, but other than that, I'm fine. Is Mel okay? Did we stop them?"

"Thank God. I was worried when I saw that you weren't stopping." His arms tightened. But then the deep rumble of his laughter filled her ears. "Didn't I tell you how great you would be at driving?"

She released a *humph*. "Where's Mel? I heard her."

"I'm here." Her nervous laughter joined Rick's, and another set of arms surrounded Chaisley. "I can't believe that you just drove the car!"

"Where's Dr. G? What *happened?*" Her frustration with not knowing what had transpired grew with every second.

"Don't worry. I'm right here too."

The man who'd been her guardian all these years joined the hug.

Chaisley wriggled her way out of their grasp and stomped a foot. "Who's going to *tell* me what happened?"

"I take it back. I think you *are* better at everything than me. Even driving a car." The relief in Rick's voice soothed her frazzled nerves.

But it was Mel who rescued her from going crazy. "My brother was the one who kidnapped Dr. G and stopped me in the road. He wanted to take me back to Berlin so I could tell him how to decipher your code."

"Oh no."

"At that point, I knew I couldn't risk any of us being taken back to Berlin. I would die before I let that happen, I just didn't know what to do. I knew you guys were out there, but I wasn't sure if you knew what was happening, so I did everything I could to keep us stuck. When I saw your car coming toward us, I knew there was hope. My brother was yelling and screaming orders at me so I burst into tears and let go of the wheel, being as dramatic as I could. He was so focused on gaining control of the car that he didn't realize you were coming. Rick shot out two of the tires, which made it impossible for us to go anywhere. I let the car stall, and then you slammed into us."

Rick pulled her under his arm even tighter. "That was when Dr. Grafton surprised us all. He yanked the door open, dragged Mel's brother out, and tied him up."

"After I gave him a sound punch in the nose and took the gun away." Dr. G sounded quite proud of himself. "That fellow whacked me over the head. I was madder than a hornet."

Chaisley put a hand to her mouth and her limbs sagged. "Is it over then? Everyone is safe? The children?"

"They had a frightening journey, but they seem to be fine." The relief in Melanie's voice was palpable.

"I was about to check them over right now." Dr. G's words comforted her.

A groan preceded some nasty slurs from the Nazi.

She tensed. "What about him?"

Rick kissed her temple. "You and Melanie need to get on the ship with the kids. I'm going to take him back with us to London."

"What?"

"Don't panic. He'll be locked up the whole time. I'll make certain of it. But I need to get him back to SIS to see what needs to be done. Attempting to murder Dr. G and kidnapping Mel are serious offenses—but more than that, they'll want to interrogate him. I'll join you at your home as soon as everything is taken care of. Shouldn't be more than a day or two at most. All right?"

"It's not what I would choose, but I know it must be done. We are over the border still, right?"

"Yes, barely." He led her by the arm back to the car. "Let me make sure the engine will still run and that it's safe to drive back to the ship."

Chaisley stood in the snow and listened to the engine crank. Granted, it didn't sound as smooth as it had, but it still purred.

"Mel, are you up for driving everyone to the dock?" The tenderness in Rick's voice was sweet. "This brother of yours and I will ride in the trunk with the lid open. That way I can keep him out of trouble."

She laughed. "Of course. Chais, you should probably ride up front with me. Dr. G can sit in the back with the children."

Rick walked Chaisley to the other side of the car. Once she was in the seat, his breath brushed her cheek. "I love you, Chaisley." Then he pressed a kiss to her lips.

"I love you, too." Her heart broke free of its confines the terror of the evening had wrought. They were safe. All of them. Now they just had to meet her grandmother at the ship and set sail for London.

The door clicked shut.

But so many others weren't safe. It broke her heart to think of men, women, and children across the continent still suffering.

As they jostled along while Melanie maneuvered the car back to the main road, Chaisley's body slumped against the seat.

"You okay?" Mel's voice was soft. Concerned.

"I am. Just thinking about all the people still suffering." She nodded and listened to Dr. Grafton tell the children silly jokes in the back seat. They giggled and chattered back. What a glorious sound. A good sign that they weren't too traumatized by the night's events.

"Me too." Mel's wistful tone preceded a quick grip on Chaisley's hand. "But we are going to keep working. Even if it's just one person at a time. We're going to do everything we can."

Lord, help us to do just that. She closed her eyes and breathed deep, allowing the voices behind her to bolster her spirit. "Sounds like the little ones have had quite an adventure." An adventure. Hopefully, they would remember it that way and not with nightmares. The resilience of children amazed her.

When they were all finally safe aboard the ship, Chaisley lay on her bed thinking that sleep would overtake her immediately.

But it didn't.

Rick was in a lower deck of the ship with his captive.

They still had to cross the channel and make it safely to London and then home.

But one hundred and three lives had been rescued from an evil man's grasp.

She hated to leave. There were hundreds, if not thousands, more. And what about God's chosen people? The Jews were being persecuted so much worse than she had ever imagined could happen.

Her heart ached with the overwhelming thought.

Father, please . . . I don't even know what to pray. Help us not to fear. Help us to be strong and courageous. Show us what You would have us do to stop the evil and hatred that keep growing.

She blinked as warm tears escaped the corners of her eyes. The world had become something she didn't recognize. But she could stand firm. Like Daniel in the Old Testament.

She prayed others would rise up.

It only took a few.

epilogue

The small chapel was decorated for the season with green boughs and beautiful candles. Rick stood at the front with the reverend as Melanie practically skipped around the room lighting each candle. He could relate to her jubilee on this day. It was hard enough to keep his own feet still. Or from grinning like a fool.

As soon as all the candles were lit, Mel disappeared through a door. A woman with a violin appeared next and walked toward them. She took her place in the corner behind Rick and began to play Beethoven's *Ode to Joy*.

Melanie reappeared with a small bouquet of flowers from the hothouse and took the ten or so steps to the front.

And then . . . there she was.

Chaisley.

His bride.

Dressed in a beautiful white gown. Simple. Elegant. Perfectly Chaisley.

Dr. Grafton took her arm and the two of them walked to the front of the small chapel.

The violinist finished the piece.

Rick couldn't take his eyes off the woman God had so graciously given him.

"I can feel you staring at me." Chaisley's soft giggle made him blink.

"*Ahem.*" The reverend cleared his throat. "We are gathered here today in the presence of God to join this man and this woman in holy matrimony."

Dr. Grafton placed Chaisley's hands into Rick's.

His mouth went dry as his heart picked up its pace. Was he supposed to say something here?

The sparkle in Chaisley's eyes calmed him. Why was he so nervous? Keep breathing. Nice and slow. Not too fast.

The message was short, and Rick couldn't even remember what was said, but it must have been good. Then they each were instructed to repeat after the reverend to say the vows.

Vows that, up to this point, Rick had heard at numerous weddings and thought for sure he could say in his sleep. Vows he had longed to say to Chaisley. But nerves abounded on this special day, and he found his heart in his throat.

His voice cracked, and his mouth felt like it was filled with sand. ". . . 'til death do us part." Whew. He made it through without too much of a stumble.

Chaisley squeezed his hands. She appeared as calm as she always did right before a concert. How did she do it?

"You may now kiss your bride, Mr. Zimmerman." The reverend's voice had changed from serious to chipper.

Rick glanced at him out of the corner of his eye.

"That's your cue, young man." The older man winked.

Melanie, Dr. Grafton, Celestia, and the violinist laughed softly.

But they all disappeared as he pulled Chaisley into his arms. His lips met hers in a sweet promise of their vows. He tugged her closer. A perfect fit.

As much as he yearned to deepen the kiss, the applause of their handful of guests reminded him they weren't alone. He released her, but kept hold of her hand. "I love you," he whispered.

She blushed. "I love *you*."

Celestia stepped toward him and hugged him tight. "I'm so glad God brought you to our family."

"Me too."

Dr. Grafton hugged him next. "Take care of our girl."

"I will."

Mel was next. Her hug was intense. "I leave tomorrow for Amsterdam to help the next group. I don't know when I'll see you again but thank you." Her eyes said more than her words.

He nodded.

And then a beautiful melody came from the small piano in the corner.

Chaisley was on the bench, playing something he'd never heard before.

The room hushed as she played. Her incredible ability mixed with the emotion she poured into each note mesmerized them all.

When the last note rang out from the piano, there wasn't a dry eye in the room.

Rick started the applause, and the reverend shouted, "Encore!"

Chaisley turned on the bench and shook her head. She held up her hands until everyone quieted. "I began to write this piece when I found out the truth of what was happening to people just like me." A tear glistened on her cheek.

"I couldn't imagine the horrors of what they were enduring. All I could think about was the first few times I opened my eyes after the accident, and I was surrounded by the dark. I couldn't escape it. Many must feel this way—that there is no escape."

She reached a hand forward, and Rick strode toward her and took it.

Chaisley lifted her face. "Music was my lifeline. At a young age, I knew God had given me a special gift. And now, He has given me a new song. Through you, Rick. Together we can be a song in the dark. Together we can fight against the evil in this world. Together we can shine the light of truth."

"No matter how much time the Lord gives us, I'll be grateful for each moment with you." Rick knelt in front of her. "That was beautiful, Chais."

She put a hand on his face, and her strong fingers caressed his cheek. "I know we have a lot of visas to try and obtain tomorrow," her voice was whisper soft, "but tonight, I just want to be your wife."

Rick lifted her into his arms and walked out of the chapel to the car as thick snowflakes fell from the sky, covering the gray ground in a fresh coat of white. "I'd love nothing more."

note from the author

To date, this is the hardest book I've written. Out of forty-plus books, that's saying a lot. And it wasn't the story—a story that's been simmering in my mind for two decades—it was the research behind it that made it so difficult.

Diving into the research on Hitler, the Nazi party, eugenics, and all the propaganda from WWII was often sickening. I can't even tell you how many boxes of tissues I went through. But it was also through that research that I stumbled upon some of the most inspiring people.

Otto Weidt is one of these inspiring people who I wish I could speak to today and tell him what an impact he had. All through a small brush and broom factory. And I wish I could thank every person on the continent who helped hide, feed, and care for the Jews and others.

Kristallnacht was a real, horrific event that happened after the shooting of Ernst vom Rath. While the Nazis tried to convince the world it was a simple retaliation for vom Rath's murder, it was not. Kristallnacht was planned and orchestrated throughout all of Germany's territories. It was a wake-up call for much of the world to see what had been happening for years and a tiny hint of what was coming.

Laurence Grand is another real person used in the story. He headed up Section D for the British SIS. When I think about what people had to sacrifice to stand up for what was right . . . I'm amazed. Especially looking at our own world today. Sometimes it can be really hard to find the truth. For me, I'm just going to keep seeking God's wisdom and staying in His Word, because this world will fail us. I pray you do the same.

My hope and prayer for you, my reader, is that God has touched your heart through this story. I'm going to leave you with the ending of my message that I wrote at the beginning of this book: "The Few."

"May we love one another above all else.
May we turn our hearts to God Almighty.
May we be . . . the few."

Until next time,
Kimberley Woodhouse

discussion questions

1. At the beginning of the book, Chaisley is delighted to receive a present she's long desired: a piano. She knows the instrument will be the key to unlocking the music she feels inside. Have you ever received a gift that meant so much to you? If so, what was it? If that longing has been unfulfilled, what gift are you hoping to receive?

2. A bombing takes Chaisley's parents from her, as well as her sight. At ten years old, her life changes dramatically. Her guardians have differing opinions about how to best help Chaisley heal from all the trauma. How do Chaisley, Dr. Grafton, and Celestia Frappier all come to terms with the tragedy that befalls them? What can you learn from each character's response? Can you relate to one character more than the other? Why or why not?

3. Rick Zimmerman is a spy for the British in the agency that eventually becomes MI-5. When we meet Rick, he sees his informant and friend arrested and taken away. What do you think about his choice to leave and take another assignment? Do you know what you would do if you were in Rick's situation?

4. Hope is a recurring theme in *A Song in the Dark*. Chaisley, Melanie, Celestia, and even the villain are all looking for hope in some way, shape, or form. Consider how each character defines hope. What does it look like to them? Do they each realize their form of hope? Discuss how do you define hope in your life.

5. The story of Esther is an example of bravery and courage in standing up for what is right in the face of great evil. The story is a constant reminder of these things to Melanie, who

battles fear throughout. How does Melanie overcome her fears? Do you relate to Melanie's fear? If so, in what way?

6. As the tour progresses, Melanie and Chaisley grow in awareness of what God's purpose is for Chaisley's tour: to help many who are blind, deaf, or disabled escape Germany. How did their plan challenge each woman in her walk with the Lord? How did Chaisley and Melanie grow? What did you learn from their individual stories?

7. Rick hides that he works for the British Intelligence Service until halfway through the book. When he reveals his secret, it deeply hurts Chaisley. What did you think about her reaction? Do you think Rick handled the situation well? What would you have done if you were in Rick's shoes? How would you have reacted if you were Chaisley?

8. Trust is another theme in *A Song in the Dark*. As the group pushes their plans to save those who are Jewish, blind, or deaf from Hitler's clutches, danger intensifies, and their trust in the Lord and each other grows as well. Talk about how Rick, Chaisley, and Melanie grow to trust in one another and the Lord throughout the story.

9. *Kristallnacht* was an event that shocked not only Europe but the entire world. Most couldn't, or wouldn't, see where Hitler was taking Germany and how he was reshaping a country, continent, and world through power and ethnic cleansing. As you read about the events that unfolded, what emotions did you feel? How can that event from history influence how you stand up for others in your community today?

10. Chaisley and Rick find each other in the midst of incredible difficulty. Their love blossoms, even as the world around them grows darker. What did you think about their relationship? Think about their choice to be together, no matter what comes. Would you make the same choice in a time of war? Why or why not?

acknowledgments

First, to the Author of all, my Lord and Savior. Thank You for the gift of story.

My incredible editor, Karen Ball, has prayed with me over this story for as long as she's known me. I wouldn't be the writer I am today without her. Karen, I love you dearly. Thank you so much for all you've invested in me the past two decades. Here's to many more stories.

I'm so grateful to Bethany House for publishing *A Song in the Dark* and for cheering me on. Jessica Sharpe, you have been such a joy to work with. Thank you for everything. All the team at Bethany House—it's hard to believe we've done almost twenty books together. Wow. Thank you for all the years and all the fun.

Jeremy, you are the love of my life. Thank you for always being the hero.

My kids and grandkids – I love you all so soooooo much. Thank you for being my cheerleaders and giving me smiles each and every day.

And to you, my readers, THANK YOU. I'll say it again, I can't do this without you.

Enjoy the journey,

Kimberley—AKA Nana the Great

one

"I cannot tell what the years may bring, life is a scene of change."

~Earl Douglass

SUNDAY, JUNE 2, 1878 · SETTLEMENT OF WALKER CREEK, WYOMING TERRITORY

Home.

A seemingly innocuous word. A place she loved.

And yet, every time Anna Lakeman returned there, her insides begged to differ.

She could see it in the distance, just a few minutes away . . . the house where she grew up, where she learned to sketch and paint.

The wheels of the wagon bumped and rolled their way along the grass- and weed-covered lane. A testament to her absence.

What was it about coming home that made her want to run away?

With each return from a dig with her father, she pondered the same questions. Never getting any answers. Or perhaps she'd been avoiding the answer for too long.

Memories of her mother were beautiful and made her feel warm and loved, so it wasn't the loss of the woman who gave her life that brought these feelings.

Then there was the loss of her best friend, Mary. It had been a decade since her friend went missing, but Anna felt the absence in her heart and soul every day. Some people said that grief lessened over time. And if she was honest, she could say that yes, the grief was less. But the loss . . . she knew that as keenly today as she had the day Mary didn't return.

Home was where she had the best memories of Mary and of Mama.

So why was it an uncomfortable place? This time she didn't silence the answer.

She knew why. Because *he* wasn't there.

It was best to face facts. Her struggle came down to the loss of her first and only love, Joshua Ziegler.

She drove her wagon up to the door and set the brake, her shoulders sagging with a long exhale. It exhausted her to deny that struggle over and over. The effort it took to shove it down so she wouldn't voice the words weighed heavier each day.

But that was the path of great loss.

And even though the loss wasn't in death, she felt it as such.

Three years had passed since he'd gone back east for medical school. Three years since their spat. Three years since they'd talked. Shared their hearts. Talked of dreams of the future. Until he left, she would've never dreamed of life without him. The community expected them to marry. Their families expected them to marry.

She'd expected them to marry.

The rumble of her father's wagon brought her thoughts around. This was no time for her pondering. She had work to do.

Every inch of Anna's body ached as she stepped from the hub of the wheel into the tall, dry grass in front of her home. She stretched but it didn't help the soreness that seemed to scream from every muscle. With a glance around, she took mental notes of the scene. One she'd sketched a thousand times and would probably do a thousand times more. Other than the growth being too tall around the house, not much had changed in the months she'd been gone with her father.

"I don't know if it's me and my old age, but the road seems to get rougher every time we travel it." Dad's soft chuckle brought her gaze around.

"It's not you, I can promise you that." Turning on her heel, she stretched one more time and then stepped toward the supplies that needed to be unloaded.

A bone-jarring wagon ride over the rough Wyoming terrain for the past five hours had given her insides the impression she was eighty years old rather than a young twenty-one. But such was the life of a traveling paleontologist and his daughter. He went wherever the bones called. She tagged along to sketch and paint everything.

As they unloaded crates, bags, and fresh supplies they'd purchased from the large mercantile up in Green River, she longed to get back to all her sketches from the trip. The bones of the horse-like creature they'd found fossilized in the rock layer weren't the greatest find her father had ever had, but they *were* interesting. Quite exciting to draw too, since she'd never seen a bone structure quite like it.

As a child, she'd wanted to be a paleontologist just like her father. She'd hung on his every word, watched his every move, and read every tome written on the subject.

But over the years, she'd learned the harsh truth.

Women didn't pursue science like that. And they most certainly didn't dig in the dirt. That was unacceptable. And vulgar—according to the women of society who knew about such things.

Although, she had to admit that she'd always admired the work of Mary Anning from Lyme Regis, England. The woman had been a fossil collector pretty much her whole life, and even though she wasn't given the credit she deserved, her name was still well-known in paleontological discussions. Why couldn't Anna do the same?

If only she could have known the woman. But Mary Anning had

been gone for thirty years and had lived half a world away. Besides, her fossil collecting had been her means of support after her father's death when she was eleven. Probably why it had been somewhat acceptable. The pity of the public gave allowances now and then.

Anna released her breath as she set down another satchel. Even though she longed to be the one to find the next great discovery in paleontology, her gifting truly was in the sketching. Oh, how she loved every little detail.

Now that they were home, Dad would sequester himself with all his notes and specimens, and she would need to put the house to order once again. After that, she could spend all the time she wanted going through the sketches and reliving their last dig.

They worked together hauling and sorting, enjoying the quiet camaraderie that had become habitual. It didn't take long to set things in their proper place since they'd left everything clean and in order. The one addition was the layer of dust, which Anna eliminated with the removal of the sheets covering the furniture and quick use of the broom.

"I'll be in my study, Anna." Dad's nose was in a book as he walked down the hall.

She'd figured as much, but unlike her usual desire to get back to her sketches, her insides swirled. The unsettled feeling called for something different from her usual routine. "I think I'll go see the Zieglers then, if that's all right with you?" she called after him. "Louise will return tomorrow to help around the house."

"That's fine." His voice vanished as the door clicked behind him. Whether or not he'd heard what she said was the question of the hour, but he'd likely stay buried in his study for the rest of the afternoon anyway.

Anna hauled the tub into her bedroom and filled it with warm water. Washing away all the dirt from the travels made her feel a bit more like herself. She dunked her head to rinse the soap from her hair. She couldn't wait to see Mary's family. When her best friend disappeared ten years ago, Anna had spent days and weeks helping the community search for her.

When no trace of her friend had been found, she'd mourned with the family, begging her father to allow her to stay at their home for a few days. Each night, she'd cried herself to sleep in Mary's bed while Mrs. Ziegler sat in her rocking chair staring out the window at the dark.

It had taken the community months to recover from the loss. Mary's parents did their best to find joy in their faith and family, but the sorrow never left.

Over the years, Anna spent a lot of time at the Ziegler home. Martha and Joshua were older but had never seemed to mind when their little sister and her best friend tagged along. After Mary disappeared, Anna continued to spend a lot of time with the family. If she wasn't at school or out on a dig with her father, she could be found at the Ziegler home.

Then Martha got married, which left Joshua and Anna. They'd been comfortable with one another the entirety of their childhoods, but things changed. In the evenings they would read with his parents, she would show them her sketches, and he soon insisted on seeing her home each night.

It didn't take much for her to develop a deep crush on Joshua. For a long time, she thought it was mutual.

Anna shook those thoughts away along with the droplets of water from her bath. There was no sense in pining for the man who hadn't even bothered to write.

After dressing and pinning up her hair, she grabbed her bonnet, went out to her horse, and saddled Misty for the short ride out to the Ziegler ranch. With the wind at her back, she hunched over the mare and gave her free rein to race along the trail they both knew so well.

The pounding of her horse's hooves shook the rest of her ill thoughts away. A chat with Mrs. Ziegler—who'd been like a mother to her—would certainly settle her down again and help Anna to get over this melancholy.

But the ranch yard was empty. No smoke rose from the chimney. The barn doors were shut. Animals corralled close to the house.

It was clear no one was home.

"Bother." Anna allowed her shoulders to slump. They must be in town.

The choice before her stretched. Go to town in search of her friends? Of course, she'd have to see other people as well. That made the option a bit less desirable. Or . . . head home?

Her shadow disappeared on the ground as she contemplated. A cloud must have covered the sun for the moment. As her gaze shifted upward, the sky darkened, and gray clouds staged themselves in the distance to roll in and cover the sun for the rest of the afternoon.

It might blow over and it might not. What to do?

A crack of thunder made the decision for her.

She'd have to head home. What had been a beautiful day now seemed downright gloomy. Sad how it matched her mood.

Turning her mount back to the trail they'd just ridden, she pulled her hat down and tightened the string. Fat drops of rain dotted the dusty road. "Time to go, Misty. Let's hope those clouds don't have much to spill."

She shouldn't have voiced the words. Because within minutes, the sky opened up, and a storm like she'd never seen before gushed from the heavens. The trail almost disappeared before her eyes and Misty's unease vibrated through Anna's knees and thighs as she held on. Slowing her horse to a trot so she could gain her bearings, she couldn't see anything but the downpour of water. Misty's head bobbed up and down with her discomfort with the thunder and lightning.

There was no shelter and no other choice than pray that her faithful mare could find her way home. Anna's dress, her underclothes, and every inch of her were now soaked.

Lightning struck a nearby tree and Misty reared. Anna held on with all her might and clung to her horse's neck. "Whoa. Easy, girl. We need to get home in one piece, all right?" She soothed the mare and rubbed her neck, keeping her words calm. Which grew increasingly difficult as the storm built.

Tension grew in her neck and shoulders as she gripped the reins. If she couldn't see where they were going, how would Misty? Her beautiful mare was getting up in years.

God, please help us to make it home. The prayer left her mind as the sky seemed to open its floodgates and dump oceans of water on top of them.

Misty's head was visible but not by much. Anna's bonnet was completely flattened from the deluge, and rivers of water raced down her face and body. Bending over her horse, she held the reins and hugged Misty's neck. "Get us home, girl. You can do it."

Misty whinnied and shook her head as thunder rumbled overhead in a constant rhythm. Then the mare trotted forward.

Anna counted each second in the minutes as they passed, hoping and praying they would reach shelter soon.

She had tallied eleven minutes when the roar sounded behind her. What was that? She sat up and looked around, but she couldn't see anything through the sheets and sheets of rain that continued to pour down from above.

The roaring grew. Accompanied by massive explosions— snapping and cracking. What was happening?

A wall of water barreled toward her.

"Giddyap, girl!" she yelled in Misty's ear.

Her mare didn't hesitate and raced into a furious pace.

But they were no match for the water.

Just as they crested a hill, Anna felt the horse underneath her lift with the wave.

God . . . help!

Kimberley Woodhouse is an award-winning, bestselling author of more than forty fiction and nonfiction books. Kim and her incredible husband of thirty-plus years live in Colorado, where they play golf together, spend time with their kids and grandkids, and research all the history around them. You can connect with Kimberley on her website, KimberleyWoodhouse.com.

Sign Up for Kimberley's Newsletter

Keep up to date with Kimberley's latest news on book releases and events by signing up for her email list at the link below.

KimberleyWoodhouse.com

FOLLOW KIMBERLEY ON SOCIAL MEDIA

Kimberley Woodhouse   @KimberleyWoodhouse   @KimWoodhouse